TODAY bestselling author **Janice Maynard** loved ooks and writing even as a child. After multiple rejections, she finally sold her first manuscript! Since then, she has written more than sixty books and novellas. Janice lives in Tennessee with her husband, Charles. They love hiking, travelling and family time.

You can connect with Janice at
www.janicemaynard.com
vww.Twitter.com/janicemaynard
www.Facebook.com/janicemaynardauthor
www.Facebook.com/janicesmaynard
www.Instagram.com/therealjanicemaynard

Joss Wood loves books, coffee and travelling – especially to the wild places of southern Africa and, well, anywhere. She's a wife and a mum to two young adults. She's also a slave to two cats and a dog the size of a small cow. After a career in local economic development and business, Joss writes full-time from her home in KwaZulu-Natal, South Africa.

D0736230

STAKING A CLAIM

JANICE MAYNARD

LOST AND
FOUND HEIR

JOSS WOOD

MIX

Paper from
responsible sources

FSC C007472

This book is produced from independently certified FSC
paper to ensure responsible forest management.

For more information visit www.harpercollins.co.uk/green

Printed and bound in Great Britain by
CPI Book Press, Barnstaple

MILLS & BOON

First Published in Great Britain 2022
by Mills & Boon, an imprint of HarperCollins*Publishers* Ltd
1 London Bridge Street, London, SE1 9GF

www.harpercollins.co.uk

HarperCollins*Publishers*
1st Floor, Watermarque Building,
Ringsend Road, Dublin 4, Ireland

Staking a Claim © 2022 Harlequin Enterprises ULC
Lost and Found Heir © 2022 Joss Wood

Special thanks and acknowledgement are given to Janice Maynard for her contribution to the *Texas Cattleman's Club: Ranchers* and *Rivals* series.

ISBN: 978-0-263-30377-3

STAKING A CLAIM

JANICE MAYNARD

For Anastasia, Ainsley, Allie, Levi and Hattie.
You are the best of all of us!
I hope you continue to stay as close
as you are now...

One

Layla Grandin hated funerals. It was bad enough to sit through somber affairs with friends who had lost family members. But today was worse. Today was personal.

Victor Grandin Sr., Layla's beloved grandfather, had been laid to rest.

It wasn't a tragedy in the truest sense of the word. Victor was ninety-three years old when he died. He lived an amazing, fulfilling life. And in the end, he was luckier than most. He literally died with his boots on after suffering a heart attack while on horseback.

There were worse ways to go. But that didn't make Layla's grief any less.

After the well-attended funeral in town, many of Royal's finest citizens had made the trek out to the Grandin ranch to pay their respects. Layla eyed the large gathering with a cynical gaze. The Grandin family was wealthy. Even folks with the best of intentions couldn't help sniffing around when money and inheritance were on the menu. That was the burden of financial privilege. You never knew if people really liked you or if they just wanted something they thought you could give them.

For that very reason, Layla had been lingering in the corner of the room, content to play voyeur. Her newly widowed grandmother Miriam looked frail and distraught, as was to be expected. Layla's father was relishing the role of genial host, embracing his chance to shine now that his larger-than-life parent was out of the picture.

Layla wished with all her heart that her own father cared for her as much as her gruff but loving grandfather had. Unfortunately, Victor Junior was not particularly interested in his female offspring. He was too focused on his only son, Victor the third, better known as Vic. Her father was grooming Vic to take over one day, despite the fact that Layla's older sister, Chelsea, was first in line, followed by Layla.

Chelsea crossed the room in Layla's direction, looking disgruntled. "I am so over this," she said. "I don't think anyone here really cares about Grandfather at all. Some of them probably haven't even met him."

Layla grimaced. "I know what you mean. But at least Vic and Morgan are genuinely upset. Grandy loved all his grandkids."

"You most of all," Chelsea said. "You were the only one who could get away with that nickname."

Layla flushed. She hadn't realized anyone else noticed. As the middle of three girls, and with Vic their father's clear favorite, Layla often felt lost in the crowd.

Suddenly, Layla realized her father was deep in conversation with a man she recognized. She lowered her voice and leaned toward Chelsea. "Why is Daddy co-zied up to Bertram Banks? Oh, crap! Why are they looking at me?"

"Who knows? Let's go find out." Chelsea, always the proactive one, took Layla's elbow and steered her across the room. Layla would have much preferred hiding out in the kitchen, but the two men obviously saw them approaching.

When they were in earshot, Layla and Chelsea's dad gave them a big smile. For such a sober day, it might have been a bit too big, in Layla's estimation.

"Here are my two oldest," he said, giving Bertram a wink. "Take your pick."

Chelsea raised an eyebrow. "That sounds a little weird, Dad."

Bertram chuckled. "He didn't mean anything by it."

Layla distrusted the two men's good humor. Both of them were known to manipulate people when the occasion demanded it. Layla had known the Banks family forever. As a kid, she had been a tomboy, running wild and riding horses and dirt bikes with Bertram's twin sons, Jordan and Joshua.

Back then, she was lean and coltish, not at all interested in girly pursuits. She could take whatever the Banks boys dished out. As she grew older, though, she'd developed a terrible crush on Jordan. It was embarrassing to think about now.

"What's going on?" Layla asked.

For once, Chelsea was silent.

Bertram smiled at Layla. This time it seemed genuine. "I have tickets to see Parker Brett in concert tomorrow night."

It was Layla's turn to raise an eyebrow. "Congratulations. I've heard those were impossible to get."

Bertram puffed out his chest. "I know a guy," he said,

chuckling. "But the thing is, I've had a conflict arise. Jordan has offered to take you, Layla, you know—to cheer you up. We all know how much you loved your grandfather."

Layla was aghast. Chelsea bit her lip, clearly trying hard not to laugh. She knew all about Layla's fruitless crush.

To be honest, Layla highly doubted that Jordan had volunteered to do anything of the sort. She wasn't even sure he liked country music. "That's sweet of you," she said. "But I don't think I'll feel like going out. This has been an emotional week."

Her father jumped in. "It will do you good, Layla. Everyone knows you've had a crush on Jordan forever."

A split second of stunned silence reverberated between the uncomfortable foursome. *Did he just say that? Oh, yes he did!* Layla felt her face get hot. *Recover, Layla. Quickly! Think!* "When I was a kid, Dad. I've moved on," Layla mumbled.

Chelsea tried to help. "Good grief, Daddy. Layla's had a million boyfriends since then. Even a fiancé." She stopped short, clearly appalled. "Sorry, sis."

Layla forced a smile. Her doomed engagement two years ago was a sore spot, more because it reeked of failure than anything else. "No worries." She faced the duo of late-fifties males. "I'm sure Jordan can find his own date for the concert."

Bertram's expression was bland, suspiciously innocent. "You're it, kiddo. He'll text you the details later tonight."

Layla glanced around the room. "He's not here?"

"He went to the funeral, but he had another commitment this afternoon."

Victor beamed. "So, it's settled. If you two ladies will excuse us, Bertram and I are going to mingle."

When the two men wandered away, Layla groaned. "You have to be kidding me. Why didn't you say something? I needed help."

Chelsea cocked her head, her sisterly smile teasing. "Well, he wasn't wrong. You *have* always had a thing for Jordan Banks. What could it hurt to get out of the house? With you swearing off men after your engagement ended and now Grandfather dying, I think it would do you good. It's just a concert."

Layla couldn't disagree with the logic. "Fine," she said. "But I hope this doesn't put Jordan in a weird spot. I'll have to make sure he knows I'm not pining for him."

"I'm sure he doesn't think that." Chelsea grinned.

Layla had been too tense and upset to eat lunch before the funeral. Now she was starving. Her mother had made arrangements for catered hors d'oeuvres to serve the dozens of guests who showed up for the reception. Judging by the crowd, it might ultimately prove to be two hundred or two fifty. But her mother, Bethany, was an experienced hostess. No one would run out of food.

"Let's get something to eat," Layla said to Chelsea.

"Good idea."

The two sisters filled their plates and retreated to a sunny alcove just off the large living room. Some people might be taken aback by the luxurious, enormous house, but to Layla and Chelsea it was simply home.

From their comfortable seats, they enjoyed the sunshine and the food. Chelsea sighed. "I can't believe it's only four days till May. Summer will be here soon."

Layla's composure wobbled. "Grandy loved the long days and even the heat. Not to mention watermelon and fresh corn. It won't be the same this year." She scanned the crowd. "I guess we should have asked Morgan to join us." Chelsea was thirty-five, Layla thirty-two. Morgan, their baby sister, was still in her twenties.

"She's hanging out with Vic," Chelsea said, stabbing a fat shrimp with her fork. "Did I tell you she sided with Vic over me yesterday? Again."

Vic was third in line, but first in their father's heart and plans.

Chelsea continued, "Every damn time she takes Vic's side. Just once I'd like her to take mine. Still, it's not their fault Daddy thinks I can't handle the ranch eventually. It makes me so angry. I love this ranch as much as anybody. It ought to be me. Or you and me together."

"Well, it won't, so you might as well get used to the idea. Besides, if genetics are any clue, Daddy will live another thirty years. You and I might as well forget about this ranch and find something else to keep us busy."

"True," Chelsea said glumly.

"Look at Mr. Lattimore," Layla said. "He must be grieving terribly, but he's as dignified as ever." Augustus was ninety-six. His wife, Hazel, was at his side speaking to him in a low voice. As a Black family in Royal, Texas, the Lattimores hadn't always had it easy, but they were equally as influential as the Grandins. The only difference was, their patriarch, Augustus, had been forced to give up the reins several years ago because of his struggles with memory issues.

"He and Grandfather were so very close. I wonder if he understands that Grandfather is gone. They've been friends for decades." Chelsea's comment was wistful.

"His memory comes in flashes, I think. You've seen people like that." The two families were so close the Lattimore kids probably felt sad about losing Grandpa Victor even if he wasn't their blood kin. It would be hard to see the oldest generation begin to pass on, especially since they adored their own grandfather.

Chelsea put her plate on a side table and grimaced. "I hate funerals," she said.

Layla burst out laughing.

Her sister gaped. "Did I say something funny?"

"Not particularly," Layla said, still chuckling. "But I've been thinking the same thing all day. When it's my time to go, just put me in the ground and plant a tree. I don't need people kicking the dirt and fighting over my estate."

"Always assuming you have one."

"Touché." Chelsea's joking comment gave Layla something to ponder. After college, she had spent the last decade pouring her energies into this place. She assisted her mother with frequent entertaining. She helped train horses. And though her father was sometimes dismissive of her expertise, she used her business degree to make sure the family enterprise was solid.

Her grandfather had been proud of her ideas and her knack for understanding the ranching business. Unfortunately, he was too old-school to ever think a woman could be in charge of anything that didn't involve cooking, cleaning or changing diapers. A woman's place was in the home.

No matter that he had been affectionate and supportive of Layla's thoughts and dreams, he had been forged in the patriarchal environs of Maverick County, and he agreed with his son. The only grandson, Vic, should be next in line to run things when it was Victor Junior's time to hang up his spurs.

Layla was at a crossroads. Her personal life was nonexistent. If Vic was going to be heir to the Grandin ranch, she might as well make a plan for the future.

Many of her friends were married and had kids by now. Layla didn't feel any rush.

Her ex-fiancé, Richard, hadn't been too excited about the prospect of starting a family. That should have been a red flag. But Layla had taken his words at face value. He'd said he was concentrating on his career.

Unfortunately, the thing he'd been concentrating on was screwing as many women as possible in the shortest amount of time. The only reason he'd given Layla a ring was that he saw the benefit in allying himself with the Grandin empire.

For Layla, the entire experience had shaken her confidence. How could she trust her own judgment when she had been so wrong about Richard?

Gradually, the crowd thinned. She and Chelsea split up to mingle, to thank people for coming and to say goodbyes. The food tables were demolished. The furniture was askew. By all accounts, the funeral reception was a success. Hazel and Augustus Lattimore were just now being escorted home. Layla's grandmother Miriam looked shaky and exhausted as she headed for her suite.

Fortunately for Layla, Bertram Banks had disappeared half an hour ago. She definitely didn't want to talk to him again. She was already planning how to ditch the concert arrangements.

She had nothing against country music. Jordan would be a fun companion. But she was emotionally wrung out. In some ways, she had never completely processed the trauma from two years ago, and now this, losing her grandfather.

As the room emptied, only the Grandins and Lattimores remained, parents and kids, though the term *kids* was a misnomer. Even Caitlyn, the youngest, was twenty-five. The reception had been advertised as a drop-in from two until five. Now it was almost six.

Layla was about to make her excuses and head to her bedroom when her mother went to answer the doorbell and came back flanked by a uniformed person holding a legal-size envelope.

Oddly, the room fell silent. The young courier looked nervous. "I have a delivery addressed to The Heirs of Victor Grandin Sr.," he said.

Layla's father stepped forward. "That's me. Where do I sign?"

Ben Lattimore, her father's best friend, joined him. "What's up? Kind of late in the day for any kind of official delivery."

Victor nodded absently, breaking the seal on the envelope and extracting the contents. After a moment, he paled. "Someone is pursuing the oil rights to both of our ranches."

"Somebody who?" Chelsea asked, trying to read over Victor's shoulder.

He scanned farther. "Heath Thurston."

Ben frowned. "Why didn't I get a copy?"

"Maybe you did at your house." Victor glared at the document. "It's in incredibly poor taste to deliver this today."

"The timing could be a coincidence." Ben Lattimore was visibly worried. "If this is legit, our properties are in trouble. We're cattle ranchers, damn it. Having somebody search for oil would destroy much of what we've built."

Vic stepped to his father's shoulder. "I thought we didn't have any oil, right? So this is probably all a hoax," he said. "Don't worry about it, Dad. At least not until we investigate."

"That's the ticket," Victor said. "I know a PI—Jonas Shaw." His gaze narrowed. "But I'll start with my mother first."

Layla shook her head. "No, Daddy. She's grief-stricken and so frail right now. We should only involve her if it's absolutely necessary." It was obvious that her father didn't like being opposed. But he nodded tersely.

"I suppose," he said grudgingly. "But *you*…" He pointed at his brother. "I'm going to need cooperation from you, Daniel."

"I'm flying back to Paris tomorrow."

"Not anymore. No one leaves Royal until we meet with our lawyer."

Layla could tell Daniel wanted to argue. But he settled for a muttered protest. "This whole thing smells fishy," he said.

Conversation swelled as the two families broke up into small groups and began to process the bizarre information. Layla was surprised that Heath Thurston would pursue something like this. From what she knew of him, he was an honorable man. But if he and his brother thought they were entitled to the oil rights, maybe they were taking the only logical step.

Still, it was very suspicious that Thurston was claiming oil rights under *both* ranches. What possible claim could he have?

Layla spotted Alexa Lattimore gathering up her purse and light jacket, preparing to leave. Layla had talked to her earlier in the day, but only briefly. "Don't rush off, Alexa. I miss you." The eldest Lattimore daughter hadn't lived in Royal since finishing college.

"I've missed you, too, Layla. I was sorry to hear about

your engagement. I wish I could have come home to give you moral support, but things were crazy at work."

Layla sighed. "It's no fun being the subject of Royal's grapevine. I don't think Richard broke my heart, but he definitely dented my pride." She tugged her friend to a nearby sofa. "I wanted to ask you something."

Alexa sat down with a wary expression. "Oh?"

"I was hoping you might think about coming home for a longer visit. I think Caitlyn would love having you around, and besides, it looks like your lawyer skills may be in demand. For both our families."

Alexa chewed her lip, not quite meeting Layla's gaze. "I don't know, Layla. I wanted to pay my respects at your grandfather's funeral, but this was just a quick jaunt. Miami is home now. There's no real place for me in Royal."

"If I know you, Ms. Workaholic, you probably have a million vacation days banked. At least think about it."

"I will," Alexa said.

Even hearing the words, Layla wasn't sure Alexa was telling the truth. Alexa had kept her distance from Royal and didn't seem eager to get involved with an ongoing crisis.

At last, Layla was free to escape to her bedroom and recover from this long, painful day. She stripped off her funeral dress and took a quick shower. After that, she donned comfy black yoga pants and a chunky teal sweater.

When she curled up in her chaise lounge by the window, the tears flowed. She'd been holding them in check all day. Now she sobbed in earnest. She would never see Grandy again, never hear the comfortable rumble of his voice. She had loved him deeply, but perhaps she had never realized just how big a void he filled in her life.

With Grandy gone, she felt adrift.

In the end, she had to wash her face and reapply mascara. The family would be gathering for dinner at seven thirty. It was the Grandin way, and old traditions were hard to break.

Just before she went downstairs at a quarter after, she glanced at her phone. All her family and friends had been at the house today, so there was no real reason to think she might have a text.

But Bertram had said Jordan would text her tonight.

It was dumb to feel hurt and uncertain. She knew Bertram. He was probably, even now, pressuring his son to take Layla to the concert. It was so embarrassing. Bertram would like nothing more than to have one of his sons marry a Grandin daughter. He wasn't picky. He would keep trying if this didn't work out.

The concert was a day away. If Layla hadn't heard from Jordan in the next couple of hours, she was done with this shotgun-date situation. She might have a long-standing crush on Jordan, but honestly, it was more like the feelings she'd had for a rock star or a movie idol growing up.

Doodling her name and Jordan's in hearts and flowers had been something fun. A fantasy to entertain herself. By the time she was an engaged woman, she had known her feelings for Jordan were mostly superficial. Still, the idea of a night on the town wasn't *so* terrible.

Layla would be the envy of every single woman in Royal, Texas.

What could it hurt to enjoy herself? She had been far

too serious for far too long. She had let her mistakes and missteps make her afraid to live life.

Jordan Banks wasn't her soul mate. But he was handsome and temporarily available. And from what she remembered of him, he knew how to have fun.

That was what Layla needed...fun. This one date might not be a long-term solution to her solitary state, but it was a start. She needed to open herself up to possibilities...to surprises. No telling what might happen.

Two

Joshua Banks felt more unsettled than at any point in his life. He'd come home to Royal hoping for a signpost pointing his feet to a next step. It was time for a change. He was determined to seize control of his destiny, no matter how grandiose that sounded. Now, after an afternoon of driving aimlessly around Maverick County, his life in Dallas seemed a million miles away. Surely he had made the right choice.

Time would tell. For now, he was checked into a hotel and about to have dinner with his twin brother. Jordan would likely press for Joshua to stay at the ranch. It was the home where both men had grown up, after all. But Joshua needed some personal space…some time to sort out his feelings about his divorce and the really good job he had abandoned amidst a surge of hope about starting over in his hometown.

Thirty minutes later, he pulled up in front of a familiar steakhouse. The ambience was laid-back, the drinks cold and the music not so loud that he and Jordan couldn't talk comfortably. When Joshua stepped out of his car, he saw his brother execute the same maneuver a few spaces away.

That was nothing new. As identical twins, they'd always had the internal radar thing between them. To be honest, though, the sibling connection had weakened during the years Joshua had lived in Dallas.

His brother hugged him. "Man, it's good to see you, Josh."

Joshua was caught off guard by a wave of emotion. "Same here."

Inside, the hostess found them a table in a corner, handed over menus and left them alone. To his dismay, Joshua realized that he felt awkward. Maybe that's what happened when you hid too many secrets.

After they ordered drinks and dinner, Jordan rocked his chair back on two legs. "Damn, bro. You look good. Why do I have the beginnings of a beer gut, but you don't?"

Joshua chuckled. "It's called being a workaholic. No time for goofing off."

"If you say so." Jordan snagged an onion ring from their appetizer sampler and popped it in his mouth. "You know I don't beat around the bush. Why is this dinner just you and me? Why wasn't Dad invited?"

Joshua winced and rubbed the back of his neck. "Actually," he said slowly, "I'll have plenty of time to catch up with Dad. I've left Dallas for good."

The chair hit the ground. Jordan stared. "No shit? What about your job?"

"I resigned." Joshua could barely say the words out loud. What kind of person gave up a high-six-figure job with cushy perks? Especially with no definite plan in sight?

Jordan frowned. "I thought you loved your job."

"I did. Mostly. But I've been missing Royal. Dumb, huh? I always wanted to head for the big city, and now I find myself envying you."

"Dad will take you back at the ranch in a hot second."

"You think?"

"He never wanted you to leave in the beginning."

Joshua sighed. "If I'm hoping to come back into the fold, I'll have to eat a lot of crow and listen to a few dozen *I told you so*'s. He never liked Becky in the first place."

Turns out, the old man had been right about a lot of things. Becky had, indeed, been more interested in the Banks family money than in Joshua, himself. When they settled in Dallas after the wedding, the cracks in the relationship began to show.

Joshua had unfortunately been blinded by great sex and a master manipulator. He was partly to blame. He had convinced himself he was in love with Becky. It was why he had married her.

He'd never been more wrong.

The server dropped off two steaming plates. Jordan cut into his steak. "So where do things stand between you and the former Mrs. Banks?"

"Luckily I haven't seen her. When the divorce was final in February, as you know, she got the house in the settlement. I moved into an apartment and never looked back."

He and Becky had separated two years ago. The marriage had been over at least a year before that. It was a sad, sucky situation and one that had taught him valuable lessons. He was glad Jordan had been there whenever Josh needed him.

Joshua stabbed a bite of perfectly cooked rib eye. "And now here I am. What have you been up to...besides working your ass off at the ranch?"

"Well, today, it was a funeral. Victor Grandin died."

"I didn't even know he was still around. He had to be older than dirt."

"Ninety-three. The grandkids were broken up about it. And his wife, of course. But I don't think Victor Junior was too upset. He's been wanting to run that ranch on his own terms for a long time. The old man never would give up the reins."

"Wow." Joshua shook his head slowly, remembering the good times he had spent there. "I guess there will be some changes on the way."

"No doubt." Jordan finished his beer and grinned. It was a sly smile, one Joshua recognized all too well. His brother was up to something. "I need a favor, Josh. And in exchange, I'll run interference with Dad for you. Soften him up. Hint that you'd like to be back in the thick of things full-time."

"That's an awfully generous gesture. What would I have to do in return?" Joshua was on his guard. Jordan was a great guy, but he was slippery.

"Hardly anything at all. Take a beautiful woman on a date to a country music concert. That's all. One brief evening. And if you want to get back on the horse, so to speak, maybe a little uncomplicated sex?"

Joshua scowled. "I may be divorced and unemployed at the moment, but I sure as hell don't need my twin brother pimping me out to some strange woman. That's a *hell no* from me."

"You didn't let me finish. You'd be doing me a favor, honestly."

"How so?"

"Do you remember Layla Grandin?"

"Of course. How could I forget? She tagged along with us when we were kids. A cute tomboy. And as I recall, she grew up to be a very nice woman, though I haven't seen her in seven or eight years."

"Exactly. The trouble is, Dad has been meddling. He went to the reception after the funeral and chatted with Layla. You know how he's always wanted the two families to hook up."

"I do know that," Joshua said slowly. "But I married Becky and you—"

"I like variety," Jordan said quickly. "The thing is, Dad spun Layla some story about how he had concert tickets he can't use, and that I wanted to take Layla instead. But it was a lie."

"So the tickets are bogus?"

"The tickets are real. But I didn't know anything about it."

"So *you* take her. What's the big deal? It's only one night."

"I have plans," Jordan said. "And on top of that, don't you remember how Layla always had a crush on me?"

Joshua grimaced. "That's old history. Besides, I thought she was engaged."

"She was. A long time ago. You need to be better at keeping up with town gossip. Anyway, I don't know who ended it, but I hear Layla hasn't dated much or at all in the meantime. Maybe some guy broke her heart."

That thought bothered Joshua, but not enough to be sucked into one of his brother's wild schemes. "I just got back into town. I've got things to do."

"Come on, Josh. You're gonna need me in your corner. Ask Layla to the concert, pretend to be me, nicely of course. And then don't call her afterward. I'll be in the clear with Dad. Layla will get the message that I'm not into her. And you'll be free to get back on your feet here in Royal. It will be fun, I swear."

"It's too complicated. What kind of arrangements have you made with her?"

Jordan's expression was triumphant. "That's the best part. None, yet. The concert is Sunday night. All you have to do is text her that you'll pick her up at six. Feed her dinner. Take her to the venue. Drop her off later. Unless the sex thing is a possibility."

"I'm not going to make Layla Grandin a one-night stand." Joshua bristled.

"Aw, hell, baby brother. You know I was kidding about the sex. Will you do it? Dad will kill me if I mess up his grand plan. He's already put the ticket stuff in my name. But I have a very special lady on the hook for tomorrow night, and I don't want to disappointment her."

Joshua felt the urge to say yes. He and Jordan used to pull this trick on Layla all the time, but she always saw through them. It might be fun to try one more twin swap for old times' sake.

"Fine," he said. "I'll do it. But what makes you think she won't catch on that it's me and not you?"

"Layla and I haven't run in the same circles in a long time. I was at the funeral today, but not the reception, so she didn't see me. Your hair is a tad shorter than mine, and you're not as tanned as me, but other than that, we could still fool ninety-five percent of the people on any given day."

"Layla was always smarter than either you *or* me," Joshua said. "I might crash and burn, but it will be fun trying."

Layla glanced at the text on her phone for what must have been the twentieth time.

Looking forward to the concert. I'll pick you up at six.
Dinner first. J.B.

Jordan Banks. Her childhood crush. Clearly, the
senior Mr. Banks had orchestrated all of this. Jordan
had had plenty of opportunities to ask Layla out over
the years if he had been interested, but he hadn't. He
wouldn't have suddenly invited her to a concert out of
the blue if his father hadn't pressured him.

But even knowing that, Layla didn't mind. She needed
a distraction.

Deciding what to wear had taxed the limits of her
wardrobe. She wasn't really into the country music
scene, but everyone in the world knew who Parker Brett
was. Tonight's crowd would be upscale, wealthy and
dressed to the nines.

Ticket prices were astronomical. Some radio personalities criticized Brett for ignoring his blue-collar base,
but Layla didn't know if that was true or not. Parker gave
incredibly generous donations to a host of charitable or-
ganizations, so who was she to judge?

Not much in her closet seemed appropriate for a concert. It was May. In Texas. Concert venues were notori-
ously hot and crowded. After some digging, she found
an item she had bought and never worn. The halter-
necked, button-up lightweight denim dress ended several inches above her knees and had a deep V-neck. She
added red espadrilles that laced up over her ankles and
a tiny leather purse that swung from a very long strap.

When she glanced in the mirror, she looked like a
woman intent on having fun.

The dress bared a lot of skin. But with her wavy blond
hair down tonight, she wouldn't feel too self-conscious.
She added enough shadow and mascara to emphasize

her blue eyes, then topped off her makeup with a light cherry stain and lip gloss.

Jewelry wasn't hard. She loved the large diamond hoop earrings her parents had given her for college graduation. They provided the final touch of glam to her appearance. She even added a dainty gold chain with a tiny diamond star.

Once she was ready and headed downstairs, it was hard not to freak out. For one thing, this was a date. With a man. After a long dry spell. For another, it was Jordan. Her crush on him had always been a combo of childhood nostalgia and female appreciation for a guy who was tall and handsome and charismatic.

As kids, she and the Banks boys had often been mistaken for siblings by strangers. Jordan's dirty-blond hair and blue eyes were enough like hers to make that a possibility. In some ways, she *had* felt like the twins were brothers.

They tolerated her and hung out with her and taught her how to climb trees and throw a baseball. Her own brother, Vic, had been a year younger than she was. Layla had always preferred the company of Jordan and Joshua, maybe because they made her feel grown-up and like she *belonged*.

At home, Vic was the only boy. Chelsea was the oldest, and Morgan the baby. Layla had always felt a bit like the odd man out. Honestly, she still felt that way even now.

When the doorbell rang, she sucked in a sharp breath and opened it. Jordan Banks stood on the veranda looking sexy enough to give any woman heart palpitations. Dark dress jeans molded to his long, muscular legs. His white, button-down shirt with sleeves rolled to the elbow emphasized his golden skin, and his hair was just tousled

enough to make him look as if he had recently climbed
out of bed.

She was mortified to feel her cheeks flushing. "Hi,
Jordan," she said brightly. Maybe too brightly, because
she saw him react. A tiny flinch? She couldn't exactly
pin it down.

At last, he returned the smile. "Hey, Layla. It's good
to see you. And man, you look gorgeous."

His sincere compliment soothed a few of the butterflies in her stomach. "Thank you." She closed the door
behind her. "I'm looking forward to the concert."

"Me, too," he said. This time, the words weren't entirely convincing.

As he helped her into the car, she grimaced. "Listen,
Jordan. I know your dad put you up to this. We don't
have to go if you don't want to."

He slid behind the wheel and gave her an unreadable glance. "Don't be silly. You're a good friend. We've
known each other forever." He paused. "I'm really sorry
about your grandfather. I remember how much you loved
him."

Layla's jaw wobbled, taking her by surprise.
"Thanks," she said huskily. "It's hit me harder than I
expected. I guess I thought he was immortal."

Jordan leaned forward and caught a tear that had escaped and clung to her lower lashes. "He must have been
so proud of you."

For a split second, the air inside the car was charged
with *something*. Layla shivered inwardly. She had always
crushed on Jordan, but this was different. His tenderness reached the grief deep inside her chest and made
her feel a little less devastated.

She swallowed hard. "I'm not going to fall apart on
you," she said. "I swear."

His smile was lopsided. His left arm rested across the top of the steering wheel. "It would be okay if you did."

In that moment, she *knew* why this felt so weird and different. In a good way.

This wasn't *Jordan*.

The man gazing at her with such empathy was *Joshua*. She would almost bet her life on it. But why? What was the point of this kind of subterfuge?

Years ago, the twins had often fooled teachers and classmates. They had tried their twin switch on Layla, too—all the time. Pranks. Silly fun. Nothing like this. Why would one brother pretend to be the other on a date?

Could she possibly be wrong?

Yet the more she stared at the man in the driver's seat, the less he looked like Jordan. Physically, yes, of course. They were two sides of the same penny.

But where Jordan was an extrovert and the life of any party, Joshua was the quieter, more thoughtful brother. The strong silent type.

Because she wasn't a hundred percent sure, she felt vulnerable. If this was a joke, it wasn't funny. Not at all.

"Shouldn't we be going?" she asked stiffly.

Jordan seemed to emerge from some kind of haze. He even shook his head slightly. "Of course. I made a reservation at Sheen."

"Oh, good. I love it there." Sheen was the perfect choice for a nondate date. The ambience was upscale and comfortable, but the tables didn't have the kind of shadowy intimacy that would have made the evening awkward.

By the time they were seated, Layla had relaxed some. If she was wrong, and the man across the table from her was Jordan, she would simply enjoy the evening. If he was Joshua, surely he would come clean eventually. In the meantime, she was determined to chill and have fun.

While they waited for their server to bring salads, Layla folded her hands in her lap. "Your father told me you were at the funeral. Thanks for coming. I'm afraid I didn't see you. It was packed."

"I was happy to be there," he said. "I'm sorry a prior commitment kept me from attending the reception afterward."

"Don't worry about it. Though you did miss some very good food."

He grinned. "Your mother always did cater a great meal."

"How are things at *your* ranch?" she asked.

Once again, she saw a tiny flinch. A weird look in his eyes. "Same as usual, I guess. Dad is always trying new stuff."

"I remember that about him."

"I suppose Victor Junior will be free to try new things, too."

Layla wrinkled her nose. "Oh, yes. He was always so frustrated by what he called my grandfather's *old-fashioned ways*. No telling what he'll be up to in the next few months. New feed, new bulls. The sky's the limit."

By the time they started on their second course, Layla was delighted with her decision to get out of the house. She was almost certain the man across the table from her was Joshua. He was thoughtful and funny. Their discussion of politics and books and movies was wide-ranging. But the most surprising aspect of the evening was how she responded to her escort physically. His overt masculinity made her shiver. She felt sexually aware of him in a way she hadn't done with any man in a long, long time.

Jordan's company might have been equally enjoyable but in a different way. Jordan would have been telling jokes and bantering with the waitress. Jordan would have flirted more. Maybe that was the origin of Layla's preadolescent crush. It had felt good to have a boy recognize the fact that she was a female.

At the concert venue, Jordan (or Joshua) kept his arm around her waist, holding her close in the midst of the crush. They each had very official-looking credentials that gave them VIP access and seating. Her date's name badge clearly said Jordan Banks. But Layla wasn't convinced.

Backstage, Layla did her best not to act like a gushing fan, even when she was introduced to the A-list movie star who was currently dating Parker Brett. When the woman's handler offered to take a photo of Jordan and Layla with Parker's lady friend, Layla almost betrayed her total fangirl status.

But she held on to her composure with an act of will. She wouldn't embarrass her date by being incredibly gushy and unsophisticated. After the photo op, Jordan and Layla were invited to partake of the buffet spread out on tables.

Because they had already eaten dinner, they skipped the main course offerings and instead sampled the desserts.

Jordan/Joshua grinned when she indulged in cream puffs. "You have whipped topping on your chin," he said.

Before she could react, he picked up his napkin and leaned in to remove the sticky, sweet mess.

They were so close for a moment she could stare into the depths of his Texas bluebonnet eyes. The shade was lighter at the edges of his irises and deeper as it moved toward his pupils. Very distinctive.

They were sitting on folding chairs in a corner. It

was still noisy, but for the moment, a bubble of privacy surrounded them.

As much fun as she was having, Layla couldn't forget about the fact that her "date" might not be who he was supposed to be. The uncertainty threatened to dampen the evening. She felt some definite chemistry with the man at her side, but her crush used to be on Jordan. Was she now flirting with *Joshua*? Because she so badly wanted to know, she decided to grill Jordan/Joshua. Maybe he would crack.

"So tell me about your brother," she said lightly. "What is Joshua up to? Still living in Dallas?"

This time she wasn't imagining the subtle reaction. The tiniest flinch. A stricken look in his gaze.

"Well, um," he said. "He's doing okay. In fact, he just came back to Royal very recently."

"Oh, how nice. Was Joshua at the funeral, too?"

Now Jordan/Joshua's face and neck turned red. He gulped his wine. "He wanted to be. But he had an important appointment at the bank. I think he may buy a house."

"So this is permanent? What about his wife? Am I remembering that right? Didn't he get married? It's been so long since I've seen him."

Layla should have felt guilty. The poor guy looked hunted. But if the Banks men thought they could pull this old trick on her, they deserved what they got. Let the games begin!

Her date paled now. "Joshua is divorced," he said.

"Oh, I'm so sorry."

He shrugged. "Becky was interested in the Banks money. Once Josh took a job in Dallas and decided not to accept any financial support from the ranch, she showed her true colors. He tried. Nobody likes to fail at marriage. But Becky wasn't interested."

Layla found herself confused. If this really was Joshua, he was being remarkably open with her. The words about his marriage were raw. She could understand his pain. Although she hadn't made it to the altar, she had thought her engagement was the beginning of a bright future.

She glanced at her watch. It was almost time to take their seats for the concert.

Jordan/Joshua leaned forward with an expression of urgency. "How about you, Layla? Any men in your life at the moment? Present company excluded." His lopsided smile made her pulse beat faster.

"I was engaged," she said slowly.

"Was?"

"My fiancé had a wandering eye."

"Ouch."

"Unfortunately, his other body parts followed."

Her companion winced. "I'm sorry."

"Thanks, but honestly, I was lucky. Being lied to is no fun. At least I found out before it was too late."

Jordan/Joshua looked desperate now. "I need to tell you something, Layla…"

Suddenly, the lights dimmed, and a bell dinged. Backstage visitors began moving toward the concert hall. Again, Jordan kept her close, his big strong body shielding her from getting stepped on.

Their seats were the best in the house—a box above and adjacent to the stage. From this vantage point, Layla could see everything, even Parker Brett's white teeth and sexy smile when he strode out onto the stage.

There was no opening musical act. Parker took command of the venue and the evening and didn't let loose for a full two and a half hours. He played all his familiar favorites plus a half-dozen new numbers.

Layla loved it. There was something about the energy of a live performance that couldn't be replicated. It was sorcery. During a slow, romantic ballad near the end of the evening, Jordan/Joshua slid an arm behind her shoulders, resting it on the back of her seat. Not touching. Just close.

It didn't mean anything. Just because Parker was singing about the spark between a man and a woman and the magic of new love… Coincidence. That was all.

She half turned in her seat, searching his face for the truth. "Thank you for bringing me," she said. "This is incredible."

Three

Joshua was in hell. He'd spent the entire concert watching Layla's expressive face. Parker Brett was a damned fine entertainer, but Josh couldn't take his eyes off the woman at his side. When Layla laughed, Josh got a funny feeling in the pit of his stomach. It felt a lot like desperation and desire.

His divorce had sent his libido into hiding for a very long time. Now he felt himself stretching, waking up from a long, painful sleep.

As they walked to the car, Layla talked nonstop. He caught whiffs of her light perfume occasionally, but it was watching her hair dance in the breeze that really got to him. The dress she wore was not particularly outrageous. Still, the way it hugged her modest curves and bared her long, toned legs made his mouth dry.

She was wearing red sandal-y things that gave her three or four extra inches in height. He couldn't help thinking that he and Layla would be a perfect match in bed. Or standing. Or pressing their bodies together in any one of a dozen other positions he could imagine.

He was sweating by the time they made it to the car, but it had nothing to do with the muggy spring night. After he unlocked her door, he rounded the car and opened the driver's side.

Suddenly, the intimacy ratcheted up about a thousand percent. "I'll turn on the AC," he said. He had to tell her the truth. It was the right thing, the only thing to do. But he didn't want the night to end with her being pissed at him.

According to Jordan's dumb plan, Joshua was supposed to wrap up the evening by saying *I'll call you.* Then Jordan *wouldn't* call. Layla would think her date was a jerk. End of story.

Maybe that was the way to go. Let this fiction play itself out. Then in a few days, Joshua could make arrangements to bump into Layla as himself. The two of them could start with a clean slate.

The trouble was, he was terrible at this kind of subterfuge. He'd been known to ruin surprise parties without meaning to…he sucked at poker. Anything that required evasion or deception was not his strong suit.

He started the car. Soon, cool air blew on their faces.

It didn't help Joshua at all.

Hang on, he told himself. *Work the plan.* Jordan's plan, damn it. Why had he ever let his brother talk him into this frustrating night? It was supposed to be lighthearted fun, not sexual torture.

As they made their way through the darkened streets of downtown Royal, Layla carried the conversation, for sure. He hoped he made sense when he responded. Actually, he didn't remember saying anything at all, but he must have.

When they finally made it beyond the town limits and out to the sprawling Grandin ranch, he pulled up in front of the beautiful main house, shut off the engine and took a deep breath. "We're here," he said.

Wow. Not smooth at all.

The ranch was quiet. There were lights on in the very back of the house and upstairs, but here in the driveway, the only illumination came from the moonlight filtering through the windshield.

Layla half turned in her seat. "Thanks for taking me to the concert, *Jordan*. I had a lot of fun."

His brain raced. Had Layla deliberately emphasized his brother's name? Did she know the truth? If so, Joshua needed to come clean now. She had been lied to before…by someone important in her life. Joshua didn't want to add to her pain or reinforce her opinion of loser guys who couldn't tell the truth, even if tonight's ruse was meant to be a nod to their childhood game of twin switch.

I'll call you. That was what he was supposed to say. Three little words.

He couldn't make his lips form the syllables. If he had never left Royal and moved to Dallas, maybe he would have eventually asked Layla to go out with him. It could have happened.

He reined in his imagination and focused on the present. He hadn't had sex in twenty months, two weeks and three days. His life was in ruins. Layla represented everything he wanted in a just-for-fun relationship.

But it wouldn't be fair to play around with her. Not at all.

Three words. That's all he had to say. *I'll call you.*

She was looking at him oddly. Had she asked *him* a question? Was she waiting for an answer?

He shifted in his seat, wanting to jump out of the car and howl at the moon. Why had he let Jordan talk him into this? The mischievous twin switch had turned into an evening of sexual hunger.

Layla's smile faded. Moments before, she had been animated and friendly. Now her expression was definitely wary. "Are you okay, Jordan?" she asked.

Her head cocked to one side. She eyed him like a science experiment she needed to study. To analyze.

When she called him Jordan he ground his teeth. He wasn't Jordan. Never had been. This was a heck of a time to remind himself that young Layla Grandin had once had a crush on *Jordan* Banks, not Joshua.

Truthfully, it was Jordan, not Joshua, who had always juggled two or three beautiful girls or women at one time. They flocked to him. He made them laugh. Made them feel special. Joshua wasn't jealous of his brother's charisma. His own hard-to-get personality had snagged him plenty of women. But right now, he wouldn't mind having a smidgen of his sibling's easy charm.

"Jordan?"

If Layla Grandin said that name one more time, he was liable to snap. His blood boiled in his veins. He was frustrated with the dumb twin switch and desperately attracted to the woman he had taken on a faux date this evening.

"Layla?" He said her name gruffly, wishing he could blurt out the truth. But his original plan was best. Let this "Jordan" relationship expire, and then Joshua could swoop in and play cleanup batter.

"Yes?" Her smile was tentative now. Perhaps the tone of his voice had spooked her. It was hard for a guy to play it cool when every cell in his body wanted the woman sitting two feet away.

"Will you have dinner with me tomorrow night?"

What the hell? Where did that come from? No way was he going to let "Jordan" go out with Layla again.

He sensed her ambivalence. His weird behavior was freaking out even him. "Say yes," he urged. Her silence wasn't a good sign.

Finally, she twisted a strand of hair between her fingers and sighed. "I honestly didn't think you enjoyed yourself this evening," she said quietly. "I know tonight's arrangement wasn't your idea. Why would you want to do it again?"

The vulnerability in her words squeezed his heart. "I had a great time," he said. "I don't know what you're talking about."

"Jordan, I—"

Hearing his brother's name on Layla's lips made him snap. Jordan had plenty of women. This one was off-limits. Besides, Jordan himself had passed her off on Joshua. What kind of way was that to treat a sweet, sexy woman like Layla?

"Please," he muttered. "We need to talk."

A tiny frown appeared between her brows. "You said that earlier. Right before the concert started."

Now he had boxed himself into a corner. How could he let "Jordan" ride off into the sunset if Joshua made a big deal about *talking*? Was he going to tell Layla the truth tomorrow night?

She touched his hand. Briefly. Placating him. "I'd like to, but I can't. Our family has a very important meeting at the lawyer's office Monday at seven. It was the only time we were all free to get together. There's a bit of trouble about the estate."

Joshua frowned. "Tuesday night, then?" Without overthinking it, he leaned in, slid his hand beneath her hair and kissed her soft, shiny pink lips.

He'd watched her reapply the gloss after dinner and again after the backstage buffet. It was a simple feminine action. Nothing overtly erotic. But it had made him hard.

Now he discovered the gloss tasted like peppermint.

The kiss deepened for a nanosecond before he pulled back. He didn't want to kiss her as Jordan, but he hadn't been able to wait another minute.

"Should I apologize for that?" he asked gruffly.

Layla touched her lips with the fingers of one hand. He wasn't sure she realized she had done it. "No apologies," she said. Her gaze was wide-eyed. Had he shocked her? Wouldn't *Jordan* have kissed a beautiful woman on a first date?

"So dinner?" He repeated the invitation.

Her silence lasted long enough to make him squirm. "Sure. Text me tomorrow night and I'll see if I'm free Tuesday. It should be fine."

Joshua's personal life had been in the pits for so long, it was shocking to realize he was actually looking forward to something. "Don't change your mind," he said.

She grinned. "I've known you a long time, Jordan. Do you ever remember me being flighty?"

This time he was almost sure she emphasized the word *Jordan*. Did she know which brother she was talking to? And if so, why hadn't she said anything?

Maybe for the same reasons he hadn't. Maybe they were both wary. A failed marriage. A broken engagement. Neither of them was batting a thousand in the relationship department. And they weren't getting any younger.

Layla gathered her purse and stepped out of the car. He hopped out, too, and eyed her over the top of the vehicle. In the moonlight, she looked younger.

"Good night, Layla," he said.

She blew him a kiss. "Good night."

He could have left. But he lingered to watch her ascend the broad set of stairs that led to the porch. When she opened the front door and disappeared inside, he sighed. This had been the best night he'd had in forever.

But he had screwed it up.

He was determined to set things straight as soon as possible. If he could exit this twin switch gracefully, maybe he had a shot at coaxing Layla into his bed. Even as a kid, he had always wanted to one-up his brother, just for bragging rights. Now the stakes were higher and far more personal.

Layla found Chelsea watching a movie in the den. "Where is everybody?" she asked, sinking into her favorite chair and taking off her shoes.

"You look super cute," Chelsea said. "Mom and Dad went upstairs an hour ago. Grandma, too. Vic and Morgan are out on a double date with some friends of theirs. How was the concert?"

"Actually, it was great." Layla could feel her cheeks burn, especially since her older sister eyed her with a grin.

"So being set up by two old men wasn't a bust?"

"Jordan was nice about it. Parker Brett's concert was amazing. I had a good time."

"Why do I hear a *but* in there somewhere?"

"You'll think I'm crazy."

"No more than usual." Chelsea laughed at her own

joke. "What aren't you telling me? Did you do the nasty with Jordan Banks?"

"On the first date? Of course not."

"Lots of women do."

"Not me."

"Then what has you all riled up?"

Layla fiddled with the hem of her dress. "I'm almost positive the man I went out with tonight was *Joshua* Banks, not Jordan."

Chelsea sat up straighter and turned off the TV. "You can't be serious."

"I am. I realized it in the first hour we were together. I know those twins. They may look identical, but their personalities are completely different."

"Did you say something?"

"No. Because I wasn't a hundred percent sure. I haven't seen either of them in a very long time."

"But I thought Joshua lived in Dallas. And was married."

"He did. But he's back. Divorced, unfortunately."

Chelsea wrinkled her nose. "Sucks for him, but it sounds like you should be glad he's single again. I haven't seen you this flustered in ages."

"I'm not flustered," Layla lied.

"Riiiggghht…"

It was impossible to fool a sister who had known you forever.

Layla decided to change the subject. "How's everybody doing after the big bombshell?"

"Daddy's freaking out, of course. And he's mad as hell. Mom spends all her time trying to calm him down. Vic and Morgan don't seem to care. Uncle Daniel was supposed to fly back to Paris, but Daddy forbade him to leave until we sort this out."

"*Forbade?* Good grief, we're not the royal family."

Chelsea snorted. "Our male parental unit has let his new position as patriarch go to his head already."

"So Uncle Daniel stayed?"

"Only until Tuesday morning."

"I don't really want to go sit in a lawyer's office," Layla confessed. "They give me the heebie-jeebies."

"I don't want to go either, but it's a command performance."

Layla rubbed her temple where a headache was beginning to brew. "Do you think our family is weird?"

Chelsea rolled her eyes. "Can I plead the Fifth?"

"I'm serious. Is it strange that we all live under one roof?"

"This place is sixteen thousand square feet. With another five thousand in the guest house. We each practically have our own suites anyway."

"I guess. But what about Vic? He always has a woman in his life. Shouldn't he want more privacy?"

"Ewww." Chelsea shuddered. "I do *not* want to talk about our brother's sex life."

"But why does he stay here? Shouldn't an unattached male want his own place?"

Chelsea shook her head slowly. "Sometimes I forget how sweet and naive you are. Believe me, Layla. I'm pretty sure our dear brother has had an apartment in town somewhere for a long time."

"But why does he still make the pretense of living here?"

"You know he likes being the favored son and grandson. He wants control of the ranch to come to him someday. Squatter's rights dictate that he shouldn't stray too far from Daddy's sphere."

"I suppose."

"We all have plenty of our own money. Any of us could leave if we wanted to. Is that it, Lay-Lay? Are you feeling the need to spread your wings?"

For some reason, hearing the childhood nickname made Layla teary-eyed. "No," she said. "I don't want to leave. At least not right now. I'm like Vic, I guess. I keep hoping Daddy will eventually see that you and I have as much right to run the ranch as his precious son."

"I wouldn't bet on it. Apparently, having a penis is a prerequisite for being a real rancher in Texas."

The sarcasm made Layla smile. "Or at least here in Royal." Layla yawned. "I'm beat. I'm gonna take a shower and go to bed."

"My movie is almost over. I'll be up in a bit."

As Layla climbed the stairs, she pondered Chelsea's half-serious question. *Did* she want to get her own place? Sometimes it might be nice to avoid all the drama.

In the bathroom, she undressed and had to avoid looking at herself in the mirror. She kept remembering the feel of a warm male hand cupping the side of her neck ever so briefly. Try as she might, she couldn't convince herself that the man at her side tonight was Jordan Banks.

If he was *Joshua*, what did that mean? Why the switch? Bertram Banks had mentioned Layla's adolescent crush. So clearly, the older man had no clue his boys had something up their sleeves.

As she climbed into bed and turned out the light, she moved restlessly under the sheet. When she closed her eyes, all she could see were those beautiful blue irises, the spark of humor and desire. Was it really desire?

She'd been fooled once.

She couldn't afford to be so stupid a second time.

But even after giving herself a stern lecture, she had a feeling she was going to dream about the man who had kissed her tonight…

Four

Lawyer's offices were about as bad as funeral homes. Layla drove her own car to the meeting. She'd had drinks and dinner with a girlfriend earlier, so she had promised to meet the family here. When she walked in, the mood was glacial and uncomfortable.

Layla took a seat beside Chelsea and prepared for a long, boring hour. Hopefully not more than that. As she scanned the room, she saw that most everyone had showed up, including her grandmother. Uncle Trent and Aunt Lisa were noticeably absent. Maybe because they didn't have anything to gain or lose, they had chosen not to attend.

The lawyer was in his late sixties or early seventies. His silver hair and conventional clothing made him the epitome of upscale legal representation. He had worked for the Grandin family for decades.

"I'll get right to the point," he said. "I've contacted

the attorney who prepared those papers you received on the day of the funeral. He has apologized for sending them at such a stressful moment for your entire family. Claims he didn't know."

Layla's father bristled. "And you believe him?"

"I have no reason not to." The lawyer addressed Layla's grandmother. "Mrs. Grandin. Did your husband ever mention anything about oil rights?"

Miriam straightened in her chair. She was a tough woman, and one who had remained in the shadow of her husband's forceful personality. "Never that I recall. But Victor kept his own counsel. If he took anyone into his confidence, it would have been Augustus Lattimore. Those two old men were thick as thieves."

Again, Layla's father was visibly upset. Layla felt sorry for him actually. It must have been hard to be shut out of all the decision-making. He was at an age where some men began to think about retiring in a few years. But Victor Junior was just now getting his chance to be in charge of the ranch.

Would *he* cling to control for three more decades? Like his father had?

Vic spoke up. "We don't really have anything to worry about, do we? Isn't this probably a scam? Anyone with a good digital printer can produce documents."

Chelsea nodded. "And according to the internet, if you wad up your paper and soak it in tea, you can make it look old."

Bethany Grandin glanced at her daughter. "Good grief, Chelsea. You're letting your imagination run away with you."

The lawyer must have sensed he was losing control of this session. He cleared his throat. "Let's stick to what we know. I asked Thurston's legal counsel for additional information about this situation." He directed his attention to Layla's uncle. "Mr. Grandin. Thurston claims you had an affair with his mother, Cynthia." The accusation was blunt.

Daniel shrugged, looking almost defiant. "Years ago. So what?"

The lawyer grimaced as if he had been hoping for a denial. "There was a baby. A girl. Ashley."

Daniel shook his head. "I did have a brief relationship with Cynthia—when I was in Royal for a couple of months. But there was no pregnancy." He ran a hand across the back of his neck, betraying his unease. He was solidly built though thinner than Layla remembered. His hair was going gray, but his dark brown eyes were the same. Layla wasn't close to her uncle, because he had lived in France for decades.

The lawyer continued. "So, you have no knowledge of this alleged child?"

Layla's uncle didn't look happy. "I do not," he said curtly. "I won't deny having a physical relationship with Cynthia Thurston many years ago. But I had no further contact with her after that."

"Is it possible she couldn't find you to tell you there was a baby on the way?"

Victor scowled. "My brother has lived in France for a long time. But he has never been off the grid. Any of us could have been in touch with him if this woman asked us to intervene. The timing of the whole claim is suspect."

Layla wondered privately if her uncle's lover would have been too embarrassed to contact a family as well-known and influential as the Grandins. Maybe she decided to handle things on her own.

Layla spoke up. "Daddy, I think you're forgetting

something. Cynthia and Ashley were killed in a car crash a couple of years ago. Heath and Nolan may have just now stumbled onto these papers."

The lawyer nodded. "Anything is possible. However, Thurston is intimating that the oil rights were due Ashley, because she was a Grandin by birth. I'm still looking into why the Lattimore ranch was included. I have a call in to their lawyer. The burden of proof is on the other side. That buys you some time. I know you're thinking of hiring an investigator. Probably a good idea. We can all keep digging. Ms. Miriam, perhaps you could look through your husband's papers for any clues."

"I'd be happy to…"

After that, the meeting adjourned, and the room began to empty.

Layla realized her uncle was standing alone. She approached him and put a hand on his shoulder. "I'm so sorry," she said. "You must be in shock."

He nodded slowly. She could see the stunned bafflement in his gaze. "It's bad enough to find out I fathered a child and Cynthia didn't say a word. But it's killing me that it's too late. I can't do a damn thing about it. I can't ask Cynthia for an explanation, and I can't get to know Ashley. I would have been better off not knowing."

Moments later, Layla left him, sensing that he preferred to defer his emotions until he had privacy to think about the situation.

She said a word to Chelsea and then headed out to where her car was parked on the street. All evening she had wanted to glance at her texts, but she made herself resist. Now was the time. She slid into the driver's seat, shut the door and turned on the engine so the car would cool down.

Then she checked her phone. She sucked in a breath.
There it was...

As promised. I'm checking in about dinner tomorrow
night. J.B.

Layla couldn't help but smile. Even if this rendezvous
resulted in an awkward moment of truth, she didn't want
to miss it. First of all, she wanted to satisfy her curiosity about which of the Banks boys had taken her to the
concert. And second—because she was almost positive
it was Joshua—she wanted to see if the spark of attraction was more than a fluke.

She responded quickly...

I'm free! What time?

Are you up for a picnic? If so, I'll pick you up at 5, and
we'll go for a drive...can you supply a quilt?

Layla was surprised, but she had no objections. A
picnic would give them more privacy to clear the air.

Sounds good to me. See you then...

She tossed her phone in her purse so she wouldn't
be tempted to continue the conversation. She probably
should be mad. Mad at either or both of the Banks men.
But maybe it was a harmless prank. She hoped so. She
would give them the benefit of the doubt, mostly because she wanted to explore the tantalizing sparks she
had experienced last night.

The following day, she was busy with a million and
one things around the ranch. And she spared a couple

of hours to help her grandmother. Miriam was intent on donating her husband's clothing as soon as possible. It was her way of coping with grief.

The two women sorted through hangers and checked pockets. The only things they found were old pieces of hard butterscotch candy, still in the wrappers.

Layla put her arms around her grandmother at one point and hugged her. "I'm so sorry about Grandy. Are you going to be okay?"

Miriam nodded, wiping her eyes. "Oh, yes. But he and I were together so long, it feels like I've lost a limb. We had good days and bad, Layla. Still, the two of us were rock solid. I hardly know what to do with myself now."

"I promise we'll all be here for you, Grammy. I know this must be so very hard."

Later that afternoon, Layla showered and changed into a new sundress she had bought recently. The material was a pale yellow gauzy cotton scattered with tiny teal flowers. The spaghetti-strap bodice was lined, so she skipped a bra.

A picnic sounded sedate enough. She settled on cream leather ballet flats. They were more cute than practical. Not the thing for tramping around the ranch, but perfect for a date with a handsome man.

When Jordan/Joshua arrived at five on the nose, she went out to the porch and down the steps to meet him, not waiting for him to come up and ring the doorbell. There were too many unanswered questions. The last thing she wanted was for her nosy family to grill whichever of the Banks brothers was picking her up.

Her date shielded his eyes from the sun. "Hey, there."

"Hey, yourself." She handed him the quilt. Again, her gut feeling told her she was being greeted by Joshua. Jordan was louder and more gregarious. This man gave her a tight smile, tucked her into the front seat of a luxury sports car and got in without saying another word. It was a different car tonight. Had the other one been Jordan's?

To be honest, Layla didn't mind that the drive was mostly silent. It had been a long, stressful week. She was happy to lean back and take a deep breath.

The car was a dream. Top-of-the-line engineering and every possible creature comfort. It was also a stick shift. Outside town when they found a two-lane road that was straight and deserted, the man behind the wheel hit the gas.

Layla smiled. There was something about speed that helped wash away tension and stress. It was one reason she liked riding horses. But today was even more exciting. She could feel the powerful engine as it worked its way higher and higher.

Watching her companion out of the corner of her eye was entertaining in its own way. Though he might not even know it, the tiny smile that tipped up the corners of his masculine lips told Layla he was enjoying himself.

He was dressed beautifully, but casually. Well-worn jeans showcased long legs, a narrow waist and powerful thighs. His expensive tooled-leather cowboy boots were the real deal. The navy-and-yellow-plaid cotton shirt was soft, the sleeves rolled to his elbows.

He also smelled really, really good.

Layla didn't ask where they were headed. It was nice to sit back and let someone else steer the ship for a change. She was, unfortunately, a bit of a workaholic. It was a tendency made even worse in the wake of her broken engagement. She had buried herself in work and scarcely come up for air.

Now she felt her muscles going lax, her body nestling into the embrace of a butter-soft leather seat. Even her bones seemed willing to loosen and unkink. Drowsy contentment wrapped her in a cocoon of well-being.

Joshua didn't know whether to be insulted or amused when he realized his passenger was asleep. She had kicked off one shoe and tucked her leg beneath her. In that position, her dress rode up, revealing a tanned, toned thigh.

His hands tightened on the wheel. He had no idea how this picnic was going to play out, but he hoped Layla would give him a chance to explain. He wasn't looking forward to confessing the twin switch, but it had to be done.

When he stopped the car at last, they were parked atop a low rise miles from the nearest house. This property was for sale. He had toyed with the idea of buying it. But such a decision would mean staying in Royal, and he wasn't sure he was ready to commit to that.

He studied Layla as she slept, glad of the opportunity to catalog how the young tomboy had morphed into a capable, extremely feminine woman. Her hair was still the golden blond he remembered. From his close vantage point, it looked soft and silky.

His sex stirred, reminding him that a man his age shouldn't be sleeping alone. Layla was the first woman in forever to tempt him. Seriously tempt him.

The dress she wore wasn't meant to be provocative. But it bared her arms and shoulders. Her legs were bare, too. In fact, she was probably completely bare underneath except for whatever underwear she wore.

Since he could see the tiny outline of her nipples, maybe nothing but panties.

He gripped the steering wheel and told himself he

had to keep a rein on his baser impulses. For one thing, Layla thought she was out on a date with Jordan. And for another, if he wanted Layla's forgiveness, he couldn't seduce her on this gorgeous spring afternoon, no matter how much he wanted to...

He said her name quietly, not wanting to startle her. "Layla. Wake up, Layla. We're here."

It took three tries, and on the last one he actually shook her shoulder. The feel of her delicate bones and soft skin seared itself into his fingertips.

Layla yawned and opened her eyes. He witnessed the exact moment she realized what had happened. Her whole face turned red.

"Oh, gosh," she whispered, scrubbing her hands over her cheeks and straightening her hair. "I'm so sorry. Did I fall asleep on you?"

"Not *on* me," he teased. "But beside me, yes."

When he realized she was genuinely mortified, he chuckled. "Don't sweat it, Layla. You've had several hard days. I'm glad you felt comfortable enough with me to relax. You must have needed the rest."

"I haven't been sleeping at night," she admitted. The embarrassed color faded, leaving her pale.

"How is your grandmother doing?" he asked.

"I helped her pack up Grandy's clothes today. She's hanging in there."

Joshua rubbed his chin. "Isn't that kind of quick?"

Layla's smile was wistful. "You'd have to know my grandmother. She's sort of the rip-off-the-bandage type."

"Everyone deals with grief differently, I suppose." He thought about his marriage—the separations, the long arguments...the realization that he couldn't save the relationship with Becky on his own. He had grieved.

Layla sat up and reached for her shoe, then slid her

foot into it and adjusted the heel. "I seem to remember you promising me a picnic?"

He nodded. Layla was hurting, too, but she was very independent. "I did, indeed. The basket is in the trunk."

Both of them exited the car. Layla stretched and looked around.

They were parked amidst a small copse of cottonwood trees. Years ago, there might have been a small creek at the base of the rise, but it had long since dried up.

"This is nice," she said, giving him a smile that made him catch his breath.

He wanted Layla Grandin on several levels, but there was a hurdle he had to clear first. He wasn't sure what he was going to say, but sooner was better than later.

While he marshalled his thoughts, he spread out the beautiful thick quilt that had probably been handed down through the Grandin family. Though it was faded, the patina of age added charm. Unlike Layla, he and Jordan had no living grandparents. Nor a mother. Only their pushy, upwardly mobile father who had always aspired to be more than what he was.

Nothing wrong with that as long as a person understood acceptable boundaries. Bertram Banks was always pushing.

To be fair, Joshua couldn't blame his father for the current situation. Jordan could have said no to his father. Joshua could have said no to his brother. But he hadn't. Because a part of him had been intrigued.

When Layla sat down, her sundress settled around her like a patch of sunshine. She was graceful and unselfconscious. Joshua couldn't help thinking about the past. Some people might wonder why twin boys had allowed a younger playmate, a girl, to tag along on their adventures. As Joshua remembered it, the reasons were at least twofold.

Layla had kept up with them every step of the way. And her presence—although she wasn't a girly girl back then—had been a way for the boys to show off, to continually try and best each other.

It was a pattern that had persisted over the years... though without their sidekick, of course.

Joshua opened the trunk and retrieved the large fancy picnic basket. "I ordered this from the Royal Diner. I hope I picked things you like. I did tell them no bananas in the fruit salad."

"I can't believe you remembered that I don't like bananas." Layla laughed, her eyes sparkling in the dappled shade. Though her irises were blue like his, the shade was different. Layla's were lighter with flecks of gold.

He toed off his boots and joined her on the blanket, crossing his sock-clad feet at the ankles. When he leaned back on his elbows, he sighed without meaning to. A weight he'd been carrying for months finally slipped away.

The past was the past. It was time for him to move on. He turned his head, looked at Layla. Took a deep breath. "I need to tell you something."

Her expression was both wistful and wry. "Is it that you're Joshua and not Jordan?"

Shock ran up and down his spine. He sat up, slinging an elbow over one knee. "You knew?"

She shrugged. "Not at first. But after half an hour, I was fairly certain. I haven't seen Jordan in a long time, nor you for that matter. So I had to question my gut feeling."

He frowned. "Not many people can tell us apart."

Layla gave him a look that questioned his intelligence. "I spent days and weeks and years running wild with you two when we were kids. I used to know you both very well."

"What gave me away?"

"Well, for starters, you're quieter than Jordan. Deeper maybe. He's a bit of a flirt."

Her comment stung, though Joshua was aware she hadn't meant it as a gibe. Becky had told him repeatedly that he was no fun. He'd heard it enough times that he eventually began to wonder if she was right.

"I'm sorry," he said, managing a grin. "Well, hell. If we're being honest, I'm not sorry at all. I had a great time with you at the concert."

"Me, too," she said. "But you still haven't explained why you and Jordan tried the twin switch with me."

"No big secret." He sighed. "Dad set all this in motion. But Jordan already had another date."

Her lips twitched. "Of course he did. I should have known."

"Otherwise, I'm sure he'd have been happy to take you to the concert."

"You don't know any such thing. I've seen the women your brother dates. I'm not exactly his type."

"Maybe." Joshua didn't want to wade into that one.

His confession hadn't extinguished the thread of heat between them. If anything, the *sizzle* intensified.

Layla tucked her hair behind her ear. "You want to start over?" she asked.

Joshua was struck by her response to the situation. She didn't sulk. She didn't hold a grudge. And she didn't punish him. Was this what normal, nice women were like? He had been ensnared with his ex-wife for so long, he had almost forgotten.

"I'd like that," he said.

"Let me help you set out the food."

They were both hungry. The conversation was light-hearted as they ate, but beneath the surface communication ran a vein of something else. Awareness.

He was in no place to jump back into anything serious. And he didn't know if Layla was the kind of woman to dabble in a short-term affair. But he was willing to find out.

She put him on the spot at one moment. "Was all that stuff you said to me the other night about your wife the truth? You know, when you were pretending to be your brother?"

He groaned. "You're not going to let me forget that, are you?"

Layla's grin was smug. "Probably not. At least for the moment."

"Yes," he said flatly. "It was true. My father warned me that Becky was after the family money. But I didn't listen."

"You were in love."

He shrugged. "I thought I was. I *wanted* to get married. I liked the idea of starting a family."

"But she never got pregnant?"

"Nope. In fact, she flatly refused to consider it. But that was the least of our problems. She loved Dallas, and the social life there. All she talked about was making the right connections, cultivating the right friends."

"And you?"

"I had a great job I loved—project manager for an energy company—but I had always assumed that one day we would go back to Royal and start a family. Unfortunately, I hadn't made those intentions clear *before* we got married. That was my mistake. I decided we should go to counseling and work on our problems. Becky agreed at first. We made it through three sessions, maybe four. But that was it. I discovered it's impossible for one person to save a marriage when the other partner doesn't care."

"I'm so sorry, Joshua." Her empathetic gaze made him feel marginally better. Rehashing his romantic past was not the way to impress a woman.

"It was for the best. We never really loved each other, I guess. We were separated for a little over two years. The divorce was final a few months ago."

Layla frowned. "But if you still loved your job, why are you here in Royal? Just for a visit?"

"Actually, I…"

"You what?" She prompted him when he couldn't get the words out.

"I quit my job. I told Jordan, but my father doesn't know."

"Wow. That's a big decision."

He gazed at her wryly. "After the divorce was final, I started feeling the pull of home, even more than I had before. I've missed the wide-open spaces. I think about the ranch a lot."

"What will your dad say?"

"Jordan thinks he'll take me back in a heartbeat."

"So, problem solved?"

"It's hard to tell. I don't want to step on Jordan's toes. I wonder if I should start over somewhere completely new."

Five

Layla was surprised by the sting of disappointment that settled in her stomach. She didn't even *know* the adult Joshua, not really. Yet maybe because of their childhood friendship, she felt a connection.

"If you don't mind a little amateur psychoanalysis on my part," she said, "I'll offer a theory."

He grimaced. "Feel free."

"I think you feel like a failure, and it has rattled your confidence."

Joshua blinked. His cheeks flushed. "You shoot straight, don't you?"

The rueful note in his words made her wonder if she had gone too far. "It's not a criticism," she said quickly. "But I've had some experience with the phenomenon. When I found out Richard was cheating on me, it shook me to the core. Here was a man I had chosen, a guy I was planning to spend my life with, and I had made a huge mistake."

"You and I are hardly the first or the last to misjudge other human beings."

"True. But up until then, I considered myself pretty smart and capable. Suddenly, everyone around me was giving me pitying glances. As if I was some poor, delicate creature. I hated it."

"I get that."

There was silence between them for a moment. Layla smoothed the skirt of her dress, not quite able to look at her companion. "I never thought this picnic was going to be a deep dive into our darkest emotions."

"Is that a bad thing? Maybe we've cleared the air."

"Maybe."

They finished their meal in companionable silence. Layla wondered if this was the last time she would see Joshua. She didn't often cross paths with the Banks family unless it was at some charity function or town event. If Joshua decided not to stay, this was it.

Something inside her wasn't willing to accept that. "You could do me a favor," she said. "If you're still around in a couple of weeks."

"What's that?"

"The Cattleman's Club is having their spring luncheon soon. I don't have a date, but I'd like to. You know how gossip in Royal is. I'm really tired of everyone discussing *poor little Layla*. They all know about Richard."

"I could do that," he said. "I'm still a member on paper. Though I haven't been inside that beautiful old building in years."

"You'll be surprised," she said. "We have an on-site day care now. And lots of other improvements. Change comes slowly, but it does eventually come."

"I take it your whole family belongs to the club?"

"We do."

"And how will things change at the ranch now that your grandfather is gone? You said your dad has been frustrated by your grandfather's old-fashioned ways."

"Ugh. Sore subject," she muttered.

"You don't have to discuss it if you don't want to."

"I don't mind. Dad is just as old-fashioned in his views, though he doesn't see it. It looks like I have a choice to make."

"Like how?"

"Chelsea and I are about to get sidelined, even though all either of us has ever wanted was to be an integral part of the ranch. She's furious about it. I'm more resigned to the inevitable, I guess. I train horses, and since my degree is in business, I keep an eye on the bottom line when no one is watching."

"Then what's the problem?"

"My father is fifty-nine years old, and he is just now getting a shot and running things his way. I don't know if my siblings and I are prepared to wait that long. It's frustrating when we have progressive new ideas, grounded in science, but Daddy won't listen. Grandy was the same in that regard, but at least he had the excuse of coming from a much older generation."

"Remind me how old your siblings are?"

"Chelsea is the eldest at thirty-five. I'm thirty-two, a year younger than you. Vic is thirty-one, and our baby sister, Morgan, is twenty-eight."

"Do all of them want to be significant parts of running the ranch?"

She grimaced. "Not Morgan. She owns a boutique in town. But it doesn't even matter. Vic has the edge in that sweepstakes."

"How so?"

"Grandy and my father were and are very patriarchal. Because Vic is the only boy, he's on deck to be the next lord of the manor."

"That doesn't seem fair at all." Joshua had reclined on his side. He looked sleepy and replete...but wickedly masculine. Layla realized she was both aroused by him and on her guard. Because Layla was lonely, and Josh was a huge part of her past, she might be tempted to wallow in sentimentality and sexual attraction and do something stupid.

"Enough about me," she said. "Maybe we should be getting back." The sun was sinking low in the sky, chasing the horizon.

"What's your hurry?" he asked with a teasing smile. That smile was deadly. It made all her secret vulnerable places tingle. As if a special kind of lightning was about to strike.

She cleared her throat. "No hurry. But I'm sure you have important things to do."

"Nothing more important than spending time with an interesting woman."

"Flatterer."

The smile disappeared. Now his gaze was warm, maybe even hot.

He played with the hem of her skirt, folding a tiny piece of fabric between his fingers. Layla was mesmerized, watching that big tanned hand so near her knee.

"Tell me something," he said, his voice deep and husky. "When I kissed you night before last, were you kissing Jordan?"

Yikes. Dangerous territory. She had a choice. Honesty or deflection. It was really no choice at all.

"No," she said. "I knew exactly who I was kissing. It was you, Josh."

The hot light in his eyes flared into male satisfaction. "Good." He leaned forward, curled a hand behind her neck and slanted his mouth over hers. No fumbling. Nothing tentative. Just a man intent on giving and receiving pleasure.

Somebody moaned. Probably her. Layla was too enmeshed in the magic of the moment to care. She trusted Joshua. She had always enjoyed his company. He was a decent, funny, kind man with a kick-ass body and worlds of experience.

Right now, he was everything she wanted.

Joshua deepened the kiss, his tongue stroking hers, his teeth nibbling her bottom lip. Eventually, he moved to her collarbone, pressing his lips to a particularly vulnerable spot. She caught her breath. Heat pooled in her sex. She wrapped her arms around his neck, trying to get closer.

She was ready to devour him, but her partner was being remarkably circumspect under the circumstances. Maybe he thought it was too soon.

"Do you have any condoms with you?" she asked.

When he froze, she felt humiliation engulf her in smothering waves. "Never mind," she muttered, pulling away abruptly. "That was the wine talking."

Joshua grasped her shoulders. His hands shook. His cheeks were flushed. "I do," he said. "But are you sure this is what you want?"

"Right now? Yes."

Her answer seemed to satisfy any doubts he had. Maybe this was reckless or even self-sabotaging, but Layla didn't care. She needed Joshua. She *wanted him*.

He eased her onto her back and leaned over her. One

big masculine hand cupped her breast firmly. When her nipple peaked, he rubbed it, circling the taut point through the thin fabric of her dress.

Fire streaked through her, incinerating her doubts. She trembled, not because she was unsure, but because the magic of the moment left her breathless. If she was this strung out from a mere touch, how was she going to survive what happened next?

She had never considered herself a passive lover, but for the moment, she reveled in having Joshua take charge. He was sure of himself. Not arrogant. Simply intent on seizing what he wanted, what she had offered.

He peeled the small straps of her sundress down her shoulders and freed her arms. Now she was bare to the waist.

She saw the muscles in his throat ripple as he swallowed. "You're beautiful, Layla."

Suddenly, she was ravenous for him. "There's a zipper in the back," she whispered. "Hurry."

His smile was crooked. "What's your rush?"

"It's been a very long time since I've enjoyed…*this*."

The grin faded. "I'll bet I've got you beat. Almost two years. My ex slept around during our separation. I still felt married."

"And since February?"

He shrugged, his jawline rigid. "Nobody. I've been a mess, Layla. Are you sure you want to get involved with a guy who screwed up his life?"

She put her hands on his biceps, loving the feel of his muscles. "We're not getting involved," she said, finding the courage to stare into his eyes. "We're living in the moment. I can't say I have much experience with that way of thinking. I'm wound pretty tight. But for you, I'll make an exception."

Clearly, she had struck the right tone with her light-hearted teasing. Joshua's gorgeous smile returned, the wattage melting her body into a pool of feminine lust.

"I'm flattered," he muttered, bending to lick the tips of her breasts.

Holy hell. Layla arched her back, trying desperately to get closer. Somehow, he reached beneath her and dealt with the zipper. Soon he had her naked except for her tiny undies. Even though the sun was almost gone, she could feel its warmth on her skin.

Or maybe she was simply hyped up on the erotic way Joshua played with her body. He seemed fascinated with her flat belly, her navel, her thighs. When he touched her *there*, she bit her bottom lip to keep from begging.

For a man who professed to be celibate in recent days, he was remarkably patient.

When she said as much—muttering her disgruntlement—Joshua threw back his head and laughed uproariously.

"I wasn't trying to be funny. You're still dressed," she wailed, aggrieved.

Lightning flashed in his eyes, turning the placid blue to stormy skies. "I don't have much faith in my control once I get inside you, Layla. At least not the first time. I wanted the foreplay to be good for you, for me."

She dragged his head down. "We can always do the foreplay afterward."

Though she initiated the kiss, Joshua took control pretty damn fast. His tongue mated with hers. He sucked gently.

Heated need made her limbs heavy. Her sex throbbed with an insistent ache that begged to be assuaged. Layla felt a sudden dollop of unease. Why was she so susceptible to this man? Were nostalgia and hormones to blame?

And then the kiss deepened, eliminating any impulse on her part to think rationally.

There was no explanation for what was happening. None that made sense.

She wanted Joshua Banks more than she wanted her next breath.

He rolled away from her, panting. She watched as he extracted a square packet from his wallet and then unzipped his jeans. When he pulled his erect sex from his snug navy knit boxers, she sucked in a sharp breath.

Thankfully, Joshua didn't seem to notice. He positioned the condom and returned to her, settling between her legs. His gaze was hooded. "You ready?"

"Yes." The word was barely audible.

Joshua entered her with one powerful thrust. The clouds and treetops cartwheeled behind her eyelids as she squeezed her eyes shut and gave in to the sheer carnality of the moment. He was careful with her, tender even. But this was raw sex. No hearts and flowers. Just a man and a woman battling a powerful need.

They clung to each other on the sun-warmed quilt, struggling for more depth, more thrust, more everything.

She nipped his bottom lip with sharp teeth. "Don't hold back, Josh. I want it all."

The groan that ripped from somewhere deep inside him echoed the madness she felt. Desperation was a tangible cloud surrounding them. She inhaled his scent, felt the odd paradox of security and exhilaration.

He came first, but only seconds before she lost her mind. The orgasm was blissful, perfect, draining and energizing in equal measures.

In the aftermath, he kissed her forehead, then shifted slightly to give her room to breathe. But they were still connected. He was inside her, mostly still erect. Tantalizingly ready for round two.

At last, she found her voice. "Wow…"

He ran his thumb along her bottom lip. "Ditto…"

"Josh?" The shortened version of his name slipped out. It was what she had called him when they were kids.

"Yeah?"

"What was that we just did?"

"If you don't know, I must have done it wrong."

The humorous, self-deprecating words didn't match the solemn look in his eyes. It was hard to meet those eyes. They saw too much, perhaps. For the first time in her life, Layla had just indulged in the equivalent of a bar pickup. A one-night stand.

To a control freak, this total lapse of judgment on her part was terrifying.

"We're practically strangers," she whispered.

"Are we?" Joshua's face closed up. He rolled to his feet, straightened his clothing and turned his back so she could do the same.

When they were both dressed, she stood up, too. "I need help with my zipper," she muttered.

She presented her back to her lover and shivered when his warm fingers brushed her spine.

It took courage to turn around and face him. "I'm sorry," she said.

Now his scowl was fierce. He folded his arms across his chest. "For what?"

She shrugged, feeling small and uncertain and insecure. "I used you for sexual satisfaction."

Those blue eyes threatened to burn her. "I see. And you think I did the same?"

"Didn't you?" She wanted badly to hear him say otherwise, but the evidence was hard to discount.

In the time it took a breeze to ruffle the new leaves overhead, every emotion disappeared from his face. "I'll take you home."

"Wait," she said. "Don't be mad. I'm just trying to understand."

"It was sex," he said flatly. "Pretty incredible sex. But if it's spooked you this badly, it was clearly a mistake."

"I'm not spooked," she said quickly.

Finally, a giant sigh lifted his chest. One corner of his mouth quirked in an almost smile. He unfolded his arms and slid his hands beneath her hair, cupping her neck. He bent his head to stare into her eyes. "Could have fooled me. Relax, Layla. We enjoyed each other. Is that so terrible?"

"I am *not* a sex maniac."

Now he chuckled. He brushed his lips over hers. "I wouldn't complain if you were. This was a hell of a way to break my fast."

"Why with me?" The words burst from her lips.

"Are you asking me to explain sexual attraction?"

She rested her cheek against his chest. "I've never had sex with someone just for the heck of it. It's always been part of a relationship."

"Are you proposing?" he asked, deadpan.

"Stop trying to make me feel dumb." She punched his shoulder.

He slid his fingers through her hair. "Can't we just enjoy ourselves? Does there have to be an answer for everything?"

She stared at him for the longest time, trying to read the mix of expressions on his face. If she didn't know better, she would think he was as surprised as she was by the connection between them.

"Why don't you kiss me again?" she said. "To see if it was a fluke."

"*It* what?" He moved closer, his big frame dwarfing hers.

Sharing the same air made it hard to breathe. "The spark," she croaked. "The fire."

That arrogant masculine grin was back. "I like the way you think." He held her head and tipped it the direction he needed, settling on the exact slant to cover her mouth with his and make them both groan with pleasure.

Layla wrapped one leg around his thigh. It was good. So good. Surely this was more than deprivation making her feel like she was melting into a puddle. She was ridiculously aroused. Clinging. Desperate.

She spared a half second to wonder who this woman was. She wasn't a version of Layla anyone would recognize.

Suddenly, Joshua scooped her into his arms and strode toward the vehicle. Layla was disappointed. She wasn't ready to go home.

But her companion had other ideas. He set her on the hood of the sports car. The metal was warm from the sun, but not uncomfortably hot.

The next round of kissing was more intense. Joshua moved between her legs, shimmying her skirt up her thighs. Getting close. And closer still.

His erection, covered in thick denim, felt good pressed against her center. When he rocked back and forth, Layla's fingernails dug into his forearms. "Please," she muttered. "Please tell me that wasn't your only condom."

Instead of answering, he growled low in his throat. His big hands cupped her butt and he lifted her into his thrusts. Like two teenagers fooling around, they tried to climb inside each other's skin.

Joshua's chest heaved with the force of his labored breathing. "Can't let go," he said.

"You have to. Right now. Please. I need you, but not without protection."

On the surface, she sounded logical and forthright. Thank goodness he couldn't see inside her confused brain. If he had told her the first condom was the only one, she might have rolled the dice and taken her chances. *That* was how much she wanted him.

"Ten seconds," he promised. He left her and jerked open the car door. She watched through the windshield as he rummaged in the glove box. His jawline was granite. His hair was tousled, his cheekbones flushed.

She rested her bare feet on the slick hood, trying not to slide off.

When he came back to her, he took care of business quickly and touched her undies. "Now?" he asked gruffly.

All she could do was nod.

Joshua didn't even bother removing her panties. He simply pushed them to one side and entered her with a raw, powerful surge that dried her throat and brought emotion to the fore. She didn't want that. All she wanted was sex.

But it was impossible not to feel things. Because she didn't know how to trust this madness, she shoved all those messy, warm responses away, concentrating on the carnal present.

Joshua Banks was good in bed. Or maybe not. Who knew? But he was a heck of a lover in the great outdoors.

Now she linked her ankles at his back. She dragged

his head closer so she could kiss him wildly. "Don't stop," she panted. "Don't ever stop."

His shoulders shook with laughter, but his eyes glittered with hunger. "I'd like to oblige, Layla, but you rev me up too damn fast."

His words were prophetic. Suddenly, he pounded into her feverishly. The hood of his car might never be the same. He moaned her name as he found his release. At the last instant, he shifted to one side and thumbed her center.

She shuddered and cried out his name as she hit the peak and tumbled over the other side.

Six

Joshua could hear his heart beating inside his ears. His knees were bruised from thumping against the side of the car. And somehow, despite their location beneath a broad, expansive Texas sky, he was starved of oxygen.

The woman in his arms stirred. "Sweet heaven."

There was no blasphemy in her awed whisper. He would have uttered words of agreement, but his tongue was thick in his mouth.

Truth be told, Joshua was as shaken as his partner. For months, he had found release with a hand job in the shower. His life had been in too much turmoil for anything else. And even after the divorce was final, he'd had a vague distaste for the idea of picking up a strange woman in a bar.

He might have done that a few times in his twenties, but he was older now. Wiser. Good Lord, he hoped he was wiser. Surely he should have something to show for a marriage that imploded. As it was, he had plenty of regrets.

The sex with Layla had been volcanic. Feelings and emotions he had ignored forever suddenly bubbled to the surface. Why had he never dated Layla? She was only a year younger than he was.

But when he still lived in Royal, she hadn't really been on his radar. She was just the funny, spunky kid who ran around with Jordan and him when they were all in middle school and early high school. Thinking of his brother brought up another sore point. What if Layla had been thinking of *Jordan* when she was having sex with Joshua?

His stomach curled. She might have done that without even realizing what she was doing. Joshua was damned if he would be a stand-in for his more gregarious sibling.

Only once had the twins fixated on the same girl. It had been eleventh grade. They both wanted to ask Tiffany Tarwater to the prom. Things had gotten ugly. After that, they made a pact. No fighting over females. Ever.

Suddenly, he realized Layla was stroking the back of his neck. His body tightened as another wave of arousal—one that had merely been simmering below the surface—seized him. His throat dried.

He had taken her like a savage. Never before in his life had he experienced more desperation, or more lust. Though he was shocked at himself, the woman in his arms wasn't trying to get away, so maybe all was not lost. Carefully, he lifted her into a seated position.

Her skin was warm and silky, her golden tresses a tangled mess. He buried his face against her bare shoulder, wanting to say something, but finding himself mute.

Layla combed through his hair with gentle fingers. Separating their bodies was an actual physical pain.

After he got rid of the condom and straightened his clothes, he turned around to find Layla looking at him.

What was that expression he saw in her beautiful eyes?

Try as he might, he couldn't come up with a single word.

Layla cocked her head, still staring into his soul...or so it seemed. "Your ex-wife is an idiot," she said calmly.

He felt his face flush. The implied compliment was reassuring, but still... "I don't want to talk about my ex," he said bluntly.

Layla grimaced. "Understandable."

"I suppose I should take you home," he said, trying—after the fact—to act like a gentleman.

His lover nodded slowly. "I suppose."

When he helped her stand, she wobbled. They both laughed.

Layla's smile was wistful, but at least it was a smile.

He retrieved the quilt along with the remnants of their picnic supper and followed her to the car. When he would have started the engine, Layla put her hand on his arm. "That was incredible," she said softly. "But I'm not sure where we go from here."

He sensed her need for clarification. But hell, he was befuddled. "What do you mean?" he asked, mostly to stall for time.

One slender shoulder lifted and fell in a feminine shrug. "You're having a personal crisis of identity. You have no idea if you're even going to stay in Royal. And my whole family is embroiled in a business emergency. Neither of us is in a healthy place to start a relationship."

Then she blushed. "Or maybe that wasn't what you had in mind."

He tried to frame a response. Honestly? He wasn't

looking for a relationship at all. But his body apparently had a different agenda. The thought of leaving the lovely Layla free and unattached didn't sit well.

"All I know is that I want to see you again."

She blinked. Maybe the staccato, machine-gun words had shocked her.

"Ditto," she said. "But this week is packed."

"Can you find time for me? For us?"

Pink bloomed on her cheekbones. "I'll try."

"Fair enough."

This time when he started the engine, she didn't stop him.

The journey back to town was slower and almost as silent as the earlier trip when his passenger had been asleep beside him. He couldn't glean much from her expression. Her face was turned away from him as she stared out the side window, apparently fascinated by the fields of Indian paintbrush.

The bluebonnets were long gone. The winter had been mild, and they bloomed early. At the time, Joshua had still been in Dallas, closed up in his office by day and in his sterile apartment by night.

Why had he ever believed a corporate job was for him? He knew a hell of a lot about the oil industry, and he had been a damned good project manager, but the work hadn't satisfied an ache in his gut.

What had he been missing? Maybe everything.

At the Grandin ranch house, he parked in front of the steps and turned to face the woman who had bewitched him. He leaned forward and kissed her long and deep, though he kept his passion reined in for obvious reasons.

When he pulled back, Layla's pink lips were puffy. She touched his cheek. "It was a good picnic," she said solemnly. "I'm glad we cleared the air."

For a moment, he had forgotten all about the Jordan/ Joshua twin swap. Embarrassment cramped his stomach. "I'm really sorry about the bait and switch. I should have said no to my brother."

Layla got out and stared at him over the top of the car as he exited as well. "But think what we might have missed." Her mischievous smile brought his hunger roaring back.

He rounded the car and pulled her into the shadows, away from the illumination of the porch lights. "We'll figure this out," he promised.

"Maybe." She leaned her head against his shoulder. "Don't make promises you can't keep. We've both failed at important relationships. We're not sure what we want. Life is complicated."

The more negatives she threw at him, the stronger his impulse to convince her.

But now was not the time. "We've always been friends," he said, his tone mild. "We still are."

"True." She patted his chest with two hands. "I'll keep in touch. You, too. Maybe we can squeeze in dinner or a movie."

"I'd rather be alone with you."

Her eyes gleamed in the half dark. "Naughty, Mr. Banks."

"My brother isn't the only one who knows how to flirt."

"I'm sorry if my comparison was hurtful. I didn't mean it that way."

He made himself let her go. "You didn't hurt anything. At least not in a bad way. Some things hurt really, really *good*."

This time, she laughed. "And on that note, I'll say good-night."

"See you soon," he said. Was it a promise or a wish?

He watched as she climbed the stairs. On the top step, she turned and waved. "Good night, Josh."

Hearing her shorten his name gave him a funny feeling inside. Few people called him that anymore. But Layla had…once upon a time.

Back at the hotel, all he wanted to do was shower, flip channels for an hour or two and crash. But his brother was waiting for him in the hotel lobby.

Jordan jumped to his feet, his expression disgruntled. "Where in the heck have you been? You just got back into town. Surely your social life hasn't heated up that fast."

Joshua counted to ten. No point in taking his brother's taunting seriously. "As a matter of fact, I was out with Layla. I told her about our little stunt."

"Was she mad?"

"Actually, she was pretty cool about it."

"Ah…"

"What does that mean?"

"I'm guessing she was disappointed that it wasn't me."

"Sure didn't seem that way." Joshua glared at his twin. "Any crush Layla Grandin had on you is so far in the past nobody has the forwarding address."

"Very funny."

Joshua shoved his hands in his pockets. "Why are you here?"

"Dad wants you to come out to the ranch. So we can all talk."

"I see." Joshua couldn't decide if this overture was a plus or a minus. "Did you already tell him my divorce is finalized?"

"I had to. Otherwise, he might have thought she was here with you."

"Perish the thought."

"Indeed." Jordan ran a hand through his hair. "So you'll come?"

"Tell him I'll head out that way before lunch tomorrow. But I'm keeping the hotel room for now. I've got a lot to think about, and I need some space to decide my next move."

"Nothing to decide. You're back. End of story."

Actually, there was plenty more to the story, but Joshua wasn't keen to get into an argument now. "Thanks for coming, Jordan. I'll see you both in the morning."

They hugged, and with a jaunty wave, Jordan headed toward the exit.

Joshua made it to his room and crashed facedown on the bed. Unfortunately, he was far from being sleepy. He was hyped up on great sex and a million questions about his future. Coming home to Royal had been a gut-level impulse. Like an animal seeking shelter in its den, Joshua had wanted a place to hide out while he made plans.

But that was the trouble with hiding from reality. A man had only himself to blame when things went sideways.

The future was murky.

The morning after her picnic with Josh, Layla found herself energized and confused. Her family was still in disaster mode. Vic was still heir to the throne. But Layla was suddenly far more interested in her own personal life than anything about the ranch.

Maybe she was practicing avoidance. Or maybe

Joshua Banks was impossible to ignore. The man was hot, sexy and too damn charming for his own good.

Her grandmother unwittingly offered a distraction. At lunchtime, she and Layla ended up in the kitchen together. While the housekeeper put together the sandwiches they had requested, Miriam leaned in and whispered, "Can we eat on the veranda out back? I need to ask you something. In private."

"Sure, Grammy." Layla was concerned. Her widowed grandmother didn't look good. She had deep shadows beneath her eyes as if she hadn't been sleeping well. But that was normal, right? The elderly woman had lost her husband. She was in mourning.

Once the two of them were settled on the wide screened-in porch overlooking the flower garden, Miriam didn't start eating right away. Her hands twisted in her lap, plucking at the folds of her faded cotton *housecoat*. Although Miriam loved to dress up and had a closet full of fashionable clothing, here at the ranch house on a weekday she reverted to the relaxed workaday style of her mother and her mother's mother.

"What is it, Grammy?" Layla asked. "What's going on? And FYI, you really need to eat something. I don't want you getting sick."

Miriam smiled. "You're a peach, baby girl. Don't you worry about me. But here's the thing." She glanced around to make sure no one was close, and then she lowered her voice. "Will you drive me to the lawyer's office? I made an appointment for 1:30. But I don't want anyone else in the family to know."

"How are we supposed to pull that off?"

"Your father is out riding the range with his foreman. Bethany flew to Houston this morning with several friends for some fashion show. It's only Chelsea, Vic and Morgan we have to dodge."

"Only?"

"We can do it." Miriam didn't offer any further details. Instead, she bit into her sandwich and managed to finish half of it.

As they ate, Layla pondered the situation. Her grandmother was obviously being secretive. Although Layla's father was acting as if he had inherited the ranch outright, on paper he and Miriam were co-owners until his mother's death. So Miriam had as much right as anyone to meet with the family lawyers.

"I think this is the day that Vic and Morgan play doubles tennis at the Cattleman's Club," Layla said. "If I can make sure Chelsea isn't around, you and I should be able to get away with no one the wiser."

"And when we come home," her grandmother said, "we'll just say we went shopping." Her face lit up as if the small subterfuge tickled her.

"Sure," Layla said. "Whatever you want." Her grandmother meant the world to her. Layla would do anything to make Grammy happy, though it might be a very long time until Miriam Grandin regained her joie de vivre. Losing a spouse after so many years was a terrible blow.

As it turned out, Chelsea was spending the afternoon with a friend who had a new baby. So no one was around to see Layla and Miriam, both nicely dressed, walk down the front steps and get into Layla's Mini Cooper. Her father had poked fun at her for buying such a small, whimsical car, but Layla liked it.

At the lawyer's office, the two women had to wait only six or seven minutes in the lobby before they were ushered into the same room where the extended family had met to discuss the oil rights situation. Though Layla was prepared to step in if necessary, her grandmother handled herself with poise and determination.

She eyed the lawyer sternly. "I am here on a private matter. Do I have your word that what we discuss is confidential?"

The man's expression was affronted. "I assure you, Mrs. Grandin, I hold myself to a high ethical standard."

Miriam made a sound suspiciously like a snort. As she sat down in the chair closest to the man's broad cherry desk, she opened her 1960s' era handbag and pulled out a three-by-five leather-bound journal. The small book was maybe half an inch thick.

She paused, perhaps for dramatic effect. "I found one of my husband's diaries. More than one, actually, but this is the pertinent time period. I always knew he hid these, but I never bothered to look for them. My husband was one hundred percent faithful to our marriage. Other than that, his little secrets didn't really concern me."

She handed the tiny book to Layla, who had taken a seat as well. "I've marked the spot with a sticky note. Please read it aloud."

Layla eyed the lawyer and vice versa. Then she took a deep breath. The ink was faded. Grandy's spidery handwriting was immediately recognizable. This particular entry had been recorded more than three decades earlier.

She could almost hear his voice…

Augustus and I did what we had to do today. We signed over the oil rights on the adjoining ranches to protect Daniel. The boy is thriving in Paris. No need for him to come home and deal with a mess. We put the rights in this Cynthia person's name and warned her not to claim anything until the baby was grown. I think she

*knows we have the money and the clout to make her life
a misery if she tries any funny business.*

Layla's nerveless fingers dropped the book in her lap.
"My God, it's true."

Even the lawyer went pale.

Miriam straightened her spine. "Those two old men
have caused untold damage with this stunt."

Layla stared at her grandmother. "We have to tell
Daddy. And everyone else."

"No. We don't." Color stained the old woman's
cheeks. "Cynthia and her daughter are dead. It's possible Heath Thurston fabricated a document based on ru-
mors he'd heard from his mother. Who knows if Daniel
was really Ashley's father? Victor has hired an investigator. For now, we let things run their course." She gave
the poor lawyer a regal glare. "I wanted you to know the
truth, so you can be prepared. We may be able to stone-
wall Thurston and buy ourselves some time."

The lawyer cleared his throat. "I can't be involved in
anything illegal, Mrs. Grandin. Surely you know that."

Miriam stood, her chest heaving with rapid breaths.
"I won't let my family's legacy be destroyed. That's all
you need to know."

Layla saw the dampness on her grandmother's brow
and the way her pupils dilated. "We can meet here again
if we need to, but, Grammy, I think I should take you
home."

Suddenly, Miriam wobbled and collapsed to the floor.

Layla's heart jumped out of her chest. "Call 911," she
yelled at the lawyer. She barely heard the man's words
on the phone as she knelt beside her grandmother. The
old woman's face was paper white.

For a few moments, Layla was terrified she had lost

a second grandparent. But finally, she located a shallow pulse in her grandmother's wrist.

The next thirty minutes were a blur. Hearing sirens in the distance. Putting wet paper towels on her grandmother's forehead. Rubbing her frail arms.

As soon as the EMTs arrived, they took over with a minimum of fuss. They spent several minutes stabilizing Miriam and then lifted her carefully onto a stretcher. Fortunately, the law office was on the ground floor.

Layla felt her heart crack as she watched the stretcher being loaded in the back of the emergency vehicle. Grammy looked so frail and ill.

"I'd like to ride there with her," Layla said, preparing to climb in.

The young female medic shook her head, though there was sympathy in her eyes. "Sorry, Ms. Grandin. It's not allowed. The area is small, and we have to be able to work on your grandmother. You're welcome to meet us at the emergency room."

Seconds later, the truck sped off, sirens blazing.

Layla didn't know what to do. Her mother was out of town. Her father was riding on the far reaches of the ranch where cell service was spotty. And besides, Grammy had wanted this outing to be a secret.

Layla stood on the street corner, frozen.

Joshua was headed back to town after a not-so-successful visit to the ranch where he had grown up. As he made the turn toward his hotel, he saw Layla standing in front of a lawyer's office. She looked upset. Immediately, he pulled into a parking spot at the curb and jumped out.

"Layla. What's wrong? Are you hurt?"

She turned her head and stared at him blankly. Her

face, even her lips, were pale. When he put his arms around her, she burst into tears.

It took him several minutes to drag the story from her. "I have to go to the emergency room," she said, looking frantic.

"You're in no shape to get behind the wheel. I'll take you."

He bundled her into the car and drove ten miles above the speed limit to Royal Memorial Hospital. Layla sat, huddled into herself, and closed her eyes. When they arrived, the state-of-the-art medical center was a hive of activity.

Layla tried to get him to drop her off at the door and leave, but Joshua wasn't about to do that. "They won't let you go back in Emergency. Not until they've fully evaluated her. I'll sit with you in the waiting room."

Joshua handed off his keys to the valet parking attendant, helped Layla out of the car and stuck with her.

No matter how upscale the hospital and how bright the paint and the floor coverings, all waiting rooms were essentially the same. Filled with antiseptic smells, the aura of fear and grief and an overwhelming sense of life and death.

Layla checked in at the desk only to be told that her grandmother hadn't been admitted yet. She looked up at Joshua, her brow creased with worry. "She's eighty-eight years old. Surely they won't send her home."

"They'll do whatever is best for her, I'm sure. Come sit down."

He tried to distract her with conversation, but to no avail.

At one point, Layla jumped to her feet and paced. "It's my fault."

"How?" He frowned, seeing her frantic state and unable to help her.

"Grammy wanted me to take her to the lawyer's office for a private meeting. She didn't want the rest of the family to know. So I said I would, but..."

"But what?"

Layla chewed her lip. "She collapsed while we were there."

"Do you want to tell me what was going on?"

"Maybe. But not now."

"Okay." He took her wrist as she made another circuit in his direction. "Sit, Layla. You're going to need to be strong to help your grandmother. Right now, you're wearing yourself out."

To his relief, Layla finally collapsed into the space beside him. It was a two-person love seat, no inconvenient metal bar in the middle. He slid an arm around her shoulders. "Breathe," he said. "Everything is going to be okay."

Layla half turned and glared at him. "You don't know that. People *die*."

Tears spilled from those blue eyes that made him weak in the knees. He pulled her closer. "Aw, hell, Layla. Don't do this. I can handle anything but you falling apart."

She had always been one of the strongest females he knew. To be honest, he and Jordan hadn't merely *tolerated* her presence when they were younger, they had *enjoyed* having her around.

Of course, being teenage boys, they never articulated those feelings.

Without warning, all the fire left her. She leaned into his embrace, not saying another word. But the slow tears didn't stop. Each one dug a little knife into his heart.

She looked even more beautiful than usual wearing a black pencil skirt, a sleeveless ivory silk blouse tucked in at the waist and low heels that matched the skirt. Her hair was pulled back into a sleek, sophisticated ponytail.

He stroked the nape of her neck and waited with her, wondering what he was doing with this woman in this spot. He'd done a lot of soul searching after he dropped her off last night. The negative column was staggering.

First of all, there was the matter of her crush on Jordan. Josh looked *exactly* like his twin. There was a decent chance that Layla was unconsciously using Joshua as a stand-in for the guy she really wanted. It was a tough pill to swallow, but Josh had to at least consider the possibility.

Second, Layla's family was in crisis mode. She hadn't opened up to him yet about the specifics, but it was something serious enough to involve the whole clan. Which meant Layla needed to be there for her parents, her siblings and, of course, her newly widowed grandmother.

Then there was the matter of Joshua himself. It was hard to be confident about a new relationship when he had so badly botched his marriage. It wouldn't be fair to any woman to get involved until he knew what he wanted out of life.

Did he want to work with his father and Jordan? Did he want to go somewhere else—create a new life on his own terms? Houston was great. The museums, the art, the music. The sporting events. He had buddies in Houston. It would be a perfect place to relocate, and the job market was solid.

But then there was Royal. This quirky town with its history and its roots and its way of pulling a guy back home. Deep down, he felt like this was where he was supposed to be. But doing what? His father and Jordan didn't really *need* him. Joshua wanted to make his own mark in the world.

If he was smart, he would put the brakes on this thing with Layla.

Yet as good and sensible as his plan sounded, he couldn't work up any enthusiasm at all for any of the choices that didn't involve her.

She made him shudder...made him yearn. In ways that made him question why he had ever thought Becky was the one.

He wasn't stupid. He knew that sexual attraction could burn hot and bright and then ultimately flame out and turn to ash...or merely cool off gradually.

He'd had enough girlfriends over the years to realize that.

Was he kidding himself to think Layla was different? There was *something* between them, something almost irresistible. Lust? He'd known lust before. He was a guy, after all. And maybe the only difference with Layla was that they shared a past as adolescents.

But he couldn't convince himself that was it. Even now, in a setting entirely nonconducive to sexual thoughts, he knew he wanted her. He felt possessive and protective. Most of all, he trembled with the need to make love to her.

Was that normal? Was he having some kind of early midlife crisis?

She stirred in his embrace, sitting up straight and rubbing her face. "Talk to me," she said. "I can't stand this waiting. Tell me about your day. Or anything."

He nodded. "Well, I went out to the ranch to see my father this morning."

"Is this the first time since you've been back in Royal?"

"Yes. I needed a few days to get my thoughts settled."

"How did it go?"

He hesitated. "Not like I thought it would. Jordan says Dad will take me back in a heartbeat, but I don't think it's that simple."

"Oh? Why not?"

He shrugged. "Just a gut feeling. He wants me to admit he was right and I was wrong. He never liked Becky and didn't want me to marry her."

"So you think he wants you to eat crow?"

"Yeah..."

"And will you?" She looked at him curiously, not judging.

"I don't mind admitting I was wrong. But I'm not sure my being back at the ranch permanently is such a good idea. Dad and Jordan have things under control. I might feel like a third wheel."

"But don't you own a share of the property?"

"I do. I've been a silent partner since I moved to Dallas."

Layla opened her mouth to say something but was interrupted when a scrubs-clad doctor pushed through the swinging doors.

"Ms. Grandin? Ms. Layla Grandin?"

Seven

Layla held Josh's hand in a death grip as she crossed the room. His strong arm curled around her shoulders, and his warm fingers twined with hers. That physical support was the only thing keeping her grounded at the moment.

Desperately, she searched the doctor's face. Was there some patient-care course in med school that taught them how to keep all expression under wraps?

"How is she?" Layla asked, her throat tight with fear.

The doc gave her an impersonal half smile. "Mrs. Grandin is stable. I've spoken with her at length. She thinks she may have forgotten to take her medication this morning. Consequently, her blood pressure bottomed out. Stress is also a factor. In addition, she hasn't been eating and drinking properly since her husband died. We're going to keep her a couple of days for observation. I've expressed to her how vital it is to care for her body while her heart heals."

That last poetic turn of phrase made Layla rethink her opinion of the young doctor. "Thank you," she said.

"Does she have anyone to stay with her when she goes home?"

"Oh, yes. Plenty of us. Don't worry, Doctor. We'll wait on her hand and foot—I promise."

When the man returned the way he had come, Layla looked up at her rescuer. His hair was disheveled. He probably needed a haircut. But the thing that stood out most in this moment was Josh's absolute strength of character. She *knew* she could depend on him. Even before today—when he had dropped everything he was doing and stepped in to care for her—she understood that about his code of conduct. "Thanks," she said. "I was a wreck, but I'm okay now. You can go."

He frowned at her. "If I'm not mistaken, you'll need a ride back to your car. Or better yet, I'll take you straight home, and someone can pick up your car later. It's in the wrong direction."

Layla hated admitting he was right. Though she was grateful to him, she didn't want to feel obligated to anyone, much less Josh. Not after he had seen her naked. There were too many unanswered questions for her to be completely sanguine about his presence at the hospital.

"That would be helpful," she said grudgingly.

Josh kissed the tip of her nose. "That hurt, didn't it? Admitting you needed help?"

She scowled. "And your point?"

"Sometimes it's nice to let someone take care of you."

Layla felt herself leaning into him, drowning in blue eyes that promised all sorts of delicious delights. "I don't need a man to look after me." She whispered the words automatically, trying to ignore the warmth spreading in her chest. The warmth Josh had put there with his kindness.

Yet, *kind* wasn't the adjective she should have used. There was banked fire in his eyes, as if the sexual connection between them was on the back burner but ready to burst into flame. The intensity of that gaze made it hard to breathe for a moment.

Fortunately for her, a nurse approached them. "Mrs. Grandin is being admitted right now. She'll be in room 317. If you want to wait for her up there, it shouldn't be long."

"Thank you," Layla said. She turned to Joshua again. "Seriously. You don't have to stay. I'm going to text my siblings. They'll all be showing up soon. And my father, too. Somebody will take me back to get my car eventually."

A second ticked by. Then five more. Joshua sighed. "I'd like to stay. When someone else in your family takes a turn, you could go back to the hotel with me and relax. Then maybe dinner in the hotel dining room. Or even room service?"

Layla searched his face. "Is *relax* code for something?"

His grin was wry. "Only if you want it to be. My hotel is near the hospital. It saves you going out to the ranch. You could take a nap. Watch something on TV."

"Make love to my childhood friend?" Rarely was she so sexually direct, but Josh might not be sticking around Royal.

He blinked. "I'm at your disposal, Ms. Grandin."

The next hour passed quickly. When they went upstairs, Josh insisted on remaining in a nearby waiting room across the hall while Layla helped get her grandmother settled.

Not long after that, Chelsea, Vic and Morgan arrived. When a nurse came to check the patient's vitals, the siblings stepped out in the hall and sketched out a quick schedule of who would sit with Miriam.

Chelsea insisted on taking first shift. "You need some rest, Layla. You look terrible. Seeing Grammy collapse must have been scary as hell."

"It was," Layla sighed.

Vic and Morgan chimed in, too. "We've got this," Vic said. "And Dad will be on his way later. Take the rest of the day for yourself. Come back in the morning."

Layla allowed herself to be persuaded. All the adrenaline had winnowed away, leaving her shaky and exhausted. After bidding her grandmother goodbye, she found Josh in the waiting room. "I'm ready," she said.

Despite the events of the day, she drew strength from his solid presence. But his hand on her elbow as they stood in the elevator made her thoughts go in a different direction. Her skin warmed and tingled where his fingers touched her.

Outside, as they waited for the valet, she decided to go for what she wanted. "Would you mind taking me to the ranch first? I can pack a bag, and then I'll probably book a room at the hotel, too. So I'll be on hand until Grammy is released."

Josh stared at her, eyes narrowed. "I like most of that plan. But there's no need for a second room. You're more than welcome to stay with me. In fact, I'll be pissed if you don't. I want to be with you, Layla."

His plain speaking touched something deep in a corner of her psyche that she seldom poked at. Her whole life she had felt invisible much of the time. Chelsea was the oldest. Morgan the youngest. Vic the beloved only boy.

Layla had gotten lost in the crowd.

Now here was Josh. Putting her first. Telling her how much he wanted her.

Was this more than physical attraction, or was she letting herself be blinded by lust dressed up as caring and connection?

On the drive to the ranch, they barely spoke.

"I'll stay in the car," Josh said as they pulled up in front.

It wouldn't have mattered. No one was home but the housekeeping staff. "Okay," she said. "It won't take me long to grab what I need." Less than twenty-four hours ago, Layla had been kissing Josh in the shadows of the front porch. Now Grammy was ill, Layla was going to spend the night in Josh's hotel room and Layla now knew for certain that Grandy and Augustus Lattimore had signed away the oil rights to both ranches.

The world didn't make sense anymore.

In her closet, she stood on her tiptoes and pulled down a medium-sized suitcase. She was an experienced traveler, so packing wasn't a problem. She would mostly need comfortable clothes for sitting in a hospital room.

Toiletries were next. A few personal items. The only thing that stumped her was what to wear in bed. It had been a long time since she had dressed up for a man at night. Though she enjoyed expensive lingerie, it felt naughty to deliberately pack things she knew Josh would enjoy. Maybe for that exact reason, she folded two beautiful gowns with matching silky robes and tucked them into her bag.

By the time she made it out to the porch and relocked the front door, Josh surprised her by showing up to carry her bag down the stairs. "It's heavy," he said when she protested.

Her nerves grew as they got closer to the hotel. Josh reached over and patted her arm. "Quit panicking. We won't do anything you don't want to do."

"That's the trouble," she said morosely. "I want to do *everything* with you."

Josh's chuckle and smug smile told her he knew exactly what was on her mind.

She kept in touch with her family via a group text. Grammy was feeling much better. She was getting IV fluids and had eaten a small dinner.

Because Josh was already a guest at the hotel, there was no need to visit the front desk. Layla felt as if every set of eyes in the lobby followed them when they stepped into the elevator. She couldn't look at herself in the mirrored walls as the numbers lit up one by one.

What was she doing? To say she was choosing to spend the night in Josh's room because it was convenient and economical was a ridiculous stretch when it came to rationalization. She needed to be honest with herself. This was 99 percent about sex. Hot, sweaty, amazing sex.

She lost her nerve when Josh opened his door and stepped back for her to enter. Layla had been hoping he had a suite. But he didn't. Although the room was very large and luxurious—even with a comfy sitting area— there was no escaping the fact that the enormous king-size bed dominated the space.

Josh set her suitcase just outside the bathroom door and tossed his keys on the dresser. "So what will it be, Layla? Room service, or dinner out?" His cocky, sexy grin told her he knew she was not as confident as she appeared.

There was really no question. She needed some breathing space. "Dinner out would be nice," she said primly.

Joshua nodded. "There's a new French bistro just around the corner. The concierge recommended it to me."

She cocked her head and stared at him. "You don't really strike me as a French bistro kind of guy."

His grin broadened, making her tummy quiver. "Maybe you don't know me as well as you think. Or then again, I might be expanding my horizons."

Layla didn't take the bait. In this battle of wits, he would probably win out, simply because it had been a very long, stressful day for her.

The outfit she had worn to the lawyer's office was suitable for dinner, so all she had to do was freshen up in the bathroom.

When it was Josh's turn, he grabbed a clean shirt and dress pants and took a five-minute shower. Though Layla seated herself on the opposite side of the room, it was impossible not to hear the water running and imagine what he looked like, his fit, muscular body wet and steamy.

The lump in her throat grew.

She couldn't look at him when he finally exited the bathroom. His scent, something lime and woodsy, invaded her senses, though to be fair, it was extremely subtle.

His damp hair was a darker blond than usual. It struck her suddenly that Joshua Banks was an incredibly handsome man. A stupid thought, probably. After all, she had known him for many years.

But now, seeing him all grown up—masculine and self-assured—she perceived him differently. Not as a preteen boy, or even an older adolescent. He had filled out. Matured. This man might still be her friend. Time would tell.

But he was also the lover she wanted.

They walked to the restaurant. It was a pleasant evening. People filled the streets. Music spilled from a nearby sports bar.

The bistro was just fancy enough to be romantic, but not so uppity that it seemed out of place in Royal. Layla was startled to hear Josh order an expensive bottle of wine in flawless French. When the waiter departed, she raised an eyebrow at the man sitting across from her. "Since when do you speak French?"

He shrugged. "College. Turns out I have a knack for languages. I do fairly well in Spanish, too. It came in handy when I was working for the energy company in Dallas. I traveled to Europe a couple of times a year."

"I see." She wanted to ask if his ex-wife traveled with him, but she couldn't bring herself to do it. It wasn't really any of her business—unless Josh somehow harbored unresolved feelings in that direction. Just because his ex-spouse had not been the woman he thought she was didn't mean he hadn't cared about her. Maybe still did at some level.

After Richard's many deceptions, Layla had learned not to take everything at face value. People told you what they wanted you to believe. She needed to guard her heart and her emotions with Josh.

Great sex didn't always equal honesty.

Despite her misgivings, dinner was delightful. The food was incredible. The wine even better. And since neither of them was driving, they lingered and enjoyed the burgundy.

Josh told her funny stories about his job. She shared a few anecdotes about college and how she and Richard had met some years later.

Josh leaned back in his chair. "So are you going to tell me what's going on with the Grandin ranch?"

She wrinkled her nose. "I can share some but not all. A few things are need-to-know."

He nodded. "Fair enough. What's the deal?"

"Basically, it seems my uncle had an affair years ago. There was a child he didn't know about. Or so we've been told. If it's true, this same source claims that my grandfather and Augustus Lattimore signed over oil rights on both ranches to this woman to hold in trust until the baby grew up. But years later, the woman and her grown daughter died in a car accident."

"That's bizarre." Josh frowned. "So the oil rights were never activated?"

"Apparently not."

"Then the story is a lie?"

"We're not sure," Layla said carefully, trying not to think about the small journal with the incriminating evidence.

"Who is it?"

"Heath Thurston."

"I don't know him."

"Our whole family is going nuts. Daddy has hired an investigator."

"Makes sense. The claim will have to be substantiated."

"I guess. And if it's true…" She trailed off, feeling sick.

Josh reached across the table and squeezed her hand. His smile was encouraging. "Maybe it's not," he said. "Otherwise, why wouldn't the girl have claimed her inheritance when she turned twenty-one?"

Layla hadn't thought of that. A tiny flicker of hope stirred in her chest, despite what she had seen in the lawyer's office.

"Let's talk about something happier," she said.

Joshua obliged. Soon they were deep into a conversation about sports and possible pennants in the fall.

They had started on the dessert course—a decadent sponge cake with fresh raspberry sauce—when someone appeared beside their table. Layla looked up, thinking it was the waiter. Instead, their unexpected guest was a man about Josh's age. He had full, dark brown hair, dark eyes and thick eyebrows. He was as handsome and striking as the Banks brothers, but in a different way. His faded jeans and well-worn cowboy boots looked out of place in the fancy bistro.

It was *Heath Thurston*, the source of all her troubles. She had googled him after the funeral to be sure she knew what he looked like.

Josh, clearly not recognizing the man, stared at him. "May we help you?"

Thurston ignored Josh, choosing instead to focus all his attention on Layla. "Ms. Grandin? Layla Grandin?"

Unease slithered in her veins. "Yes."

A smile added charm to his serious face. "I'm Nolan Thurston."

Nolan... Her brain scrambled to keep up.

When Layla was silent, he elaborated. "My brother is Heath Thurston."

Layla shook her head slowly. "What is it with this town and twins? I can't believe you have the nerve to speak to me, especially in public."

Josh rose to his feet, tossing his cloth napkin on the table. "Get lost, Thurston."

Again, the man ignored Josh. When he addressed Layla again, his expression was conciliatory, his words couched in pleasant tones. "I wondered if you and I might have lunch together soon. You know. To talk things out. It's possible we can find some common ground before all of this gets blown out of proportion. And you could bring your sister Chelsea. She's the oldest…right? I've been told the two of you are close."

Layla stood as well, now flanked by two imposing men. "You're out of your mind," she said tersely. "No lunch. No dinner. No nothing. And stay away from my sister. Your brother is trying to destroy my family's livelihood."

Nolan's smile faded. "*Destroy* is a harsh word. Heath only wants what's fair. The oil rights are ours. Surely you can understand that. Take a step back and look at the situation unemotionally. What would you do if the situations were reversed?"

Eight

Josh had seen enough. Layla looked as if she might punch the guy. He lowered his voice and infused it with an audible threat. "Go. Away. Or I'll call the cops."

Nolan Thurston was a cool customer. He didn't seem at all rattled by Josh's posturing. "I'm not trying to cause trouble," he said. "Besides, what's it to you? I fail to see your connection to the matter. Unless you're a fiancé? Or a boyfriend?"

Josh ground his teeth, wishing he could wipe the smug smile off Thurston's face. "My relationship to Layla is none of your business."

Nolan shifted his gaze back to Layla. "Lawyers are expensive. I think it would be much more civilized if you and I—or any other of your siblings—could arbitrate a fair outcome that will satisfy us all."

Layla's spine stiffened. It almost seemed as if she grew two inches, like an Amazon in training. "To be honest, Mr. Thurston, I don't give a rat's ass about what might satisfy you and your avaricious brother. Your mother is gone. Your sister, too. Even if such an agreement ever existed—and I doubt that it did—any obligation ceased with your sister's passing."

Nolan scowled. "You don't know that. Sounds more like wishful thinking on your part. Have lunch with me. Soon. It's in everyone's best interests."

Layla placed her hands on her hips and lifted a haughty eyebrow. "Don't presume to know what's best for me *or* my family, Mr. Thurston. Grandins have worked that ranch for generations. We don't intend to let you and your brother ruin a single blade of grass."

Josh moved toward the man, fully prepared to usher him out of the restaurant by force, if necessary.

Fortunately, Thurston got the hint. He tossed his business card on the table and sighed. "Think about what I've said. Let me know if you change your mind. I'll be in touch."

When Nolan Thurston turned on his heel and walked rapidly out of the dining room, Layla sank into her chair as if her legs had collapsed. She rested her elbows on the table and put her head in her hands. "This has been the week from hell."

Josh didn't say a word. But he sat down quietly. Thirty seconds later, Layla lifted her head and gave him a sheepish smile. "Present company excepted, of course. You've made my soap opera of a life bearable."

Her pink lips curved in a self-deprecating smile that sent a shiver down his spine. Suddenly, he was calculating how quickly he might persuade her to go back to the room. "You've had a rough go of it," he agreed. "I'm sorry Thurston interrupted our meal."

Layla poked at her now-soggy cake. "It's still good.

Go ahead. Finish yours. Or I will." She laughed at him with her eyes. Her mouth was full of syrupy dessert.

Damn. How did she do that? One minute he wanted to comfort her. The next he was ready to strip her naked and take her right here on the table. To be honest, his impulses when he was around Layla were beginning to freak him out.

He didn't have a shrink on retainer, but if he did, this would have been a good time for some intensive *what-in-the-hell-are-you-thinking* therapy.

But that was the problem. He wasn't thinking. At all. He was only reacting and lusting and generally acting like the poor little sphere in a pinball machine, getting whacked from one side of the game to the other with flippers. Everyone who played knew the outcome of pinball was hard to predict. All the bells and whistles served as a distraction. The ball could end up anywhere.

He suddenly had an epiphany. He didn't need to find all the answers today. Or even tomorrow. The important point was not to lose sight of the prize. One thing he knew for certain. Layla Grandin had skin in this game, whether she knew it or not. They had both been burned by love. They had that in common. But so had lots of people. Knowing what relationships *didn't* work was easy.

Predicting the future was a lot more difficult.

Layla swallowed the last bite of her cake and chased it with a final sip of wine. Then she sighed. "I'm stuffed. Do you want to go for a walk?"

Hell, no! He swallowed, praying he hadn't said those two words out loud. "Sure," he said, hoping his smile looked more genuine than it felt.

After he paid the check and they made it back out onto the street, his mood mellowed. The sun was down.

A light breeze fluttered new leaves on the trees. He took Layla's hand in his. "You choose the path, Layla. I'll follow your lead."

They walked for half an hour, barely speaking. Enjoying the spring evening. He wondered if Layla was worrying about the Thurston brothers, but he didn't want to bring up a sore subject.

Eventually, their circuitous route took them back to the hotel. In the elevator, he tucked a strand of silky blond hair behind her ear. They were alone. No one to see when his thumb caressed her cheek.

Layla blushed. She searched his face, her long-lashed eyes locked on his. "Thank you," she said softly. "It's been a very long time since I've had somebody looking out for me. I may not *need* it, but that doesn't mean I don't appreciate everything you've done for me today. I'm not sure what would have happened if you hadn't shown up when you did."

"You would have thought of something."

"Maybe. But then again, I might have gotten behind the wheel to drive myself to the hospital. I was in shock, I think."

"Yeah."

In the room, he could see Layla's nerves. "I need to make a phone call," he said. "Why don't I do that downstairs to give you some privacy while you get ready for bed?"

The relief on her face almost made him laugh, but he didn't.

"Sounds good," she said breezily.

Though her words were light, her body language and the wariness in her gaze told him she wasn't sure of herself...of the situation...of him.

He needed to earn her trust. A woman who had been

lied to and cheated on would look for honesty in a man. Faithfulness.

The relationship was new. At the moment, it was fueled by a palpable sexual chemistry. He didn't know where this was headed. But for now, he would give Layla what she needed. He would keep her safe.

Layla took a hot, super-quick shower. She had washed her hair that morning, so all she had to do was tuck it into the hotel-provided shower cap and use the extra time to shave her legs.

The bathroom door was locked. By her. Was that weird? Now, when she turned off the water, she listened carefully. If Joshua had returned already, he wasn't making a sound.

Staring at herself in the mirror was a mistake. She looked more scared than aroused. But that wasn't true. She wasn't scared of Josh.

Her body ached for his touch.

Maybe she was so comfortable being sexually vulnerable with him because their relationship hadn't begun recently. Admittedly, a years-long gap meant she didn't know him as well as she once had.

But she was convinced the essence of the man was the same.

She dried off and slipped into one of the silky nightgowns she had packed. Lots of women preferred black when they wanted to look sexy for a partner. Layla fared better in lighter, brighter colors. This sapphire blue set flattered her pale skin and blond hair.

Finally, she knew she couldn't dally any longer. She brushed her teeth. Put everything back in her toiletry kit. Took a deep breath. Showtime...

When she entered the bedroom from the bathroom,

she thought for a moment that Josh still wasn't back. But then he moved, and she saw him. He had been standing at the window, half hidden by the heavy navy drapes.

A streak of dark red colored his cheekbones. "You look amazing," he said gruffly.

"Thanks." She didn't know what to do with her hands. Suddenly, she felt awkward, really awkward. "Your turn in the bathroom," she chirped brightly.

Josh closed the distance between them, took her in his arms and kissed her hungrily. "Don't be nervous, angel. That's what you look like. The angel on top of a Christmas tree. Perfect in every way."

She shook her head. "I'm not perfect, Josh. Nobody is." His embrace made her melt. All her reservations vanished. "I'm just a woman who wants to enjoy a sexy, interesting man. All night long."

"Hell, yeah," he muttered.

She pushed at his shoulders. "Go. I'll be waiting."

When he vanished into the bathroom, she folded back the covers on the bed and tested the sheets with her hand. Smooth as a baby's bottom. Cool and pristine.

She tossed aside most of the decorative pillows and chose two of the best ones to prop against the headboard. For the first time since meeting Josh again, a thought flitted through her mind. What if Josh was her forever guy, her chance to start over, to have a *real*, lasting relationship?

After her engagement to Richard ended, she had been more dispirited than heartbroken. She had known for some time that he wasn't the man she thought she knew. It showed up in little things. The way he was careless with her feelings. The many times he broke simple silly promises. Or forgot plans they made together.

With the hindsight of two long years, she had come

to believe that she *made* herself think Richard was her heart's desire, because she was hitting that dreaded "thirty" mark, and she had wanted what so many of her friends had. Love. Stability.

In retrospect, Richard wasn't entirely to blame. The signs had been there, but Layla ignored them.

The cheating, though, that had broken her. It made her feel cheap and used, as if all Richard wanted was an in with her family, and once he accomplished that, he no longer had to pretend. Honestly, she stayed with him longer than she should have, because she was embarrassed to admit to her family how badly she had messed up.

It had been Chelsea who first saw the problems, Chelsea who encouraged Layla to dump a toxic relationship. For that, Layla would always be grateful to her older sister.

When the bathroom door swung open, Layla lost all interest in the past. The tall, lanky man—naked except for the fluffy hotel towel wrapped around his narrow hips—stood framed in the doorway with a charming grin.

Layla pretended to fan her face. "Oh my," she said. "I'm feeling a little woozy. All that testosterone…"

Josh chuckled. "That's the Layla I remember. Smart and sarcastic." He dropped a handful of packets on the table, crawled in bed beside her and nuzzled his face against her belly. "You smell delightful," he said, the words muffled.

She combed her finger through his thick, damp hair. "It's the hotel shower gel. You do, too."

Josh lifted his head and frowned. "I remember you always did have trouble taking a compliment. Even as a kid."

"I guess I thought you and Jordan only tolerated

me. So if you said something nice, I didn't know how to take it."

He sat up. "And now?"

His gaze was serious. Her fingers itched to explore all that smooth, tanned skin. But he expected an answer.

"Well," she said slowly. "I think men tell women what they want to hear."

His expression darkened. "I'm neither a liar nor a cheat. And I was faithful to my wedding vows, for what it's worth."

"I know that, but…" She wrinkled her nose. "I was expecting more crazy sex with you, not a heart-to-heart."

He leaned on one elbow now, his head propped on his hand. She didn't like the way he seemed able to see inside her brain.

Josh's sculpted lips twisted in self-derision. "So you're not really interested in us getting to know each other better? You'd rather me bang you on the hood of a car and call it a day?" His mood was surly.

"Don't be crude. Of course not."

"Sure sounds like what you said."

"I'm not great with feelings." The words slipped out, involuntarily released from the truth vault. The Grandin family wasn't mushy.

His expression softened. "Come here, sexy thing."

She allowed him to tug her down and ease her onto her back. Now he leaned over her, surrounding her with his warmth and his delicious masculinity. "I thought guys liked to get straight to the main event," she muttered, feeling incredibly vulnerable amidst a warm, sultry arousal.

Josh toyed with one narrow strap of her nightgown. His fingers felt hot against her skin. The air-conditioning in the room worked very well. In fact, she *could* blame her tightly furled nipples on that very thing.

But again, she would be denying the truth. She ached to feel his hands on her bare body.

Her partner had more patience than she did. He traced her collarbone, then pulled both straps off her shoulders, trapping her upper arms. He kissed the sensitive skin below her ear. Nibbled her earlobe. Rubbed the curves of her breasts through thin silk.

"Josh…" She said his name raggedly. Pleading.

His smile was oddly sweet. "I'm glad my brother asked me to take his place on that date."

"Me, too," Layla said. "Very glad." She paused, wanting him to understand. "Everybody thinks I had a crush on Jordan when we were kids, and it's true, I did. But that's because he was easier than you. With Jordan, what you see is what you get."

"I'm not sure I understand." Josh's gaze was watchful, his expression wary.

"You're deeper. You have layers. That was true even back then. I was a little scared of you, I think, especially when we got to high school. You made me feel odd. I didn't know what to do with those emotions. They were the beginnings of sexual awareness. I realize that now. But for a girl of fifteen, those reactions were intimidating. It was simpler to field Jordan's dumb jokes than to talk to you."

"If I hadn't been a clueless adolescent boy, maybe I could have made it easier for both of us."

"Maybe." She ran her hand over the stubble on his chin, glad he hadn't felt the need to shave. "I sometimes envy those people who find their soul mate in high school. But broken engagements…broken marriages. They feel like failures, don't they?"

"Definitely. I guess most of us have to learn life's lessons the hard way."

She tugged his head down and kissed him, shivering when his tongue stroked hers possessively. When she could breathe, she rested her cheek against his chest. "I'm happy to continue this conversation later. But the gorgeous man in my bed needs attention."

Josh laughed. "*He* does, or you do?"

When she slipped her hand beneath the towel and wrapped her fingers around his erection, he groaned. It was Layla's turn to grin. "Both, I think."

Perhaps because things had moved so fast between them in the beginning, now they were able to momentarily harness the need, to bank the embers.

"I want to touch you all over," she complained. Her arms were still trapped at her sides.

Josh ignored her pleas. Slowly, ever so slowly, he dragged the bodice of her nightgown to her waist. As he tongued her nipples and bit them gently, Layla clenched her fingers in the sheet at her hips. The sensation was indescribable.

His voice, when he spoke, was low and raspy. "You were a cute kid…and an even cuter young teenager. But, Layla, you've grown into a stunning woman."

The raw sincerity in his words couldn't be feigned. The way he looked at her made Layla want to believe in fairy tales. The ones where the prince claimed his maiden.

Her body was on fire. "Get me out of this," she begged.

He finished removing her nightgown. Now she was naked. She tugged at his damp bath towel until she could pull it from under his hips and toss it on the floor.

Josh stared at her. "I want to devour you, and I'm

not sure how I feel about that. You make me reckless. Desperate."

"It must be contagious." She ran her hands over his taut abdomen and up his broad chest to his pecs. Her fingernails dug into his shoulders. "Maybe foreplay is overrated. I need you now. I want you now."

The relief on his face told her they were on the same page. He grabbed protection, sheathed himself and moved between her legs. But he paused, the skin stretched tight over his cheekbones, his eyes glittering. "Maybe after the first fifty or sixty times, we'll want to slow down."

Layla wrapped her legs around his waist. "Don't bet on it, cowboy."

When he surged deep, she couldn't breathe for a moment. It wasn't his weight on top of her that was the problem. He had braced himself on his elbows.

The lack of oxygen was *forgetting* to breathe. As Josh buried himself inside her, bumping up against the deepest reaches of her sex, shock jumbled her synapses. All of her senses went on overload. She was hot and cold at the same time. Trembling with exhilaration and at the same moment teetering on the brink of despair.

Nothing this good could last. Nothing this good was real.

Were they both courting sexual oblivion to avoid their problems?

It felt as if she was flying without a net. Perilously close to crashing into oblivion.

His harsh breathing mingled with hers. The words he uttered were sexual and earthy. Praise and pleading. Her body raced to a climax that exploded in her pelvis and behind her eyelids in shards of blinding light.

She whimpered and lifted into his thrusts, desperate for every last ounce of completion.

When Josh cursed and went rigid, she knew he had found the same bliss.

They dozed afterward. She didn't know how long. When she tried to get up and go to the bathroom, Josh clasped her wrist. "Don't go," he said, slurring the words.

"I'll be right back." She kissed his hand and freed herself.

A few minutes later, she crawled back under the covers and burrowed into his embrace. His body was hot and hard and so wonderfully different from hers. She slipped one of her legs between his powerful thighs and stretched an arm across his chest.

For the first time in her life, she didn't question her future. It was enough to let things unfold one day at a time. She would live in the moment.

She yawned, replete and content, and let the waves of mental, physical and emotional exhaustion wash over her.

Nine

When Josh jerked awake in the middle of the night, he had no clue where he was. Gradually, his racing heart slowed. Had he been dreaming? A nightmare?

Then reason returned. And a grateful embrace of reality. Layla was in his arms. Soft, warm, deeply unconscious. She made the cutest little snuffling noises when she slept.

He cataloged his physical state. Sexually sated, but with a boner that could pound nails. Still unsure about the future except to know that at this very moment an anonymous hotel room with this very specific woman was exactly where he wanted to be.

They had fallen asleep early. Now he'd had enough rest to be energized already. But it would be selfish to wake Layla.

Surreptitiously, he peered at his watch. One thirty in the morning. His stomach was growling, and he needed to visit the john. Carefully, he moved a feminine arm. Then a leg. Layla grumbled in her sleep, turned away from him, but didn't wake up.

While he took care of business and washed up, all he thought about was making love to her again. He was rusty about dating rules. Could a guy get in trouble for coaxing a drowsy woman into having sex?

When he rejoined her, she recoiled from his cold feet. He moved them, but drew her closer, spooning her and filling his hands with her breasts. The curves and valleys were delightful. He could almost be satisfied with this.

But his body urged him to take more.

He wanted more. In fact, he trembled with the need to be inside her.

"Layla." He whispered her name, willing her to wake up. "Layla, sweetheart. Can you open your eyes?"

It seemed like eons, but it was probably only a minute or two.

She rolled onto her back and shoved the hair out of her eyes. "What?"

That single grumpy syllable didn't bode well for his plans. "I was hoping you might want to…you know…" He stroked her center.

Layla made a noise that was halfway between a protest and a moan.

"Was that a *yes*?" he asked hopefully.

"Do you have something against sleep?" Her sarcastic question was clearly rhetorical.

He kissed her, sliding his tongue deep into her mouth. Then he nuzzled her nose with his. "How can I sleep when a gorgeous, naked woman is in my bed driving me insane with her incredible body?"

"Over the top, Banks. Over the top."

He rubbed his erection against her thigh. "I'm dead serious. So serious."

Because there was a light burning in the bathroom, and he had left the door cracked, he could see the grin that finally lifted the corners of her mouth, even though her eyes remained stubbornly closed. "Single-minded, aren't you?"

He played with her breasts one at a time, teasing the nipples. Plumping the curves. "I'm gonna need a clear affirmative from you, Ms. Grandin. Audible consent. Please."

Finally, her long lashes lifted. Her blue eyes looked darker in the dim light. "Yes, Mr. Banks. I agree to have sex with you. Under one condition."

He tensed. "What is it?"

"You've got to feed me afterward. I'm starving."

Twenty minutes later, Josh flopped onto his back, his chest heaving. "Damn, woman. What was that thing you did with your tongue?"

Layla giggled, a young, innocent sound that was more like the girl he had once known than the sophisticated, capable woman with whom he had recently reconnected.

She yawned and stretched. "If we're going to have sex this much, I may need to bring snacks and a cooler."

"Okay, okay," he said rolling out of bed to fetch the room service menu. "What do you want?"

With a naked Josh sitting four feet away in all his glory, Layla *knew* what she wanted. But at this point in the relationship, it seemed prudent not to give the man any more ammunition than necessary. "Nachos?" she said.

He winced. "Seriously?"

"Fine," she huffed. "You throw out a suggestion."

"No. I'll give you one more chance."

"We could split a burger."

His gaze narrowed. "Medium rare?"

"Is there any other way?"

"Cheese?" he asked.

"Swiss and cheddar both."

"I can see you like to live on the edge."

She stretched her arms over her head, enjoying the way his gaze settled on her breasts and glazed over. "You would know. And it's all your fault. I was practically a nun before you came back to town. I think you've corrupted me."

Josh tossed the menu aside and ran a hand up the inside of her thigh, his eyes flashing fire, his cheeks flushing. "Room service can wait," he groaned. When he buried his face between her legs, she shrieked.

It was three o'clock before they got any food.

Layla sighed. "That might be the best cheeseburger I've ever eaten."

They were tucked up in bed, shoulder to shoulder, devouring their meal. Layla had insisted on protecting the fancy comforter with a couple of bath towels.

Josh leaned toward her and licked her chin. "Ketchup," he explained solemnly.

She batted his hand away when he tried to tug at the sheet she used to protect her modesty. "Behave."

He shrugged. "If you insist." After snitching a handful of fries from her plate because his were all gone, he shot her a sideways glance. "I want to know more about the grown-up Layla. What is it you love about the ranch?"

She smiled. "That's easy. The horses. I tell them all my secrets. I love the way they move and the joy they feel when they gallop. The smell of hay in the barns. The way the mares whinny when they want the colts to settle for the night."

Josh was silent for so long, she felt self-conscious.

"What?" she demanded. "Was that more than you wanted to know?"

"That was beautiful," he said gruffly.

She ate another french fry, because it was something to do. "Not everything at the ranch is so poetic. I'm handy with the business part. I've got an MBA that I put to good use when Grandy and Dad let me." She stopped, overwhelmed anew by the remembrance that her grandfather was gone.

Josh slid an arm around her shoulders, comforting her without words. He sighed. "They're lucky to have you."

"I don't know," she said honestly, ruefully. "I've been thinking it might be time for me to move on."

"Why?"

"Well, if Daddy goes by Grandy's example, he'll clutch the reins until he's old and gray. And even then, Vic will be the one to take over. I'm not sure there's any point in me staying in the long term. I've thought about finding something else to do with my life. Maybe after my grandmother is gone. I don't want to disappoint her."

"I can't imagine you being a disappointment to anyone."

"That's sweet," she said. But Josh didn't see the whole picture. Layla had disappointed her parents right out of the gate by not being a boy. Chelsea was bad enough. But now *two* girls? Only the advent of Vic had satisfied the familial expectations. And poor Morgan was likely supposed to be a boy, too, to even the scales.

Layla set her plate on the bedside table. "I should probably get some more sleep," she said. "I need to be at the hospital by nine."

"Of course."

They put the room service tray out in the hall and locked the door. Josh turned out the light. It was silent for a moment as they got comfortable under the covers. He didn't allow any distance between them.

Layla's eyes were closed when he spoke.

"You can stay here as long as you want, if you can be away from the ranch."

She studied his words for hidden meanings. Was he simply being nice, or was that an ongoing booty call? "Thank you," she said. "I suppose it will depend on Grammy. When they release her, I'll need to be out there to help."

"Makes sense."

She rested her cheek on his shoulder. "Why are you staying in this hotel instead of with your dad and brother?"

Something in him reacted. He either flinched or froze or *something*. At last, he answered her. "My brother asked me the same thing. I've been gone for a long time. I've needed space to do some thinking about what comes next."

"I thought you wanted to come home."

"I did. I do. But sometimes life takes a turn we don't expect."

Layla pretended to fall asleep after that. What did he mean?

Soon, she heard him breathing deeply. He was out cold.

Unfortunately, Layla was awake far longer, wondering if she was making a huge mistake. She liked Josh a lot. They had a history of sorts. He was the kind of man she could fall in love with…could marry. Start a family with.

Was she weaving crazy dreams?

Maybe *she* needed some space, too. Her world had been turned upside down in the last month. She was emotionally vulnerable. Perhaps it was time to take a step back and protect herself.

Josh ordered breakfast from room service while Layla was in the shower. The sun was bright, too bright for his eyes, which were gritty from lack of sleep. But he wouldn't change a thing.

When Layla exited the bathroom, she was fully dressed. And in a hurry.

She grimaced when she saw the food. "I'm so sorry, Josh. I don't have time to linger. I'm trying to get to the hospital before the doctor comes by." She kissed his cheek on the way to the door. "I'll let you know how Grammy is doing. Bye."

The door closed with a gentle slam. And then Josh was alone.

He ate two thirds of the food and left the rest. When he was dressed and ready, he pulled out his phone and checked flight schedules. If he hurried, he could catch a midmorning hop to Dallas and be back before bedtime. He had a few loose ends to tie up.

It was a long day. Air travel was becoming more and more of an endurance test. He could have chartered a small jet. But it seemed like an unnecessary expense at this juncture. So he endured the packed plane and the inevitable delays.

By the time he made it back to Royal, retrieved his car and drove from the airport to the hotel, he was exhausted. Only the prospect of seeing Layla again kept him going.

It was an unpleasant shock to enter his room and

find no sign of the woman who had kept him awake half the night.

Only a note on the pillow gave him a clue.

He read it with a sinking feeling.

"Hey, Josh—Grammy was doing so well the doctor released her right after dinner this evening. We've all headed back to the ranch. I stopped by to grab my suitcase as I'm sure you've noticed. Thanks again for rescuing me on the street and for such a fun night. Talk soon, Layla."

He crumpled the sheet Layla had torn from a hotel notepad. Tossing it in the nearest wastebasket gave him a moment's satisfaction. But then he reneged and rescued it, flattening the paper between his fingers.

The depth of his disappointment was significant. Instead of another night of hot, wonderful sex, he was going to sleep alone.

Without Layla.

How had she come to be so important to him so quickly?

He slept fitfully and awoke at dawn. Though he had put it off, he knew it was time for a serious talk with his father and brother.

Three cups of coffee later, he was headed out to the Bankses' ranch. Their property was prosperous and productive, but not on the scale of either the Grandins' or the Lattimores'. Those two families were Royal royalty. He grinned at his own joke.

When he came here recently, the three men had spent most of their time in the barn and on horses riding the property. Today, as Josh walked into the warm, cozy kitchen at the old farmhouse, it was almost as if nothing at all had changed in the last week or the last decade.

His dad and his twin brother were seated at the scarred oak table eating pancakes.

Jordan looked up with a grin. "We saved you some," he said. "Pull up a chair."

While Josh ate, his father read the *New York Times*. Jordan stared at his phone.

They had never been the kind of family to wade into deep conversational waters. Which made what Josh was about to do all the more difficult.

Eventually, he finished his meal and screwed up his courage. "Hey, you two. I have a question to ask. And I need you to think about it before you answer."

Each man looked up with an identical expression of bewilderment.

Bertram waved a hand. "Well, don't keep us in suspense."

Josh swallowed hard. "Would the two of you consider buying out my share of the ranch?"

Jordan's mouth fell open.

Josh's dad paled. "Hell, son. We were just razzing you the other day…giving you a hard time. Of course we want you back. You have to know that."

Josh's brother nodded. "We're excited to have you home."

"I believe you—I do. But I'm not sure staying is the right choice for me. Clearly, I don't have a great track record with big life changes. Still, it seems to me that the two of you have things running smoothly here. I know I could help, but it would be the path of least resistance. I really want to try something new."

Bertram stood and refilled his coffee cup. "Like what?" His father had been perturbed to hear Josh had quit his job.

"I'm not sure. I don't have everything pinned down

yet. But as soon as I land on a plan, you'll be the first to know, I swear."

Jordan shook his head slowly. "Cash flow is not a problem. We're doing better than we ever have. If you want us to buy you out, Dad and I can swing it. But you wouldn't be a third wheel here at the ranch. You're family. You're my brother, my twin."

Josh was taken aback when Jordan hugged him spontaneously. He returned the hug, realizing how much he had given up when he moved away. "Thanks," he said, his throat tight. "That means a lot. You know I love this ranch. It's home. But you two have made it what it is. I think I need to let this be your baby. I'm going to carve out something for myself—or I will if I'm lucky. Call it an early midlife crisis, I guess. The divorce rattled me. I don't want to screw up my life that badly ever again."

Layla hadn't seen Josh in ten days. It seemed impossible, but the hours flew by. Taking care of Grammy kept the family busy. Her medications had been worked out, of course, but she seemed frail after her collapse. Too much stress, perhaps.

The family had fallen into a schedule that was working for the moment. Chelsea, Layla and Morgan split up the waking hours. Layla's parents and brother took turns occupying the extra twin bed in Grammy's bedroom overnight. It was the one Victor Senior had slept in.

Miriam was grieving. They all were. But each day got a little easier.

One afternoon when Layla was off the clock, she went for a drive, needing to get out of the house and clear her head. Caring for her grandmother had turned out to be the perfect distraction to avoid thinking about Josh.

What was she going to do about him?

The two of them hadn't even talked on the phone. But they had texted now and then. She presumed he was busy, though he didn't give her any details, and she didn't ask. Miriam's health was the usual topic of conversation.

One night late, Layla got a short text.

I miss you...

Her heart did a funny little flip in her chest. She felt like a teenage girl crushing on a boy who smiled at her.

I miss you, too...

That was it. Just those two texts. And then nothing. But she wondered if Josh was just missing the sex, or did he really have feelings for her?

It was hard to read his mind. Not that she had been particularly forthcoming about her own feelings. Thinking about Josh made her ache. Though she had tried to downplay her emotions, even to herself, the truth was impossible to ignore. She was maybe/possibly falling for Joshua Banks.

He was likely being a gentleman, trying to respect the fact that Layla had a lot of responsibilities at the moment.

She drove aimlessly at first, leaving the town limits and seeking out the open road. Sunshine and blue skies were mood boosters, but it wasn't enough.

Eventually, she found herself headed toward the spot where Josh had made love to her for the first time. When she found the small hilltop, she parked her car and got out. If she closed her eyes, she could remember that afternoon in Technicolor detail.

There had been so much urgency, so much heat. The attraction wasn't one-sided. That much she knew. They had both been hungry, desperate to connect in the most intimate ways possible.

Thinking of those hours made her face hot with a blush that emanated from deep inside her. *Wanton* and *reckless* were not words she associated with herself.

But with Josh, she felt like a different person.

When she spent the night with him at the hotel, the magnetic lure had only strengthened. Pheromones on steroids.

Could that kind of sexual compatibility be only physical? Sex with Richard had been enjoyable. But not earth-shattering. Why were she and Josh combustible?

She didn't want to believe she had deep feelings for him. He was coming off a messy divorce. Admittedly, he and his wife hadn't been together in over two years before that. But still. The man might have a few *issues*.

Most friends she knew who had divorced weren't eager to jump back into any kind of serious relationship.

The Spring Luncheon at the Cattleman's Club was coming up very soon. Josh had agreed to be her date. Would that be the end of this fling or the beginning of a new chapter?

Truthfully, she was scared to make the next move. Josh had the power to hurt her, though he might not realize it. If he wasn't interested in anything more than sex, she would have to extricate herself gracefully.

She knew people who enjoyed physical affairs without messy entanglements, but Layla wasn't made that way.

As the wind cooled her skin and sent her hair flying

around her head, she knew this was a critical point in her life. She had never found validation in her family. Not really. To them, she was just Layla. Always around. Always available.

But surely there was more to life than being the middle child of four, as odd as that sounded. Who was she? What did she want? Was she willing to fight for Josh? Really, it was more than that. She could bring peace and purpose and challenge to her life with or without a man. Suddenly, one of the puzzle pieces fell into place.

Excitement buzzed in her veins. She spared one last wistful glance for the place where she had first felt the warmth of Josh's single-minded lovemaking, and then she drove quickly back into town.

One of her college classmates was a Realtor now. Layla burst into her office, out of breath and hopeful. Shana was a successful Black woman who possessed the kind of personality that made her a natural with customers.

After they exchanged pleasantries, Layla handed over her phone, where she had captured a screenshot of latitude and longitude. "I want to find out about this property," she said. "It looks like an old farm that hasn't been worked in years. I might want to buy it if the price is right."

Shana stared at the photo and then typed something into her computer. And then more. She frowned. "The owners were elderly. They died back in January, both of them. They had two heirs, a son and a daughter in their sixties. The property was definitely for sale, but now the listing says *not available*."

Layla's heart sank. "What does that mean? It doesn't say *sold*?"

"I'll get to the bottom of it," Shana promised. "And in the meantime, why don't I start looking for other properties? You can email me a list of what features you're interested in…acreage…etc. I know I can find something you'll like."

"Thanks," Layla said. "I appreciate it."

Ten

Back in the car, Layla blew her nose, trying to swallow the disappointment that made her eyes sting. She'd been on an impulsive errand anyway. In her head, she had already been building a cute house, right on the spot where Josh parked his car with a view of the surrounding countryside.

How silly and sad was that? Memorializing one amazing encounter with a man who was as mysterious as he was sexy.

Back at home, she found Chelsea on the back porch having coffee. "Where have *you* been?" her older sister asked.

"I went for a drive."

"To see Josh Banks?" Chelsea asked it with a teasing smile. Layla had shared only the G-rated details of her time with Josh.

"Nope. I don't think he's interested in anything serious. And besides, I've had far too much humiliation to go chasing after another man who doesn't know what the word *commitment* means."

"I can't imagine Joshua Banks cheating on a woman. He's always been a straight arrow, hasn't he?"

"He has. But I think that proves my point. It's been over a week. He hasn't asked me out again. I imagine he has other things on his mind besides me."

"I'm sorry, Layla. I could hear in your voice how much you liked him."

"It's not just that. I'm thinking about leaving the ranch. Dad is hung up on this Vic idea, and even if he ever relents, *you'll* be the logical choice to run things, not me. I've been the invisible Grandin my whole life. Is it selfish of me to want a guy to think I hung the moon? To give me his undying devotion?"

That last part was tongue-in-cheek. Chelsea heard the underlying plea and hugged her tightly. "You have to know that you're always welcome here, no matter who's in charge. And as for wanting more in the relationship department, well, don't give up on men."

"I'm not. But they sure make life complicated." She was ready to shift the subject to something less personal. "By the way, I forgot to tell you about one unpleasant experience I had."

"With Josh?" Chelsea seemed shocked.

"Not exactly. He and I were having dinner when this strange man showed up at our table. He introduced himself as Nolan Thurston, *Heath* Thurston's brother."

Now Chelsea's face reflected even more shock. "What did he do? What did he want? Did he threaten you?"

"Oh, no. Exactly the opposite. He asked if you and I might have lunch with him to *talk things out*. He thought we could come to some kind of understanding, I guess.

But you know he was probably a spy for his brother… trying to find out what our family knows about the oil rights situation…what we're thinking."

"He hasn't contacted you again?" Chelsea asked.

"No. That's why I forgot about it until now. Why on earth do you care?"

"Well, it might not hurt for us to do the same. Get information from him. Strengthen our position."

"I don't want to have anything to do with either of the Thurstons." Layla still felt guilty about keeping her grandmother's secret.

"Oh, well. It may be a nonissue." Chelsea stood and collected her cup and saucer. "Will you sit with Grandmother for half an hour? I'm supposed to relieve Morgan, but I've got an important Zoom call. Won't take me long."

"Sure," Layla said.

When she reached Grammy's room, Morgan put a finger to her lips. "Shh," she whispered. "She just fell asleep."

The two women stepped out into the hall. "How is she?" Layla asked.

Morgan smiled. "Really good overall. She's eating well. But I know she's grieving more than she wants us to see. You hear about people in long marriages dying of broken hearts when they lose a partner. It's selfish, I guess, but I hope she won't go too soon. I need Grammy. We all do."

"Definitely." Layla surveyed her baby sister's red hair and blue eyes and the shadows under those eyes. Morgan was the only one in the family who didn't work on the ranch. She owned a boutique in town called The Rancher's Daughter. It surely hadn't been easy to find the time to help out, but she had carried her share of the load.

Layla spoke impulsively. "Why don't you let me cover your hours tomorrow? You look beat."

Morgan's expression was wistful. "I'm tired, yes. And I appreciate the offer. But I feel so conscious now that our time with her is limited. I don't want to have any regrets."

"I understand. Still, if the shop and all this gets to be too much, let me know."

When Layla slipped quietly into the dimly lit bedroom, her grandmother opened her eyes, her expression mutinous. "I could hear the two of you whispering out in the hall. Talking about me, I'll bet. I'm not an invalid."

Layla sat down beside the bed. "Of course you're not. We were just being quiet because Morgan said you were asleep. Were you playing possum?"

That made Grammy smile. "I *was* asleep," she said. "But it was just a catnap." She sat up in the bed. "Will you take me to the back porch? I need some sun."

"Sure. It's a beautiful day."

Miriam Grandin wasn't about to accept help she didn't need. Though Layla held the wheelchair steady, her grandmother stood up and then seated herself. Layla tucked a fluffy afghan around her knees. "Here we go."

The old woman perked up even more when they got outside. When the housekeeper checked on them, Layla asked for cookies and cocoa. The calendar might say spring, but it was never out of season for Grammy's favorites.

With the wheelchair by the porch rail, Miriam could tip her face toward the sky. "This is nice," she said. "I'm damn tired of staying inside."

Layla smothered a snort of laughter. She loved her grandmother's indomitable spirit. Morgan probably didn't have a thing to worry about.

"Well," she said. "You're doing great. I don't see why you can't gradually get back to your normal schedule."

"The new normal, you mean."

The gentle rebuke reminded Layla that Victor Grandin Sr. still cast a long shadow. "Yes, ma'am," she said meekly.

"So tell me what's going on with you and the Banks boy."

Layla flushed. "This family gossips more than the old biddies in town."

"You can't blame us. After the debacle with your Richard person, we just want to see you happy again."

"I'm happy," Layla muttered.

"Doesn't look like it at the moment. You should be out having fun. Now that I'm not at death's door anymore, I'll hire a nice girl to sit with me during the day. The rest of you need to get on with your lives."

"We love you, Grammy."

"I know that. But you've done enough."

Layla wouldn't win that argument, so she changed the subject. Her grandmother was strong enough now to have this discussion. "Grammy," she said. "Don't you think we need to tell the others about Grandy's journal? I feel bad keeping it from them."

Miriam shrugged. "No point in it. Without the paperwork, that journal doesn't mean a thing. It wouldn't hold up in court. Relax, girl. That fancy-ass investigator my son hired will follow the trail. Time enough to worry about things when his work is done."

"Okay..." Layla didn't want to go against her grandmother's wishes. And in this case, maybe she was right. The legalities were what mattered. No substantiated paperwork, no claim.

Three days later, Layla stood in front of the full-length mirror in her closet and surveyed her choice of outfit. Josh was picking her up for the noon event at the Texas Cattleman's Club in an hour. She had already changed three times.

First, she had picked out a tangerine Jackie O–style dress. It was sophisticated and springlike, but she didn't feel quite right in it. Next there was a trendy pantsuit, teal with a floral silk blouse to match. The cut of the jacket and pants flattered her figure, but again, she gave it a thumbs-down.

Now she wore a riskier choice. The dress she had chosen was blush-pink silk with a low neckline and spaghetti straps. The waist was fitted, then flared into a flirty skirt that stopped a few inches above her knees.

The layered skirt alternated between the lighter pink silk and a more vivid rosy shade of tulle that peeked out when she moved. Her shoes were three-inch heels in a nude color that didn't detract from the dress.

Jewelry had been a hard choice, but she settled on a single-diamond pendant that rode demurely on the slope of her breasts. Matching studs adorned her ears.

Last, but not least, she carried a pink-flamingo clutch that perfectly completed the underlayers of her skirt.

On a normal day at the club, this outfit would definitely be over-the-top. But the Spring Luncheon was a notable social event. Layla wouldn't stand out for being overdressed. Though the men would be in dark suits, the female plumage would run the gamut.

Last year, one of Layla's old high school classmates—renowned for making an entrance wherever she went—showed up in skintight silver lamé. The gossipmongers had a field day with that one. But not long after, the woman snagged husband number two, so as a strategy, it worked.

Layla's heart raced, and her cheeks matched her

dress. The wardrobe choice wasn't the only thing giving her heartburn. It was the text she'd received earlier from Josh.

I'd like for you to spend the rest of the afternoon and evening with me. If you're interested, pack a bag...

On the one hand, she loved his direct communication. It was clear and to the point. But why had he waited so long to coax her into his bed again? To be fair, she had disappeared from his hotel room after the first time and only left a note. But surely he understood why.

Though she had a ton of reservations about getting in deeper with a sexual relationship that might never progress to anything else, she didn't have the will to say no.

She wanted Josh. It was risky. It made her vulnerable.

But she couldn't give up a man who made her feel both exhilarated and safe. It was a fascinating combination.

Though it seemed silly, she didn't put her suitcase on the bed. She kept it in the closet and packed it surreptitiously, not wanting Chelsea to wander in and ask uncomfortable questions.

A family friend was coming to sit with Grammy. No one had been hired yet. Only Grammy thought that was a good idea.

The remaining six Grandins were going together to the club. Except for Layla. She had invented an excuse about having to leave earlier. No one had questioned her. If she was lucky, she could go down the stairs that exited the side of the house. She had asked Josh not to ring the bell, but to text her when he arrived.

If he thought the request odd, he didn't let on.

Her phone dinged at exactly 11:13. Her ride was two

minutes early. It wasn't a forty-five-minute drive to the club, but Layla wanted to disappear from the house before her parents and siblings congregated.

She tucked her purse under her arm, checked her reflection one last time and picked up the small suitcase. It wasn't heavy. A woman didn't need much when she was planning on being naked most of the time.

She choked back a laugh as she tiptoed down the stairs. When she rounded the corner of the house, Josh was standing beside his car. From the look on his face, she had to assume her outfit was on point.

He shook his head slowly as he looked her over from head to toe, his eyes flashing with male appreciation. "You look incredible, Layla. Are you sure we have to go to the Cattleman's Club luncheon?"

The question was clearly rhetorical. She hoped. "Thank you for the compliment, but I need to see and be seen," she said, smiling. "We're fighting this oil rights claim, so all the Grandins will be front and center today."

He reached out and took her suitcase. After placing it in the trunk of his car, he came around and opened the passenger side. "In you go." He tucked pieces of her flyaway skirt beneath her leg before carefully closing the door.

When he was behind the wheel with the engine started and the AC blowing cool air, he faced her. His expression was not so lighthearted now.

"What's wrong?" she asked, experiencing a fillip of alarm.

"I've missed you," he said gruffly. Carefully, he leaned forward and kissed her cheek. Then he followed it up with a second one just below her ear.

Everything inside her went on high alert. Wow. With

only two chaste kisses, the man could make the cells in her body sizzle with wanting him.

When she would have pressed closer, he held her at arm's length with a rueful smile. His hands were warm on her bare shoulders. "No more," he said. "If I start kissing you like I really want to, we'll never get to the club."

For half a second, she debated blowing off the big event and going back to Josh's hotel room. Unfortunately, she had always been the conscientious type.

Sometimes being a mature, responsible adult sucked.

Josh gripped the steering wheel with damp hands. His throat was dry. His chest was tight. Layla was everything he wanted in a woman. Smart. Funny. Sexy as hell. The faint scent of her perfume made the confines of the car a torture chamber for a man desperate to get laid ASAP. Seeing Layla appear with suitcase in hand moments ago had been a huge relief.

He hadn't been one hundred percent positive she wanted a do-over.

She looked different today, and it wasn't just the clothes, though that dress was tantalizing and provocative. Her body was curved in all the right places.

Maybe it was the way she wore her hair. This morning, it was twisted on top of her head in the kind of intricate style women seem to instinctively know how to do.

Unfortunately, the updo bared the provocative feminine real estate at the top of her spine. Which made Josh's hungry fascination about a thousand times more intense. All he could think about was nibbling the back of her neck while he reached around and cupped her bare breasts.

And they *would* be bare. No matter how gorgeous the dress, he planned to have her out of it as soon as possible.

Already, he was calculating how long they would have to stay at the club before he could spirit her away.

"You're awfully quiet today," he said as he threaded his way through the streets of Royal proper.

Layla sighed. "I've been looking forward to seeing you again, but I'm worried about the two of us."

"Why is that?"

"I'm in my thirties already. I should have my life together by now. But I've held men at a distance, because I felt so betrayed and rejected by Richard. I wish I could say I was in love with him, but I wasn't. And you've admitted you weren't in love with your wife. Not the kind of forever love we're supposed to want."

"Where are you going with this, Layla? No offense, but we're pulling up at the club in about six and a half minutes. Not exactly the time for a heart-to-heart."

"That's probably why I did it," she said. "I'm scared to get hurt again." She half turned in her seat. Now he sensed her staring at him, even though he kept his eyes on the road. "You're a great guy," she said. "But…"

"But what?" He felt his blood pressure rise, and not in a pleasant way.

Layla twisted a piece of her skirt restlessly. "Statistics for divorced people aren't good when it comes to future success with new partners."

"You sound like you've been reading encyclopedias," he grumbled, feeling his neck get hot. He *was* divorced. No way around it. If he could go back and undo all his mistakes, he would. But he was stuck with his checkered past. The missteps had taught him what was valuable and what was dross.

"I don't think encyclopedias exist anymore, do they?" she said.

"We're getting off track." He pulled into a parking space, slammed the car into Park and faced her, trying not to glower. "If you and I together is such a risky proposition, why did you bring a suitcase?"

Layla's bottom lip trembled. Her dewy cheeks were flushed—a shade of pink that almost matched her dress. Her blue eyes shimmered with something he couldn't quite decipher. It almost looked as if she might cry, but that made no sense.

They were together. On a day that was supposed to be fun.

"You didn't answer my question," he said quietly. "Why did you bring a suitcase if you're breaking things off?"

Her chin came up. "I never said that. Besides, there's nothing to break off. You and I are friends."

"With benefits." He wouldn't let her brush aside the incredible moments when they had been intimate—first at the picnic and later in his hotel room. "I assumed you didn't have sex with me on a whim."

"I didn't," she whispered.

"But you've changed your mind? Because you think I'm on the rebound, and you've got sucky taste in men? Is that it in a nutshell?"

"You should have been a lawyer, Josh." Her eyes shot blue sparks. "And for the record, I don't like being interrogated."

Years ago, he had learned to keep his temper under control. Now it popped and sizzled, dangerously close to igniting. "Then what *do* you like, Layla? Tell me."

Even though they were early, he had deliberately chosen a parking space at the far reaches of the parking lot.

It meant they would have to walk a fair distance to get to the club entrance, but for now, there were no cars anywhere close to them. Which was a good thing, because this argument didn't need witnesses.

Her continued silence pushed him closer to the edge. "What *do* you like, Layla? If we're such an unlikely pair, what *do* you like?"

Without warning, she put both hands on the sides of his neck and pulled him closer. Now he could see the layers of blue in her pupils, layers that threatened to submerge him and drown him.

"I thought it was obvious," she said, the words husky. "I like having sex with you."

When Layla pressed her mouth to his, he jerked, shocked and stunned and crazy in lust with her. "Yes," he stuttered as her tongue and lips dueled with his.

He slid a hand inside the top of her dress and found bare skin beneath what appeared to be a lacy nothing of a bra. He squeezed reverently. "I've laid awake every night thinking about this. About you."

She groaned, wrapping her arms around his neck and teasing the whorl of his ear with her talented tongue. "Yes."

What was she saying yes to? Was she having the same sleepless nights?

He rubbed her nipple, feeling it peak beneath his fingertips. "It scares me how much I want you," he confessed. It was true. Layla brought him peace and agitation in equal measure. Her presence in his arms helped him reclaim the contentment of his childhood when his biggest problem was how to keep his brother from eating the last ice-cream sandwich in the freezer. But touching her, making love to her, created the frenzied agitation of knowing he had no control when it came to Layla.

He was moments away from dragging her into the back seat and taking her wildly when some tiny voice inside his head whispered reason. Already, cars were lining up closer and closer in the parking lot. Today was a big deal, especially so for Layla and her family.

It took every ounce of determination he could muster to peel her arms from around his neck and ease her over into her seat. "Fix your lipstick," he muttered, already missing her warmth.

Her gaze was hazy and unfocused. There was a tiny red patch on her collarbone where he had nibbled her like the rarest of gourmet delights. She put a hand to her mouth. "What time is it?"

"A quarter till twelve."

"Oh my gosh." Frantically, she searched for her purse. The flamingo nested in the floor of the car. Layla grabbed it and found what she needed.

He pulled the visor down for her. "Don't worry. We didn't mess up much."

Not for the world would he mention that she had the look of a woman who had just experienced orgasmic pleasure. The dreamy expression in her eyes. Warm, glowing skin all over that made her seem young and lush. Lips puffy from his hungry kisses.

She was no ingenue, and yet she projected innocence and sweetness. The fact that she seemed unaware of her appeal made her all the sexier. When Layla was satisfied with her face and her hair, he shut off the engine. It was going to be a scorcher today.

He touched her arm. "Shall we make an appearance, Ms. Grandin?"

He saw Layla take a deep breath as she checked her

reflection one last time. Then she curled her hand around his. "Thank you for bringing me today."

"Of course. And by the way, am I supposed to play the part of your adoring boyfriend, so the whole town will know Richard the ass is a distant memory?"

Her lips tilted up in a smile. "I like the way you think."

"The role isn't much of a stretch," he said, brushing the backs of his fingers across her soft cheek.

Big blue eyes searched his. Was she looking for assurance? The best way he could give her that was to keep showing up.

"Come on," he said. "Let's do this…"

Eleven

Layla had been coming to the Texas Cattleman's Club since she was a child. Sometimes her family enjoyed Sunday brunch on the terrace. On other occasions, she tagged along when her mother met friends for lunch. And then there were the holiday memories. The huge tree in the lobby entrance. The lavish parties. Cookies and stockings and other goodies. Adult laughter and conversation. Usually an appearance by Santa Claus.

As the daughter of a wealthy rancher, she had always been welcomed at the club. But even as a teenager, she had been aware of a rigid hierarchy that took some in and kept others out. Fortunately, in recent years as some of the old guard passed on and newer, more progressive ideas were incorporated, the membership had become more inclusive. Now she paid her dues like all the other members.

Josh had her arm tucked in his elbow. She liked how

that felt. Honestly, she enjoyed the way other women in the room looked him over with interest. Though he'd told her he still maintained his TCC membership, it had probably been at least six or eight years since he had entered this historic building.

Appetizers were being served on small tables scattered around the main hallway. Fresh flowers hung from brass sconces. Someone had even whimsically decorated a stuffed moose head with a tiara of daisies.

Layla wasn't a particular fan of hunting trophies, but some of them remained, even after renovations and redecorating. A small brass plaque below each specimen recorded the hunter and the date. Taxidermists in Royal would always have a job.

She and Josh grabbed a couple of plates. The shrimp and cocktail sauce were legendary. Not to mention the tiny Angus beef sliders. "Pace yourself," she warned her companion. "You'll want to save room for lunch." She wiped her lips with a napkin. "Would you mind if I touch base with a few folks?"

He grinned. "With or without me?"

"Don't you know people?" she asked, cocking her head and staring at him to see if he was kidding.

"Go," he said. "It's been a while, but I still recognize half the folks in this room. I'll be fine."

She squeezed his hand and walked away, conscious of his gaze on her back. That little interlude in the car had left her with quivery knees and a marked lack of enthusiasm for socializing. Even so, she had work to do.

She found the Lattimores standing in two tight circles and greeted them a few at a time. Jonathan and Jayden. Alexa and Caitlyn. Their parents, Ben and Barbara.

Even though Alexa had flown in to attend the funeral of Layla's grandfather, she had returned for this event, probably at her parents' urging. Layla tugged her to a quiet corner. "How are things at your house?" she asked.

Alexa grimaced. Her long black curls and dark brown eyes made her stand out. The gorgeous Black woman sighed. "Like your family, everyone is worried about the oil rights business. And absolutely no one can understand why my grandfather would put *our* ranch at risk, when it was your uncle who fathered a child."

"I know I said it once, but you should really come home and help them. They need a lawyer they can trust. Surely your firm will give you a leave of absence…right? For a family crisis?"

"Poor naive Layla." Alexa grinned so Layla would know she was kidding. "My bosses are all about billable hours."

"But you'll try?"

"I don't know," Alexa said, looking torn. "It's not a good time for me."

"Emergencies never are."

Chelsea appeared at Layla's elbow, seeming out of breath. "Hey, Alexa," she said. "Glad to see you again. If you don't mind, I need to borrow my sister for a moment."

Alexa waved a hand. "She's all yours."

Before Layla could blink, Chelsea had backed her into a corner. Literally. Her older sister frowned. "I just peeked in the dining room. Your place card isn't at our table. Are you planning to skip the meal? Geez, Layla. You know this is an important day."

Layla shook her head slowly. "Calm down. Of course I know. Show of strength and all that."

"So why aren't you going to eat lunch?"

"Did it ever occur to you that my place card might be at another table?"

Chelsea's jaw dropped. "You're with someone?"

"Joshua Banks."

Chelsea's expression of bewilderment was comical. "But I thought you said that situation wasn't going anywhere. You told me you wanted someone with no emotional baggage, a man who would worship the ground you walk on."

"Now, you're editorializing." Layla laughed. "Relax. I'll be in the dining room the whole time. But Josh and I have a table for two."

"And *after* lunch?" Chelsea raised an eyebrow.

Layla felt her face get hot. "After lunch, we'll see." She took her sister's arm. "Come on. Let's mingle for a few minutes. We need the support of the town if this oil rights business gets ugly. Schmoozing 'R' Us."

She and Chelsea worked the room for fifteen minutes. Then the president of the club announced that lunch was ready to be served. En masse, the crowd of people began moving toward the dining room.

Chelsea went up on her tiptoes. "So where *is* Joshua Banks? Surely you didn't leave him alone in this room of female piranhas."

Layla might have miscalculated. Josh was fresh meat on the social scene. Why hadn't she thought of that? "He'll be fine," she said, hoping her words were true.

Suddenly, she spotted him, and her vision narrowed. *Wow.* Chelsea saw him at the same moment. She whistled under her breath. "Your man looks pretty darned gorgeous in that tailored suit. The Joshua I remember didn't have a body like that. He was skinny and quiet and barely looked at girls."

"He's changed," Layla muttered. Suddenly, she wanted nothing more than to be at his side. But there were several hundred people separating them.

She and Chelsea allowed themselves to be jostled forward in the direction of lunch. Once they were inside the dining room, guests milled about, finding their spots. A few families, like the Grandins and the Lattimores, had tables for six or eight.

There were multiple two-tops, including the one where Heath Thurston sat alone at first. But the crowd parted when *Nolan* Thurston strode through the melee as if he owned the place. He shook his brother's hand and sat down.

Behind Layla's shoulder, she heard someone whisper. *I thought those two were estranged. Nolan hasn't lived here in years.*

Chelsea bristled and leaned in to whisper in Layla's ear. "There's our arch enemy Heath Thurston. Have you noticed that *he* hasn't spoken to us? At all? He's letting his lawyers do the dirty work."

"That makes sense," Layla said. "Keeps everything professional and clean. The other guy is the one I told you about who wants to have lunch with us. *Nolan* Thurston. The two Thurstons are twins in case you can't tell."

"Too many of those in this town," Chelsea muttered. "I guess we should sit down."

But Layla noticed that her sister's attention lingered on Nolan.

Layla was just about to cross the room to her table when someone came up behind her and put a hand on her shoulder. "Layla Grandin," the voice boomed. "Hot damn. If I'd known you grew up so beautiful, I'd never have let my brother take my place."

Before she could protest, Jordan Banks whirled her around, hugged her and kissed her square on the lips. Even for a childhood friend, his greeting was a bit much.

She freed herself as quickly as she could. "Hello,

Jordan. How are you?" He did look very much like his
brother, but Layla could clearly see the differences.

Jordan shoved his hands in his pockets and rocked
back on his heels. "I'm great. Texas-size great. Sorry I
couldn't take you to the concert."

"No worries. I had a lovely time with Josh. I guess
you and your dad are pretty happy to have him back at
the ranch."

Jordan's expression changed visibly. In fact, he looked
uncomfortable. That was so unlike him, Layla's stomach
flipped. "What did I say?" she asked, trying to make a
joke of it and failing miserably.

"I assumed he would have told you," Jordan said.
"Joshua has decided he wants Dad and me to buy out
his share."

Layla's chest tightened. "Well, he probably hasn't had
a chance to say anything," she said, doing her best to
pretend this was no big deal. "My grandmother has been
ill, and I've been staying with her a lot. This is the first
time Josh and I have seen each other in days. Two busy
people. You know how it is."

Her scrambled explanation wiped the uncertainty off
Jordan's face. Relief tinged his expression. "I'm sure
he'll catch you up," he said. "I'd better get to my seat.
Dad and I are together today."

"No date?" she asked, wondering if she could make
him squirm. Jordan laughed and gave her a naughty grin.
"She'll be waiting on me later," he said.

Layla made her way across the room, realizing as
she approached her table that Josh had a frown on his
face. "Sorry," she said. "Did you think I was never
coming?"

"Nah." His smile didn't reach his eyes.

"Are you okay?" she asked, flipping out her napkin and spreading it in her lap.

"Sure," he said. "I see you and Jordan ran into each other."

Her mind raced. Was that pique in his voice? Surely he didn't think Layla had invited the over-the-top greeting or that she was at all interested, despite her old crush. "Your brother can be a bit much," she said. "But yes. We haven't seen each other in at least four years, I think."

The conversation was suspended when the emcee stood at the podium, made a few announcements and then handed out several awards for businesses that had grown substantially in the past year. Finally, the salad course came out.

Thankfully, Josh seemed to shake off his funk. He was funny and charming, and everything a woman could want in a date.

At one point, he grilled her. "You didn't tell your family that you and I were coming to this shindig together, did you? They've all been staring at us for half an hour."

She winced. "Sorry about that. They would have made a fuss. I thought it was easier this way."

"Do I embarrass you, Ms. Grandin?" he asked in a gentle voice.

"Of course not," she said, avoiding his perceptive gaze. "Don't be silly. But I didn't see the point in making a big deal about our date. It's not like we're official or anything."

"Official?" Some of the humor left his face.

"Don't be difficult," she said, lowering her voice. "You know we're just having fun. Who knows what the future will bring?"

"Indeed."

She never knew blue eyes could freeze ice cold. Josh's

snarky response lit her temper. *He* was the one making plans to cut himself loose from the ranch where he owned a third of a share, the ranch where he had grown up, the ranch where he had spent many an hour raising hell with his brother and Layla.

The curl of hurt in her stomach grew tighter.

She pushed her uneaten salad away and then had to face the main course.

The pasta primavera was both beautiful and delicious. She poked at it, managing to eat enough bites not to draw attention to herself.

In the end, she focused her unhappiness on the Thurston brothers. "Look at them," she hissed in a low voice. "Sitting there in front of God and everybody as if they're pure as the driven snow."

Josh had been quiet throughout the meal, but unlike Layla, he had cleaned his plate. "They're not criminals. Just because they're claiming oil rights that they think belong to their family doesn't mean they're being vindictive."

"So you're taking their side?" She knew she was being unreasonable, but why wasn't he telling her about his decision not to work on the Bankses' ranch? That was news. Big news.

The dessert course was mostly silent.

Josh had no clue what was going on with Layla. She was upset. That much was clear. He didn't want to think her mood had anything to do with Jordan. Josh had felt sick to his stomach when his brother kissed Layla right on the mouth.

To be fair, Jordan's ebullience was nothing unusual. He was like that with most women. Heck, Josh had seen him hug men and lift them off their feet.

Abruptly, Josh stood. "If you'll excuse me, I need to go to the restroom." He exited the dining room and exhaled. Though the club was well air-conditioned, with that many people in one place, the temperature was rising.

When he came out of the men's room, he nearly bumped into Nolan Thurston. Both of them paused, feeling the awkward moment.

Josh stared at him. "Maybe you and your brother should rethink this oil rights business. The Grandins have a lot of clout in this town."

"Is that a threat, or are you pissed that we're upsetting your girlfriend?"

"If your mother or your sister was entitled to something—and that's a big *if*—it doesn't follow that the two of you automatically have a claim. Why don't you let this go? Do you have a grudge against Layla's family? Is that it?"

Nolan's gaze narrowed. "What my brother and I are doing is up to us. You wouldn't begin to understand. So I think you should stay out of it. And a word of warning—if you're interested in anything serious with Layla Grandin, you'd better stake a claim. You aren't the only man in Royal to notice her. Things you care about can be taken away in a heartbeat. Be grateful for what you have."

Before Josh could craft a cutting response, Nolan disappeared down the hall.

The man's words lingered, though.

Oddly, Josh didn't think Nolan was a bad guy. But he couldn't figure him out.

Back in the dining room, the luncheon was winding down. People were beginning to leave. He saw Layla with the Lattimore crew.

When Josh joined them, Layla made a general introduction. "I don't know if you all remember Joshua Banks. He moved to Dallas a number of years ago. His dad is Bertram Banks, and Joshua's brother is Jordan."

After a round of handshakes, Layla filled in the gaps. "Jonathan and Jayden Lattimore. Next, their sister and my good friend Alexa, who now lives in Miami, and last, but not least, the baby of the family, Caitlyn."

Josh nodded. Caitlyn's smile was shy, but charming.

"Nice to meet you all," he said.

Alexa raised an eyebrow. "I noticed the table for two. Are you the new man in Layla's life?"

Silence fell. Layla's cheeks turned pink. The four Lattimore siblings gave him measured glances as if to say he might not be good enough for their friend. Josh cleared his throat. "Well, I'm a man, and Layla is spending the day with me. As for the rest of it, I guess that remains to be seen."

Layla shot him a look of gratitude and took his arm. "It was great to be with you all today. I'm sure Josh has appreciated the third-degree, so he and I are going to scoot out of here. I'll see you soon."

In the parking lot, they strolled toward the car. He shot his quiet companion a sideways glance. "You up for a drive?"

"I'd love that," Layla said.

He still couldn't pin down her mood. But he was relying on sunshine and speed to smooth any rough edges. It was an impulse on his part to return to the spot where their physical relationship had begun so spectacularly.

When he parked on the exact same hilltop, they got out. Layla's shoes weren't suitable for the rough ground, so she took them off and tossed them in the car.

"Too bad we don't have a quilt," he joked.

Layla's expression was hard to read. "Can I tell you a secret?"

"Sure."

"I spoke with a Realtor this week about buying this property."

"You're kidding."

"Nope."

"But what about the Grandin ranch?"

She shrugged, her expression mutinous. "They don't really need me. Vic is going to take over one day, and if not him, then Chelsea. I've started thinking about…"

"About what?" Josh prompted. He took a strand of hair that had escaped the knot on top of her head and curled it around his finger.

"About having something that's my own. I'm tired of being second-best. Or third or fourth. I'm smart and organized. Nothing says a woman can't own a ranch."

"Of course not." He kissed her nose. "Especially a woman like you."

"So you don't think I'm crazy?"

He saw by her vulnerable expression that she really wanted to know his opinion. "You're a lot of things, Layla, but crazy isn't one of them. You're creative and hardworking. You have everyone's best interests at heart. You're a devoted granddaughter and daughter and sister. I'm damned grateful we reconnected."

Those eyes that kept him up at night darkened. "Me, too," she said softly.

Suddenly, his patience ran out. He cleared his throat. "Are you still interested in going back to the hotel with me?"

Her gaze widened. "It's the middle of the afternoon."

He kissed her long and hard, pressing her body to

his. Feeling the way her fluttery skirt tangled with his pants legs. When he could speak, he rested his forehead against hers. "Do you have a problem with that?"

"No." Her voice was barely a whisper. "Not at all."

Twelve

Layla had a decision to make, and she was running out of time. As Josh sent the car hurtling back toward Royal, she leaned against the headrest and closed her eyes.

She wasn't drowsy this time. Far from it. Her body hummed with sexual energy and anticipation.

Was she really going to sleep with a man—again—who was only interested in having a good time? The truth was brutal. She was halfway in love with Joshua Banks, but she was almost certain he was simply using her for sexual gratification.

Could she handle a physical relationship knowing they were both going to walk away when it was over?

Ever since her conversation with Jordan, she had waited for Josh to tell her that his dad and brother were buying him out...that he planned to take the money and run.

The question was—run to where?

She knew he had no interest in going back to his ex-wife, but Dallas had been his home for a long time. Surely he would tell Layla if that was what he had in mind. Or maybe he was keeping her in the dark because his plans didn't involve her at all.

Maybe he was enjoying the sex. Maybe she was convenient.

It was all well and good to think about principles and self-respect and doing the right thing.

The truth was, Layla couldn't walk away. He had hypnotized her, enchanted her. That one slender connection—their childhood friendship—had lowered her defenses and let this complicated, devastatingly handsome man walk back into her life with impunity.

From the beginning, he had told her he wasn't sure he was going to stay in Royal. He had admitted that his life was in turmoil…that he needed and wanted to start over. Heck, the man had even confessed to being an emotional mess.

It was her own fault if she had been weaving fantasies about happily-ever-afters with Joshua Banks.

At the hotel, things got real. She knew if she stepped into the elevator with him, the rest of the day was a foregone conclusion. Still, her feet carried her on a path that led to infinite pleasure but an uncertain future.

Josh must have sensed her unease. He took her suitcase from the trunk of the car and handed his keys over to a dark-headed, bright-eyed young man who looked too young to shave, much less park expensive vehicles.

Layla stood on the curb, waiting. Josh joined her and cocked his head, his smile rueful. "This isn't an all-or-nothing deal, sweetheart. I can always take you home."

She searched his face, looking for a sign that she wasn't making a huge mistake. He was kind and sexy and had just enough bad boy in him to make a woman weak in the knees. "I don't want to go home."

It was true. She didn't. *Please don't break my heart, Josh Banks.*

He held her hand on the way upstairs. His palm was warm and slightly rough against hers. She gripped his fingers, telling herself this was light and fun.

But in her heart, she knew. This was Layla putting her heart on the line. Letting herself be vulnerable. Telling the Fates she was ready to try again.

Josh's hotel room was the same. Which meant she couldn't help staring at the bed and remembering the night she had spent here.

She kicked off her shoes and curled her toes in the thick, luxurious carpet. "Do you mind if I freshen up?"

"Help yourself. Then I'll take a turn." He opened the mini fridge and extracted a beer. "We're not in a rush." His teasing smile connected with something deep in her core, setting off a chain reaction of raw need and desperate longing.

Unlike before, it wasn't bedtime. In fact, it was a heck of a long time until lights out. How were they going to fill all those hours?

It was a hot day. At first, she thought about simply using a damp washcloth to remove her makeup and run over her arms and legs. But it seemed dumb to try that when she could simply strip down. She didn't want to get in bed and feel icky.

After the world's quickest shower, she dried off and debated her options. She had imagined Josh removing her fancy dress. But now she didn't want to put it on again. Instead, she grabbed one of the hotel robes on the back of the door, the one that had clearly not been worn.

It swallowed her. She belted it tightly and opened the bathroom door.

Josh looked up, his gaze hooded. Heat flared between them, invisible but undeniable. She thought he would say something. Instead, he brushed by her and entered the bathroom. Moments later, she heard the shower.

His was even shorter than hers. She was still dithering about whether or not to get in bed when he reappeared, wearing the second robe.

A man should look more relaxed, more approachable without his fancy suit. In this case, it was the opposite. Stripped of the traditional clothes he had worn to the luncheon, Josh was even more stunningly masculine.

His damp hair was tousled. Because the robe was belted loosely, a large portion of his beautiful, lightly hair-dusted chest was exposed. His shoulders were so broad, the hotel robe strained to fit them.

Layla found courage and went to him. In her bare feet, the difference in their heights was pronounced. She grabbed the robe's lapels and went up on her tip-toes. "Thank you for being my plus-one today," she said. "Every woman in the room was jealous of me." Then she kissed him.

She took her time, enjoying the taste of his mouth, feeling the intoxicating way their lips clung and parted and pressed close again.

Josh was breathing heavily, his chest rising and falling rapidly. Her own pulse was racketing along at about a thousand beats a minute. So far, he was passive beneath her kiss, mostly letting her take the lead.

She stroked his tongue with hers, growing bolder. He groaned low in his throat. The hair on her arms stood up at the guttural sound.

At last, he gripped her shoulders. "I've wanted you for

days, Layla." Was that a note of desperation in his voice?
He shed his robe and removed hers. Without warning,
he scooped her into his arms and carried her to the bed.

Perhaps he meant to lay her carefully on the mattress,
but when Layla bit his bottom lip, his knees buckled,
and they tumbled onto the bed together.

Still feeling her power after that sensual, explorative
kiss, Layla straddled his waist. "I'd like to be on top.
Any objections?"

Josh stared up at her with a narrowed gaze. "Not a
single damn one."

Now that she had assumed the position, she was left
with a plethora of choices. There were plenty of condoms
on the nearby table, but she wanted to play.

Carefully, she stretched out on top of him. She could
feel his hard sex against her lower abdomen. Her breasts
squished against his powerful chest. Now she could nes-
tle her head on his shoulder and listen to him breathe.

"This is nice," she said primly.

Josh's laughter threatened to tumble her off her comfy
perch. "*Nice* wasn't the adjective I had in mind," he said.
He cupped her butt in his hands and squeezed. "Interesting. Stimulating. Tormenting. Any of those?"

She put her hands on his shoulders and pushed up
so she could see his face. "Sure. I'll take them all. You
looked very handsome today. I think I like a man in a
suit."

He pinched her ass. "How about a cowboy in dirty
boots?"

Awkwardly, she sat all the way up, straddling him.
"Do I have to choose? Can't I have both?"

Josh touched her intimately. "If you'll give up this
torture, you can have whatever you want."

Without meaning to, Layla closed her eyes. Seeing

Josh's hands on her body was too much. Every light in the room was on. What was she doing? She'd never had an exhibitionist bone in her body.

"Josh," she whispered, not even knowing what she wanted to say.

He was a gifted lover. Soon, he had her at the edge of climax, her breath lodged in her throat.

Hazily, she remembered the condoms nearby. "I can't reach them," she said, waving a hand.

"Way ahead of you." The husky words were accompanied by action. He shoved her gently to one side and grabbed a single packet.

When he ripped it open, she stared at him. "Let me do it."

The stain of red on his cheekbones darkened. He handed over the protection. "I said it before. Whatever you want, Layla."

He reclined again and watched her. Her hands shook. This intimacy wasn't one she had initiated very often or at all. During the time she was engaged to Richard, she had been on the pill.

Now when she took Josh's erect shaft in one hand, he shuddered from head to toe. As if she really was torturing him.

His sex was fascinating, long and hard…covered with hot silky skin. She pressed a kiss to the head, eliciting a feral sound from her lover. He grabbed her wrist in one hand. But she ignored his unspoken command.

"Relax," she said softly. "I want to taste you." Taking him in her mouth, she sucked gently, feeling him flex and swell. Feeling the power she had over him was both exhilarating and humbling. But she didn't want power, not really. She wanted a lover who would be her mate, her equal, her partner.

In that instant, she recognized what she hadn't allowed herself to acknowledge. She was not *halfway* in love with Joshua Banks. She had fallen into the deep end—the water over her head. Offering her heart to him madly, passionately, extravagantly.

And yes, he was an enigma. He probably didn't feel the same. Even so, she was helpless to fight the emotion that stung her eyes or to ward off the wave of love and longing that tightened her chest.

"Enough," he said, the word barely audible. "Now, Layla."

She smoothed the condom into place and rose over him, then took him into her body like a silent pledge. This was what she had waited her whole life to find. A man who was worthy of her love.

Soon, she was no longer able to think rationally. Josh filled her completely. Even in the less dominant position, he took control. His hands on her hips might leave bruises. Layla didn't care. His firm hold was the only anchor in her universe.

His gaze locked on hers. "Are you taking what you want, my love?"

She nodded, mute. His beautiful sapphire eyes seemed to be telegraphing a message that was apparently coded in another language, because she couldn't read it. And when he said *my love*, that was just sex talk—right? He couldn't really be as besotted with her as she was with him.

Without warning, he rolled over, taking her with him, never breaking their connection. "Nice trick," she panted.

His low, amused laughter made her blush.

"I don't think I'll let you leave this room," he said, lazily stroking deep.

Layla wrapped her legs around his waist. "We can't screw 24/7."

"Wanna bet?"

She clung to him, feeling the cataclysm build. Josh seemed to know her better than she knew herself. Physically, he met her every need.

When he lost it and pounded hard, head thrown back, cheekbones tight with strain, Layla hit the peak and cried out. It was even better than the last time. Higher. Hotter. More out of control.

Josh came, too, his large frame vibrating. He moaned her name and slumped on top of her. She held him close. Feeling his strength. Memorizing this moment against the day when it might be nothing but a faint recollection.

Like every woman insecure in a budding relationship, she wanted to find the courage to ask where this was leading. But she was afraid of the answers. Maybe the really brave thing was not to ask at all, but to take what Josh had to give and offer him her heart in return.

He would never know how she felt, perhaps. But a gift was only a gift if it was freely given.

They both dozed for a few minutes.

When Josh finally roused, he yawned. "Wow. You turn me inside out." He was rumpled and heavy eyed and so beautifully male it hurt to look at him.

"Same." She laughed, her heart squeezing.

"We have the rest of the day," he said. "What would you like to do?"

She wrinkled her nose, unwilling to state the obvious.

Josh nuzzled her cheek, kissed the sensitive spot below her ear. "Besides that, naughty woman," he said.

"I'm feeling mellow. You choose."

In the end, it turned out to be a perfect afternoon. They watched a movie in bed with room service snacks.

Before dinner, they changed into running gear and did a quick five miles around downtown.

The shared shower afterward turned into something more. Josh took her up against the wall, face-to-face, her arms locked around his neck. It was the most intimately personal thing she had ever done with a partner.

She could swear she saw love and tenderness in his gaze, but the stubborn man never said a word about his ranch share or anything else that mattered.

After dinner in the hotel dining room, they danced to the romantic music of a small orchestra. Layla had packed a full-length red jersey dress that didn't wrinkle. With Josh's warm hand splayed on her bare back, she could have nestled in his arms for hours. But eventually, they went upstairs again.

Josh stared at her when she kicked off her shoes. "Are you happy, Layla?" he asked.

She tensed. "What do you mean?" He might be talking about this day in particular or life in general.

He shrugged. "It's a simple question."

Perhaps this was the opening she had been looking for. Maybe he was waiting for a sign from her. She looked him straight in the eye and smiled wistfully. "Meeting you again has been the happiest thing in my life for a long time, Josh. I have no regrets." That last was to let him off the hook if he was thinking about leaving.

He owed her nothing. No promises had been exchanged, no vows made.

Instead of continuing the conversation, he kicked off his socks and shoes. Then he removed his jacket and shirt and tie. While she watched, he took her wrist and reeled her in, pulling her tightly against his body so they were touching from shoulder to hip. He found the zip at the back of her dress, lowered it and shimmied her dress to the floor.

Now Josh was bare from the waist up, and Layla wore nothing but a strapless black bra and matching panties. "Are *you* happy, Josh?" she asked, her heart in her throat.

He held her tightly, his face buried in the curve of her neck. "You're a very special woman," he said gruffly. "And yes, I'm happy."

She winced. It wasn't exactly the answer she was looking for. When they made love this time, it was markedly different. Less urgency, more tenderness. Was this what goodbye sex felt like?

The question haunted her. She thought for a few moments that she wouldn't be able to have an orgasm, but Josh was endlessly patient. He touched her as if she was infinitely breakable, yet he coaxed fire to the surface. When she finally came, the pleasure was blinding, but tears clogged her throat.

Afterward, they slept, wrapped together in each other's arms. As dawn was breaking, Layla got up to go to the bathroom. When she returned, she climbed back into bed, determined to wring the last drops of pleasure from this interlude.

By the time Josh took her home today, they would have spent the last twenty-four hours together. It felt like forever, but it was far too short, especially since she was no closer than ever to understanding him.

When Josh's alarm went off, they got up and dressed. They both wore jeans and casual shirts. He talked. She answered. But the words were meaningless, utilitarian.

Josh took her suitcase as they made their way downstairs. He kissed the top of her head right before they stepped off the elevator and into the lobby. "This was great," he said. "Thanks for sneaking away a few hours."

"It was fun for me, too," she said. "But I do need to get home and check on Grammy."

Josh stopped suddenly when he saw a trio of men standing on the sidewalk just outside the portico. "I've been trying to get in touch with one of those guys for two weeks." He handed her his wallet. "Would you mind asking for the car? The claim ticket is in there. And give the kid a fifty. He's heading off to college in a couple of months."

Layla nodded. "Of course."

Josh set her suitcase at her feet and jogged over to join the group.

When Layla opened the billfold, she found the claim ticket immediately and passed it to the man at the podium. Then she looked for a fifty-dollar bill.

The money was easy to spot, but as she extracted it, a folded slip of white paper fell out. When she picked it up, her stomach clenched. It was a boarding pass for a flight from Royal to Dallas. Dated the day after Layla first spent the night in Josh's hotel room.

She stared at it blankly, trying to process what she was seeing. Most people had boarding passes on their smartphones now. But in the case of a seat-assignment change or an upgrade, a gate agent might print out a paper boarding pass.

Unfortunately, this was only one leg of the trip. She had no idea when Josh returned.

Why had he gone to Dallas? Why hadn't he mentioned it?

Was this the reason she hadn't heard from him in a string of days while Grammy was recovering at home?

Heartsick and confused, she stood frozen, praying the car would show up soon. The same bright-eyed young man from yesterday handed over the keys. Layla offered the tip. "This is from Mr. Banks," she said, managing a smile.

The boy's eyes widened. "Wow. Thanks."

Layla put her suitcase in the trunk and sat down in the passenger seat. She was numb. Hurt. Stunned.

She must have greeted Josh when he slid behind the wheel. Obviously, they chatted on the way out to the ranch. But she would have been hard-pressed to remember a word.

When Josh pulled up in front of the ranch house, it was all she could do not to bolt up the steps. Instead, she waited while he retrieved her bag. He insisted on carrying it to the front door.

"I'll call you," he said.

"Sure..."

When he bent to kiss her lips, she turned her head at the last minute, making it look casual. Josh's kiss landed on her cheek, not her mouth.

"I'd better get inside," she said, not quite able to meet his searching gaze. "Thanks for going to the luncheon with me."

He frowned, perhaps for the first time realizing something might be wrong. "I'm glad you asked me. Will you let me know if there is any news about the oil rights?"

"Okay."

"Now that the Thurston twins showed up at the luncheon, I doubt they are going to ride off into the sunset."

She grimaced. "Probably not."

He kissed her again. This one landed smack on her lips—the same traitorous lips that returned the kiss in spite of everything.

Josh pulled back, his expression lighter. "Goodbye, Layla. We'll talk soon."

Thirteen

We'll talk soon. That stupid throwaway phrase rattled around in her head for the remainder of the day. The time to talk was over.

Clearly, Josh's agenda and Layla's were vastly different.

One upside of having a big family living under the same roof was that there were always plenty of distractions. She visited Grammy in her room and was happy to see her looking perky and healthy, even for a woman her age.

After that, she spent a couple of hours in the barn doing her own personal brand of equine therapy. Even though the horses couldn't talk back, Layla told them a few of her secrets. Their soft whinnies and the way they bumped her with their heads eased some of the pain in her heart.

Unfortunately, there was no family dinner that evening. Everybody was either on the run, or like Grammy, eating in their room.

Layla wasn't hungry. She made herself a smoothie with protein powder and forced herself to drink it. At nine thirty, she knew she couldn't procrastinate any longer. Though it was cowardly, she couldn't face Josh. This breakup was happening via text.

Josh...

She typed the single word and stopped, not sure how to say what she wanted to say. He didn't need to know she was in love with him. That would be the ultimate humiliation. Doggedly, she continued.

I know you and I have enjoyed reconnecting after so many years, but my family is in the midst of a crisis, as you've heard. Plus, by your own admission, much of your life is up in the air. I think it would be best all the way around if we don't see each other anymore. I wish you every happiness...

Layla

Well, that was it. Short, sweet and to the point. She felt sick. Deliberately torpedoing a relationship that had given her so much joy seemed self-defeating. But she had no choice. She had too much self-respect to let another man keep her in the dark.

When she hit Send, the tears started. She didn't try to stop them. It was natural to grieve. Joshua Banks was a wonderful man, but he wasn't for her. Clearly, his needs had been sexual, first and foremost.

She hadn't expected a grand gesture. But *something*… Even a generic *I care about you* would have been nice.

Five minutes after she sent the text, her phone rang. If a ringtone could sound angry, she fancied this one did. Of course the caller ID said Josh Banks.

Just this one more conversation and she would be done.

She wiped her face with the back of her hand and answered.

"Hello?"

Josh's voice reverberated with confused rage and maybe even a hint of desperation. "What the hell, Layla? What's going on?"

She swallowed hard. "I think the text was self-explanatory. I've said all I have to say. Goodbye, Josh."

"Wait," he said urgently. "Don't hang up. Did something upset you? Is it your grandmother? Or the Thurston brothers? Let me be there for you."

"It's none of that, Josh. Just what I said in the text. Besides, I don't think you and I have much in common. Please let this go."

Dead silence gripped the phone connection for long seconds.

"You didn't seem to mind our differences when I was giving you multiple orgasms," he said tersely. "Talk to me, Layla. Please."

He was breaking her heart into tiny little pieces. She almost capitulated. But then she reminded herself that Josh Banks was only interested in sex. He had kept Layla on the periphery of his life. She needed to make a clean break.

"Goodbye, Josh."

Heartbreak was a funny thing. Layla was able to function almost normally during the daytime. But the nights were long. And painful.

After spending hours in Josh's bed, it was impossible to pretend that her own lonely room was where she wanted to be. She had done the right thing. No question about it. But oh, how it hurt.

In fact, her intense suffering told her more clearly than ever that Richard had damaged her pride and her self-respect, but he had never really possessed her heart. How had she believed she was in love with him?

It was possible Chelsea sensed something was wrong, but she gave Layla her space. That was a good thing, because Layla was holding herself together by sheer will. Sympathy from her sister would have pushed her over the edge.

In the midst of her grief, she struggled with her grandmother's secret. And she finally decided that she had to tell her family at least the bare bones of it.

Three evenings after her exchange with Josh, the whole clan was in residence for the noon meal. Grammy had been picked up by a friend whose granddaughter was taking both women to lunch in town.

When the housekeeper had served the main course out on the back veranda, Layla set down her fork. "I have news," she said, keeping her voice low. "Grammy didn't want me to tell any of you, and I promised, but you deserve to hear at least bits of it."

Her father scowled. "My own mother conspiring behind my back?"

Chelsea thumped the table. "Oh, for heaven's sake, Daddy. Don't be so dramatic. Let Layla finish."

Five sets of eyes stared at her with varying degrees of suspicion. Only Morgan smiled. "Go ahead, Layla."

"Because of Grammy's wishes, I can't tell you all the details, but suffice it to say that she came across some of Grandy's scribbles. I've seen them. Unfortunately, it does seem as if Grandy and Augustus Lattimore offered the oil rights to Heath Thurston's mother."

Three beats of silence passed. "Hell," her father said. "I didn't want to hear that."

Vic stood and paced. "What are we going to do?"

Layla exhaled. "I thought we might be morally bound to produce this *thing* Grammy found. Grammy says not. It's not anything close to being a legal document. Simply a passing reference. The burden of proof is on the Thurston brothers."

Chelsea stood as well, running her hands through her hair. "Good Lord. Are we really going to let them dig up this ranch?"

"We may not have a choice," Layla said. "Still, that photocopy we got from the lawyer has to be substantiated before things go any further."

The housekeeper returned, and all serious conversation was abandoned. But Layla could see from the expressions on everyone's faces that they were all concerned.

She was, too. Of course she was. But her breakup with Josh loomed larger at the moment. Maybe that made her a bad daughter. She didn't want to see her family's ranch ruined. Truly she didn't.

Despite that, Heath Thurston and the contested oil rights were the least of her problems.

When ten days had passed after the spring luncheon at the TCC, her nerves reached a breaking point. No one needed her at the moment. She had to get out of the house, off the ranch.

When she was in her car and driving, one particular spot called to her. She tried not to go. It was pointless to make herself miserable for no reason. But by the time she had traversed all the back roads of Maverick

County, she discovered she couldn't return home until she made one final pilgrimage.

The Realtor had never called Layla back. Maybe she was too busy selling actual houses and ranches to deal with a tract of land out in the middle of nowhere.

Layla made her way to the very same hilltop where she and Josh had first made love. Was that why she wanted to buy the land? Was she trying to preserve that day forever in her memory?

She got out of the car and leaned against the tree. A light breeze made the afternoon heat bearable. Overhead, a buzzard flew in ever-widening circles. Maybe he sensed the death of Layla's love life and was waiting to pick at the bones.

Even in her pain, she had to laugh at her own joke. She wasn't the first woman to want a man she couldn't have. And she wouldn't be the last.

It was just that the moments with Josh had seemed so very *real*. So perfectly intimate. So natural. So right.

The truth was, her romantic judgment still sucked.

She felt the tree bark against her back. Bits of sunlight made their way through the leaves and branches overhead. Time passed. Layla wasn't wearing a watch, and she didn't care. Maybe she had a bit of Irish in her. Perhaps she was holding a wake for the death of her dreams.

Loss was hard any way you looked at it…

Eventually, heavy clouds began to build, and the humidity increased. Texas weather was capricious. A storm was on the way…

She honestly didn't know how long she had been standing there when she heard an alien noise. Not a bird. Not the wind. Not even an animal.

Instead, as the sound grew closer, it became clear that she had a visitor. When she glanced behind her where the road wound down the low rise, she clenched her fists. How could he possibly have known she was here?

When Joshua parked beside her car and got out, she schooled her face to show indifference, despite the fact that her heart was bouncing all around her rib cage.

"Are you psychic?" she asked with an edge in her voice.

"No. I went out to the ranch. Your sister told me you had gone for a drive. I took a shot." His voice was flat.

Layla didn't move. But she managed to gaze at him without flinching. He looked terrible, frankly. His beautiful hair hadn't been combed. His mouth was set in a grim line.

She went on the attack, hoping he would leave. "What do you want, Josh?"

He leaned against his car, arms folded across his chest. "I think I deserve an answer. Something other than the bullshit you gave me in a text and over the phone. One moment I had a warm woman in my bed, the next she was colder than a witch's tit in December."

"Charming," Layla drawled. "Is that the way men talk to women back in Dallas?"

"Cut the crap, Layla," he said sharply. "Why did you bail on us?"

Temper was better than despair. The hot rush of anger and indignation felt good. "There was no *us*," she said. "*Us* implies a relationship. You saw me as a fuck-buddy."

"Don't be crude," he snapped. "It doesn't suit you."

She infused her voice with ice. "Your opinions are irrelevant."

Suddenly, the aggression in his stance disappeared. For a split second she witnessed uncertainty. And pain? Surely not.

He stared at the ground and then back at her. "I

thought we had something special, Layla. I could swear you felt it, too. What happened?"

She'd had enough. The Band-Aids she had slapped over her emotional wounds were being ripped away by this postmortem. "I'll tell you what happened, Joshua Banks. You lied to me, just like my ex-fiancé. You and Richard are cut from the same cloth."

Fury flared in those blue eyes she saw in her dreams. "I *never* lied to you," he shouted. "Never."

Could she jump in her car and drive away? Would he stop her? She honestly didn't know. And if he touched her—at all—she feared she would let him lie to her again.

She took a deep breath, wanting to destroy him with the force of her disappointment. But rational, cooler thoughts prevailed. "Lying by omission is still lying. I get that you weren't sleeping with other women when you were with me. But the end result was the same. I told you I had trust issues with men. You knew my weakness, and you exploited it."

Bewilderment brushed his features. "I honestly don't know what the hell you're talking about. I thought we were getting closer every day."

Either the man was a very good actor, or he thought what he had done wasn't wrong. Probably the latter.

It angered her that she had to spell it out. Because it made her humiliation complete.

"Okay, Josh," she said. "Here it is. You asked your father and brother to buy out your share of the ranch, but you never thought to mention it to me. You flew to Dallas for some unknown reason, and again, I didn't merit even the briefest of explanations." She swallowed, her heart aching. "Those are not the actions of a man involved in a relationship. You're a loner. Or maybe you just don't see me as having any lasting effect on your daily life. Either way, I don't want or need that. I don't want or need you."

Whew. That last sentence was a huge lie. And with the clouds churning overhead, the possibility of a lightning strike was not merely theoretical.

During her big speech, Josh went white. In fact, his pallor was disturbing. Grief and shock turned his eyes dark. "Oh, God, Layla. I—"

Just as he started to speak, a powerful bolt of lightning split a small tree less than three hundred yards away. The thunder was simultaneous.

His face changed. "We've got to get out of here."

Huge drops of rain began to fall. "Goodbye," she said, tears filling her eyes.

Josh took her shoulders in his hands. "I need twenty minutes," he said, his eyes as wild as the sky. "Swear to me you'll listen for twenty minutes."

A second beautiful but deadly lightning strike sizzled the air a little farther away. "Why? It's pointless."

He had to raise his voice to be heard over the wind. "Come to my room at the hotel. We need a quiet place to talk."

"Oh, no," she said, horrified at that idea.

"Please, Layla. You can sit by the door if it will make you feel better. Twenty minutes. That's all I ask."

It began to rain harder. Soon, they would be soaked. "Fine," she said, swallowing the pain of being near him again. Surely she could endure twenty minutes. Then this would all be over.

"We'll go in my car," he said. "I'll send someone for yours later."

"Absolutely not. I'll follow you."

They faced off, Layla resolute, Josh increasingly frustrated. A third lightning strike settled the matter. She dove for her car and locked herself inside. Josh stared at her grimly, got into his own vehicle and then began carefully turning around.

When he started down the hill, she followed him. They had made their decision in the nick of time. The clouds opened up, and the rain let loose in huge driving sheets. The noise inside the car was deafening. Even with her wipers on high, she could barely see out the front windshield.

It didn't help that the rough lane they had come up was little more than two ruts in the ground. The entire hilltop was turning to mud.

She breathed a sigh of relief when they made it out to the paved road. For a few moments she considered eluding Josh and driving home. Unfortunately, she knew him well enough to assume he would simply follow her.

There was no way in heck she wanted to handle this volatile situation with her family looking on. She wouldn't put it past Josh to enlist their help.

The drive back to town shouldn't have taken more than twenty-five minutes. Today, it was almost twice that. Josh was forced to creep along at fifteen miles an hour. In some places, flash flooding was a definite risk.

Her hands were clenched so tightly on the steering wheel that her neck muscles gave her a headache.

It seemed like an eternity.

Finally, they pulled up beneath the hotel's portico and got out. Though she hadn't gotten drenched, she was wet enough to know she looked bedraggled. She grabbed her purse and joined Josh.

Neither of them spoke in the elevator.

Layla stared at the floor. No matter what he said, she

wouldn't be manipulated. His behavior was clear. He only wanted Layla in bed.

At last, Josh unlocked his hotel room door and stepped aside for her to enter. Immediately, Layla grabbed a desk chair and dragged it to a position right beside the door. Josh's lips tightened, but he didn't respond to her deliberate provocation.

Instead, he went to the bathroom, grabbed two towels and returned, handing one to Layla. She pulled a tiny mirror from her purse and checked her reflection. Not one-hundred-percent drowned rat, but close enough. She ran the towel over her damp hair and then combed it out.

When she was done, Josh sat down on the side of the bed. He looked so defeated and miserable that she almost relented.

She glanced at her watch pointedly. "The clock is ticking."

His spine straightened. He looked at her, an intense gaze that seemed to see inside her soul. "I love you, Layla."

Shock reverberated through her body. And stunned joy. Though it took all she had, she kept her expression impassive. What kind of ploy was this?

"I suppose you forgot to mention that, too?" she said.

He flinched visibly. Perhaps her sarcasm had been over the top, but for him to pretend now made her angry. She wanted so badly to believe him, but she couldn't trust that his words were real.

"I am *so* sorry," he said.

She shrugged. "For what? Things are what they are."

He rested his elbows on his knees, staring at her, coaxing her by the sheer force of his personality to look at him. "This isn't a game. I love you. I suspected it the first time we made love, but I knew it the night you spent in this very room."

Inside, she began to shake. "No."

He stared at her. "Yes. I've lived through what love isn't...which is why I knew so quickly when the real thing hit me hard."

"You don't have to do this, Josh." Her throat hurt from holding back tears of emotion. Everything he was saying delighted her. But was it sincere?

"Layla..." He looked frustrated now. "I know I messed up, but not for the reasons you think."

"What are you trying to say, then?"

Josh shrugged. Unbelievably, his face flushed as if he was embarrassed or bashful or both. What was going on?

He rubbed his jaw. "I was trying to make a grand gesture. All the planning and juggling was falling into place. I was almost ready."

"For what?"

"To make my pitch. To propose."

The joy tried to return, but Layla kept a lid on it. She shook her head slowly, wondering for a moment if this was an odd dream. "You were going to propose to me when you hadn't even said *I love you*?"

He muttered a word she had never heard him use. "I screwed up, okay? I was so busy trying to surprise you that I made you feel shut out and unimportant. That was never my intention."

Now he was definitely embarrassed. She didn't know what to say. Did she believe him? Could she?

When she didn't say anything, Josh doggedly plunged on with his explanations. "The reason your Realtor couldn't find any information about that piece of land you wanted to buy is because my sale was already in progress. I thought you and I could start a ranch of our own. Partners. Lovers."

She was dumbfounded. "You bought a ranch. For us. But you didn't think to include me?"

He stood now and paced. "I was all into this big surprise idea."

"I *hate* surprises," she said.

"Well, I know that now." He went to the mini fridge and grabbed two bottles of water, then tossed her one of them. "Drink something. You're kind of pale."

Layla caught the plastic container automatically. When she opened the lid and took a sip, she realized how thirsty she was. The whole encounter had made her dizzy and uncertain. This wasn't how romance unfolded in rom-coms. She was so tied up in knots, she didn't know *how* to feel.

When she finished two-thirds of the bottle, she sighed. "Go ahead. Finish your story. Tell me about your secretive trip."

He clearly didn't like the adjective, but he didn't quibble. "I went to Dallas twice actually...for a couple of reasons. I met with my ex-boss and pitched him the idea of me working remotely. It's not really a stretch, and I was pretty sure they needed me."

"And did they?"

"Apparently so. He gave me my job back with a raise. I figured if I was going to have a wife and a brand-new business venture, I was probably going to need some income flowing in until the ranch was up and running."

"A wife?" Her stomach quivered. Maybe dreams really did come true.

"A wife," he said firmly.

Layla was giddy, but she wanted the whole story. "You said *two* reasons. What was the other one?"

He stopped by her chair and rubbed the back of his hand over her cheek. His gaze narrowed, those beautiful blue eyes dark with intensity. "Do you love me, Layla?"

She hesitated. She couldn't help it. Trust was hard. She saw that her reaction hurt him.

When she didn't say a word, he crouched beside her. "Don't be afraid of me, Layla. I can't bear it. Don't be afraid of us."

He was so close. So very close. All she wanted was to launch herself into his arms, but this was crazy. Wasn't it?

"We barely know each other," she whispered. She waved a hand. "Give me some space, please." What she wanted him to do was ignore her demand, but then he wouldn't be the honorable guy she loved.

A frown line appeared between his brows, but he went back to his seat on the bed. "We've known each other for years," he said, the words flat. "Lots of people are still close to friends they met in grade school. Our connection may have weakened with time and distance, but once we were together again, I *knew* you."

"But love?"

His jaw was tight. "Men and women come from different planets, right? We look at the world differently."

"What's your point?"

"When you and I were intimate, our bodies connected in more than a superficial way. We saw each other's weaknesses. Our failures. Our hopes for the future. That kind of sex is rare, Layla. Tell me you realize that."

"I haven't had a lot of sex," she admitted. "Except with Richard the rat."

"And was that sex good?"

Fourteen

The room was so quiet, a person could have heard the proverbial pin drop. She thought about it for a moment. "It wasn't *not* good," she said. "Besides, my mother always warned Chelsea, Morgan and me not to ever confuse sex and lust with love. She told us it was a common female mistake."

"Was that what happened with Richard?"

That one stumped her. "Not exactly. I thought he was something I was *supposed* to want. Love and marriage and kids."

"And how did you feel the first time you and I were intimate?"

She thought back to that day. The quilt. The sunshine. The remarkable way she was at ease with Josh and yet so intensely aroused. "I felt like I was flying," she admitted.

At last, a tiny smile of relief tipped up the corners of his mouth, that mouth and those lips she wanted to devour. He watched her closely, so very closely. She didn't know whether to be flattered or worried. And he seemed to be waiting for something more. So she kept talking. "I don't think you know me as well as you think. I'm pretty boring—an introvert for the most part. And I'm not very adventurous. I like tending to the animals at the ranch. It grounds me, makes me feel safe."

He stood again. This time, he took her hands and pulled her to her feet. "And what about me, sweet Layla. Do I make you feel safe?"

It was an odd question, perhaps. And not very sexy according to the rom-com script. But he was so close and so very dear to her.

She took one step and rested her cheek over his heart. "You do," she said. And it was true. No matter how bizarre his behavior, now that he had explained, all her feelings for him came rushing back. She wasn't mad or angry or uncertain.

All she felt at this exact moment was *safe*. And relieved. And if she allowed herself to relax—so very, very happy.

Suddenly, one last question bumped up against her burgeoning peace. She was afraid to ask it. With Josh's big warm body pressed against hers, all she wanted was to bask in the incredulous glow of this man's confession of love.

But the tiniest doubt remained that perhaps he had unresolved issues with his ex.

She swallowed the lump in her throat. "I still haven't heard that second reason you went to Dallas."

Deep in his chest, a groan rumbled. He pulled back, looked in her face and bent his head to kiss her. Tenderly at first, but then with that wild passion that always washed over them and birthed insanity.

"Don't move," Josh said.

She put her fingers to her lips. They tingled. As she watched, Josh rifled in what looked like a piece of carry-on luggage and extracted a turquoise box. When he turned around, his expression was a mix of sheepish defiance.

"A buddy of mine manages the Tiffany store near University Park," he said. "I picked out a ring two days ago and made him swear I could return it if you wanted something else."

Before she could react, he knelt in front of her, tossed aside the outer package and white ribbon and flipped open the real box. "Marry me, Layla," he said, his voice husky. "I adore you. I want to spend the next fifty years making you happy."

He pulled the ring out of its nest and slipped it on the third finger on her left hand.

Somewhere along the way, Layla forgot to breathe. It seemed to be a common problem when Josh was around.

The ring was stunning. A single, flawless, round diamond. At least two carats, maybe more. The platinum setting included a duo of blue baguettes flanking the solitaire.

Josh rubbed his thumb over her knuckles. "Two sapphires," he said. "One for your eyes and one for the wide Texas skies where I found my soul mate."

She tugged him to his feet and searched his face. "Are you sure?"

His gaze was clear and heated. "Absolutely. But you still haven't answered my question. Do you love me, Layla Grandin?"

She sighed happily, holding up her hand to make the ring sparkle. "I definitely do."

Her honesty was rewarded with a world-class kiss.

He held her tightly. Enough that she felt the evidence of how much he had missed her pressed against her.

His voice rumbled in her ear. "Will you marry me, Layla? Will you be my wife and my lover and my best friend? Will you build a ranch and a home and a family with me?"

For the first time in her adult life, she was absolutely sure she knew the right answer to a very grown-up question. She pulled back and smiled at him, her eyes brimming with happy tears. "I will, Josh. I will."

Epilogue

Five days later... Las Vegas, Nevada

Josh held Layla's hand as they stood outside the wedding chapel. Even with dark sunglasses on, he had to squint against the blinding sun. He bent his head so he could see her face. "It's not too late to change your mind, sweetheart. You're a Grandin, the first in your crew to get married. You should be wearing a ten-thousand-dollar dress and having the entire population of Maverick County come out to see society's latest bride in all her finery walk down the aisle."

He worried that she would regret what they were about to do.

Layla removed her own sunglasses and gave him a sweet but naughty smile. She was wearing white, a sexy sundress that bared a lot of skin and showcased her body. "I don't want that," she said firmly. "In fact, it sounds dreadful. We can always have a fancy reception later. Besides, with this oil rights controversy dragging on, I don't think the timing is right for a big splashy wedding."

It was also why they weren't taking a honeymoon right now, other than two nights in Vegas. Josh kissed her forehead, not wanting to muss her makeup before they tied the knot. "If you're sure. I don't want to upset your family."

She laughed. "I guess that's one benefit of being the forgotten child. No one cares what I do."

He had a hunch she was dead wrong about that one, but he was getting his beautiful bride, so he was willing to be convinced. "Come on, darlin'. Let's do this."

Hours later, Layla couldn't remember a word of the vows she had spoken. Nor the officiant's face, or even the flowers she carried.

But what stood out was Josh's steady gaze and the unmistakable love in his eyes. When he looked at her like that, she knew she had won the jackpot.

At the moment, he was downstairs procuring some kind of surprise. When he told her that a few minutes ago, she had gaped at him and then rolled her eyes.

Josh swore this was one surprise she would be happy to receive.

When a knock sounded at the bedroom door, she checked the peephole and let him in. "That was quick."

Josh grinned. "All I had to do was check at the front desk." He handed her a large white envelope. "Happy wedding day, Ms. Banks."

Layla, definitely puzzled, opened the flap. She'd halfway been expecting another box with jewelry inside.

Even when she extracted the sheaf of papers, it took her a second to understand what she was looking at. And then it sank in.

Her heart raced. "I thought we couldn't close until next week." They had added her name to the pending sale several days ago.

Josh kissed her forehead on his way to open the bottle of champagne that was chilling in a bucket on the dresser. "The sellers were eager to be finished. All the paperwork is final. You and I will sign on the dotted line day after tomorrow when we get back to Royal, but the deal is done." He lifted his glass and handed her one. "We own a ranch, Layla. Just the two of us."

Her heart fluttered in her chest. "Do you really think we can do this?"

"Of course we can. It's going to be the best damn ranch in Texas."

She drained her champagne and put her arms around his neck, pressing close, hearing him inhale a sharp breath. "I adore you, Joshua Banks."

He nuzzled her nose. "The feeling is mutual." His big warm hands settled on her ass. "I like this wedding dress. A lot. But you'll be more comfortable if you take it off."

"Josh…" She ran a fingertip over his lips. "You're so thoughtful."

He shrugged, feigning modesty. "I'll do anything for my sexy bride."

"Anything?" She unbuttoned his shirt.

His face flushed. She had a feeling it *wasn't* the alcohol.

"Anything," he muttered. He picked her up and carried her to the bed. They had both laughed about the candy-apple-red bedspread with the embroidered cupids. Josh flipped back the covers and set her on her feet. Then he undressed her in record time. He took a deep breath and exhaled slowly. "I wish we hadn't wasted so many years."

Layla shook her head slowly. "Not a waste, Josh. Not entirely. We've grown. Pain and heartache do that to a person. But now I *know* what I want. I want you. For better or for worse. I love you."

She kissed him, trying to tell him without words how much joy he had brought to her life. Josh trembled as he held her tightly. Layla trembled, too. They were so lucky to have found each other.

He rested his forehead against hers. "Vegas is all about gambling, but what we did today isn't a risk. Not to me. I've never been surer of anything in my life. You're my one and only, Layla. I love you."

His words healed the scars on her heart.

They scrambled into the bed, and Layla helped with the rest of his clothes. When they were both naked and panting, he went up on one elbow and stroked her hair. "How do you feel about having twins?"

Layla gaped at him. Her heart raced in fear and delirious joy. "Oh my gosh. I never even thought about that."

Josh rolled to his back and laughed so hard tears filled his eyes. "If you could see your face," he gasped.

Happiness filled the room, swirling in the air. Fizzing like the champagne.

Layla stroked his chest, enjoying the buzz of sexual anticipation. She had no doubts. Not a one. This man would be by her side until they were old and gray.

"We did all this so fast I didn't have a chance to get *you* a wedding present," she said, feeling guilty.

Josh pulled her close. Kissed her hard. Settled between her legs, ready to go. His hot gaze stole her breath. "I have everything I could possibly want right here, my love. Now, close your eyes and let's see if we both remember how to fly…"

* * * * *

LOST AND
FOUND HEIR

JOSS WOOD

One

Garrett Kaye wasn't having fun—he didn't know if he'd recognize fun if it bit him in the ass—but he was less bored than usual.

And that had to be a win.

He was at Ryder International's Annual Valentine's Day Ball seated at an exquisitely decorated table. The monotony of the black, white and silver theme—the ceiling was covered in a shimmery silver fabric interspersed with fairy lights, and the round tables were covered in an expensive white fabric printed with black roses—was broken by three-foot-high wineglasses standing in the center of the table, the bowls holding deep pink, red and white tulips and pops of bright greenery. The dinnerware was pure white, the cutlery a heavy silver, and the wine and champagne glasses were crystal.

The food, produced by a James Beard award–winning chef, was Michelin-star standard, the champagne was ridiculously tart and ludicrously expensive, and judging by the *ooh*s he'd heard, the swag bags were impressive. The smiles on the faces of his fellow guests told him that everyone was having a decent time. They should be, since they'd paid upward of one hundred thousand dollars for a ticket. Though, to be fair, for most of the guests, Garrett included, dropping so much money wasn't a problem.

Would he be here if it was anyone other than the Ryder-White clan hosting the ball? Probably not. To the members of that illustrious family, he was simply the son of Callum Ryder-White's assistant, a local boy and an international success story.

Yet, Callum and clan had no idea that with no effort at all, Garrett could tip over their carefully constructed applecarts.

"My first job was in Panama City, doing a gin promotion on the beach…"

At the sound of the melodious voice, Garrett pulled his attention back to the conversation at the table, where Jules Carlson—she of the abundant curls, warm brown skin and rocking body—was holding court. Her hazel eyes, a complex combination of green, gold and brown, fascinated him. When she looked or spoke to someone she liked, they sparked with warm gold flecks. When she laughed, those flecks turned to copper. Occasionally, he saw green-colored flames, but only when she spoke to him. He seemed to annoy her, and the thought amused him.

Hers was an abnormal reaction and one that piqued his interest.

Garrett knew he was a good-looking guy. That was fact, not ego. He was tall—at six-four, some would say too tall—and he kept his body fit and muscled. He was also a realist and knew that, thanks to his fat bank accounts, women would always treat him like he was a combination of a bachelor prince, bad-boy rock star and Mr. Universe.

Money, he knew, could whitewash everything.

But Jules Carlson—a world-famous mixologist and bartender—was comprehensively unimpressed by him. Interesting.

He liked interesting.

Garrett leaned back in his seat and undid the single button holding his tuxedo jacket closed, listening as Jules regaled the table with a story of one of her first pop-up bars where everything seemed to go wrong. She'd dropped a bottle of tequila on her foot but carried on working with a broken toe, a fight broke out, and she had a clothing malfunction: her bikini top slipped sideways, showing the customers more of her breast than she intended.

She had lovely breasts, Garrett decided, as his eyes skimmed her narrow frame. She was tall and slim with great curves. Curves her dress—a bold tangerine skirt and top comprising laser-cut geometric shapes in white, orange, gold and black baring patches of her torso, leaving much of that golden-brown skin uncovered—showed off to perfection. With its beaded spirals and shapes, the dress was a nod to her distant African ancestry. It was bold and sensuous and stood out in the sea of understated, mostly monochromatic dresses in the room.

"That pop-up bar was sponsored by Crazy Kate's Gin, wasn't it?" Tinsley Ryder-White asked, a tiny frown marring her pretty face. Like him, Tinsley had dark brown hair and blue eyes and the same angular face. It wasn't surprising that they looked a little alike: he was, after all, her uncle.

Garrett stared at his tumbler of whiskey before lifting his head to rake his eyes across the room. Callum Ryder-White, looking older than Garrett remembered, stood next to the bar, his once-dark hair now streaked with white. He'd be—what?—in his early eighties now... Garrett paused and did some mental math.

He was thirty-five, so Callum was around forty-eight or -nine when he impregnated his assistant, Garrett's mother, Emma. Callum had been married at the time and had an adult son, James.

Garrett moved his gaze to James. He and his half brother looked like two peas in a pod. Garrett was taller by five inches or so, and more muscular, but there could be no doubt they were related.

It was weird that no one, bar him, had ever picked up on the family resemblance. Well, he presumed his mother saw their similarities, but since she refused to confirm or deny whether Callum was his father—sparking their two-decades-long cold war—he couldn't ask her. He tried not to talk to his cold, ambitious mother any more than he had to.

As the unacknowledged child of ruthless, ambitious and determined Callum Ryder-White and Emma Kaye, emotionally remote and obsessed with her position as personal assistant to one of the East Coast's most powerful men, Garrett was a problem to be solved, an afterthought and a burden.

He'd learned early on that he was stronger on his own and that seeking love and approval made one weak.

But he was thankful for the trust fund that Callum bequeathed to him on the day he turned twenty-one. Oh, he couldn't swear on a Bible that it was from him, but who else would've left Garrett five million dollars? He'd taken that money and invested it all in an internet start-up business. By the time he'd finished grad school two years later, his investment was worth twenty-five million, and the proceeds of that sale gave him the funds to open Kaye Capital.

His skin prickled remembering the risk he'd taken. He

could've lost everything in one roll of the dice… He'd gotten lucky. So lucky. He was grateful his intuition paid off, but a big part of him wanted to go back and smack his younger self for taking such a stupid risk. Jesus, he'd had rocks for brains back then.

But, as his mother said, God protected the young and dumb.

A burst of laughter pulled him back to the conversation at his table, and he saw Sutton Marchant, bestselling author, and Cody Gallant, owner of a famous events company, wiping tears of laughter from their eyes. Apparently, Jules was a talented storyteller and could charm and entertain.

Garrett was better known for being gruff rather than garrulous.

"I'm looking forward to being involved in the cocktail competition as a judge, Tins. It's such a great idea," Jules stated, looking at Tinsley sitting across the table from her.

"What cocktail competition?" Sutton asked.

Tinsley explained that, as part of their centennial celebrations, Ryder International was sponsoring a contest to find the best cocktail in the world. The competition was open to mixologists and bartenders, the contestants had to make cocktails inspired by world events, and Jules was to be one of their judges.

"What would you make, Ju?" Tinsley asked Jules.

Jules placed her pointed chin on her hand, looking like a bright and bold butterfly. "Mmm, good question. So many things have happened since George Ryder-White opened Ryder's first bar a hundred years ago, and the last century was one of incredible progress and change. The space race, computers, contraception, the internet." She paused, her pretty nose crinkling. "I think I'd do something with equal parts, something feminine and fantastic and fierce, inspired by amazing women who fought for equal rights, women like Ruth Bader Ginsburg, Sojourner Truth, Frida Kahlo and Audre Lorde, among others."

Sutton frowned. "I know who Ginsburg and Kahlo were, but I'm not familiar with Truth and Lorna—"

"Lorde," Garrett corrected him. "Sojourner Truth was born into slavery but escaped and became an outspoken abolitionist who dedicated herself to gender equality. Technically, she's a nineteenth century heroine."

Jules's glare was hot enough to incinerate.

"Audre Lorde was a poet and feminist who, despite being legally blind and having a speech impediment, became an incredible force for change in the movement," he continued.

Jules's eyebrows shot up, and Garrett thought he saw a flash of respect in her eyes. "I'm impressed, Kaye."

Her tone implied the feeling wouldn't last. Garrett felt his lips lift in amusement. "I read."

He read a *lot*, all the time. Reading, he realized at a young age, was an escape from reality, from loneliness, from always feeling on the outside of his mother's life and career. In books, he found new worlds, ideas, concepts and galaxies he could explore to his heart's content.

"The cocktail competition was my dad's idea," Tinsley said. "He's good at coming up with high-concept ideas. He's wasting his talent working for Callum."

No one at the table needed an explanation, as it was common knowledge that Callum Ryder-White kept James on a short leash. Callum was in complete control of anything and everything that happened at Ryder International.

Fascinated by Jules's hazel eyes, he watched them soften to a gentle, warm green-tinged gold as she sent Tinsley a sympathetic look. Jules was quite fascinating, he thought, sipping his whiskey. Sultry and sensational. In fact, those adjectives were the perfect description for Jules Carlson: sultry and sensational. And, seemingly, sensitive.

He wanted to see her with her clothes off, wrapped in his sheets. He could see them together—just for one night, maybe two—but he'd taste her mouth, the honey between her legs, discover her curves, run his hands over her skin.

He'd seen her interest when she'd looked at him: it was in the way she lifted her fingertips to her throat, the hint of her tongue touching her top lip. She might not like it— she definitely didn't like him—but she liked what she saw. Liked the way he made her feel...

Yeah, they'd end up together, maybe tonight, maybe in two months or two years. He shrugged, unconcerned at the time line. When you were certain of something, you could wait without worrying.

Jules took a sip from her champagne glass, her perfectly shaped eyebrows pulling into a thin line. "I saw that Crazy Kate's Gin is listed as one of the companies you're considering as sponsors for the competition. Is that right, Tins?"

Tinsley nodded. "Yeah, as you know, they have been one of our most important suppliers for the past few years." She smiled at Jules, her expression revealing her fondness for her friend. "And Kate introduced us to you, and for that, we'll always be grateful."

Jules's responding smile could power the sun. Garrett felt his sudden intake of breath, the pounding of his blood rushing south. Dammit, that smile should come with a warning, it was that powerful. He wondered what it would feel like under his lips...

"You should rethink Kate as a sponsor, Tinsley, because I doubt they are going to come on board. They have laid off employees and scaled down their operations," Jules explained. Her tone sounded breezy, but the anxiety in her eyes suggested she was downplaying the situation, and he wondered why she would do that.

"What?" Tinsley demanded, shocked. "But why?"

Jules looked a little sick. "So many factors, including the effect of the COVID-19 pandemic."

Garrett noticed that both Cody and Sutton were listening to their conversation. "Crazy Kate's is the one based in North Carolina, right?" Cody asked.

No, it was out west somewhere.

Garrett ran through his mental database of companies, easily pulling up the necessary information. He had a photographic memory, and once he read something, it stayed there forever. Crazy Kate's was a Denver-based boutique gin manufacturer with a small plant and modern, engaging branding. Just before the pandemic, they'd signed loans to expand into what he called the *Big Boy* market, and then lockdown hit. With bars, clubs and restaurants closing, the hospitality sector had taken a hell of a hit. Because he held interests in all sectors of the economy—he believed in having many eggs in many baskets—he'd come through relatively unscathed. That couldn't be said of many businesses.

Jules shook her head. "Denver. Crazy Kate's was the first company I did promotions for. Kate herself suggested that I do pop-up bars. She was instrumental in getting my business off the ground." She looked at Cody. "Ryder's and Crazy Kate's did a joint promotion, and that's how I met Tinsley and Kinga."

Garrett spoke, his deep voice cutting through the buzz of the room. "They recently upgraded their bottling plant, right? And built a brand-new distribution depot?"

He saw their surprise at his knowledge of the small company. As a venture capitalist, companies big, small and in-between were his stock in trade. But he didn't elucidate. He rarely—okay, never—explained anything to anybody.

Jules pointed her spoon in Garrett's direction, her glare hotter than a supernova. "Do not go anywhere near them, Kaye," she told him, her expression fierce.

Right, so he wasn't the only one who read extensively. Judging by her fierce frown, she knew his reputation. As well as being one of the most successful venture capitalists in the world, he was often thought of as someone who preyed on businesses in financial distress by purchasing their debt or their assets at rock-bottom prices and moving them on at a huge profit. It seldom worked that way.

Garrett didn't pull his eyes off Jules, knowing that if he backed down, she'd take that as confirmation of her suspicions.

Sure, he'd made some business decisions that some might call, from the outside looking in, morally ambiguous. He knew he had a reputation for being a flesh-stripping bastard, but sometimes, more often than people realized, some businesses were in such financial distress that the only solution was for someone like him to swoop in and denude the company to cover its debt. Hell, he was often a better bet for the owners than bankruptcy, but his critics were always happy to portray him in a negative light.

Good thing he didn't give a shit.

Garrett saw that Jules was still frowning at him, waiting for a reply to her order to stay away from Crazy Kate's. He lifted his hands in mock surrender. "What? I just asked an innocent question!"

"I only just met you tonight, Kaye, but I suspect that, even as a baby, you weren't innocent," Jules told him, her voice frosty.

In a way, she was right. Emma had never made allowances for his age. He'd never been conned about Santa Claus or the Easter Bunny, told that pixies lived in forests or that the tooth mouse brought you money. No, Emma didn't believe in what she called *all that crap*. Neither had she shielded him from the realities of life. From a young age, he'd been encouraged to watch documentaries and the news and was still haunted by some of the pictures he'd seen.

He wondered whether Jules would be the type of mom who'd tell her kids about Santa Claus, who'd get up on the roof to make the sound of bells jingling, who'd hide chocolate eggs in the garden for her children to find. Would she slip money under their pillow and put their teeth into a special container and stow it away in a keepsake box? He'd heard that some mothers did that.

Jules was passion and heat and life so…yeah, she'd spin tales of fairies and bunnies, magical mice and a bearded man who brought presents.

"I'm flying out to see Kate next weekend, so I'll see what's going on," Jules told the table, her eyes worried. She bit her bottom lip. "God, I hope she isn't too deep in the hole that she can't find her way out."

Sutton, who in a previous life was a successful trader on Wall Street, sent her a sympathetic smile. "It's probably not as bad as you think," he told her. Garrett, unfortunately, knew better. He had more chance of getting pregnant than Crazy Kate's had of becoming financially viable again.

Jules didn't look convinced. "She's had calls from various companies, offering to buy her debt from the bank."

Sutton exchanged a long look with Garrett, and he saw the question in Sutton's eyes, knew what he was asking. He shook his head. No, he wasn't one of the vultures circling.

"If she agrees to that, she'll lose everything. Her ranch, her savings, everything is tied up in the business," Jules stated, her voice a little wobbly. It was obvious this Kate person meant a great deal to Jules, and Garrett wondered why. It sounded like their relationship went deeper than business. Emotions and business, as he knew, were not happy bedfellows.

"Someone called Volker won't stop calling her," Jules said, not noticing when Tinsley abruptly pushed her chair back and stood up and hurried away. Cody followed her, but Jules, so wrapped up in her subject, was oblivious.

"Do you mean Valder?" Sutton asked, his tone careful.

Hearing the name of his archenemy and industry competitor, Garrett leaned forward and rested his arms on the table. He looked at Sutton, saw the annoyance in his eyes and sighed. Yeah, he didn't always get the best press, but Valder was the king of the vultures, happy to strip businesses of every asset that could turn a profit. Garrett was okay with dismantling businesses and making a buck, but Valder didn't stop there: he also took the shirts off the owners' backs while he was at it. Garrett never advertised his actions and couldn't have people thinking he was a sap, but he always made certain to leave the debt-ridden owners something to show for their hard work, an asset they could build or live on until they got their feet back under them.

Valder was bad news.

"Tell your friend to stay far away from him," Sutton told Jules before standing up. "I'm going to the bar. Can I get either of you another drink?"

They both declined, and then they were alone, sitting opposite each other. Jules lifted her eyes off the bubbles in her champagne to look at him. "Do you agree with him?"

"About Valder? Yeah."

"Is there anything anyone can do?" Jules asked, sounding a little desperate.

He wanted to reassure her but knew that it was better to hurt her with the truth than comfort her with a lie. And what the hell did he know of comfort, anyway? "If Valder

is circling, then the situation is dire. He rarely steps in before it's too late."

Jules released a low curse, and Garrett wondered if
he'd imagined the gleam in her eyes that suggested tears.
"You have a personal relationship with this woman, this
Crazy Kate."

The edges of her sexy mouth pulled up at the corners.
"Yeah, I do." She pushed back a corkscrew curl, one of
two that had been left to hang loose to frame her face. "I
spent every summer on her Colorado cattle ranch from
the time I was ten. She's my second mom."

Garrett tried to imagine this glamorous woman on a
ranch, mucking out stables and wrangling cows. Wrangling cows *was* what they did, wasn't it? Having been
brought up in an apartment, he was a city boy to the core
and didn't have the first clue. He couldn't imagine this
gorgeous woman in her stunning dress shoveling shit. He
grinned.

"What's so funny?" Jules demanded, green fire in her
eyes again.

"I'm just trying to imagine you on a farm, doing farmy
things."

"Farmy things?"

He spread his hands. "Can you ride a horse? Do you
know how to muck out a stall?"

Jules rolled her eyes. "And how to service a tractor,
break in a horse and plow a field." Her smile turned sin-
ister. "I also know how to castrate a bull."

His balls pulled up and hit the back of his spine. "I'll
take your word for that," he replied, annoyed to find his
voice an octave higher than it was before. "Seriously? You
really know how to do that?"

"And more. You should know that I never lie, Kaye. Ever."

Garrett stared at her, surprised to find his lungs tight

and his ability to breathe compromised. He hadn't been this affected by a woman since he'd lost his virginity when he was sixteen. She'd been twenty and, in his eyes, experienced. She'd also lost her shit when she found out—thankfully only after the deed was done—that he was four years younger.

It wasn't his fault he looked older than he was.

But like that long-ago woman, Jules made his heart bounce off his rib cage and his mouth go desert-dry. He felt like he was dancing on the razor-sharp edge of a knife, on the whirling bands of a hurricane. She was dangerous, he realized.

But, damn, what was life without taking the occasional risk?

It wasn't like he was going to hand over his heart to the woman. It was said that he didn't have a heart, and his critics could be right.

The tempo of the music changed, and Garrett heard the familiar notes of an old standard. It was one of his favorite songs. Few people knew he adored music and that he'd briefly considered studying it as a subject at college. But the thought of being a starving artist didn't appeal so he used music, spending hours at the piano, as a way to de-stress. He tipped his head to the side, waiting for Griff O'Hare to murder the song. But Griff hit the opening note perfectly, and Garrett nodded in appreciation as he sang the lyrics, effortlessly and with emotion. Since the singer was also playing piano, Garrett decided the guy wasn't just a pretty face but a serious musician. His respect for the man inched upward.

Standing up, Garrett rebuttoned his jacket and walked around the table, stopping next to Jules's chair. She looked from his hand to his face, puzzled.

"Are you asking me to dance?"

"Yes. I presume that a woman who can neuter a bull can also sway?"

Her hand slid into his, so much smaller and so much softer. She released a light snort. "Oh, I can do more than sway, Garrett Kaye. I've taken dance classes all my life."

That didn't surprise him. Every movement she made, whether it was to cock her head or lift her hands, was filled with grace. "Is there anything you can't do, Ms. Carlson?"

"Not much," Jules admitted as she stood up. "There are, however, many things I won't do."

He placed his hand on her lower back, keeping his touch light. Her perfume hit his nose, and Garrett was transported to hot summer nights filled with stars and the scent of jasmine.

"What won't you do, Jules?" Garrett asked her, as they hit the edge of the dance floor. He lifted her right hand in his and curled his left around her hip.

"I won't cave-dive, eat guavas or sing in public."

He smiled. "What else?" he asked, a little charmed. And more than a little scared to realize that he could actually *be* charmed.

"Eat snails, bungee jump or pierce my tongue. Oh, and I'm definitely never going to sleep with you."

Garrett Kaye was the most infuriating, irritating, arrogant man she'd ever met.

Yet here she was, in his muscular arms—she could feel the bulge of a big bicep beneath her hand—and inhaling his too-sexy scent, a combination of expensive soap, an even more pricy cologne and testosterone.

Testosterone. Garrett Kaye had it in spades.

Jules lifted her eyes from his perfectly knotted tie and looked at his short beard. His facial hair was at that perfect length between stubble and beard, soft enough to rub your cheek against, short enough for it to tickle in the most delicious way. Jules pulled in a deep breath, held it and released it.

She should not be having salacious thoughts—hell, any thoughts!—about Garrett. He was the embodiment of the type of man she avoided.

She liked slim and small men, gentle men, unambitious men, intelligent men. Okay, Garrett was obviously smart—one didn't reach his level of success without some smarts—and he was well-read, but he was too blunt, too direct, too damn masculine.

Too damn alpha...

Too much like her dad.

Big, bold and overconfident men didn't interest her, and he embodied all three.

But, damn, her body wasn't getting her brain's warning signals. Her left hand wanted to trace the curve of his huge shoulder, and she kept reminding herself that she couldn't move closer, that she must not press her aching-to-be-touched breasts against his acre-wide chest. Her stomach kept doing a slow roll, and the space between her legs felt like it was on fire. Her body wanted him, but her brain was urging her to run for cover.

Garrett's thumb brushed the bare skin on her lower back, and Jules shivered. "I can't decide whether that's a good shiver or a bad one," Garrett said, his deep voice sliding inside her and turning her blood to hot molasses.

Jules tipped her head back to look into his astonishing eyes, blue with more than a touch of teal. "I'm not sure what you mean," she said, happy to hear that her voice sounded like it normally did.

Another swipe of that thumb, another shiver. "I think you are attracted to me, but your brain is flashing ten-foot warning signals, telling you to run."

Jules stopped abruptly, shocked at his perception. She pulled her hand from his and took a step back. "Why would you think that?" she demanded. Did the guy have X-ray vision? Was looking below the surface his superpower?

She didn't like it. At all.

Garrett picked up her hand again and pulled her back into his embrace.

She was ironing-board stiff but she couldn't unbend, because if she did, she might be tempted to snuggle in and rest against that broad chest, to feel safe.

Nobody else could protect her; she was responsible for her safety. That was why she held a black belt in judo and knew how to use a knife. She stayed away from guns, as having one put to your temple as a six-year-old tended to lead to a lifelong hatred of them.

"Come back to me right now, Jules," Garrett ordered her. "Wherever you are is not the place you want to be."

Jules's eyes flew up to meet his, and her mouth dropped open in shock. How could he possibly know that she was back in their kitchen in Detroit, that her mom was begging her dad to let her go, telling her that she'd do anything—*anything!*—if she didn't hurt their little girl.

Her dad had flung Jules away and grabbed her mom's arm, and the two-hundred-fifty-pound man had dragged her tiny mom to their bedroom. The next day, as soon as her dad had left for work, she and her mom left town and hit the road.

In the following months and years, Jules got very used to moving, very quickly. It was now a habit, and instead of bouncing from town to town, she bounced between countries and continents.

Garrett gave her hand a quick squeeze. "Are you okay, Ju— What's your real name, by the way?"

She blinked at the sudden change of subject. "Juliana-Jaliyah, hyphenated." Whoa.

Only a handful of people knew her real name: she was Jules to her friends and Joolz, no surname, when she was working and on all her social-media accounts.

Why on earth had she told Garrett Kaye her real name?

"Juliana-Jaliyah... That's quite a mouthful."

"Tell me about it," she muttered. "And I had a lisp."

Garrett's sexy mouth pulled up into what had to be the first real smile she'd seen from him this evening. It hit his eyes, made the crinkles at the corners deepen and turned the teal blue lighter and greener. Yeah, he should laugh more. He was a masculine type of beautiful when he laughed.

"It's a mouthful but a pretty mouthful. And it suits you."

Jules poked him in the chest. "Everybody calls me Jules," she told him. Nobody ever called her by her full name. Since her teens, she'd introduced herself as Jules. It was stronger, a name that kicked ass.

"When I was young, I went through a stage of refusing to answer to any name other than Hedwig."

It took her a while to make the connection. "The famous owl from *Harry Potter*?"

His big shoulders rose and fell. "I liked to read. And waging war with my mother. I'd bring back books from the library, and she'd look at them and decide they weren't age-appropriate."

She smiled, intrigued. "Like?"

"Well, I do remember her having a shit fit when I brought home *Go Ask Alice* at twelve."

Jules winced, remembering the book's themes of drug use, rape and sexual abuse. She could just imagine the tug-of-war. "Who won the argument?"

Garrett flashed a grin that would have looked more at

home on a pirate. "Neither, or both. I read the controversial books at the library and brought home the books that I wanted to read and knew she'd approve of."

"Smart, willful and a little arrogant," Jules commented. She lifted her eyebrows. "Nothing much has changed in—what?—twenty-eight years?"

"I'm thirty-five, not forty..." Garrett muttered.

Jules hid her smile at his annoyance. "Really? You look older," she lied.

"Haha, funny. What were you like at twelve?"

Introverted, scared, scarred. Jules tossed her head and looked him dead in the eye. "Fabulous and flirty. And absolutely nothing has changed," she stated, her voice defiant. Nobody but Kate knew about her childhood, not even Tinsley and Kinga, her best friends.

Garrett's eyes bored into hers. "Liar," he softly responded. He moved their joined hands so that the knuckle of his thumb rested on her bottom lip. Jules resisted the urge to touch the tip of her tongue to his skin.

"Why do I think that your supposedly fabulous life—I did a quick online search under the table while Callum Ryder-White did his speech—is carefully constructed? You *want* the world to think you are this carefree creature with the world at her feet."

Jules stared at him, her heart in her throat. "Why would you think that?"

He shrugged and dropped their hands. "Your bio is littered with words like *nomadic*, *interesting*, and *free and easy* and gives the impression that you are happy-go-lucky and insouciant. You're not."

Wow. He'd just stabbed through her layers, his words piercing her carefully crafted cloak. She was both fascinated and horrified but couldn't resist her next question.

"So who do you think I am, then, O Wise One?" Jules

intended her tone to be mocking but wasn't sure she hit her target. She sounded a little off balance and, worst of all, a tiny bit scared.

"I think the world sees your beautiful face and rocking body and gets sucked in by your bright, bubbly personality and decides that's who you are."

"So who do *you* think I am, Kaye?" Jules challenged him. And why did she care?

"Honestly, every time I look into your constantly changing eyes, I get this impression of a woman who's walked through hell and has come out the other side, pulling a tank of water in case of random flames."

The music stopped, and so did Jules's ability to breathe. No one had ever, in so short a time, found all her protective layers and pushed them aside to get to the heart of her. Who was this man with his wizard-like abilities?

Before she could gather her words, Garrett dropped his hand from her back and stepped away. He pulled their still-linked hands to his mouth and kissed the ridge of her knuckles. "Thank you for the dance. And, Juliana-Jaliyah?"

"Yes?"

"We *are* going to sleep together. Sooner rather than later, and you will be the one doing the asking."

Then he walked away, leaving her speechless and discombobulated on the edge of the dance floor.

Two

Garrett didn't want to leave Jules—why would he when she was both gorgeous and interesting, the best combination?—but he'd noticed James Ryder-White's eyes following him around the dance floor.

What was up with that? Why was he the focus of his half brother's attention?

Because he was a guy who preferred to confront a situation rather than walk away and worry about it, he thought it was time that he and James had a little talk. Oh, he wouldn't tell James what he suspected—that they were related—as he'd made a promise to his mother a long time ago that he would never raise the subject of his parentage with any Ryder-White, ever.

He regretted making that promise, but he still intended to keep it.

That long-ago argument with his mom was the root of their still-dysfunctional relationship. They weren't estranged. They still occasionally spoke, but since that summer, they didn't venture beyond inquiries about each other's health and the weather. And whenever they found themselves alone, it wasn't long before a two-ton elephant strolled into the room and plopped itself in the corner...

I know who my father is, Mom. Why won't you confirm it?

I don't have to confirm a damn thing and never will.

Unlike many people, he hadn't found a letter or his birth certificate or read any of his mom's private correspondence. No, his discovery of his father's identity was completely random, the strangest, weirdest fluke.

A few weeks after he'd turned sixteen, he'd swung by her office to pick up her bank card—visiting her at work was strongly discouraged!—because his had expired, and he couldn't use it to do the grocery run, one of his many chores.

She'd been angry at his sudden appearance and had told him to wait in the break room, telling him she'd get to him as soon as she could. Wanting to be outside, he'd walked onto the balcony off the break room and, as he always did when he walked from a dark room into sunlight, released a huge sneeze.

He waited forty-five minutes, becoming increasingly more irritated. His vigil was broken when his mom's boss, Callum Ryder-White, walked outside, too, and, like him, immediately sneezed into a snow-white handkerchief.

Because he'd been a brat and thought that everybody wanted to hear his opinions, he'd informed Callum that sneezing in sunlight was called ACHOO, or Autosomal Dominant Compelling Helio-Opthalmic Outburst. He'd been about to tell Callum that he had it, too, but the man's ice-blue eyes and why-are-you-talking-to-me look cut off Garrett's words. His mom hurried onto the balcony at that point, apologized to Callum for her son's presence—children of staff members were not welcome at Ryder Tower—and shoved some money into his hand and told him to beat it.

But Callum walked ahead of him, and Garrett couldn't help noticing that as he walked, Callum repeatedly touched his right index finger to his thumb...

It was a nervous tic that Garrett had, too.

On returning home, he went online and, because Callum was one of the best-known businesspeople on the East Coast, saw photographs of him when he was a young man. Like Garrett, Callum was tall, and their face structures were the same. They had the same bold nose and deep-set eyes. Garrett could dismiss their physical similarities, but a little further research told him that the ACHOO syndrome was mostly inherited...

His mom didn't have it, so it had to come from his father.

Garrett and Emma had their first fight about his parentage that evening, and their fights over her lack of honesty and transparency didn't stop until he left for college. She did, however, manage to elicit that promise from him not to say anything about his suspicions to anybody, ever.

Garrett took his promises seriously so, to this day, his hands were tied.

Garrett slid into the empty spot next to James, rested his elbows on the bar and ordered a fifteen-year-old whiskey.

"Care to tell me why you are watching me?" Garrett demanded.

James jerked at his blunt question, obviously caught off guard. He scrambled for an answer. "I've known Jules for a long time. She's Tinsley's best friend, and I'm protective of her."

Good catch. "And you think she needs protection from me?"

James nodded. "Something like that."

"Bullshit," Garrett retorted. "First of all, Jules needs no help. Her tongue is more effective than industrial-strength paint stripper. And you weren't looking at her, you were looking at me."

It seemed to Garrett that James was using a hell of a lot of willpower to keep his expression impassive. "If you say so," he said, allowing a trace of derision to touch his voice.

Was that snotty voice supposed to intimidate him? Sure, his half brother was nearly twenty-five years older than him, but if Garrett allowed himself to be intimidated by men who had years on him, he wouldn't own and manage a multibillion dollar company.

Garrett sipped from the glass the bartender slid his way and looked over it at James. "Why have I caught your attention, James? Why am I in your crosshairs?"

Shock jumped into James's eyes. Gotcha, Garrett thought. What was going through his half sibling's head, and how did it affect him? He looked down, saw the tremor in James's fingers and frowned. Something was bubbling under his seemingly calm surface. He reminded Garrett of one of those prank cans, the ones that, when opened, shot out a snake or a clown.

Garrett saw that the two men on the other side of James were far too interested in their conversation, so he lowered his voice. "Why do I sense that you, the son of my mother's boss—" Yep, something flared in his eyes with that comment. James definitely knew more than he let on. Join the freakin' club. "—can disrupt my life?"

He was fishing here, hoping that James would let slip something to confirm his suspicions that they were related. And if he did, what would Garrett do with that information? He wasn't angling to become part of a family—he had no idea how to be a son, a brother or an uncle. Hell, his mother had barely allowed him to be a son. They'd been two strangers living in the same house for much of his life. His mom was physically present, but she'd been consumed with her job, with her position as Callum's right-hand person.

He'd been very young, too young, when he first realized that Callum and her career were higher up on her priority list than he was.

No, a family wasn't for him. But he wouldn't mind knowing if there were any health concerns he needed to be aware of. He already had ACHOO. Was there anything else he'd inherited from his father? Didn't he have a right to know that information?

Garrett sighed, turned and looked across the room to see Jules dancing with Sutton Marchant. He was laughing, she was laughing, and they looked good together. Garrett felt the intense urge to plow his fist into Sutton's aristocratic face.

Mine! Mine! Mine!

Crap, if they could hear his thoughts, every feminist in the country would strip him of a few layers of skin. Women were not possessions; men didn't get to own them. He knew this—of course he did; he wasn't a Neanderthal. He didn't have gender, racial or any other kind of pay gaps at his firm: as far as he was concerned, if you did the same job, you earned the same salary. Promotions were based on performance. Anyone, male or female, who engaged in sexual harassment got their asses fired.

So why did he want to storm across the room and haul Jules out of Sutton's arms and drag her into his? Garrett ran his hand over his jaw. He was losing his goddamn mind. No, he'd lost his mind when he agreed to pay a stupid amount of cash to attend this super exclusive event. Mind gone, he was now descending into madness. It was the only rational explanation.

Even from a distance, he could see that Jules was back to being her charming, charismatic self. But it wasn't her, not really. Charming Jules was a carefully concocted version of herself, the person she thought the world wanted to see.

Juliana-Jaliyah was deeper, smarter, and she was, like him, scratched and scarred.

"I'm not aiming anything at you, Garrett," James said.

Garrett turned back to look at James, taking a minute to make sense of his words. He felt shocked that just looking at Jules could shift his laserlike focus.

"My gut is insisting that you are up to something, and it's never failed me before," Garrett told him, getting his thoughts back in the game.

"Maybe your Spidey sense is wrong," James suggested. James didn't sound as confident as he had a few minutes before. Garrett thought that he might've inadvertently stumbled across something here.

Yeah, this ball was turning out to be far more interesting than he'd expected.

"It's never wrong," Garrett retorted, banging his glass on the bar. He looked down at James—thanks to his height, he pretty much looked down on everyone—knowing his eyes had turned dark and dangerous. They always did when he was upset. Or frustrated.

"What's going on, James? What are you thinking, planning? Want to save me the hassle and tell me now?"

James opened his mouth to speak but slammed his jaw closed again, so hard that Garrett thought it might hurt.

"I think you have either had too much to drink or have an overactive imagination, Garrett."

Garrett shook his head. "Nah, that's not it." Garrett clamped his hand around James's shoulder and squeezed.

"You don't have to tell me. I'm good at ferreting out secrets, and I'll discover yours."

James looked like he'd popped the lid on that gag can, but the snake inside it was real. And poisonous.

Interesting, Garrett thought, walking away.

Jules smiled at Sutton as he pulled her hand through his crooked elbow and led her off the dance floor. He was a nice guy, and dancing with him had been fun...

But he was not, in any way, compelling. She wasn't attracted to Sutton, not like she was to Garrett Kaye. Being up close and personal with Garrett's spectacular body made her feel like she was plugged into an electrical socket. Her body—stupid thing!—craved his.

But conversing with him made her feel like she was jamming an acid-tipped fork into her eye.

She'd beg him to sleep with her? When unicorns made a comeback and she could hire Snow White's dwarves to clean her apartment.

And, let's be clear here, she didn't like his ability to see past her skillfully molded public persona to whom she was below. Not that he'd managed to peel off too many layers, but he'd definitely gotten further than most.

Irritating man.

Jules saw Kinga standing next to the stage, holding a champagne glass against her chest, swaying as she watched her fiancé sing. Jules grabbed her elbow and tugged her away.

"Hey, that's one of my favorite songs!" Kinga protested when they stopped in a quiet corner of the ballroom, far away from the bar and the dance floor.

"I love you, King, but since meeting Griff, you've turned into such a sap," Jules told her, rolling her eyes.

Kinga's grin told her that she wasn't offended. "I

know! But he's so talented and so hot, and he does this thing that just—"

Jules placed a hand over her mouth and shook her head so hard that her curls bounced. "No, no, no, *no*! I do not need to know what kinky stuff you get up to, thank you very much!"

Kinga peeled her hand off her mouth, grinning. "You are such a prude!"

No, she wasn't. Or at least she didn't think she was. Okay, she didn't *want* to be a prude...

What would Garrett think if she told him that she was one of the few twenty-eight-year-old virgins left in the Western world? Would he laugh, mock her, denigrate her? Or would he see her as a challenge? Really, his notion that she'd beg him to take her to bed was laughable.

It would never happen.

But she was annoyingly tempted. She wanted to peel back his layers of clothing and see if that big body was as fit as he felt, if she was exaggerating the circumference of his big biceps and if she could curl up on his chest.

She was a smart, independent, capable woman—life had taught her to be that way—so why did she look at him and think...*protector*? She didn't need one of those, just like she didn't need a husband or a significant other. She was fine on her own. Better than fine: she was *safe*.

After being chased around the country by her obsessive and possessive father, knowing that if he caught them, they might end up, well...*dead*, feeling safe was high on her list of priorities. And, yeah, she now had issues. And one of those was sex...

No, that was wrong. She didn't have a problem with sex per se—at least she didn't think she did, as she'd gotten pretty damn intimate with a few guys—but she did have a problem with bedrooms. And that was where most guys thought sex should take place.

Jules didn't like bedrooms. It was where bad things happened behind closed doors.

Grunts, screams, tears, sobs. Fists hitting flesh...

As far as Jules was concerned, bedrooms were only good for storing clothes. She hadn't slept in a bed behind a closed door since they'd left Detroit more than twenty years ago.

And she liked it that way.

Jules looked across the ballroom and, because he was so tall, immediately spotted Garrett. Her stomach rocketed up to her throat and plummeted down to her toes, and her skin prickled with goose bumps. And annoyingly, she felt that insistent tingle between her legs. Normally, when her body reminded her that she was a woman in her sexual prime, she used a vibrator to take the edge off. Jules winced, remembering that it was in a box in her cupboard gathering dust. She'd been busy lately, running from country to country and city to city, and she was usually too tired to feel horny.

But tonight, she was beyond horny. She wanted to *jump him now*.

She might think he was gorgeous, but she didn't like him and especially didn't like how perceptive he was. But for the first time, her body's desire was strong enough to dampen her mind's insistence on caution, its need to keep her safe.

But Jules knew, deep down inside where truth resided, that Garrett Kaye—he of the sharp mind and blunt tongue—would never, ever hurt her.

Kinga lightly pinched her wrist, and Jules jumped. "What?"

"You dragged me over here, remember? And now

you're just standing there, staring off into space," Kinga replied. Jules turned to look at her, and her eyes immediately softened, and she ran her hand up and down Jules's bare arm. "Are you okay, honey? What's up?"

Jules played with her thick, faux-diamond-and-beaded bangle. "Weird evening, that's all."

"Are you not liking the people at your table?" Kinga asked, immediately concerned. "I thought that sitting with Cody and Tinsley would be where you'd be happiest."

While she earned a good living, she wasn't in the can-spend-the-price-of-a-house-to-buy-a-ticket bracket. Ryder International, or, to be precise, her friends, comped her ticket to the ball. They'd told her that they'd be happy to give her another complimentary ticket so she could bring a date, but Jules hadn't wanted to take advantage of their friendship. Besides, she wasn't dating anyone—she didn't have time for that ritual—and wouldn't invite some random man to such an exclusive event.

"It's not that, Kinga." Well, it was partly that. Jules sucked in some air and tipped her head back to look at the fabric-swathed ceiling. "Do you know Garrett Kaye?"

Kinga frowned. "Sort of. I mean, I've met the guy a few times. Gorgeous but not chatty."

A perfect summation. "We've been trading barbs all evening, and I danced with him. There's some sort of weird chemistry bubbling between us."

Kinga's eyebrows flew up. "Really? I didn't think you were his type."

Not his type? What the hell did that mean? "Because I'm of mixed heritage?" Jules demanded.

Kinga waved her words away. "No, you know I don't mean that! What I meant was that, according to the East Coast gossips, Garrett always chooses a very particular type of woman when he's looking for a date to an event or to grace his bed."

"And what type is that?" Jules asked.

"Cool, snotty, someone with impeccable connections and an amazing pedigree."

Kinga made them sound like the nonhuman entrants in a Crufts dog show.

"You couldn't be more different. And different, might I remind you, is good," Kinga added.

"How can I want to jump his bones when I don't know him? And the little I know, I don't like!"

"People have sex for different reasons, Jules. Sometimes that reason is love, a soul-deep connection with a partner. Sometimes that reason is stress relief, a need to feel connected to another human being. And sometimes because it just feels so damn good!"

Jules placed her hands behind her back and rested her palms against the wall. "I don't have casual sex, Kinga. I'm not cut out for it."

"You've never had a one-night stand?"

"Uh...no." She felt the urge to tell Kinga that she'd never had penetrative sex, but she held back. Would her friend even believe her? She liked men, she dated all the time, she'd received and given oral sex, but whenever a potential lover suggested they take it to the bedroom, she called a halt to proceedings. As a result, men faded from her life as mist did from mountains on a hot summer's day.

Kinga cocked her head to one side, thinking. "You like olives, right?"

"Yes."

"And anchovies?"

"You know I do." Where was Kinga going with this?

"And you hate snails."

Jules shuddered. "Yuck."

"How did you know that you liked those foods? By trying them, right? So give a one-night stand a go. If you don't like it, because not everyone does, don't do it again." Kinga squeezed her hand. "But there's no shame, either way, Ju. Your body, your rules. No exceptions to that rule, *ever*."

It was excellent advice, Jules thought as she followed Kinga back to the main area of the ballroom. But maybe, before she ventured down the one-night-stand road, she should have sex first: penetrative sex.

That, she thought, should be step number one. But allowing Garrett to be her first would be a mistake. He was someone who'd expect his partner to be experienced, to know what the hell they were doing in bed. He'd have no patience for an inexperienced virgin, and she didn't want to feel like a fumbling idiot.

But she didn't want to sleep with anyone else.

Catch-22, she thought.

Marvelous.

Nearly a month had passed since the Valentine's Day Ball, yet to Garrett, it felt like last week. He'd spent most of the last two weeks crisscrossing the country, and he was glad to be spending Friday morning in his office, catching up.

After a crack-of-dawn five-mile run, he'd made the minute commute to his office from his penthouse apartment on the top floor of his office building, determined to work through his mile-long to-do list. But being back in Portland—wet and cold—made him think about Jules, where she was and what she was up to.

According to her social-media pages, which he, embarrassingly, checked every day, she was currently stateside and taking a minibreak from demonstrations and manning pop-up bars in exotic cities like Cartagena and Cape Town.

She was taking the weekend, maybe the week, she told her million-plus followers. She needed to breathe deep, slow down, do a digital detox.

She'd been on his mind, more than he'd expected. She'd pop in at random times—while he was inspecting a plant, or in the middle of a cash-flow projection—and he'd remember her lithe body in his arms, the feel of her golden skin under his hand as they danced, her dizzy-making scent.

Thoughts of her had even prompted him to make inquiries into Crazy Kate's, and he'd winced when he'd received detailed reports from his most experienced researcher. The company was so far in the hole they were knocking on hell's door...

They'd run out of cash, creditors were baying, and the bank had given them minimal time to make a massive balloon payment. Because her house, buildings and the ranch Jules mentioned were mortgaged to the hilt, Kate had more chance of taking a magic-carpet ride than she did of making that payment.

To save the company, she needed an angel investor, someone who was prepared to put a load of cash into the organization and not see results for five, maybe ten, years, if they ever did at all. It was that far gone...and nobody he knew, including him, was fool enough to touch it with a barge pole. Even Valder had backed off, knowing that there wasn't enough value in the assets to cover the debt.

Kate was facing bankruptcy and the loss of everything she owned. It was a scenario he'd seen played out so often before. Sad but inevitable.

Jules, he was sure, would be devastated to learn that the ranch would leave Kate's hands. It was obvious, to him at least, that she had an emotional connection to the property and that she loved Kate. He wondered how they'd met, how an East Coast girl had come to spend time on a ranch in Colorado.

He spent an enormous amount of time—far too much—wondering about Jules Carlson.

Garrett lifted his head at a discreet knock on his door. His assistant stepped into his office, the sleeves of his button-down rolled up past his elbows, displaying colorful ink. Sven refused to wear anything other than jeans. He had two piercings through his right eyebrow, a ring through his lower lip and a stud in his cheek. He was built like a tank, and he had the most extensive vocabulary of curse words of anyone Garrett knew.

He also had a postgraduate degree in ancient languages, could tiptoe into any computer anywhere in the world and was the most efficient, organized soul Garrett had ever encountered. They had an understanding. He organized Garrett's life, occasionally did some not-always-legal digital breaking and entering, and managed his office with startling efficiency.

Garrett's part of the deal was to pay him an enormous salary—he was worth every penny—and not give him any crap about his clothing choices, piercings and tats. Garrett also gave him an afternoon off a week to visit his brother who lived in a residential home for people with intellectual disabilities, and Garrett had to fund Sven's addiction to expensive coffee.

It was a deal that worked for both of them.

"What's up?" Garrett asked as Sven dropped into a chair opposite his desk.

Sven nodded at his stack of requisition forms. "Accounting is bugging me for those."

Garrett pulled a face. "I'm getting there." He'd get there faster if he stopped thinking about Jules.

"You wanted to keep your day free of appointments, but

James Ryder-White wants to meet with you. He wouldn't tell me why, but he insisted it was important."

Shock flashed over Garrett, then curiosity. He'd vowed to dig into James: he knew the man was up to something, but the month had run away from him.

"You heard that Callum Ryder-White had a heart attack, right?" Sven asked.

He hadn't. He lifted his eyebrows. "When did that happen?"

"A week, ten days ago? Apparently, it's quite serious. He's going to be out of the office for a while."

"He should've retired years ago," Garrett told him. His father was in the hospital, and Emma hadn't bothered to tell him. Then again, he hadn't spoken to his mom for six weeks—or was it eight? Garrett ran a hand over his face. Man, they were the definition of *dysfunctional*.

"So, do you want to meet with James? And when?"

Garrett leaned back in his chair, propped his feet up on his desk and stared up at the ceiling. It was his favorite thinking position. He was curious as to why James, who had to have his hands full running Ryder International, was asking for an urgent meeting. With him. Of all people. Why?

And that's why he'd meet with his half brother: because he was so damn curious. But he'd meet when it would be convenient for him, not James. "He can come by, but later. Kaye Capital business comes first."

"Around six?"

Garrett nodded. "That'll work. Anything else?"

Sven nodded to the requisitions. "Yeah, those. Marge needs them, and you know she scares the hell out of me." Garrett rolled his eyes. Nobody scared Sven, not even him.

Sven lumbered to his feet and headed to the door.

"Is there any chance of getting a decent cup of coffee?" Garrett asked him.

"When you are done with those reqs," Sven told him. At Garrett's scowl, he grinned. "Everybody needs motivation, even you."

"How about this for motivation? Make me a cup of coffee, or else I'm going to fire your ass. Or cut off your supply of Jamaican Blue," Garrett mildly suggested.

They both knew that the threat of losing the supply of his favorite coffee was the direr of the two options. "Requisitions first, coffee later," Sven told him, closing the door behind him.

Garrett glared at his closed door, muttered a curse and picked up his pen. He was about to dash his name across the bottom of the page when his smartphone signaled an incoming message. Garrett picked it up and swiped the screen, frowning. Few people had this number, and most messages came through to the cell phone Sven managed for him.

He opened the messaging app and saw an unfamiliar number but when he tapped the profile picture, a very familiar face appeared on his screen. His heart lurched as he took in Jules Carlson's fresh and lovely face. In the photo her eyes looked green, her curls hung down the sides of her face, and he could see tiny freckles on her nose and across those amazing cheekbones.

God, she was stunning.

Garrett, I heard that you are back in town and was wondering if we could meet. I'll buy you a drink. Whatever time and wherever suits. It's rather urgent. Jules Carlson.

Garrett wanted to think she was asking him out on a date, hopefully to bed, but he knew he was chasing rainbows. There was a formality to her message, an underlying tension he hadn't expected.

She wanted something from him, and he suspected that it had something to do with Kate Kennedy of Crazy Kate's.

But, hell, he didn't care. She'd reached out, and he'd meet her, anytime and anywhere.

What about at the Portland Harbor bar around eight?

That would give him an hour with James, twenty minutes to freshen up and twenty minutes to get to the hotel. He only needed ten. Her reply came a few minutes later, just a thumbs-up. Yep, definitely not a date.

Garrett sighed. Crap, he thought, as he dashed his signature across the bottom of the page of a requisition which he hadn't actually read.

The woman fried his brain cells, and if they got to bed, he had no doubt she'd short-circuit his brain.

He had to be careful with this one.

Three

Across town, in the exquisitely decorated living room in his wing of Callum's estate, James paced the area in front of the fireplace, listening for the sound of Penelope's footsteps.

He wiped his damp palms on his thighs and stared into the fire, not hearing the hiss and crack of the burning wood.

James placed his forearm on the marble mantel and stared down at his five-hundred-dollar shoes. This was not going to be a fun conversation, but it needed to be held, things needed to be said.

They couldn't keep living like this.

He couldn't keep living like this.

James strode over to the art deco drinks trolley, picked up the crystal decanter and sloshed a hefty amount of whiskey into a tumbler. He tossed the liquor back, gasped at the burn and poured himself another glass.

He needed liquid courage…

Penelope stepped into the room, tall and slim and effortlessly graceful. She raised her eyebrows at his whiskey glass and looked at the diamond-encrusted watch—Piaget? Cartier?—on her delicate wrist. It was a silent rebuke, and James flushed.

Yeah, it was midmorning, but there were times when a man needed help to get him through a conversation. This was one of them.

James gestured to the cream-colored sofa. "Take a seat. Can I get you a drink?"

"It's far too early for me," Penelope replied, sending him a cool look. His aristocratic, cool-as-mountain-water wife had a way of castigating him without saying a word, and still, after more than three decades of marriage, could make him feel like an awkward teenager.

It was her superpower.

James hitched up the fabric of his trousers and sat down opposite her, turning his head to look out onto the cove below them. He loved this property on Cousin's Island with its massive house, private stretch of beach and purpose-built marina, and he'd imagined he'd grow old here, looking at his view.

But if he put his plan into action, everything that was familiar, including this house, would be taken away.

But he'd be free.

"You asked to speak to me, James," Pen said. When he looked at her, he saw the hint of a frown between her jet-black eyebrows, her tense full mouth and the anxiety in her eyes. She was still a beautiful woman and looked like Tinsley and Kinga's sister rather than their mother.

Looking good, her position in East Coast society and being married to the heir of the Ryder-White fortune were important to Penelope and had been some of the main reasons she'd married him in the late eighties. James didn't think much had changed since then.

He tapped his index finger against his knee. How should he start this difficult conversation? "I'm considering challenging the status quo."

Penelope's gaze sharpened. "And what, exactly, does that mean?"

He gathered all the courage he had. "I've been thinking about what Tinsley said about secrets a few weeks back, how the truth needs to come out," James stated. "I think she's right. I think there are a bunch of Ryder-White secrets that need to see the light."

Penelope placed her hand on her chest and played with the pearl pendant on her thick gold chain, something she only did when she was feeling nervous. The observation calmed him; it was good to know that he wasn't the only one feeling off balance.

"We are rapidly heading toward retirement, and we've danced to Callum's tune all our lives, Pen. I'm sick of it."

"Our dancing ensured that we had access to this house, to a certain standard of living," Penelope pointed out. "It allowed us to send our girls to the best colleges, to set up trust funds for them."

"I think that's what Callum's trained us to believe," James responded. He'd been thinking about this, a lot.

"I was twentysomething when I took my uncle Ben's side against Callum, and at the time he told me I'd pay for my disloyalty. For thirty-plus years, Callum's pushed the guilt button, the you're-a- useless-son button, the you're-nothing-without-me button. And I believed him," James responded. God, being honest, with one's spouse and with oneself, was both hurtful and liberating.

"I've been conditioned to believe that we would be nowhere without Callum. He's always said that he and Ryder

International are the sources of all our good fortune, but that's not true."

Penelope cocked her head and gestured for him to continue.

"We've bought and sold property all our lives, and we've made some tidy investments, made quite a bit of money independent of Callum." He'd been the one to play the property market but thought it advantageous to include her in the statement. "That's how I set up trusts for the girls, good trusts." And the trust for Garrett.

"What's your point, James?"

James uncrossed his legs and placed his arms on his forearms. "I'm tired of dancing to Callum's tune, Pen. I want to live my own life…"

Penelope held her thick gold rope in a tight grip. "Are you asking for a divorce?"

Her voice never wavered, but he saw the nervousness in her eyes. They weren't the happiest couple in the world but they rubbed along well enough. He'd had a couple of mistresses and had never asked or wanted to know whether she'd had lovers herself. Some questions were better left unanswered.

"No, I'm not asking for a divorce." He saw her shoulder slump in relief, and his ego grinned. "I just want to step away from Callum, live our own lives on our terms."

"If you do that, you'll lose your inheritance. So will the girls."

"What, exactly, will we lose, Pen?" James demanded.

Her answer came quickly. "The Ryder-White shares, the art and car collections, the access to the apartments in London and France, the investments. This house."

"When did we last use the European apartments?" James replied, trying to keep his tone mild. "I don't even know what's in the art collection. It's tucked away in a cl mate-controlled warehouse, and even if Callum did grant me access, everything is wrapped up and hidden away. Callum never allows anyone into the facility where he keeps his collection of rare and classic cars. God knows the last time any of them were driven. Besides, how many cars can we drive at one time?"

"And this house?"

"I'll miss this house, of course I will. But we have other houses, and we have money, lots of it. If we need to, we can rent a hotel suite in Paris and London and stay as long as we like, and we can spend hours in museums and galleries looking at fantastic art."

He pushed a hand through his graying hair. "Callum has never allowed me to make any decisions about the company. It's never felt like mine, anyway," James told her. 'I'd rather be free than be controlled by him anymore."

"And the girls?" Penelope asked.

It was a fair question, and most of his worries centered around them.

"I've spent so much time thinking about how this will impact them. If I walk, they won't inherit anything from Callum—"

"They are girls. They wouldn't have inherited anyway," Penelope said, her words bitter.

True enough.

"They are both wealthy in their own right and are exceptionally well educated. They'll inherit millions from us when we die. They have also found the men who make them happy. Wealthy men, I might add. If I walk away and Callum fires them in retaliation, they could open up a PR business and make a killing all on their own. None of us need Callum." James looked away from her and stared down at his hands. "I am almost sixty years old, and I need to be my own man, Pen. I also need to know you'd support me in that."

Penelope stood up and walked away from him to stand by the bay window. She placed her hand on the glass and stared down at the gunmetal gray water churning in the bay below. "I'm not opposed to your idea, James. You can walk away, right now, today, and I'd go with you, if that's what you want," she stated.

Yes, that's what he wanted.

"Except you've overlooked one important factor. When Callum dies, everything will come to you, anyway. You'd still have the responsibility of everything. Whether it's today or ten years from now, it's going to be yours, and walking away now won't change that. You are Callum's only male heir."

And there it was, the opening he needed. James stared at Penelope, and she knew him well enough to know that there was something she was missing. "What?" she demanded.

He simply looked at her, waiting for her to connect the dots on her own. Then her eyes widened, and the color in her face faded. "There's another heir out there, one that you know of," she whispered.

One that you know of... Did he imagine her emphasis on the *you*? He pushed the thought aside. It wasn't important, not right now. James sucked in some much-needed air and gathered his courage.

"Garrett Kaye is my son. That's why I'm meeting with him tonight to suggest he take over as CEO of Ryder International. If I acknowledge him as mine, if he acknowledges me as his father, I assume that Callum will immediately change his will, and I will be edged out. I'm okay with that."

Penelope held up her hand. *"Wait! What?* Garrett is your son?"

"We'd need a DNA test to confirm it, but yeah, he's mine." James explained the circumstances of his birth, that he found out he was a father after their marriage. "Emma would not admit he was my child, and I kept demanding answers. She wouldn't discuss Garrett with me, and I wouldn't drop the subject so she threatened to tell you and Callum, and the police, that I'd raped her. I couldn't risk the gossip and the nastiness, so I backed off."

"That bitch!"

Yep, he agreed.

"I love our daughters, you know I do, but I've missed out on thirty-five years with my son. I'd like to get to know him, if he'll let me." James stood up and jammed his shaking hands into the pockets of his suit pants. Pen looked as shocked as he'd expected her to: her face was ghost-white, and a fine tremor racked her slim frame. But she was holding up better than he'd thought, and he was proud of his strong wife.

He wanted to go to her, to pull her into his arms and comfort her, but he knew she needed time to take in this earthshaking news. She wouldn't yell or scream—Pen wasn't dramatic—but she'd need time to process what she'd heard.

"If you tell me that I can't acknowledge him, that you don't want to rock the boat, I'll respect that. We'll just keep on keeping on as we've done for the past three and a half decades." He'd be disappointed, but he'd learned to live with that particular emotion.

"And neither of us will be happy," Penelope whispered.

James shrugged. They hadn't been happy for a long, long time. That was the price they'd paid for him standing up to his father, for taking his uncle's side when Ben told

Callum that he'd never marry, that he was in love with, and wanted to marry, another man.

Penelope dug her nails into her biceps and looked at him, her expression reflecting her bone-deep fear.

"I know you're scared. I am, too. But I genuinely believe that we will be fine, that we'll be happier if we walk away," James said, trying to reassure her.

"Walking away from Callum doesn't scare me, James," she said, a high, shrill laugh following her words.

He sent her a sharp look. "Then what does, my dear?"

"Your reaction to what I'm about to tell you. Sit down, darling. You're not the only one who has a bombshell to drop."

Jules spent two hours enduring pitying looks, drinking one too many wine spritzers and batting off too many men looking for company.

How dare Garrett Kaye stand her up? Jules paid the taxi driver and stepped onto the sidewalk outside Garrett's building, watching the taxi pull back into the traffic. She'd have to call for another one later as she'd left her car in the parking garage because a) she'd had too many wine spritzers and b) she was mad, and it was her rule that a person shouldn't drink and drive or drive and fume.

Jules tipped her head back to look up at the sleek facade of Garrett's building. She counted the floors—eleven—and lights blazed from the tenth and eleventh stories. Prior to deciding to ask for his help, she'd researched him, annoyed at how little information she could find on the internet. But she did discover he lived in a luxurious penthouse apartment on the top floor of the building and that his office was one floor down. His employees' offices were another floor below, and she rented out the rest of the space to a prominent law firm.

Jules bit her bottom lip and jammed her hands into the pockets of her coat. It was late and she was a little buzzed, but she had to see him, now, *tonight*. She hated asking anyone for help—that wasn't what she did—but she didn't know where else to turn, what to do.

Kate was in a bad, bad way, racked with debt and floundering. When they'd spoken earlier in the day, Jules offered up savings, a not inconsiderable amount, but Kate, after thanking her profusely, refused her offer, telling her that her half a million wouldn't make a jot of difference. She owed tens of millions, and she was going to lose her business, all her properties and, horribly, the ranch.

She'd be left with nothing.

Jules immediately told Kate she could live with her, that she'd support her...well, forever, if she had to. Kate had been Jules's port in a very violent storm, and Jules had no idea what she would've done without her. Kate had also launched Jules's career, and she basically owed her everything.

But she couldn't stand by and watch Kate sink, see the ranch that had been in Kate's family for generations pass into a stranger's hands. She had to do all she could to find the miracle Kate needed.

Garrett Kaye wasn't in the miracle business, but he dealt with ailing companies all the time, and maybe he knew—wunderkind that he was supposed to be—something no one else did. Maybe he could give her some advice on something, *anything*, Kate could do. Oh, she knew there was little chance of the business being saved, but maybe Garrett had an idea of how she could save the ranch.

She didn't have anyone else to whom she could turn. Her best friends were dealing with their family issues. Calum was still in the hospital after suffering a massive heart attack and was fighting off an infection after undergoing a triple bypass. Tinsley and Kinga were both helping James manage the family's massive international company, and her friends didn't have any experience dealing with a failing business. She only knew one person who did: Garrett.

She hadn't wanted to call him—she felt completely out of her depth with the man—but she'd walk through the flames of hell for Kate. She'd mustered the courage to text him, and he'd agreed to meet, but then the blasted man had stood her up.

Jerk.

But he was a jerk whose brain she needed to pick so here she was, determined to ask her questions, to interrupt whatever he was doing. God, she hoped he didn't have a woman up there. That would be awkward.

Awkward be damned. Kate's financial and emotional well-being were more important than Kaye's sex life. In Jules's mind, at least.

Jules walked to the main doors of the building and wasn't surprised to find them locked. She stepped over to a discreet door to the side but couldn't see an intercom. There was no way to call up to ask the occupant to let her up.

Dammit.

Good thing she had his number. Jerking her phone out of her bag, she found his contact details and tapped her foot as she waited for him to answer. And waited some more.

"Jules, hell, sorry, something came up."

"Apologize to my face, Kaye," Jules told him. "I'm outside your door. Let me in."

"Listen, it's not a good—"

"I waited two hours for you to show, Kaye," Jules interrupted him, her voice dripping acid. "Let. Me. In."

Jules heard Garrett's muttered curse, but the door

clicked open. She stepped inside and realized she was in a private elevator. After the door shut behind her, the elevator whizzed her up with dizzying speed.

Seconds later the door opened to reveal a dark hallway. Jules dropped her bag to the floor and slowly unwound her scarf, her attention caught by the massive, abstract oil painting taking up most of the wall. She shrugged off her coat and, unable to find a coat hook, draped it over the arm of a chair in the corner, her head cocking as Tchaikovsky's *Sixth Symphony* washed over her, bleak and beautiful.

She recognized it immediately. Her mom—a talented musician—used to play Tchaikovsky on an old LP player after fighting with her dad. Growing up, Jules had heard this symphony, a terrifyingly sad piece of music, more often than a young child should.

Knowing that Garrett wouldn't hear her call his name over the sound of the alternating notes between the first and second violins, she walked into a large mostly empty great room. His penthouse apartment covered the entire top floor, and this room was situated in the corner of the building. Arched windows reflected the lights from the neighboring buildings and the harbor below. The space echoed the mood of the music. It was austere and a little desolate, with just a freestanding island with a marble top, a sleek dining table in front of the rectangular window in the corner and a long, low couch in front of the far wall to break up the vast space.

His apartment went beyond minimalist to stark. And cold. Jules shivered as the music turned ferocious, the sound of the snarling horns filling his space. Wishing she could switch it off, she looked around and saw Garrett next to the last window, his forearm resting against the glass above his head, watching the activity in the harbor.

As the instruments dropped out of the symphony, Jules

wondered why Garrett was listening to such an emotive piece, what prompted him to choose the hauntingly sad symphony to accompany his thoughts.

"It's not a good time, Juliana-Jaliyah," Garrett told her, his voice a low growl in the sudden silence of the apartment.

He held a half-empty whiskey bottle in his right hand, and Jules stared at his hard profile, debating whether to leave.

"Interesting choice of music, Kaye. I never would've pegged you as someone who loved the classics," Jules stated.

"I love all music, classics included," Garrett said, without turning around. "It's said that Tchaikovsky wrote that piece as an elaborate suicide note."

"Because he was dead nine days after conducting the premiere, struck down by cholera he caught from drinking contaminated water." A sudden thought horrified her: he wasn't contemplating harming himself, was he? He didn't strike her as being depressed, but she needed to check. "Are you planning on drinking water contaminated by cholera, Kaye?"

She heard his hard snort and was immediately reassured. He looked like he had the weight of the world on his shoulders, but Jules knew he could handle whatever came his way. Even so, he looked very alone.

Jules walked across the vast space and stopped next to him. Taking a chance, she placed her hand in the center of his back and rested her head against his bicep. He'd either talk or he wouldn't, but for as long as he tolerated her presence, she'd stand here, giving him any comfort she could.

She felt his tension and watched as he lifted the whiskey bottle to his lips and took a long sip. A memory from her childhood slapped at her—bourbon instead of whiskey—and she tensed. How long had he been drinking, and how drunk was he? She was alone in his apartment, in this building, with a man she didn't know, a man with a bottle in his hand, someone who was upset.

Maybe she *should* leave...

"I'm not drunk, and I'd never hurt you," Garrett told her, in a clear, calm voice.

Jules stepped back and tipped her head to look at him. In the low light she saw that his eyes were clear.

He lifted his whiskey bottle. "I've only just opened this, and that was only my second belt."

He had a way of looking inside her and reading her, and it unsettled her. "How do you do that?" she asked him, genuinely curious. "How do you know what I'm feeling?"

He shrugged, turned, walked to the sleek dining table and banged the whiskey bottle on its surface. "You have the most expressive eyes—and face—of anyone I've ever met. And when I took a sip of whiskey, your entire body tensed."

So observant, even while upset.

Garrett picked up a tablet, hit a button and a series of lights came on, making Jules blink. Yep, his apartment was starker than she'd thought, dominated by white walls and those awesome windows. There was a basin and sleek cooker buried in the island but she couldn't see any appliances, cupboards or anything that hinted at a kitchen. How the hell did he cook?

Jules turned her attention back to Garrett. He looked... well, not awful—he was too good-looking for that—but like he'd had a day hand-delivered from hell. Blue stripes ran under his deep-set eyes, and his mouth was tight with tension. He still wore his suit, a deep navy and designer, but his tie was pulled loose, and his wavy hair looked messier than usual.

"Want something to drink?" Garrett asked her. He gestured to the whiskey bottle. "I have fifteen-year-old Scotch, but if you want something special, I have a full range of spirits and mixes as well."

Jules looked around for a drinks stand, or a cupboard that could hide a bar, but didn't see anything. His stash of liquor was probably hidden in his yet-to-be-revealed kitchen. Jules shook her head. "I already had a couple of drinks, while I waited for you."

Garrett stared at her, frowning, and then he winced. "Shit, I stood you up."

"You did," Jules agreed.

Garrett dropped an f-bomb and slapped his hands on his hips. As if only just realizing that he was still wearing his suit jacket, he pulled it off and threw it onto the couch. His tie followed its arc, and then he rolled up his sleeves. "I'm sorry. I should've let you know that I couldn't make it. That was rude of me."

It was. But Jules now suspected he had an incredibly good reason for standing her up. Walking over to the piano, she sat down on the stool and draped one leg over the other. "You offered me a drink, but I'd prefer coffee. Any chance of a cup?" She turned and looked at the marble island and lifted her eyebrows. "That is, if you have a machine. Or even a kettle."

Garrett stared at her for a long minute before nodding abruptly. He picked up his tablet and hit another button, and the far wall behind the marble island slid away, disappearing behind another wall. Jules blinked at the sleek kitchen in front of her, complete with high-end appliances and a coffee machine complicated enough to power a spaceship.

The disappearing wall also revealed a hallway. "What'

beyond the kitchen?" Jules asked, fascinated by his high-tech, low-on-stuff apartment.

Garrett walked across the living area to his coffee machine. "Guest bedroom, my gym, a home study. Sauna and Jacuzzi." He hit a switch on the coffee machine, and the thing lit up like a UFO. "What do you want? Latte, cappuccino, espresso?"

His machine-gun questions amused her. "Black is fine."

"Jamaican, Kenyan, Colombian?"

Oh, God, the man was a coffee snob. "Surprise me," she told him. She looked around, eyebrows rising at the massive black-and-white painting on the far wall. "I presume the master suite is behind that sliding wall?"

"No sliding wall," Garrett told her, pulling levers on his machine. "Just a hidden door." He smiled, but Jules noticed that it was forced. "Why? Are you angling to see it?"

"In your dreams, Kaye," Jules tartly responded.

"Actually, you have been," Garrett muttered. Really? Had he been thinking about her, like that? She'd imagined she was the only one indulging in late-night, X-rated, naked-together fantasies.

He pulled her cup from the machine, placed it on a saucer and carried it over to her, pushing it into her hand. "The beans are from Sri Lanka... Tell me what you think."

Jules lifted the cup and hesitated. She frowned at him. "They had better not be the beans that have passed through the digestive tract of some primate, Kaye."

This time, Garrett's smile almost reached his eyes. "Not this time, Juliana. But if you are feeling adventurous..."

Jules scowled at him. "I will never feel that adventurous."

"Pity, because the coffee made from those beans are what angels drink in heaven," Garrett told her.

Jules took a sip of her coffee, sighed at the rich, complex taste and shifted in her seat. Her hand wobbled, and the coffee sloshed in the cup. Garrett quickly pulled the cup and saucer out of her hand.

"Hey!" she protested.

"That's a Fazioli, a limited-edition piano," Garrett told her, holding out his hand to her. "I don't know how clumsy you are, so let's move you, and your coffee, away from it."

"I'm not clumsy at all," Jules told him as he led her across the room to the long, uncomfortable-looking sofa. "I juggle bottles of expensive liquor for a living, and my clients don't like me breaking their bottles or their glasses. And it makes me look like an amateur."

His hand was warm and broad, and hers felt like it belonged there. And wasn't that one of the more stupid thoughts she'd had lately? Garrett Kaye wasn't for her. Nobody was. She'd never allow a man to get close enough to hurt her.

But when Garrett's thumb skimmed the skin above her thumb, she felt a bolt of pleasure slam through her, and she stumbled.

Garrett's mouth kicked up, mocking her previous statement. Jules didn't know whether she wanted to smack him or kiss him.

"You are very annoying," Jules told him, sitting down on the cold gray couch. But when she hit the cushions, she realized it was spectacularly comfortable. Garrett placed her coffee on the wood-and-steel coffee table and sat down next to her, resting his forearms on his knees, his hands dangling.

He'd made an effort to be hospitable, but she'd noticed the storms in his eyes, the tension in his shoulders. He looked like a man who needed a friend, someone to talk to. Didn't everybody, even reticent, arrogant billionaires, need a sounding board occasionally?

"Do you play?" Jules asked, gesturing to the piano.
"Yeah."

Right, she was going to have to pull some teeth to get
him to open up. Jules took another sip of coffee, wondering why she felt compelled to dig a little deeper, to scratch
away some of his layers. Maybe it was because his eyes
were dark and turbulent. Maybe it was because his shoulders were halfway to his ears. Maybe it was because she
was curious.

No matter the reason, she was going to dig.

"When I walked in, you were standing in the dark,
looking like you were carrying the world and its baggage on your shoulders," Jules said, keeping her voice low.
"And, annoying as you can be, I don't think you make a
habit of standing women up, so something must've happened to upset you."

Embarrassment flashed across his face. "Sorry. Again."

"I wasn't looking for another apology, Garrett," Jules
replied. She placed her hand on his thigh, sighing at his
strength and heat. What would it be like to be surrounded
by both?

Pulling her hand back, she lifted her coffee cup, surprised by the fine tremor in her hand. "I just wanted you
to know that you can talk to me...if you want to." She
shrugged, tried to smile. "And I'm a bartender, and whatever you say will be treated in the strictest confidence."

"Yeah, I don't think so," Garrett said, his voice rough.

His response wasn't a surprise. From the moment she
met the man, she knew he was emotionally unavailable,
someone who didn't open up easily. Or at all. Abrupt,
direct, unemotional, he was the type of man she usually avoided. But yet here she sat, completely fascinated
by him.

Jules put her cup on the table, folded her arms and gave

the inside of her arm a hard pinch. Her objective was to help Kate, and help Kate was what she'd do.

And if that meant dancing with this devil, she'd do that, too.

Four

Her scent—light and lovely—was driving him mad. Because the urge to kiss her was nearly overwhelming, Garrett stood up and walked over to the window, leaning his shoulder into the cold pane. He eyed the whiskey bottle on the island, considered taking another drink and shrugged the urge away. His drinking made Jules tense up, and until he knew why it made her uncomfortable, he'd abstain.

Garrett looked at her, sitting there in her cranberry minidress that ended a couple of inches below her butt. His heart flipped over, and his stomach did a long roll as his eyes skimmed her curves. Below the hem of her dress, her solid black tights showed off her shapely thighs before disappearing into a pair of knee-high boots.

Her hair tumbled to her shoulders and down her back, and through her makeup, he could see the entrancing spray of freckles across her nose and over her cheeks. He wanted to play connect the dots, to see how far down her body those lovely spots went.

He wanted her, wanted to lose himself in her, in her slim body and delicious scent. He wanted to kiss that wide mouth and allow her taste to whirl him away from reality...

He wanted to forget, just for a little while, the conversation he'd had with James Ryder-White a few hours before, wanted to ignore James's request and his absurd statement that there was a good chance that Garrett would one day inherit a vast fortune.

That he was, by birth, a Ryder-White.

But Callum wasn't his father. James was.

Garrett still couldn't process the news, wasn't able to make sense of the bombshell James had dropped. He was his father, James stated, and he needed Garrett to manage the international empire. Hell, if he chose to let the world know he was James's firstborn, everything James would inherit—the Ryder International shares, the properties, Callum's wealth—would all pass to him. It was, James told him, a risk he was willing to take.

Ryder International needed an experienced CEO at the helm, and James wanted to get to know his son.

What. The. Hell?

The rumble in Garrett's stomach pulled him back to the present, and he couldn't remember when last he ate. And if Jules had been waiting for him for two hours, then she had to be hungry, too. And maybe after some food, he could start thinking properly, *unemotionally*.

"Have you eaten tonight?" he demanded, internally wincing at his terse tone.

"No, not yet."

"What if we ordered takeout, and while we're waiting, you tell me why you wanted to see me tonight?"

Jules stared at him, as if he were the spider and she the fly. After a tense thirty seconds, she finally nodded. "Okay."

Relief washed over him, as sweet as a soft spring morning. "What do you feel like eating?" he asked, pulling his phone out of the back pocket of his pants. "Pizza? Chinese? Indian? I eat everything, so you choose."

"There's a low-key but fantastic Korean place a few blocks north of here, The Homesick Korean. Do you know it?"

He shook his head. "I don't."

Jules got up and walked toward his hallway, and Garrett sucked in a harsh breath, wondering if she'd changed her mind and was leaving. When she returned holding her phone to her ear, his heart settled.

"Have you eaten Korean food before?" Jules asked. When he shook his head, she nodded and spoke into the phone and ordered a range of dishes in what sounded to him like passable Korean. After giving his address, she disconnected and tossed her phone on the couch.

"Do you speak Korean?"

Her smile finally hit her eyes. "Just enough to order."

Garrett followed her to the couch and sat down, keeping a broad cushion between them. Why tempt himself? "What are we eating?"

"Sweet and sour pork, spicy seafood mix served with udon noodles, and seafood and spring onion pancakes."

"Sounds good," Garrett commented. He rested his arm along the back of the sofa, his fingers very close to her sweet-smelling, bouncy hair. God, he loved her loose, natural curls, her exquisite profile, the way her dress flowed over her breasts.

"Tell me why you wanted to see me tonight," Garrett said on a long sigh. It would be at least twenty minutes before their food arrived, and he needed something to think about other than what she looked like naked.

Jules turned to face him and gestured to her boots. "Do you mind if I get comfortable?"

Garrett shook his head and watched as Jules slid down the zip on the backs of her boots and pulled them off. She wiggled her toes, sighed and then rotated her feet, groaning a little.

All his blood went south at hearing that little sound. Would she sound as breathless when he slid inside her?

"That feels so much better," Jules said. She tucked her feet under her bottom and turned to him, her face serious. "I need your help," she baldly stated.

That was the second time he'd heard that phrase tonight. People never asked him for help, but today, in the space of four hours, he'd had the same request twice. Since he doubted that Jules was about to ask him to run a multibillion dollar company, he told himself to relax.

Garrett gestured for her to keep talking.

"At the Valentine's Day Ball, I told you about Kate Kennedy, the owner of Crazy Kate's."

Yeah, he remembered.

Despair dropped into Jules's eyes and pulled her wide mouth down. "She's about to lose everything, Garrett. Her house in Denver, her business, her assets. And her beloved ranch."

Judging by the wobble of her bottom lip, the possibility of losing Kate's ranch was eating Jules alive. He waited for her to explain, and when she just stared at her toes, he placed a hand on her foot and squeezed. "I'm sorry to hear that, Jules, but I'm not sure how I can help."

When Jules looked at him, her eyes were large and sad, green instead of gold. "I need you to look at her business, find a way for her to keep it going."

Garrett stared at her, wincing again. He knew that there was no chance of that happening. What Kate needed was someone with deep pockets, a person who didn't care when he'd see a return on his investment, someone who didn't care if he ever saw a profit.

Those sorts of suckers were few and far between.

"Honey, I've been keeping an eye on the company, and I think Crazy Kate's is beyond help," he told her, trying to be as gentle as he could.

Jules's curls bounced as she shook her head. "I refuse to believe that. Surely something can be saved? She doesn't have to lose everything!"

"She's mortgaged every property she owns, and the bank needs a way to recoup some of those losses."

"The ranch is her home, dammit! Kilconnell Ranch has been in her family for six generations. She's emotionally attached to that land."

And so are you. "It's really bad business to mortgage a property you love and never want to lose."

"I know that, but desperate people do desperate things." Jules rubbed her forehead with her fingers. "Everybody has written her off. Everybody wants her to fail. I just want someone to go and talk to her, look at her business and her books and see if there's a way to get her to succeed. Or if not succeed, to help her keep her ranch."

Jules was tilting her sword at a windmill, and she was going to stab herself in the foot. Or in the heart. "Banks don't want businesses to fail, Jules. Foreclosing isn't good for business, and if she's that deep in debt, they'll probably also take a hit."

"So you're telling me to accept it?" Jules demanded, her expression suggesting that he'd asked her to kick a kitten.

"I'm trying to be realistic, Juliana. Giving you false hope won't do anyone any good."

Jules stared down at his hand still holding her foot. "I just need to do anything I can, Garrett."

Her compulsion to help her friend touched him, and he sighed, knowing that he might regret his next words. "What, exactly, do you want from me, Jules?"

Jules pushed an agitated hand through her hair. "Would you consider coming to Denver with me this weekend? I'd like you to talk to Kate, look at her books and try to find something, anything, to help her save the business."

Garrett stared at her, trying to make sense of her words. "You're asking me to fly to Denver to look at someone's business, hoping that I will be able to save it?" he clarified.

Jules nodded. "Even if you can just find a way to save the ranch, I'd be grateful."

He looked into her astounding eyes and found himself on the point of saying yes, of agreeing to her absurd proposal. He shook his head, trying to harden his heart.

He was the owner of a massive company. He had far more important projects demanding his attention. He needed to wrap his head around his parentage and James's offer for him to take on the CEO position at Ryder International.

Even if Garrett had some spare time and the emotional energy to help her out, there wasn't anything he could do.

"Garrett, you're her only chance!"

That was where she was wrong: not even he could rescue Crazy Kate's and the ranch. Well, he could, by throwing fifty million at the problem—fifty million he'd never recoup. He was a businessman, not a philanthropist.

Garrett pulled in a deep breath and looked for his patience. It was a commodity in short supply. He squeezed her foot and waited until she looked at him. "What do I do, Jules?"

Jules frowned at his question. "You buy struggling

companies and either put them back on their feet or you buy them and strip them of their assets."

Close enough. "As I said, I've been keeping an eye on Crazy Kate's. I had my people research the company. If there was a chance the business could be rehabilitated, I would've looked into it some more, but it's too far gone, even for me."

Jules lifted her face, and her eyes collided with his, fierce and fantastic. "I wish that everyone would put as much effort into proving it viable as they do into believing it's not!"

This was why emotion and business were such bad bedfellows. "It isn't a matter of belief but of numbers. The numbers are goddamn awful, Jules."

And he, like others in this game, didn't believe in flogging dead horses. Or businesses.

"What does the ranch mean to you, Jules?" he asked, curious.

A rich cloud of emotions turned her eyes to gold, then to copper, to green and then back to gold. "The ranch is happiness, stability, security. Kate is, and always has been, my rock and my anchor, the one person I have always been able to rely on."

"Are you related to her?" Garrett asked.

The shake of her head told him that she wasn't. "But she's family, someone I *chose*, someone who chose *me*. I travel a lot, Garrett. I'm never in one place for long, and I like it that way. It suits me. I have an efficiency apartment, a place where I can dump my stuff. But Kilconnell Ranch is my *home*. And the thought of anyone else but Kate living there is driving me crazy."

And making her sad. And he'd do anything not to make her sad.

"Okay."

Jesus, what? Had he just said yes to visiting the ranch?

Garrett, wondering what alien had invaded his brain, turned his head to look outside, seeing the wet streets of Portland, the heavy clouds blotting out the stars. If he stayed in the city for the weekend, he'd spend most of his time in his office one floor down, working and brooding, fixating on his parentage and digesting James's news. He tasted anger in the back of his throat and knew it was coated with bitter hurt.

Thanks to his mother's stubbornness, he'd been father-less for thirty-five years. And it didn't escape his notice that James had only come clean when he needed help. It wasn't about what Garrett needed. His mother had put her career above his need for a father; James needed Garrett's business expertise to steer Ryder International through rocky waters. His parents, such as they were, only looked after themselves and their interests.

And it made him goddamn furious.

James had suggested getting together this weekend, but Garrett wasn't ready to see him again, didn't know if he ever would be. So maybe it was better that he did leave town, that he put a little distance between the situation and his turbulent emotions. He could go to Colorado with Jules, paw through Kate's papers and set her mind at ease that there wasn't anything anyone could do.

He'd breathe the mountain air, maybe take a hike— when was the last time he had spent any time in nature or even outdoors?—and figure out what he wanted from the Ryder-White family.

If he wanted anything at all.

One of the perks of being wealthy was owning a plane, and Garrett loved the freedom it gave him. Twelve hours after agreeing to accompany Jules to Colorado, he was winging his way west, Jules sitting in the enormous leather chair opposite him looking excited and happy.

His pilot announced they were starting their descent to Durango-La Plata County Airport, and Garrett asked Jules to fasten her seat belt. She sent him a quick smile, her eyes shining with eagerness. And hope.

"I can't wait to get to the ranch, to see Kate," she told him, not for the first time. "As soon as you get there, you'll understand why I—we—love the place so much and why we think it's worth saving.

"It's a sunshiny place, especially in summer, and the wildflowers in spring are brilliant. It's an alpine paradise, with these incredible views of the mountains. The wildlife is incredible and there's an alpine lake stocked with brown trout. It's right next door to a national forest so there's a lot of land to explore…" Jules nibbled on her bottom lip, and Garrett thought he saw the sheen of tears in her fantastically expressive eyes. "God, I sound like a tour guide… It's worth saving, Garrett," she quietly added.

He'd done his research on the property. With its stone-and-wood mansion and extensive outbuildings, the ranch sounded amazing but, unfortunately, banks and lending institutions didn't care about amazing vistas and alpine lakes. They dealt in certainties and cash, both of which were in noticeably short supply.

"Thank you for doing this, Garrett. I am so grateful." She placed a hand on her heart and tapped her fingers against her chest. "I know you will find something to help save the ranch."

Hope flared in her eyes, and her complete confidence in his abilities made him feel ten feet tall, like he could jump mountains and swim oceans. She looked at him like he'd hung the moon and stars. Nobody had ever, ever looked at him like that before.

This was why men did stupid things for women, he decided. Why they bought flowers, wore cologne, kept their cars clean… Just to see a woman looking at him like this.

Garrett knew she was about to launch herself into his arms, but if she did that, he'd be French-kissing her in two seconds, and she'd be naked in three.

Get a grip, Kaye. You know how this is going to end, so be an adult and prepare her for disappointment.

He held up his hand and frowned, trying to tamp down her enthusiasm. He needed to bring her back down to planet earth because he was certain looking at Kate's financials would confirm what he already knew. "Jules, this is a long shot. There is a less-than-zero-percent chance of me finding anything that can help her. You know this, right?"

Her pretty nose wrinkled, and irritation flashed in her eyes.

"I'm not going to lie to you. Or give you false hope," Garrett warned her. "I know how much you want a miracle, but I'm not in the miracle business."

"I get it," Jules said, all but bouncing in her seat.

Garrett gripped the bridge of his nose with his thumb and index finger. He lowered her hand and scowled at her. "I don't think you do," he growled. "There's a really good chance that her business troubles will be worse than you expected."

A little of her excitement dimmed. "I just want someone to look at it from another angle," she muttered.

This was such a goddamn waste of time. Why had he agreed to this madness? Oh, right, because she looked so damn sad. He was such a sap.

Garrett closed his eyes and shook his head. This wasn't going to end well. He could feel it in his bones. He might be selfish, but the best he could hope for from this weekend was that the quiet and the sweet mountain air, and being out of Portland, would help him to decide whether he was going to, on a very temporary basis, run Ryder International.

He should say no, keep his distance... He was in his midthirties; he didn't need to be part of a goddamn family. He didn't need Callum's inheritance or the burden of Ryder International, and if he kept his father's identity to himself—James promised that he would respect his wishes in that regard—his life needn't change at all.

James, as per Callum's instruction, would find another CEO and would inherit the company and Callum's assets. That was fair and right. James was, after all, the next in line.

But James told him, with unexpected candor and sincerity, that he wasn't interested in his inheritance. He'd far rather have a relationship with his firstborn and pass Ryder International to the next generation. James's only proviso was that it was an all-or-nothing situation. Garrett had to be all in or all out; there was no in-between. While James wasn't asking him to change his name—not that he would—Garrett couldn't pick and choose how he wanted to be involved with the famous family.

All in. Or all out. It was a helluva decision to make.

"You have that same look on your face as you did last night," Jules commented.

Garrett's eyes slammed into hers. "What do you mean?"

"Now and again, when you think I'm not paying attention, you look a little sad, a lot lost and very confused," Jules explained. She cocked her head and her eyes drilled into him. "What happened yesterday, Garrett?"

He wasn't going to tell her. He couldn't.

"James Ryder-White came to see me yesterday, a few hours before you did. He was my last meeting of the day."

Garrett heard the words tumble from his lips and cursed himself. Why the hell was he telling her this? This was super classified information, and if it got out, the share prices of both Kaye Capital and Ryder International would dip, rise and swirl around.

Jules narrowed her eyes at him, her mind obviously going a mile a minute. "What did he come to see you about? As far as I can tell, you have nothing in common. You are different ages, different industries, and, judging by your tense, quick conversation at the Valentine's Day Ball, you aren't friends. So what did he want with you?"

He didn't answer her question. Not that she expected him to.

They were in a holding pattern, high above the airport, waiting to land, and if Jules didn't get Garrett talking now, she never would. Jules tapped her finger on her thigh, wondering how to get him to talk. He'd told her, more than a few times, that there was no chance of him finding any solution to Kate's horrible dilemma, so she couldn't help wondering why he'd decided to accompany her to Colorado, why he was using his considerable resources on what he kept saying was a wild-goose chase. If the chase was so wild, and the goose so elusive, why was he here, with her?

No, there had to be another reason why he was flying west with her. And it had something to do with James Ryder-White. She thought she'd try another question but didn't expect to get anywhere. "If you think that there's no hope for Kate, why are you here? With me?"

"As you said, if anyone can find a solution, it'll be me. But I don't want you getting your hopes up and then blaming me when it comes to nothing."

Nope, not buying that. "Then why do I feel like you are

running away from Portland, Garrett? And what does it have to do with James Ryder-White?"

"I don't run. From anything," Garrett told her, sounding annoyed.

Jules fought the urge to roll her eyes. "Okay. Then why are you wanting to put some distance between you and James?"

Garrett ran both hands over his face, dropping them to glare at her. "You're going to keep nagging me for an answer, aren't you?"

"Probably," Jules cheerfully replied.

"Shit. Well, this is classified information, so if you blab, I'll know it came from you."

Jules nodded and waved his words away.

"Callum Ryder-White recently had a triple heart bypass and is still in hospital fighting an infection."

"I know. Tinsley and Kinga are my closest friends."

He glared at her. "Did you know that Callum asked James to find a temporary CEO to run Ryder International while he was incapacitated?"

No, that was news. "James has worked for Callum all his life. Surely he can run the organization?" Jules asked.

"You'd think," Garrett snapped. "But no, Callum doesn't think James has enough of a killer instinct. He instructed James to find someone to run the organization."

A bank load of pennies dropped. Jules gasped. "You?"

"Me," Garrett confirmed.

Jules frowned, puzzled. James's request made absolutely no sense. Garrett had no connection to Ryder International—okay, his mother had held the position as Callum's personal assistant forever, but Garrett and Callum had no business ties or shared business interests.

"Why you?" Jules demanded.

He opened his mouth to answer her but then turned

away to look out the window to the ground below. Right, so he knew the reason why James approached him but wasn't ready to share that with her yet.

Silly to feel so hurt, but she did.

Jules stared at his broad chest, noticing the way it tapered down to his waist. He had a great chest, with wide shoulders, and his legs were long and muscled. He really was the most masculine guy she'd ever met, an intriguing combination of power and grace.

"Why me?" Garrett repeated her question, handing her a self-mocking smile. "Well, I do have an MBA and am one of the most successful venture capitalists in the country."

Probably in the world and the galaxy. Jules released an annoyed puff of air. "We both know you can do the job, Kaye! But why did James ask you? Especially since you are known to be a workaholic and have a revolving door of projects."

"Have you been researching me, Juliana-Jaliyah?"

"Stop trying to provoke me, and answer the damn question," Jules snapped. "And if you don't want to tell me why, then just say so."

"I don't want to tell you," Garrett replied. "It's personal…and I'm still wrapping my head around all that he said."

Annoyance and hurt rolled over her, and Jules nodded. The man, she reluctantly conceded, was entitled to his secrets. She barely knew him, so she couldn't expect him to confide in her. But she wanted him to. She wanted him to trust her and to talk to her. She wanted to peel back his layers and see who he was beneath the cool composure.

But that wasn't in the cards…

Jules played with her seat-belt buckle and forced her mouth up into an impersonal smile. She heard the sound of the engines changing, knew they were descending and looked out the window onto a clear but cold late winter's day in Colorado. This weekend might be the last weekend she spent at Kilconnell Ranch, and she wouldn't let Garrett's terse and uncommunicative manner taint her memories. She'd laugh with Kate and Peta, take a horse for a ride, stare at the mountains and take a thousand mental snapshots.

And pray that Garrett would find something, anything, to save the only home she'd ever known.

Five

Storm clouds chased them from the airport in Durango to Silverton, where they stopped for coffee. The town was busy with tourists who'd come to enjoy the March snow. They didn't linger to explore the town—filled with boutiques, shops and restaurants—and were soon on the road to Kilconnell Ranch, a half-hour drive away.

Garrett handled the SUV he'd rented with cool competence, tackling the curvy road with confidence. Happy to let him drive, Jules sat back in her seat and watched the passing scenery, marveling at the views of the majestic peaks, picking out familiar landmarks as the vehicle flew down the road.

It was a wild, desolate, primal area, but she loved it for being untouched, lovely and fierce. And as she always did when she traveled this road, she felt like she was on her way home and would soon be stepping into a house filled with love.

Talking about love…

"So Kate lives with her wife, Peta. They've been to-

gether for many years and married two years ago." She
darted a look at Garrett's profile. He was gorgeous and
hot and ripped, but if he was intolerant, it was going to be
a very long two days.

The edges of his mouth lifted. "I don't give a rat's ass
how people love each other, Jules. None of my business."

Thank God.

"We'll be there in about fifteen minutes. You'll be
sleeping in the guest suite in the east wing. It has amazing views of the mountains," Jules informed him.

"And where will you be sleeping, Juliana?" Garrett
asked, his voice silky.

"Not with you," she quickly responded.

"Pity."

Jules stared out the window, wanting to tell him that,
while she dumped her clothes and toiletries in the attic
bedroom, she never slept upstairs, preferring to sleep on
the couch in front of the fire or on the sofa in the study.
He'd think her weird if she told him she used bedrooms as
a place to store clothes, to dress and put on makeup, but
that she hadn't slept in a bed since she was six or seven.

She could lie in a bed and read but she couldn't fall
asleep in one and found bedrooms claustrophobic and con-
fining. And yeah, her aversion was why she hadn't managed to have sex yet.

That meant going without sex, and that totally sucked.
But she couldn't tell anyone about her phobia, didn't
know how to explain that sleeping in a room with a bed—
or the thought of making love to a man in there—made
her want to hyperventilate.

Thanks, Dad.

"I want you, Jules. You know that."

Actually, he'd been thinking about little else since he'd

met her. He kept imagining her lithe body naked, the color
of her nipples, whether she waxed or was au naturel. He
didn't have a preference: it was her body, and it would be
a privilege to enjoy it however she presented herself. And
yeah, he wasn't going to lie to himself, a part of his rea-
soning for accepting her invitation to accompany her to
Colorado was to see if they could take their chemistry up
a notch, to share her bed. She was such a curious, wonderful combination of sarcasm and strength. She was tempting and tantalizing and, yes, trouble.

He liked sex, was good at it, but Jules was the only
woman who'd caught his eye in over three months, maybe
four.

He wanted sex, but more than that, he wanted sex with
her.

"You make it sound so easy, so rational," Jules said, and
Garrett heard the tremor in her voice. "So damn natural."

"It is natural," he stated, confidently steering into a
sharp bend.

"To someone who's had a lot of it, I suppose it is," Jules
mused. "I haven't had enough of it to know."

Garrett frowned. Did she really think he would judge
her for not being experienced?

"There's nothing wrong with not having had many lovers," Garrett quietly stated.

"Or any at all."

It took him a minute to understand what she was trying to say. He swallowed, then swallowed again. She was
a virgin? No, he had to have misunderstood her. "You've
never…?"

He looked at her, caught the flash of green before she
spoke again. "I'm not completely inexperienced but… I've
never had penetrative sex. God, this is embarrassing."

It shouldn't be. "I don't believe in slut-shaming women

If guys can enjoy sex, so can women. Fair is fair," he stated. "Conversely, I would never judge anyone for staying celibate, for being choosy. I believe in personal choice."

He saw her shoulders drop an inch and some of the tension leave her face. He returned his attention to the road, his brow furrowed in thought. How the hell was she still a virgin? She was in her late twenties. Surely there must've been someone who'd caught her fancy over the years? She was gorgeous and a minor celebrity; she had to have had offers.

She said that she wasn't inexperienced... But what the hell did that mean? Was she implying that she'd had oral sex? But that didn't make sense, either. Oral sex was as intimate, if not more intimate, than penetrative sex... Why would she have one and not the other?

His mind was spinning, and there was only one thought that stayed front and center.

He still wanted her more than he wanted to breathe. And it wasn't because he'd had weird news from James and was feeling off balance but because she was a sexy, smart, forthright woman, and being naked with her would be a pleasure. And a privilege.

"Do you think your virginity is something to be saved for marriage?"

"Not particularly," Jules replied.

Her short, snippy reply told him that she was done discussing the subject, but he wasn't. He still had a point to make. "To me, sex is natural, recreational, fun, something I do because I enjoy it and I'm good at it. Virgin or not, I want to make love to you...with you. It will be phenomenal."

"How do you know that?" Jules threw up her hands, and when she looked at him, he saw the flush on her cheeks and the embarrassment in her eyes. "You can't know that! We haven't even kissed yet!"

That was what she was worried about? Hell, he could fix that immediately. Garrett peered through the windshield, saw the turnoff to a logging road coming up and pulled into it. After making sure he was completely off the road, he hit the button to undo his seat belt and turned to face Jules, who looked at him with wide eyes.

"What the hell are you doing, Garrett?"

"Kissing you, Jules." Because her eyes held a hint of anxiety, he grinned at her. "Pucker up, princess."

Amusement pulled her lips upward. "You are ridiculous."

Garrett smiled at her as he lifted his hand to her soft cheek, his thumb brushing over her lovely cheekbone. "Let me show you just how much chemistry is arcing between us, Juliana."

He lowered his head to hers and butted his forehead against hers, keeping his touch gentle. He looked into her eyes—how could he not?—and then scanned her lovely face. Looking at her was such a pleasure and made his heart sigh, then sing. Needing to feel her skin, he used his thumb to graze the side of her face, exploring the skin below her ear. He moved his head slightly and used his cheekbone to connect with hers and rubbed their skin together, and when he heard her shaky breath, he knew she was as turned on as he was.

"Can I kiss you, sweetheart?" he murmured, needing to know.

Her yes was shaky but there, so he placed light kisses on her mouth, her jawline and her neck as his hand slid over her hip and flirted with the top of her ass. He came back to her lips, not afraid to linger a little. When her mouth parted and the hand on the back of his neck tightened, he slid his tongue between her teeth and...

Another big bang, greater and more intense than the original boom that started life on earth, rocked him off his feet. Garrett found himself falling, coming apart, re-amalgamating in a way that he didn't recognize.

Her hand on his face scorched him, her tongue branded him and his mind dissolved and only contained one word... maybe two.

Mine.

More.

He was standing on a precipice, and if he allowed this to continue, he'd take her now, on the side of the road. And judging by the way she was kissing him back, she might just let him.

It took everything he had, every last ounce of will-power, to pull back, to rest his cheek against hers. They'd just kissed, yet he felt like he'd been ripped apart by a tornado, smacked by an avalanche.

"Wow," Jules murmured.

He pulled back to look at her. Her eyes were glassy with desire, and the pulse point in her neck was beating as fast as a hummingbird's wings. Oh, yeah, *chemistry* was too small a word to describe what was bubbling between them.

Jules stared at him, wide-eyed, and he dragged his thumb across her bottom lip, telling himself that he couldn't, shouldn't—mustn't—dive back in.

Because if he did, he wouldn't be able to stop. And their first time—because there would be a first time—would not take place in the front seat of a car.

She deserved a soft bed, fragrant-smelling sheets, a warm room. Everything that was magic.

At Kilconnell Ranch, Garrett followed Jules's instructions to park in the empty bay of the detached garage. On potting Peta walking up from the stables, accompanied by a lone mixed-breed dog, Jules bounded out of the car. She ran to meet Peta, Kate's forewoman and wife, and wrapped her arms around the slim and wiry woman. Peta looked and smelled the same.

No, Jules thought when she pulled back to gaze into her old friend's face, maybe not quite the same. The wrinkles on the edges of her eyes and around her mouth were deeper, she looked thinner and her eyes were definitely worried.

Jules squeezed her again and placed her cheek against Peta's to whisper in her ear. "I'm trying to find a solution, Pete."

Peta patted her cheek. "I know you are," she replied, before turning to Garrett and holding out her hand and introducing herself.

Garrett, dressed in designer jeans, brand-new boots and a fancy jacket, dropped the luggage he was holding to shake Peta's hand. He rubbed his palms together. "Holy crap, it's cold."

"We're expecting a storm to roll in later," Peta told him. She glanced at her watch, looking worried. "Kate and I need to go into town, and if we want to get back before the conditions turn ugly, we've got to leave soon. Let's get you guys inside."

Jules followed Peta toward the wooden front door. Garrett walked next to her, carrying their overnight bags in one hand, his other hand low on her back. Her shoulder brushed his, and she felt like she belonged at his side. One kiss and she was having silly notions, ones that didn't have any basis in reality.

No matter how good a kisser he was, how many wildfires he ignited inside her, he wasn't for her. She couldn't cope with hard, reticent men dealing with demons. She had too many of her own to be able to take on someone else's

"Where is Kate?" Jules asked, conscious of the heat of Garrett's body and big hand as they walked into the spacious hallway of the ranch house. A pack of dogs bolted out from their beds by the fire in the great room and swarmed them, shoving noses into hands and crotches, demanding attention.

Jules greeted them all, smiling when she saw Garrett on his haunches, enthusiastically handing out ear and tummy rubs. Being such a city boy, she was surprised to see how comfortable he was around dogs. She was stupidly attracted to the man, that much was obvious, but seeing him with the dogs upped her *like* factor.

The attraction she could deal with and ignore—kinda, sorta—but *like* was much more dangerous.

"Kate is trying to get all the documents in some sort of order for your man here," Peta told her. "She had an offer on the building, and she moved all the records from the plant in Denver to the ranch."

An offer on the building had to be good news and Jules felt a spurt of excitement. "Did she get a decent price for the building?"

Peta shook her head. "Sale fell through."

Crap. Jules slumped and felt Garrett's big hand squeezing her shoulder, a quick, silent gesture of encouragement. She wasn't in this alone; he was here to help.

If he could. But as good as Garrett was, he wasn't a miracle worker, as he kept reminding her.

Jules walked into the great room with its huge, exposed beams and stone wall behind the oversize fireplace. Double-volume windows brought the outside in, and the view was all the artwork the room needed. Plump, inviting couches, bright cushions and a massive fire made the huge room seem cozy and homey. Jules, so in tune with this place, immediately noticed something missing. There were no animals in the fields. "Where are the animals, Pete?"

Peta turned oh-so-sad eyes on her. "We were offered a really good price for the herd, and a neighbor agreed to take the horses."

Jules felt tears sting her eyes. The ranch wasn't the ranch without animals milling around. The land felt desolate and empty. "Could you not keep them?"

"Animals cost money, Jules," Garrett told her, his deep voice rolling over her. "Selling them is a quick way to cut costs."

"You're not just a pretty face," Peta told him, in her blunt way of speaking. "Kate cried for a week after the animals were hauled away."

Jules didn't blame her. She felt like crying, too.

"Juliana!"

Jules spun around at the sound of Kate's voice, and she saw her second mom standing in the doorway to the great room, dressed only in a thin cashmere sweater and blue jeans. Jules ran to Kate, flinging her arms around her slim frame and rocking her from side to side.

"God, I missed you. I've been so worried about you," Jules told her when she finally let Kate go. She frowned at her drawn face and worried eyes. "Are you okay?"

Kate lifted a thinner-than-normal shoulder. "As good as anyone can be when facing becoming homeless."

"You and Peta will always have a home with me," Jules told her, squeezing her hands.

"Oh, there are places we can go, but this is home, this is our place," Kate told her, her eyes bright with tears. "This is where I was born, where we got married, where I want to die."

Jules hugged her and placed a kiss on her temple. "

know. That's why I brought Garrett along. He's brilliant, and hopefully he'll find a way to save the ranch."

"From your words to God's ears," Kate said. They both looked at Garrett, standing by the bank of windows with his back to them, taking in the breathtaking view of the mountains looming over the ranch. Jules called his name, and Garrett turned, smiled and headed toward them. Jules turned to look at Kate, saw her eyes widen and a small smile touch her mouth.

"My, my, he's a long, lovely drink of water." She smiled at Jules. "Are you two together?"

Jules rolled her eyes. "No, Kate. I asked him out here to help you!"

"Pity," Kate said, leaning against the eight-foot doorframe and watching Garrett.

"He's not my type, Kate," Jules said, her voice harder than usual.

Kate gave Garrett another up-and-down look. "Tall, big, muscular. What's not to like?"

She did like him, wanted to get naked with him, but she was still trying to convince herself that her attraction to him was an aberration, a step out of time. He wasn't anything like the guys she normally dated. She normally batted away the testosterone types and had drinks and dinner with guys who were gentle, sensitive, sometimes meek, always mild. They were, she realized, easy to handle and very easy to walk away from.

"Nothing can, or will, happen between us," Jules told Kate, keeping her voice low. Was she assuring Kate or herself?

After being introduced to Garrett, shaking his hand and exchanging small talk, Kate thanked him for his offer to help and explained that the Crazy Kate paperwork was in her study upstairs.

"I hope Jules hasn't oversold my expertise, Kate," Garrett told her, sliding his hands into the back pockets of his jeans. "I think the chances of my finding a solution are minimal, at best."

Kate nodded. "I appreciate you trying. There are also records on my computer. Don't feel shy about digging in."

"Kate, if you still want to go to town, we need to leave now," Peta told her.

Jules cast a questioning glance at Kate.

Kate rubbed her arm. "Frank fell and broke his hip, and Goldy brought him home this morning. I promised to take them some supplies as they are out of everything. And Peta says we need to get back before the storm hits."

Frank had worked as a ranch hand for thirty years and Goldy as Kate's housekeeper for almost as long. They'd retired to a small house on the outskirts of Silverton two years ago. Kate took her responsibilities to her people seriously—whether they were retired or not—and wouldn't be able to rest until she knew they had food in the fridge and were as comfortable as they could be.

"Send them my love," Jules told them.

"Will do," Kate said, taking her coat from Peta, who was looking impatient. Jules glanced at the patchy blue and cloudy sky. Experience told her not to dismiss Peta's gut. If she said a storm was rolling in, then it was.

"I've put Garrett in the east wing, Ju. There's stew and freshly baked bread for lunch. Help yourselves to anything else you need." Kate kissed Jules's cheek and sent Garrett a friendly smile. "Make yourself at home."

Garrett inclined his head. "Thank you."

Kate and Peta left the house, slamming the door behind them. Jules turned to Garrett and nodded to the stairs.

"Well, at least they stayed long enough for me to introduce you," Jules said.

"No worries. I don't need to be entertained," Garrett told her. He looked down at their bags, still lying in the middle of the hallway floor. "Shall I take these up?"

Jules used her foot to push them to the side. "We can take them with us when we go up. The house is enormous by the way. Kate and Peta's rooms are to the right of the staircase—they occupy the west wing. The guest bedrooms, including yours, are to the left of the stairs. Kate's study is in the center of the two wings, the door directly in front of you as you hit the top of the stairs. There's also a guest suite on the third floor. That's my space."

Garrett walked back into the great room, and Jules followed him. It looked, smelled and felt like home, somewhere she could breathe.

"It's a beautiful place," Garrett mused. "How big is the ranch?"

"Eight thousand or so acres," Jules immediately answered. "With two lakes and a river running through it, it has ample water. The house, as you can see, is stunning. There are three barns and another guesthouse."

Jules knew she sounded like a real estate agent, but she needed Garrett to understand that this property was worth saving, that he needed to find a way to save the land that had been in Kate's family for over a hundred years.

"I'm trying to be strong for them, upbeat and positive," Jules said, keeping her eyes on the highest peak in the distance. "But the thought of losing this property makes my throat burn and my heart weep."

Garrett walked across the room and through the door leading to a huge country kitchen. His voice floated back to her, asking her if she wanted coffee. When she stepped into the kitchen, she noticed that he'd found the coffee machine she'd bought Kate and Peta for Christmas two years ago.

"Where do they keep the mugs?"

"In the cupboard beneath the machine," Jules told him. She admired the way his jeans tightened to show his perfect butt as he bent down to open the cupboard door.

Garrett stood up, holding two huge mugs, one of which had been her favorite mug as a teenager.

"You are obviously attached to Kate and this property," Garrett said, checking the level of beans and water in the machine.

"I spent every summer holiday here since the time I was ten. For two months of the year, from the time I stepped out of the car to the moment Kate took me back to the city, my life made sense."

Garrett shoved the cup under the spout and tapped the side of his fist against the relevant button. It had taken her a year to figure out the intricacies of the machine, yet Garrett seemed to know exactly what to do. He was a coffee savant, she decided. Jules hoped he was also a save-the-ranch savant.

"But you're not related to her?" Garrett asked, whipping away a cup and repeating the process.

Jules stared past him to look out the bank of picture windows to the back pasture. In spring, it would be covered in wildflowers. God, she hoped she got to see it.

She felt Garrett's eyes on her face, knew he was waiting for her answer. How much to tell him? "There's a women's shelter in Denver. We happened to spend some time in it."

"*We* being who?" Garrett asked, his focus completely on her.

"My mom and I," Jules told him, pulling out a kitchen chair and sitting down at the long, rustic-chic table. "Before she went insolvent, Kate was seriously wealthy. She comes from old money. And her family were big-time philanthropists, but Kate gets…involved. She gets her hand dirty. She works in homeless shelters, volunteers at animal-rescue centers, shelters for women and children on the run."

The coffee machine hissed, but Garrett kept his eyes on her, his attention laser-sharp. He gestured for her to carry on talking.

"Kate was working at the shelter we found ourselves in, and we just clicked. And when my mom started feeling unsafe, terrified to stay in one place in case my abusive father found us, she told Kate we were going to leave. It was the end of spring, and Kate offered to take me home for the summer. Thanks to some fake identity documents Kate paid for, we remained in Denver, and the next summer I came back here. And all my vacations after that. This place became my second home."

She wasn't looking in his direction, but she felt his tension, knew his eyes had sharpened. She never spoke of her childhood and her father's abuse. It was a secret she never shared with anyone. Jules didn't understand why it felt so natural to explain a little of her sordid past to Garrett. But she couldn't sit still, so she jumped up and walked over to the window in the alcove adjoining the kitchen and rested her bottom on the windowsill, stretching out her legs.

"You said your mom was scared... Was your dad actively looking for you, or was your mom just being cautious?"

"Nope, he was tracking us," Jules told him, keeping her voice flat. Unable to look at him, she stood up and turned to look out of the window. The view always soothed her. "He nearly found us in Minneapolis, and in Wichita. Once we turned a corner and saw him standing on the doorstep o our apartment building. Another time a neighbor told is that he'd been around, inquiring after us."

"Jesus."

She heard Garrett's footsteps approaching and sighed when his arms slid around her waist, pulling her up so that she stood flush against him. He rested his chin in her hair. "Did he find you?"

"Not me, but he did find my mom. We heard, through someone back in Boston, that he was tired of tracking us, that we could stay gone as far as he was concerned. We decided to stay in Denver and put our faith in Kate's fake documents," Jules told him, her voice scratchy. "We're still not sure how he found my mom, but when he caught up with her, he put her in the hospital."

She felt Garrett's sudden intake of breath. "What happened?"

"He beat her up, sexually assaulted her and, after realizing she was more hurt than he thought, took her to the hospital. He told everyone she was in a car accident, and because he's charming and polished and educated and because he flashed his police creds, they believed him. He was told that she'd be in hospital for a week, so he returned to Boston, which was where we were from originally. He asked for some vacation time…"

"What work did he do for the police?"

"My father was a lieutenant in the Boston PD, highly decorated, highly respected. Highly connected."

Garrett's arms tightened, and he released a low curse. Lifting his arms, he crisscrossed them across her torso, holding her a little tighter. "Tell me all of it, Jules."

No, she couldn't. Not all of it. But she'd tell him enough. "He picked up his truck and drove back to Denver. It took him two days. Somewhere around Des Moines, he fell asleep, and his car veered into oncoming traffic. He had a head-on collision with a truck and was killed instantly."

He didn't say anything and for that she was grateful.

"I was here, riding with Peta, playing with the dogs

in my happy place, blissfully unaware of all the drama. A few weeks later, my mom came to get me, and they told me that my dad was dead. I couldn't mourn him, and I was…relieved, I guess. He couldn't hurt my mom anymore, and we were free."

"Totally understandable," Garrett murmured, his breath warm against her temple. "I'm so glad that you were here, with Kate, and that you didn't have to see your mom in the hospital."

She was, too. "I feel safe here, like nothing can touch me. If I feel upset or stressed, I come to the ranch, and I find myself again."

He tightened his hold, and Jules felt safe in his arms, like he was the steel barrier between her and the often-ugly world. Then Garrett kissed the top of her head before stepping back. "Our coffee is getting cold. And then I think I should head upstairs and take a look at Kate's paperwork."

Jules took the cup of coffee he held out and wrapped her hands around the warm mug. She blew across the steaming liquid and took a sip. It wasn't as good as the coffee at his place, but it warmed her up from the inside out. Or was that Garrett? Was having him stand next to her, albeit temporarily, making her feel optimistic, more centered and a lot more at peace?

It was most likely the ranch, she decided. Being here, in the middle of nowhere, surrounded by the mountains, always made her feel less stressed and more settled. She cocked her head to the side, remembering how devastated Garrett had looked the night before.

"If you take some time, walk the land, breathe its air, this place has a way of seeping into your soul. I've always found the answers I need here."

"What makes you think I need answers, Juliana?" Garrett asked, his tone light. But he couldn't fool her.

She knew he had problems to work through. There was far more to his conversation with James than a simple job offer.

"Everyone has questions and we all need answers, Garrett. Step outside, get out of your head and let the mountains talk to you," Jules suggested, walking toward the door that led into the great room. "There's magic in the air here, Garrett. And it can heal you if you let it."

Six

Over the years, Garrett had developed the ability to look at financial documents and analyze and identify anomalies while mentally working his way through other issues.

In Kate's book-filled study, he perused Crazy Kate's profit-and-loss statements and thought about Jules's past. Anyone looking at her social-media platforms would think that she was a free spirit, a hardworking but fun-loving minor celebrity. But there was so much more to her than the facade she presented to the world. She was born into a life filled with tension, uncertainty and violence. Thinking of a young Jules being scared made him wish he could go back in time, as he'd find great pleasure in rearranging her father's face. Violence against women and children was the hallmark of a petty, small-minded man who, in his opinion, had some pretty major psychological issues.

Kate should never have built a new bottling plant.

Garrett was grateful Jules had Kate to run to, that she'd

found freedom and love and affection. He had never had a ranch or a place or a person to give him comfort, to guide his way. He'd had to figure it out on his own.

Mmm, it's obvious Kate expanded too fast and too aggressively...

Jules and Kate were close, but he'd never been able to talk to his mom, and when he tried, she shut him down. Hard. His efforts to corroborate that Callum was his father had never borne any fruit, and her inability to explain the circumstances around his birth left him confused. Was he not worth an explanation? Did he mean so little? Why was protecting Callum more important than knowing how he came into the world?

But, as it turned out, all his conclusions and assumptions were false, and he felt like a fool. James, not Callum, was his father, and for some reason James no longer wanted to keep his identity a secret.

Damn, Kate's interest charges are through the roof...

Why did James want to kick over the Ryder-White applecart?

By asking him to become Ryder International's new CEO, by explaining that he and Emma had had a hot love affair when he was in his early twenties that had resulted in a child, James was risking everything: his home, his position and his goddamn inheritance. Was James at war with Callum? Was Garrett being used as a weapon? A pawn? As a means to an end?

Garrett hadn't built up an empire by rushing blindly into situations, and he didn't intend to make any impulsive moves. Besides, he wasn't a kid anymore who craved a family; he was perfectly fine on his own.

Games were being played, and Garrett still needed to learn the rules. So, for now, he'd keep James at arm' length until he had a better handle on how this situation would play out.

Why the hell did Kate sign a new distribution agreement when things were so dire?

Garrett promised to give James an answer about the CEO position within the next week, and he regretted doing that. He needed a lot more time. Honestly, he should've refused on the spot, as he didn't have the time, or the energy, to run another multibillion dollar organization. He'd sweated blood and tears to establish Kaye Capital, and he was not going to put his business at risk for someone else's.

He also needed to speak to his mother, to get confirmation of James's wild claims.

Garrett raised his head and looked out the window, expecting to see a clear day. But heavy, dark clouds had rolled in, covering the amazing view of the Rocky Mountains. Peta had called it: those clouds looked ominous. Man, he was so sick of winter.

Garrett turned his attention back to Kate's computer, scanning the files for an asset register. He was hoping to find something massively undervalued, a cache of items that someone had overlooked.

The bottom line was that she'd experienced chronic cash-flow problems and had needed a loan to cover her expenses. Then she'd needed another loan when her cash flow didn't improve. Because she was overextended and because she was emotionally attached to Crazy Kate's, she had remortgaged this property, thinking that it was a temporary bump, something she could easily recover from. She had been wrong.

Garrett looked at his watch, raising his eyebrows at the time. Thanks to the low-lying clouds blocking out the sun, two in the afternoon felt like dusk. He wondered how much more time he should give Kate's financials, as he knew, deep down in his gut, that she was bankrupt and would soon be homeless.

And Jules would lose her happy place.

He could go downstairs, tell her that Kate didn't have a chance of saving her ranch, and their weekend would end abruptly. Or he could delay. Would it make any difference if he told her tomorrow, before they left? It was the weekend, and thirty-six hours wouldn't make an iota of difference, and he'd get to spend some more time with the very intriguing Jules.

She fascinated him, as she was far more than a pretty face and a quick quip. Beneath the charming bartender was a woman with more layers than he could ever have imagined. Judging by their kiss, their sexual chemistry was off the charts, and he really wanted to see her naked.

But sex with Jules would be more than a way to get his rocks off. It wouldn't just be stress relief or something to do to pass the time. Making love with her would be more... Damn. More *what*?

He couldn't define it; he just knew it would be different. And after years of the same, he was in the mood for something a little out of the ordinary. Nothing permanent but something to break up the sameness.

Work, exercise, sex. Work some more.

He was at a luxury ranch. He'd found out who his real father was. He'd been offered a new job. Wasn't that enough to shake him out of his complacency?

No, not nearly. He wanted Jules. But having her wasn't going to be easy. She was a curious mixture of street smarts and naivety, of confidence and fear. She was attracted to him, of that he was sure, but he had no idea whether she intended to act on their mutual attraction. And how far would she go to explore the passion bubbling between them?

She'd said she was a virgin, and her reasons for remaining so were a mystery. What was she waiting for? Love? Marriage?

She was looking in the wrong place if she expected either from him. He was the son of a woman who wore her single-mom status as a badge of honor—as she should. But he sometimes felt that Emma used him as a weapon to advance the idea of how capable she was, how much she didn't need anyone else. She'd taught him, from a young age, to be independent, and he wasn't ready to make space for another person in his life. He didn't think he'd ever be.

But Jules did intrigue him…

Garrett turned at the sound of footsteps on the stairs, and there she was, looking relaxed and five years younger in a pair of loose jeans and a moss-green slouchy sweater. Only thick socks covered her feet, and the side of her face bore the unmistakable imprint of a ridged cushion.

"Have you been sleeping while I toiled away up here?" he mock-demanded, surprised to hear the teasing note in his voice. He never teased anyone, didn't even know if he was doing it right.

"I was reading a book and drifted off," Jules admitted, walking into the room and approaching the wooden desk. "Sorry, that was rude of me. And I didn't give you lunch."

Garrett waved her apology away. "I never sleep during the day, and if I was hungry, I'm perfectly capable of finding something to eat."

Jules picked up a folder, read the label and put it down again. "Did you find anything?"

Yeah, he'd realized that things were worse than he'd thought. Instead of telling her the truth—he'd decided he wanted the rest of the weekend with her—he shrugged.

"Still looking at files," he replied. It wasn't a lie.

Jules rested her hip against the desk and wrinkled her

nose. "Kate and Peta are running later than they thought they would be. It's already started snowing in town, and it's about to dump down here. The weather service has upgraded the report, suggesting the storm is intensifying. There are warnings about slick roads and dropping temperatures. Peta has a little phobia about driving on icy roads, so they are going to stay in town tonight. If the weather clears, they'll be back tomorrow."

Jules nodded to the window, and Garrett saw snowflakes drifting in on the wind. "I don't know if we can drive out tomorrow. We might be stuck here for a day or two."

He needed to be back in Portland, but he couldn't control the weather. Because he was a practical guy, he asked whether the house had a generator and an adequate supply of water, food and wood.

"Kate's been living here all her life, Garrett. She's ready for anything. So, yes, yes and yes."

Right, they wouldn't starve or freeze. It was a good start. "If we're going to be stuck indoors for a while, do you want to take a walk while we can?"

Jules, to his surprise, nodded. "Kate asked me to feed their horses. Apparently they couldn't bring themselves to sell their favorite animals."

Garrett pushed his chair back and stood up, stretched. He walked around the desk and held out his hand. Jules placed her hand in his and flashed him a heart-stopping grin. "I also need to collect eggs. C'mon, city boy. Let' see how you do with chickens."

After feeding the two remaining horses—Kate's pinto and Peta's Arabian—and replacing the straw in their stables, Jules efficiently collected eggs from the chicken coop and filled up the feed troughs.

Despite being away for so long, her movements were familiar and instinctive, and there was peace in seeing to the livestock, what little of it there was.

Jules was conscious of Garrett's eyes on her, watching her work. He'd offered to help, but there was sadly so little to do that it was quicker to do it herself than to hand out instructions. She glanced at him, his hands bunched into the pockets of his parka, the beanie covering his eyebrows. Although he was from Portland, he moved from heated car to heated office to heated home and wasn't used to spending any amount of time in the cold.

To be honest, neither was she. She'd lost feeling in her nose twenty minutes ago, and her fingers were cramping with cold. It had been a long, long time since she'd spent a winter in the Rockies.

Jules shut the door to the chicken coop and stamped her feet. "Let's head back. I could murder a hot chocolate."

"I could murder a whiskey," Garrett countered. Taking her hands, he lifted them to his mouth. He blew on her icy fingers before taking off his soft leather gloves and rubbing her hands between his. "Man, your hands are freezing, Ju."

He had no idea. Thinking that he looked and felt far too warm, she lifted her free hand and slid her fingers down his neck, digging under his scarf and the collar of his jacket. He yelped and danced away. He mock-frowned at her, but she caught his small smile, the amusement flashing in his thunderstorm eyes.

"Let me warm them up on your hot, hot skin," Jules said in a breathy, baby-doll voice, fluttering her eyelashes for added effect.

She expected him to bat her away, to tell her she didn't have a chance in hell of warming her ice-block hands on him, but he surprised her when he lifted his arms away from his body. "Go for it."

Jules bit her lip, off guard. "I was just messing with you, Garrett."

"Hey, when a gorgeous woman asks to put her hands on me, I always, always say yes," Garrett replied, his husky voice causing little fireworks to pop on her skin.

Jules saw the challenge on his face, in his eyes, and her inner bad girl told her not to be a sissy, to accept the dare. Lifting one eyebrow, Jules moved closer to him and pushed her hands under his jacket, then under his cashmere jersey. She found the soft cotton of his Henley and tugged it from his pants, burrowing her hands under it to find his skin.

She placed her palms on the ridges of his stomach. Yum. It was like putting her hands in front of a fire.

But better. A thousand times better.

Her thumb drifted through the hair of his happy trail, and she wondered what he'd look like naked. Utterly fantastic, she suspected.

She heard Garrett release a hiss and felt his stomach muscles contract, but he didn't pull back. Moving her cold hands to his hips and then to his back, she burrowed in closer, burying her cold nose in his soft, woolen scarf. He was heat and heart, and she could stand here forever.

Just like this.

Jules felt his thumb skimming her cheek. She tipped her head back and saw desire blazing in his eyes. He tapped her cheekbone with his thumb. "You are so incredibly beautiful, Jules."

She knew she was pretty and, with a lot of work, could sometimes hit stunning. But she knew she wasn't beautiful. "I'm not wearing a stitch of makeup, and I have a red nose and red cheeks," she told him.

"Naturally beautiful," Garrett whispered. He tipped his head to the side. "Can I kiss you, Juliana-Jaliyah?"

Hell, when he used her full name in that particular voice, he could strip her naked and take her up against a wall. "I'd like you to, Garrett." But they had to be sensible. "But we're in a stable, the storm is picking up and I think it's best we went back to the house."

Garrett frowned, then sighed. "Sexy and sensible."

Jules reluctantly removed her hands from his body and lifted her still-cold fingers up to her mouth and blew hot air onto her hands. Garrett handed her his gloves. "Use these."

Jules shook her head. "I'm fine. We'll be back at the house in five minutes."

"You've been hauling water and working with cold buckets, so put them on, Jules," Garrett told her.

He had that stubborn look on his face that she was coming to recognize. He wasn't going to budge until he got his way. The wind was now howling, and she didn't want to stay in this barn arguing with him. Glaring at him, Jules slid her hands into the too-big wool-lined gloves. Her fingers immediately started tingling with relief.

Satisfied, Garrett put his hand on her back to usher her toward the barn door. "Anything else you need to do in here?" he asked.

"No, I think we're good. The horses have blankets, the barn is insulated and they'll be fine," Jules replied.

Garrett stepped in front of her to push open the big barn door, leaving them just enough space to slip into the night. Snow slapped her face, and Jules put her back to the barrage, watching as Garrett closed and latched the door.

Jules instinctively turned to the left, holding her hand out for Garrett to take. They hustled, hand in hand, back to the house, trying to ignore the icy pellets in the wind and the wet sludgy snow hitting their faces and sliding down the backs of their collars.

Turning the corner, they saw the door to the kitchen and increased their pace, desperate to get back into the warmth and the light.

Garrett reached the door first, but instead of barreling inside, he yanked it open and waited for her to reach him. He shut the door behind them and, to her amusement, engaged the never-used dead bolt.

The nearest neighbor was ten miles away, and they were in the ass-end of nowhere. Who did he think would pay them an unexpected visit?

He saw her laughing and sighed. "City boy, remember?"

Jules took off her beanie, unwound her scarf and dropped both on the small table in the mudroom. She hung her jacket on the hook by the door and stamped her feet to dislodge the stubborn snow before stepping out of her wet boots. Garrett followed her lead, and they walked into the kitchen in stocking feet.

Jules nodded to the door that separated the kitchen from the mudroom. "You're not going to lock that one, too?"

"Hey, there might be a psychotic Bigfoot wandering around out there."

"And you think a thin door is going to stop an eight-foot, big-as-hell man-ape?" Jules teased him.

Garrett started to reply, stopped and threw up his hands. "I've got nothing."

Jules laughed and walked over to the stove, where Kate's stew sat in a huge pot. She turned to face Garrett. "Are you hungry? We can have a late lunch, and if we get hungry later, I can warm up some soup. There's always soup in the freezer."

"Not right now," Garrett told her.

Jules turned to look at him, and all the moisture in her

mouth disappeared as he stared at her, his expression intense. All his focus was on her, and she placed her hand on her heart as he walked around the table to reach her.

She expected him to place his hands on her and yank her to him, to plunder her mouth and sweep them away on a tsunami of heat and hunger.

But Garrett stopped a foot from her and simply lifted his hand to swipe his thumb across her bottom lip. "You have such a sexy mouth, and I need to have it under mine again."

She couldn't speak, couldn't move, scared that this perfect, perfect moment would dissolve like a bubble hitting a spike of grass.

"I want to kiss you, Ju."

Words were impossible, so she simply nodded and waited for his mouth to reach hers, for their passion—so combustible—to ignite.

Initially, his kiss was soft, almost chaste. His lips nibbled hers, feeding her small, soft kisses. Jules released a growl of frustration, and she felt his lips curve against hers.

"More?" he whispered.

She draped an arm around his neck and stood up on her tiptoes. "More," she replied.

He laughed at her impatience and simply resumed his teasing. Frustrated, Jules palmed the back of his head, held his jaw in her other hand and pressed her mouth to his, sliding her tongue past his teeth.

Her tongue wove around his, and she felt him tense. He stepped into her space and, with one hand on her lower back, pulled her closer, so close that her stomach pushed into his hard, oh-so-lovely erection.

Better, Jules thought.

But it could be so much more. She pulled her mouth off his and looked up at him. "Kiss me, Kaye. Properly."

"Your wish is my command, princess," Garrett replied.

Just to tease her, he waited another ten seconds, but when he resumed kissing her, he dialed the heat up to nuclear, and suddenly, Jules didn't know which way was up or down. His mouth ravaged hers—there was no other word for it—and she, in turn, wanted to inhale him. To climb inside him and hang out there…

Garrett's hands skated over her butt and snuck up and under her sweater, bare fingers dipping down the gap between her jeans and her lower back. She shivered as his long fingers ran up her spine, skirting her rib cage, inching closer to her breasts.

She wanted him to touch her there, to touch her *everywhere*.

Needing her hands on him, she pulled up his Henley and placed her cold hands on his skin. Her hands discovered the light covering of hair on his pecs, his flat nipples, the hard muscle under his masculine skin. Her fingers danced over his ladderlike stomach and flirted with the band of his pants, knowing that if she moved an inch, she'd be able to press her palm against his hard length.

She wanted to do that, she really did…

So she did.

God, this wasn't like her, allowing passion to take her on a dizzy ride. She never allowed things to move this fast, but then again, this was Garrett, and he was different.

"I want to look at you, see you naked. Is that okay?"

Jules nodded, and he pulled her sweater up and over her head, stepping back to look at her in her thin lacy bra, her nipples visible.

He ran a finger across one nipple, then the other. "So beautiful."

Without giving her time to react, he dropped down to kiss her, tugging her distended bud into his mouth. Jules whimpered, and before moving to the other breast, he pulled the lace away. Then his tongue was on her skin, and she arched her back, shoving her fingers into his hair to keep him there, doing that. Hopefully forever.

Garrett adored her breasts for a long time before sliding his mouth down her sternum, kissing her stomach, licking her navel. He sank to his knees, and Jules was so caught up in the way he made her feel that she didn't protest when he slid down the zipper to her jeans, placing kisses on the triangle of her lacy panties. Her jeans slid over her hips, and at his order, Jules lifted her foot and stepped out of one leg.

"Widen your legs, sweetheart."

Oh, no, he couldn't be doing this, not in Kate's kitchen. Embarrassed, Jules was about to call a halt to the proceedings, but Garrett placed an openmouthed kiss on her inner thigh, gently nipped her skin and soothed it with his tongue. He nuzzled her mound, making approving sounds and, with one gentle finger, pulled her panties aside. He blew warm air onto her, and Jules gripped the counter with both hands, wondering how much longer her legs would hold out.

Garrett rubbed his knuckle over her feminine lips, finding her bundle of nerves with unerring accuracy.

As his fingers and lips worked in unison to toss her toward the stars, Jules allowed her mind to soar and her spirit to dance with the night sky. Was that a comet to her right, a shooting star to her left? As her pleasure inched higher and higher, she saw black holes and supernovas, space dust and fairy lights.

And then, when Garrett slid two large fingers inside her

and placed his skilled tongue on her clitoris, she stepped into the sun and detonated.

She didn't know if she screamed or cried or laughed—probably all three simultaneously—but her legs did buckle, and her knees liquefied. Garrett's arm encircled the top of her thighs, and he took her weight, tonguing her until she hit another, even bigger orgasm. Then her legs failed, and she dropped down, her thighs resting on his, her forehead on his shoulder.

"GodohGodohGod…"

Garrett's hand smoothed her hair. "That good, huh?"

"Geh…geh…gump…" Lord, she'd lost the ability to talk.

Garrett's laugh was low and completely wicked. "I'll take that as a yes." Wrapping his arms around her, he stood up, lifting his body weight and hers in one easy movement. He sat her on the kitchen counter and stepped between her legs. Holding her face in his hands, he dropped an openmouthed kiss on her mouth. She tasted herself—a little sweet, a lot sexy—on his tongue. God, that was hot.

"Take me upstairs, Juliana-Jaliyah," he murmured between kisses. "Take me up to your room, and let me make love to you, in a bed, as the snow falls outside."

Jules tensed and pulled back, ice invading her veins. Oh, God, she wanted to. She wanted him to carry her to her room and lay her down on her bed.

Up there she'd be able to see his strong, amazing body, experience what making love to a man was really about. In the silence, she'd hear his deep breathing, his voice on her skin.

She tried to hold on to that image but slamming doors, her father's drunken insults and her mother's cries, accompanied by the unmistakable sound of the bed slamming against a thin wall, rolled over her.

She heard his grunts, her sobs, and every muscle in her body tensed. Words like *slut* and *you'll take it and you'll damn well like it* echoed in her head, and she lifted her bunched fist to her mouth and cursed her shaking body.

"Jesus, Jules."

Strong arms picked her up off the counter, and Garrett walked her over to the rocking chair in the corner and sat down with her in his arms. He pulled the blanket lying on its back across her. Jules remembered that she was wearing nothing more than her panties and bra, both of which were askew. Under the blanket, Garrett pulled her bra cup across her breast, and she slid her hand between her legs to rearrange her panties.

Jules buried her face in his neck and tried to stop shaking. She'd been in this position before with other guys, she thought, but the memories had never been this vivid, her reaction so strong.

Why was she falling apart with Garrett?

And, God, he had to think her the biggest tease in the history of the world. Jules sniffed and wiped the ball of her hand across her burning eyes. "I'm so sorry. I shouldn't have let you go so far."

"Shh," Garrett murmured, his hand running up and down her bare thigh.

"I'm sorry."

"Nothing to be sorry for."

"But you didn't—"

"Not coming won't kill me, Jules." Garrett forced her head back onto his shoulder and gently held her. Jules breathed deeply—in for four, hold for four, out for four— and felt the memories recede, her tension fade away. She felt warm and relaxed, and if she closed her eyes, she could sleep.

"I suppose you want an explanation," she murmured, on a huge yawn.

"Only if you want to give me one."

She didn't, not now, possibly never. "Please don't be mad at me, Garrett."

She'd had anger from guys before. A few who told her she'd led them on, that she was a prick-tease and that she should be grateful for what she'd been offered.

"I'm not mad, sweetheart. Consent is me asking whether you want to be intimate with me. But it's also respecting your right to say no, at any point in the process."

This guy…

"I chose to love you like that. I enjoyed every second of it. But there's no expectation of quid pro quo."

She couldn't tell him everything, but maybe she could shed a little light on her messed-up mind. "It's not that I don't *want* to. I would've, if we'd stayed right there. Hell, if you'd hauled a condom out of your pocket, we might've even christened the table where Kate and Peta eat breakfast. I want you. Don't doubt that."

She felt his chest swell, as if he was holding his breath. "So correct me if I am wrong. You're not averse to sex per se, just sex in a bedroom?"

God, he was sharp. She'd tried to explain before, using the same words, but nobody understood. Or made the effort to understand.

"Well…*huh*."

Jules dropped her head back to look at his profile. "Is that all you have to say?"

He turned his head, smiled at her and dropped a kiss on her nose. "For now. Snuggle down and close your eyes… Feeding those horses exhausted me."

She smiled. "You just watched me. I did all the work." Jules felt his kiss in her hair as the chair started to rock.

"If you keep rocking the chair, I'm going to fall asleep," she told him.

"Good, do that."

Feeling warm and relaxed and oh-so-lazy, Jules obeyed.

Seven

"How did Kate come to start up a gin-making business?" Garrett asked as Jules put a plate of steaming stew in front of him. The enormous wooden dining table stood in front of a massive window, and beyond the insulated panes, heavy snowflakes danced on the wind.

He'd never known darkness like this: it was complete, stygian, horror-movie black.

He rather liked it.

Garrett watched as Jules, after putting a plate of homemade bread between them, took her place next to him so that she could also, he presumed, look out onto the night.

She'd slept for about an hour, and strangely, he'd been happy to hold her, enjoying the quietness, letting his thoughts roll in and out, not feeling the need to solve any problems or plot strategy. He might even have dozed off, but if anyone asked, he'd deny that with his dying breath.

He never napped. It wasn't what a constantly-on-the-go workaholic did.

Hell, Jules had a way of making him step out of the normal and embrace the...unexpected.

He didn't accompany acquaintances to ranches high in the Rockies to try and save a stranger's family farm. He didn't muck about in stables in the bitter cold. He didn't hold a woman while she slept.

Jules had the strangest effect on him.

"Before she met and married Peta, Kate was in a long-term relationship. He hated ranch life, she loathed the city and they quickly realized they were better off living apart. Seth bought a house in Denver, and Kate spent nights and weekends with him there," Jules explained, leaning back in her seat. The wide neck of her sweater exposed her shoulder and the strap of that lacy bra. He recognized that brand of lingerie. Their items were gloriously feminine, custom-made and brutally expensive.

Vouchers to order off the brand's online shop made excellent thanks-for-the-fling-we're-over gifts.

Garrett pulled his attention back to his earlier question and told himself to concentrate.

"They did marry at some point, shortly before I met her, I think. Seth owned a company making craft gin, and built up a small name for himself online and at gourmet-food markets. He named the company after Kate. He called her his crazy, wild child."

"So she wasn't always gay?"

Jules shrugged. "Kate told me that she's always been sexually fluid, more attracted to the mind than the body. Seth was an artist, a hippy, and from all accounts, he made her happy," Jules explained, after taking a couple bites of stew. "I never knew Seth but I think I would have liked him."

He followed her lead and sighed at the explosion of flavors on his tongue. "God, this is good."

"Kate can cook," Jules agreed. "Anyway, I was in my late teens when Seth was diagnosed with stage four pancreatic cancer. He died six weeks later."

Garrett stared at her, aghast. "That's quick."

"So quick. She was heartbroken."

"So to honor him, she took over his craft-gin company," Garrett said.

Jules took a bite of bread and waved her hand from left to right. "Sort of. She became a recluse for six months, maybe more. Then she started to work at the women's shelter in the city, and I met her maybe nine months after Seth died.

"She let the company languish, and it faded away. A couple of years later, Kate got a call from someone asking if he could buy Seth's gin recipes, his equipment, the Crazy Kate's name and his branding. Kate nearly sold it to him."

"What stopped her?" Garrett asked, interested.

"She'd met Peta by then at a grief-counseling group— Peta had lost her partner of twenty years in a car accident—and Peta suggested that before she sold anything to anybody, she should understand what she was selling and why. So Kate started working the business and soon found herself loving it. She made gin following Seth's recipes and then added flourishes of her own. She redesigned his website and reached out to his previous suppliers, and they were all ecstatic to carry her product. Soon, she couldn't keep up with demand."

Garrett could guess the rest. She bought a building and set up a commercial gin-making process. The orders, bigger and better, started rolling in, and to fulfill them, she borrowed more and more, thinking she'd repay the loans out of profits. But one client went into liquidation, another ran into cash-flow problems themselves, and she found herself in trouble. It was a book he'd read so many times. One he could've written himself.

"You said Kate gave you your start as a mixologist. How?" Garrett asked, wanting to move the subject off Kate and onto Jules.

She smiled. "She hired me to promote Crazy Kate's at state fairs and music festivals. I learned to make all the gin classics, but then I started experimenting with making other cocktails, some of which were horrible, some okay. I always seemed to have a crowd at my stand—" he could understand why as she was both gorgeous and charming "—and other drinks companies started hiring me to promote their products. When I finished college, I went to bartending school." Pointing her fork at him, she said, "And yes, there is such a thing. The jobs kept rolling in, and I was never short of work, and I loved traveling from town to town. I still do.

"During one of my trips back east, I auditioned to run a pop-up bar for Ryder International, and I met Tinsley and Kinga."

"You mentioned that, at the ball."

She wrinkled her nose in apology. "The three of us clicked straight away, and they hired me to fly to Hong Kong and do a demonstration in their newest Ryder Bar. I pretty much haven't stopped moving since."

"Don't you get sick of living in hotel rooms and eating restaurant food?" Garrett asked. He was on the road a lot, and after a couple of days, all he wanted was his own bed and fridge.

Jules ate a little stew before answering him. "Moving around was what I did for many, many years with my mom," she quietly explained. "Moving makes me feel secure. Staying in one place makes me antsy."

"Because of your dad," Garrett stated.

"Yeah, because of him." Jules stared down at her plate, idly pushing her food around. "Can we not talk about him or me?"

He didn't like people pushing him to open up, so he respected her wish to move on from her past and her parents. "One last question?" he said, as a thought popped into his head.

She lifted her eyebrows.

"Where does your mom live? You don't talk about her. You talk about Kate all the time, but your mom? Not so much."

Jules wrinkled her nose and placed her elbows on the table. "My mom still lives in Denver. She works as an aid in a retirement home. We don't talk much." She dredged up a smile. "I know you are going to ask me why not, and I'll tell you, but then we're done talking about me, okay?"

Garrett nodded.

"After my father died, life was good. Really good. We were so happy for a few years. In my final year of school, luckily just a few months before I graduated, she met a guy and fell for him. He moved in and within weeks was physically abusing her. She stayed with him and they are still together."

Garrett stared at her, astounded. "No way."

"After *everything* my father did and what she went through, it's hard to believe, right?"

Garrett stared at her, unable to believe what he was hearing. "I'm sorry, I don't understand why she would do that."

Jules's shoulders hit her ears before dropping again. "I asked her the same question. She told me that it's not an issue and that he's nothing like my father. That she loves him and can't live without him." Jules rubbed the back of

her neck. "I told her I couldn't watch it happen again and
that she had to choose him or me. She chose him."

"Aw, baby."

"I don't like it, but I've learned to accept that it's her
life and her choice to make."

Yeah, behind the gloss and the glamour was a woman
who'd been hurt a hundred times over. Garrett wished he
could go back in time and kick some ass.

Jules wiped up some gravy with a piece of bread and
popped it into her mouth. She gestured to the window
and the darkness beyond it. "God, it's so beautiful and
so quiet."

Garrett pushed his plate away and reached for his tumbler of whiskey. It was great whiskey, one of his favorites. He took a sip and felt the burn slide down his throat.

"Do you not drink anything other than whiskey?" Jules
asked. When he shook his head, she looked horrified. "No
wine, no beer?"

"Wine gives me a horrendous hangover, and beer
doesn't float my boat. Cocktails are normally too sweet
or taste like chemicals."

"Sacrilege!" Jules sent him a horrified look and placed
her hand on her heart. "I have to change your mind. I have
some kick-ass combinations for other spirits that you'll
love."

He didn't think so, but he'd play this game as long
as it made her smile. He placed his elbows on the table
and smiled at her. "You can try, but my mind is not easily changed." He gestured to the drinks stand where he'd
found the bottle of whiskey. "But do your best."

Jules sent it a sour look. "I'll have to take a rain check
on that because Kate, despite being a crafter of one of the
best gins I've ever tasted, doesn't keep much liquor in the
house, and Peta doesn't drink at all." She smiled. "When

we get back to Portland, I'll invite you to Ryder Bar downtown and show you what I can do."

He'd suffer through a couple of revolting cocktails if it meant spending more time with her. Garrett ran his hand through his hair, thinking that he was a fly trapped in a particularly sticky web. And that he wasn't fighting too hard to extricate himself.

"What's your favorite cocktail?" Garrett asked, leaning back in his chair.

"I make an amazing version of a Moscow mule."

He pulled a face. "What's that, again?"

Jules grinned at him. "Vodka, ginger beer, lime juice. My version uses vegetable juices, carrot mostly, lots of fresh ginger and cilantro."

It sounded awful, and he told her so. "That's a salad, not a drink," he grumbled.

"Don't knock it until you try it, Kaye." Jules pointed her finger at him. "And you will try it."

He laughed at her fierceness, amused that she thought she could get him to do something he didn't want to do. That hadn't happened in a long, long time. But deep inside, Garrett suspected this woman might be the person he'd make an exception for. She'd gotten him to fly to Colorado ahead of a record-breaking snow dump. Hell, who knew what he'd be agreeing to next?

Feeling uncomfortable with the direction of his thoughts, Garrett pulled his eyes off her lovely face and looked outside. "Hey, it's stopped snowing, and the wind has died down."

"Not for long," Jules muttered. "I checked the weather report, and it's supposed to snow all night."

"But it's not snowing now."

Jules looked outside and shrugged. "So?"

"Let's take a walk," Garrett suggested. It was either

walk or kiss her senseless, and he didn't know if he'd cope with another bout of lovemaking that was interrupted half-way through. No, it was better to find something else to do, some other way to distract them.

"In subzero temperatures?"

It was a reasonable alternative to a cold shower.

Jules, looking like the Abominable Snowman, plod-ded along next to Garrett, her rain boots sinking into the snow. The clouds had parted, just for a moment, to show a star-studded sky and a full moon. It wouldn't last, but she was happy to stand next to Garrett and imagine plucking the moon from the sky, as if it were a bright, silver apple.

Jules thought that she would be quite content to stand with Garrett anywhere.

He was blunt and terse but so honest, and the way he looked at her heated her blood.

She wasn't an idiot: she knew he wanted her with a fe-rocity that shocked her. That she could turn him on—this man who dated movie stars and models—was a hell of an ego boost. And his willingness to stop—to hold her when she freaked out, to not complain or demand an explana-tion—warmed her.

Jules felt like she could tell him anything, that he was pretty much unshockable. Could she tell him about her father, how his actions led to her fear of sex…?

No! She had to stop thinking that.

She didn't fear *sex*. She would've happily allowed Gar-rett to finish what they'd started if he hadn't mentioned them moving to the bedroom. Hell, he could've taken her on the kitchen floor or on Kate's sturdy dining table. No, the act itself didn't frighten her, but she didn't want her first time to be tainted with the memory of her father gripping her mom's hair, pulling her to their bedroom at the end of the hall.

Why had she never realized this before? Why had it taken her so long to work this out? And why hadn't she asked any of those other guys to do her on the couch or the dining table or the rug in her living room?

She was pretty sure they wouldn't have minded. She enjoyed kissing, touching, the feel of a man's body plastered against hers and the different textures, smells and sounds they had.

So why had she hesitated?

Jules forced herself to dig deep, to get to the heart of the matter. Surely, if she was so affected by how her father treated her mother after a fight, she'd be terrified of the sex act, not just scared of being alone in a bedroom with a man? What was the difference with being alone with a man in her living room? She was still behind a closed door.

Jules thought about her previous relationships, remembering the few hot-and-heavy encounters of her past. They'd get down and dirty, indulge in some heavy petting and maybe some oral sex, but when the man of the moment asked to move to the bedroom, she shut down… just like she had with Garrett earlier.

He'd phone the next day, and the day after, send emails and text messages, and eventually she'd reply, quickly finding an excuse not to see him again.

Months would pass, she'd meet someone else, and the whole dysfunctional cycle would repeat itself.

At this rate, she'd be an eighty-year-old virgin.

Had she been using her fear of sex to avoid starting something with somebody? Was she scared that opening the door to her sexuality would open the door to love, to commitment, a future? It didn't have to be like that. Having sex didn't mean that she had to commit to a guy. Sex was sex; love was different.

Garrett didn't want a relationship. That wasn't something he expected from her. If she slept with him, nothing would change between them. And wasn't it time to get past this, to put her issues behind her?

She was almost thirty years old and was a modern woman in thought and deed. She deserved an active, fun sex life. And if anyone could help her move past this, Garrett—the first person who fried her brain and caused a massive lowering of her inhibitions—could.

"Would you sleep with me?" she demanded, her voice loud in the silent night.

And just like that, a cloud covered the moon. Jules imagined it slapping its hand over its eyes, mortified at her blunt, out-of-the-blue question.

Garrett turned to face her, his expression inscrutable. "That came out of nowhere."

"Tell me about it," Jules grumbled, kicking a clump of snow with the toe of her boot.

"What's changed since earlier?" Garrett asked her, using a bland, nothing-to-see-here voice.

"I'd like to..." God, this was embarrassing "...complete the act. I'd like to stop feeling like a jittery spinster and have a life that includes sex. And I'd like you to help me with that."

Garrett ran his hand over his face. "Maybe you should think about this, Jules. Choose someone who's a little kinder, someone with more patience."

Jules stomped her foot. "I tried that, and it didn't work." She looked away, conscious of the heat warming her face from the inside out. "Look, nobody has ever made me feel the way you do."

She saw horror drop into his eyes and saw him pull

back, as if he were stepping away from her words. She waved her hands around. "I'm not asking you to marry me, Kaye! I'm just trying to tell you that I've never felt so physically attracted to anybody as I do to you."

"Okay...right. Good."

Jeez, he didn't have to look so relieved.

Garrett rocked on his heels, his face an unreadable mask. "I'm not sure if this is a good idea, Jules."

"For you or me?" Jules challenged him.

They stepped onto Kate's wraparound deck, and thanks to the outdoor lighting, Jules could see the hesitation on his face. "Look, if you don't want to, then just say so, and I'll move on."

"To what? To whom?" Garrett demanded.

"I don't know, but I can't keep living like this! I can't keep bailing, running from the memory!"

Garrett's eyes sharpened. "What memory?"

"He'd beat her and then drag her into the bedroom. She'd cry, plead, but...crap, the walls were thin." Jules rubbed the back of her neck, feeling uncomfortable. "As I said, I have a thing about bedrooms."

Garrett stared at her for the longest time, his expression inscrutable. Was he regretting being here with her? Thinking that this was too much information, that she was being too dramatic? Damn, she shouldn't have let that slip. It was her biggest secret, something she'd never shared before. She gestured to the door leading into the great room. "I'm going in."

Garrett looked up at the sky where clouds were rolling back in. "Yep, here comes round two."

Jules walked down the side of the house until she came to the door to the mudroom and yanked it open. They shed outer layers and shoes and, in silence, walked into the large house, the silence broken by the crackle of logs in the overlarge fireplace.

Jules put her hands out to the flames, sighing when she heard Garrett running up the stairs. A door opened and closed, and she wondered where he'd gone and whether he was coming back.

Who'd have thought that asking for sex would be so hard?

Jules stared into the gold-and-blue flames, remembering how many times she'd fallen asleep on that leather couch, staring at the fire. How secure and safe she felt with Kate upstairs and the dogs gently snoring in their dog beds scattered throughout the room.

This was her happy place, her refuge, her safe place.

God, what was she going to do if it passed out of Kate's hands? Jules sighed, embarrassed at her selfishness. She made it out here a few times a year, but this was where Kate and Peta lived. They had an emotional connection to this ranch that was far stronger than hers. She'd be so sad to lose Kilconnell Ranch, but Kate would be devastated.

There had to be something someone could do. But Garrett had looked at the books earlier and hadn't found anything. What if there was nothing to find? What then?

Jules felt Garrett's arms encircle her waist, sighed when his lips touched the spot where her shoulder met her neck. He was so much taller than her, so much stronger, yet she felt safe with him, protected. Was that why she'd asked him to sleep with her?

Why did she instinctively know that he'd never hurt her? Was she confusing lust with trust, thinking that, because he'd set off a series of explosions in her womb, between her legs, he was trustworthy?

No, she wasn't that easily confused.

"Do you want to explain some more? Talk about it?" he asked, his question gentle.

"No, I want you to love me."

Garrett lifted the hair off her neck, pushed it over her shoulder and, using his tongue, painted streaks of fire over her skin, along the cords of her neck. Gently turning her around, he placed his mouth on hers, his tongue between her lips, asking her to let him in. Jules placed her hands on his pecs and stood on her tiptoes, eager to explore his mouth, to have him in hers.

His hand skimmed down her throat, across her shoulder and down her torso, his fingertips coming to rest on her puckered nipple. She arched her back, wanting to get closer to him, needing more.

"Let's get your clothes off, baby," Garrett whispered.

Jules tipped her head back and looked up into his serious face. "So are we doing this?"

"We'll go as far as you want. And if you want to call it quits, we stop. You're in control here, Ju."

Jules swallowed as he gently pulled her sweater up her body and over her head. The appreciation in Garrett's eyes made her feel supermodel gorgeous. He ran a finger down the slope of her shoulder, down her arm. "You have the most beautiful skin."

Jules tugged at his sweater, and Garrett reached behind him and, with one hand, pulled his sweater and T-shirt over his head and dropped them to the floor. Jules immediately placed her hands on his chest and her mouth above his heart, inhaling his sexy, turned-on, shower-and-soap smell. Gorgeous.

With a twist of his hand, Garrett undid her bra and pulled it down her arms, dropping the lacy fabric to the floor. One hand covered her breast, and he played with her nipple, his long fingers sending ribbons of pleasure dancing through her. Garrett bent his knees, wrapped his arms around the back of her thighs and easily lifted her so that her torso was aligned with his mouth. He pulled her nipple, flattening the bud against the roof of his mouth.

So strong, so powerful.

After telling her to wind her legs around his hips, he walked backward and lowered them both to the leather couch, with Jules sitting astride him, his hard shaft between her legs. There was too much fabric between them, and she wanted it gone.

Jules lifted her hands to hold his face and stared into those blue-green eyes. "I'm loving this, but..."

"But?" Garrett asked when she hesitated.

"We do it here, we don't move," Jules said.

Garrett nodded, his gaze solemn. "Deal." He kissed her again, starting slow and letting their passion build, his hands exploring her torso and back, occasionally swiping her nipples with his thumb before darting off to discover her ribs, her lower back, the soft skin above her jeans-covered hips.

Garrett pulled away from her mouth and ducked his head to kiss her breast, curling his tongue around her nipple. Jules closed her eyes, thinking that this was the best sexual encounter of her life.

"I need to see you naked, baby," Garrett suggested. He easily lifted her off his lap and tugged her between his legs, flicking open the button to her jeans and pulling down her zipper. He placed kisses on each inch of bare skin he exposed, and by the time her jeans skimmed down her hips, Jules was shaking with need.

She felt the throbbing between her legs, the warmth and the wet, and when Garrett pushed her panties down, she stiffened.

"Shh, Jules," Garrett murmured, dragging his finger

down her narrow strip of hair. He slid his fingers between her feminine folds and into her wet channel, skimming her happy spot.

"So, so lovely," Garrett muttered. "The things I'd love to do to you, Juliana-Jaliyah."

Right now, she just wanted him inside her, stretching her. Rocketing her to an intense orgasm.

"You've got too many clothes on," Jules told him, shocked by the need in her voice. Reaching down, she aimed for the button on his jeans, but Garrett pushed her hands away, flipping open the top button, then the next. He slid his hands under his underwear—plain black and expensive—and lifted his hips, pushing his jeans and briefs down his hips. Jules couldn't take her eyes off his shaft, as big and long as he was, jutting out from a thick thatch of hair. She swallowed, wondering how she could accommodate him…

Garrett sent her a smile. "It'll be fine, Jules. Trust me."

She nodded, saw the reassurance in his eyes and nodded again.

Garrett lightly stroked her right thigh. His touch was both reassuring and sexy, a curious combination of heat and encouragement. His hands skated down her legs in a tactile assault that liquefied her knees. She rested her hands on his shoulders and stared down at his wavy hair, wishing he'd return to that place between her legs where she ached the most. Garrett looked up at her, and she swallowed when she noticed the passion in his now-dark eyes, his needy expression.

"Kiss me, Ju," he commanded, and Jules hooked her thighs over his and slid down his legs, her mouth connecting with his as her hot core slammed against his shaft.

So, so good.

Their lips locked, tongues intertwined, and his fingers

traced patterns on the bare skin of her butt. Her panties created friction between them that they both liked, the lace scratchy against her core. Garrett's hand moved up and down her side, from ribs to breastbone, occasionally spreading his fingers so that he brushed her nipples. She felt enveloped by him, surrounded, and she loved it. Her breasts pushed against his strong chest, her hard nipples pressing into his skin. Needing to touch him, to stoke his fire, she stroked his ribs, tracing her fingers over his washboard stomach. He felt amazing, and he made her feel desired, hot, horny.

Jules pushed her hands behind her, running them over the parts of his thighs she could reach, rocking her core against his erection and feeling her heat build. His hands cupped her breasts, teasing her nipples. He ducked his head, kissed her jaw, sucked on her earlobe and told her that he wanted her mouth again. Sitting up, she leaned forward and slapped her mouth against his, their kisses turning feverish. She wanted to get closer, climb inside him, have him be inside her.

She'd never wanted anything more.

Unable to wait, she wrenched her mouth off his and pulled back to meet his eyes. She needed his complete attention, needed him to know that he was what she wanted, in every way that mattered. "I want you... Now," she added, her tone fierce.

"Not yet," Garrett muttered, lifting her off him. He lowered her to the Persian rug on the floor, and Jules looked up at him, her body pulsing with need.

"Garrett, please," Jules begged, trying to wrap her hand around his biceps to tug him down. But Garrett simply shook his head and moved his hands to her panties and, with one quick twist, snapped the thin cord at her hips.

He slowly pulled the fabric out, dragging the lace across her clit, causing Jules to arch her back.

"More...of that!" she gasped.

"As you please, princess," Garrett said, amused. He slid his hands between her legs, brushed her clit and slid two fingers deep inside her. He did something, hit something, and Jules felt herself rocket up, releasing a series of low moans. He kept moving his fingers inside her and, with his other hand, rolled her nipple between his fingers. Jules closed her eyes in exquisite pleasure. He sat back on his knees and reached for his jeans, pulling condoms from the back pocket before tossing the pants to the side. He tore a condom off the strip, removed the latex from the packet and pushed it into Jules's hand.

God, they were really doing this.

"Put it on me, Jules. Touch me."

At his words, Jules realized that she'd been the one receiving pleasure and had handed out little herself. Sitting up, she wrapped her hand around his erection, exploring his silk, satin and steel member. She looked down and realized that even this part of him was beautiful.

At some point, not now, she wanted to kiss him, to take him into her mouth...

"Condom, Jules," Garrett reminded her.

At his gruff suggestion, her eyes flew to his face, and she saw the impatience in his eyes, the need on his face. Smiling, pleased that she could make such a powerful man shake with desire, she slowly, oh-so-slowly, rolled the condom down him, letting her fingers drift lower.

Garrett sucked in a harsh breath, and he put a hand on her shoulder and pushed her down. Reaching up, he snagged a cushion from the couch and told her to lift her hips, then he shoved the cushion under her bum.

He tested her readiness again—she was even wetter

than before—and he positioned himself above her, his palms flat on the carpet next to her head, his penis sliding over her clitoris.

"Are you sure you want this, Jules?"

She nodded.

"Not good enough. Tell me," Garrett insisted as his tip rested against her bundle of nerves.

"I want you, Garrett. I need you," Jules said, almost weeping with frustration.

He slid inside her with one smooth stroke, pushed through the thin barrier and seated himself deeply.

He pulled back, and she protested. Garrett pushed her hair off her forehead, before sliding into her again. He started to repeat the action, cursed and tensed, choosing to move into her with care.

She didn't need that: she wanted him wild and unrestrained. "Take me, Garrett."

Garrett rested his weight on one elbow to push a strand of hair off her cheek. "We need to go slow, take it easy."

"I don't want easy or slow, I want hot and wild."

"Baby, you've never done this before…"

"With you, I feel like I have, like this is familiar," Jules insisted. She stroked his jaw with her fingertips. "Take me, Garrett. Hard."

He searched her face again, frowned and then sighed. His hand moved between their bodies and he slipped his finger down, finding her bud, which he stroked. Once, then twice, his hips lifting when Jules lifted her hips to slam herself against him. Heat and power and electricity and pleasure rolled through her, and she pulled Garrett's hand away.

Garrett heard her silent pleas and slammed into her. Jules sucked in a deep breath, thinking that he felt bigger than he had moments before. He rocked back, withdrawing to his limit before pounding into her again, and Jules, for the first time in her life, saw stars.

On the next thrust, those stars exploded, and on the next, her world disintegrated in tiny pinpricks of luminescent fragments.

From a space a million miles away, she felt Garrett's release, heard his shout, but she was spinning away on a tornado of color and sensation.

Eight

Jules, shattered and shaken, pulled the multipattern blanket off the back of the couch and wrapped it around her. She looked over to the window to where Garrett stood, magnificent in his nakedness. His forearm rested on the glass above his head and she wondered what he was thinking about as he looked out into the night.

She didn't regret making love to him. It had been a wonderful experience that she'd always remember. But while she might've lost her virginity, she was only halfway to resolving her bedroom problem. She'd never feel comfortable in an old-fashioned marriage, one where the man was the dominant partner, where his career took precedence over hers, where he got the final say on all decisions made.

She was scared of strong men, domineering men, men who were like her father. But more than that, she was scared that she would turn out to be like her mother, sacrificing herself to love and be loved.

Frightened that the deeper she immersed herself in the relationship, the less empowered she would be. Jules knew she was a lot like her mother, in both looks and personality, and she was terrified that if she fell in love, she'd lose herself.

Just like her mom had.

So don't fall in love.

Jules stared at Garrett's broad back, the way his spine dented in a masculine sweep just above his buttocks, his long, muscled legs. She'd never give a man the power over her, but she wouldn't mind having someone in her life, someone to come home to, a manly someone who would be glad to see her after days or weeks away. A man to wake up with, whose shoulder she could fall asleep on.

But that meant breaking through the final barrier and taking Garrett up to her bedroom and making love to him in her bed. In any bed. Maybe if she got past this hurdle, she could also sleep in a bed by herself, like everyone else.

Her breath hitched, and a vision of her father's big hand wrapped around her mother's hair, her neck bent at an impossible angle, flashed through her mind. She remembered a slick of drool in the corner of his mouth and a dangerous cocktail of power and passion in his hard, dark eyes.

Even as young as she was, Jules had known that bad things happened behind closed bedroom doors.

But her father had had a hold on her for too long, and she was still letting his actions affect her life. It had to stop.

She'd given Garrett her body, and he'd treated her well, very well indeed. And intellectually, she knew that nothing would change if she walked up the second flight of stairs to her attic bedroom. But her heart still wanted to beat out of her chest, and her mouth felt like she was trying hard not to swallow spiders.

But she had to do this. She had to cross this bridge.

Garrett was here, and she didn't think he'd turn down an offer of round two.

Be brave, Jules.

"Will you come upstairs with me?"

She saw his spine straighten, the tension in his shoulders. He stepped back from the glass, and she saw that he was looking at her reflection in the window, just as she was looking at his. "I presume you are not asking me to come up to your room to play tiddlywinks?"

She hauled a deep breath into her collapsed lungs. "No, I'd like you to make love to me again, in my bedroom."

"Are you using me to banish some ghosts, Juliana?"

It killed her when he said her name in that way, all deep and dangerous. Jules thought about lying to him but lifted her shoulders in a quick shrug. She gestured to the carpet. "That was an amazing experience, and I'd like to do it again. This time I'd like to change the venue."

"Are you going to ravish me again, Juliana? Twice in one evening?"

She rolled her eyes at the hand he placed on his heart, his look of mock outrage. A small smile tipped the corners of his mouth up and the anticipation in his eyes told her he was up for, and looking forward to, round two.

"I'm sure you can handle me." She had no doubt about that.

Jokes aside, Garrett could and would handle whatever life threw his way. Because he was unemotional and practical, he stood his ground as emotion rolled over him, not allowing his feelings to move his eyes off the goal.

She needed someone like him to help her over this final hurdle, someone steady and sure. Someone she could lean on.

Someone she trusted.

Why did she trust him? She barely knew the man, but

he had a mile-wide streak of integrity running through him. Yeah, his rep in the business world wasn't teddy bears and roses, but the world saw what they wanted to see. Hell, her followers assumed she was a super confident, kick-ass mixologist who frequently spoke out against domestic-and child-abuse issues, sexual harassment and humanitarian crises. Nobody, not even her best friends, knew she was scared of bedrooms…and what happened between those four walls.

It was time to get over it.

Garrett slowly turned and glided toward her, stopping a few feet from her. "Are you sure that's what you want to do?"

No. But Jules nodded.

"I don't want to kill the mood but I'm not your therapist," Garrett growled, but the worry in his eyes negated his harsh words.

No, he wasn't. But he was a way for her to move on, to have a seminormal life, to get her sexual mojo on track. Or to find it. Whatever.

"You don't have to say or do anything but make love to me," Jules assured him.

"Do you need a safe word?" Garrett suggested.

Jules's eyebrows flew up. "A safe word?"

Garrett pushed his hand through his hair, impatient. "In certain situations, a safe word is agreed upon so that if the—"

"What situations?" Jules demanded, trying not to laugh.

"In certain situations when one partner has complete control over the other, a safe word is used when someone is feeling out of their depth—"

"I know how BDSM works, Garrett," Jules told him, trying to hide her smile. "Obviously, I've never indulged." She tipped her head to the side. "Have you?"

He stared at her, completely unembarrassed. "Once. It

wasn't my thing. I prefer more give-and-take in bed, both of us holding equal power."

Jules released a little sigh of relief. She wasn't a prude, and she knew that people enjoyed that kind of stuff, but it wasn't for her. And, honestly, it sounded like a *lot* of work.

"But the thing with a safe word is that it gives you an out, a way to cut through everything to call it quits when the experience becomes overwhelming."

Jules thought about his offer, understood why he was making it and appreciated the gesture. But then she shook her head. "Thanks, but I think we're good. I know I can tell you to stop and that you will."

Something flashed in his eyes that she couldn't identify, something warm and deep and wonderful. Her trust pleased him, she realized. And then Garrett ran the edge of his thumb down her jaw. "Okay, no safe word. I've got the gist of your fear but will you tell me all of it, sometime?"

"I'll try," Jules replied. "And will you tell me what caused you to stand me up in Portland?"

Garrett's thumb tapped against her jaw. "Maybe."

She wanted to ask for more but knew she couldn't. His small concession was enough for now.

"Take me to bed," Jules asked him, holding out her hand.

It was such a simple phrase, one that women used all over the world in different ways and languages, but they both knew that, this time, it held a deeper meaning.

It was a bridge to cross, a new start, the destruction of an old demon.

It meant more.

And Jules was terrified that Garrett did, too.

On Sunday morning, Garrett walked up two flights of stairs carrying an overloaded tray, which contained the biggest coffee carafe he could find—he needed more than one cup to get his brain to work—two big mugs and a box of doughnuts he'd found at the back of the fridge.

Because he was a guy, he figured that if he couldn't see mold growing on them, they had to be edible.

Kicking open the door, he immediately noticed that in the short time he'd been downstairs, Jules had pulled on an oversize sweatshirt and finger-combed her hair. She sat curled up in the bay window, her feet up on the long cushion, staring out over the snow-covered fields. The sun was out, the wind had died down, and the sky was stunningly blue.

He wasn't anxious to get home, despite there being a million Kaye Capital tasks he should be tackling. He also needed to think about James's offer and the role, if any, he was going to play in Ryder International.

He should be listing the pros and cons of having half sisters, a stepmother, the drama that would accompany the announcement that he was James's son. Did he want the burden of inheriting all of Callum's wealth, the shares in the company, being responsible for carrying forward the Ryder name? He wasn't a Ryder, hadn't been for thirty-five years, and probably would never feel like one. He owed them nothing...

But the chance of being part of a family, of spending Christmases and Thanksgivings together, birthdays and pool parties, was an annoying dream that wouldn't completely dissipate, no matter how hard he tried to force the images away. As a child, he'd always wanted a big family but quickly learned that you frequently didn't get the things you most wanted.

Hell, he'd barely had a mother. A family was beyond all possibility.

If he outed himself as a Ryder-White by birth, the most

likely outcome was that Tinsley and Kinga would hate
him, Penelope would, at best, be wary of him, and James
would kill himself trying to make them all happy. Garrett
had no idea how Callum would react. No, it wasn't worth
it. He was better off alone.

"Coffee's getting cold, Kaye," Jules told him.

He jerked his head up and realized that he'd stopped
just inside the room and was staring at nothing. He never
lost focus. Annoyed with himself, Garrett placed the tray
on the bench at the end of the bed and poured coffee into
one of the mugs. He doctored the coffee with cream and
handed it to Jules before picking up his cup of black.

Yeah, a good cup of coffee and an excellent view—of
woman and scenery—were a great way to start the day.

He could take today, Garrett told himself. Tomorrow
was Monday, and he had to get back to Portland and make
some decisions, either to keep his world as it was or to flip
it on its head. The first was safer, the second more exciting, more tempting.

But temptation frequently came back to bite him in the
ass, so he'd go for safe, for what he knew. He was dealing
with people, not companies, and humans were inherently
unpredictable. With them, it was always better to take the
path of least resistance.

But sometimes it was damn boring.

"Sit down, Garrett," Jules softly commanded him.

Garrett sat on the opposite side of the bench, leaned
into the wall and placed his feet on either side of Jules's
hips. He rested his cup on his thigh and looked at her.
The sweatshirt hit her knees and, hopefully, she was
still bare-ass naked underneath. She seemed okay, he
thought. There had been a few minutes last night when
he suspected that she wanted to bolt—not from him but
the room—but every time that happened, he dialed up

the passion, trying to make her forget where she was, to remind her that the only thing she needed to focus on was him. It had worked.

But he thought he should check, just to make sure. Assumptions were not always accurate. "Are you okay?"

She looked at the rumpled bed, the pillows on the floor and smiled. "Yeah, I'm good."

"And did I cure you of your bedroom phobia?"

She smiled at his deliberately cocky comment. "You banished some demons. Send me your bill," she flippantly instructed him.

"Honey, you can't afford me," Garrett said with an easy grin.

Jules held her mug to her chest and tipped her head to the side. "It seems that I am the one doing all the talking, Kaye, all the time. How about you telling me something for a change?"

He rolled his shoulders, trying to ease the tension. "I don't like talking about myself, Jules."

"I don't like vegetables, but I eat them because they are good for me," Jules replied, not backing down. "Talk to me, Garrett."

He didn't want to. This extraordinary woman, who'd already slipped under his skin, would make inroads into his heart, and he couldn't let her do that. His heart had to remain impenetrable, its many barriers intact. All his life he'd felt like he was a problem to be solved, and he couldn't bear it if Jules looked at him the same way. He was fine on his own, always had been, always would be.

"It's not healthy to keep everything bottled up inside," Jules told him, sending him a self-deprecating smile. "If you don't talk about it, deal with it, you end up being an almost-thirty-year-old virgin with bedroom issues."

Before he could turn the conversation back to her,

she spoke again. "What scares you about talking to me, Garrett?"

Everything?

"I'm a vault. If something is told to me in confidence, I never break it." He believed her and knew that he could trust her to keep her mouth shut. And that was a good thing because his family situation was explosive news.

"And us talking doesn't mean that I'm going to suddenly fall in love with you and demand you give me babies."

He slapped a hand against his heart in mock horror. "You're not?"

"I'd like kids, someday, but I'm not sure about marriage, about being legally bound to someone. I certainly never intend to *obey* any man, ever."

"Now, there's a shocker," Garrett drawled jokingly.

"Ha! You laugh, but so many men think they want an equal partnership, yet when it comes down to it, his career always becomes more important than hers. And when the kids come, the woman is forced to compromise her ambition to be the caregiver, while the man's life doesn't change much." Jules waved her hands in the air. "Stop trying to change the subject, Kaye. We were talking about you, not me."

Unfortunately.

She wouldn't give up. She'd harangue him until he told her something. And he wanted to share, he realized. He wanted to bounce James's wild idea off someone. Jules was here, and he trusted her...

They were lovers, but somehow, in an incredibly short space of time, they'd become friends.

Jules plucked the coffee cup out of his hands, walked over to refill it and handed it back to him. She sat cross-legged in front of him, her jaw resting on her bunched fist, elbows pressed into her knees. Her full attention was on him. "I recently discovered my mom was in her midthirties when she had an affair with a much younger man. He was twelve, thirteen years younger than her. He was completely in love with her, but she didn't love him with the same intensity."

Jules's eyes didn't leave his face.

"He was only twenty-two or twenty-three, and they'd been sneaking around for months. He wanted to come clean, to show the world that they were a couple, but she was terrified she'd lose her job, and, God, she loved her job. She loved her job more than she ever loved me."

He hadn't meant to verbalize that truth, but it rose to the surface and bubbled over. Around Jules, he kept doing things that weren't in his nature: trying to find a way to save her ranch, sleeping with virgins, playing hooky from work, telling her stuff he never told anyone before.

Jules didn't say anything. She just looked at him, empathy in her amazing eyes.

"I'm an afterthought to my mother, a hassle, someone she had to deal with but would rather not have. I'd nag her to tell me who my father was, and she promised to tell me on my tenth birthday. I turned ten, and she promised to tell me when I was thirteen. Then fifteen, and so it went. I'm still not sure what I'm angrier about, her broken promises or her refusal to tell me about my dad. I believed I had a right to know. Was I wrong?"

"I don't think so," Jules softly replied.

"By the time I hit my midteens, my frustration with her was at an all-time high, as was hers with me. We argued about everything. I said the sky was blue, she said it was green. It wasn't...pleasant."

Garrett went on to explain that Emma was Callum's secretary and that he'd met him, heard him sneeze in the sunlight and seen his strange actions with his fingers. As he expected, Jules's eyes widened in shock. "You're Callum Ryder-White's son?"

"That's been my assumption for the longest time."

"Did you confront your mother?" Jules demanded.

"I did, and she denied it, vehemently. Sometime during the argument, she got me to promise that I would never talk about my theory, that I'd never approach Callum for confirmation." He sipped his coffee and scowled. "She's held me to that promise, and I haven't broken it. I don't break promises, Jules, ever."

"Because your mom broke so many promises to you. That's why you wouldn't promise me that you'd save the ranch. Because you didn't know if you could, and you won't make a promise unless you can deliver on it."

"It's a silly thing, but…yeah. In my business, which is cutthroat as hell and can sometimes be shady, I stick to the truth, always. I've lived with lies and obfuscations, and I hate dishonesty. All I have is my word, and, unlike my mom, I must keep it."

"I get it, Garrett. I do."

"It's equally important that the people I care about keep their word," Garrett told her, the warning in his voice unmistakable.

"You either trust me or you don't, Garrett," Jules quietly told him, her expression dignified. "I'm not going to beg you to."

He saw something in her eyes that reassured him, but being cynical, he wondered if he was seeing something that wasn't there because he *wanted* to trust her. It scared him shitless, but it was novel and exciting and felt like he was riding a roller coaster blindfolded.

He was going to tell her. He simply couldn't hold back.

"As I was recently, and reliably, informed, Callum

isn't my father," Garrett released the words and opened the door.

Her eyes widened. "And do you know who is?"

He nodded. He bent sideways to put his coffee cup on the floor and bent his legs, resting his arms loosely around his knees. "James came to see me just before I was supposed to join you at that bar."

He remembered James's nervousness, the fear mixed with determination on his face. He hadn't known how Garrett would react, but he'd walked into his office, spine straight and shoulders back, and done what he'd come to do.

Offer Garrett the job as CEO and inform him of his parentage. It had been hard for him, but he'd done it, and Garrett had to admire his resolve.

"Callum is in the hospital, and they are looking for a CEO. James offered me the position, and I laughed in his face. Why would I want to leave my kingdom for a place I don't know and an industry I know next to nothing about?"

"C'mon, Garrett, you have an encyclopedic knowledge of many different industries, and the basics of any business are the same. Buy low, sell high, cover your costs and make a profit. You could run a trading store on Mars if you wanted to."

Her faith in him warmed him. And, yeah, he did have a knack for business, could see trends and anticipate big-picture results. He could run Ryder International. He just didn't want to.

He didn't think.

"You were telling me about James and his CEO offer..." Jules nudged his knee.

Yeah. "I refused him, laughed in his face. He sat down in a chair, crossed his legs and told me, with remarkable sangfroid, that with one word in Callum's ear, he could dump Ryder International in my hands whether I wanted it or not."

Jules lifted her hands, asking for an explanation.

"Callum and James have a very rocky relationship."

Jules nodded. "He treats him like a servant. I don't know why James puts up with Callum."

"Because he's the sole male heir, the last Ryder-White male. Callum won't leave the business to Tinsley or Kinga. They don't carry the necessary equipment."

Fury jumped into Jules's eyes. "The misogynistic bastard."

"Yep." Garrett raked a hand through his hair. "Apparently, Callum informed James that should he become aware of a male son, grandson or nephew, someone else who carries the Ryder-White genes, that man will inherit Callum's wealth, not James. If Callum dies and the executor of the will becomes aware of another Ryder-White, James will be shoved aside in favor of the new heir."

It sounded unbelievable… It was unbelievable.

"But why? What could James have done that Callum would turn on him like that?" Jules asked, shocked.

It was a question he'd asked himself, many times. "I don't know."

Jules's arched eyebrows pulled together. He watched as she worked her way through his words and when her eyes widened, he knew she'd hit on something. "James said that he could dump Ryder's on you whether you wanted it or not."

Garrett nodded.

"Does that mean that you are a son, a grandson or a nephew?" Jules said.

God, she was quick. And he loved her mind, the way it worked. He nodded.

"So which are you, Garrett?"

Garrett inhaled, filling his lungs. "James was the young man who got my mother pregnant. I'm Callum's grandson. My teenage observations weren't that wide of the mark."

Her mouth dropped open, and he could see words forming on her tongue, yet she made no sound. Garrett gripped her chin and pushed her jaw up. He managed a wry smile. "Welcome to my world, Juliana- Jaliyah. In the last two days, I've acquired a father, a stepmother, two sisters and a company. And it's all up to me if I want to acknowledge them. James has handed the decision over to me. I can either acknowledge everything—and run Ryder International—or not. It's my decision."

"Holy hell. What are you going to do?"

"I don't have a freakin' clue."

Nine

Jules finally understood why Garrett had looked so agitated on Friday night. It was a hell of a thing to discover that you were someone's son, and the additional burden of hearing that he held the fate of the Ryder-White family, who were little better than strangers to him, in his hands had to weigh heavily on his mind. Jules knew that Garrett was a loner, self-contained and emotionally independent, so hearing he had a father who wanted to acknowledge him, a stepmother and two half sisters must have made the earth shift below his feet.

With all that going on, why did he head west with her to help someone he didn't know? Who was this man? He was a mass of contradictions—tender and tough, sweet and so smart—and she could spend a lifetime trying to figure him out. She doubted she ever would, but she'd sure like to try.

*Wow, Carlson! You barely know the man, and you're
making plans... What is wrong with you?*

He wasn't her forever guy; she didn't think such a creature existed. And she didn't believe in tying herself—legally—to a man. It was too big a risk, too huge an ask.

She'd seen all the facets of love, and many of them were
ugly and violent. She never wanted to run the risk of being
caught in that particular trap.

Her heart was convinced he'd never hurt her, that he'd
rather die than lift a hand to her, but her brain—suspicious
organ that it was—kept reminding her that her father was
perfect-husband material before he'd placed a ring on her
mom's finger. He first hit her on their honeymoon, before
the ink on their marriage certificate was dry.

Her father had fooled so many people: his friends, his
family, his work colleagues. At a very young age, Jules
promised herself that she'd always remain alert, that she'd
never allow herself to fall in love, to hand a man enough
power to hurt her, physically *and* emotionally...

But, damn, Garrett tempted her to do exactly that. She'd
listen to her brain, thank you very much...

But her body was demanding another bout of bed-based
fun. If she'd known that sex was this much fun, she'd have
pushed herself to get over her little phobia sooner.

She twisted her lips. No, she wouldn't have... It had
taken Garrett striding into her life for her to face her fears.
She wanted him more than she wanted to hold on to the
safety her issues afforded her. Jules looked out the window,
squinting against the bright sunlight. The snow, which was
less heavy than expected, would melt fast, and if memory
served her correctly, by this afternoon the roads would be
navigable. She had, maybe, half a day left with Garrett,
and she intended to make the most of it.

And while she indulged, she'd hopefully banish some of his blues, too.

Jules placed her hand on his knees to push them down and then straddled his thick thighs and lowered her head to allow her lips to meet his. She felt his smile against her lips, full of sunlight, and kissed the corner of his mouth. Garrett allowed her to play, his hands coming to rest lightly on her hips under her sweatshirt. She blushed as his hand swept over the curve of her bare buttock, embarrassed that she hadn't pulled on any underwear.

Then again, she loved her pretty bras and gossamer-thin panties and paid a fortune for them. She couldn't afford to replace more ripped-away underwear.

"You are so lovely, Juliana," Garrett murmured, as his fingers dug into the skin on her lower back. "Being here, with you, has been a step out of time, a lovely distraction."

Jules frowned. She didn't want to be a distraction; she wanted to be a necessity... *No!* What was she thinking? This interlude with Garrett was exactly that: a blip, a never-to-be-repeated weekend. She couldn't allow herself to get emotional or sentimental. She had to be practical.

"You stopped kissing me—" Garrett spoke against her lips "—and I miss your mouth."

Jules gave herself a mental slap and lowered her lips back to his, telling herself to enjoy him, that she was running out of time to kiss and touch this gorgeous man. Shuddering, she slipped her tongue inside his mouth, allowing passion to swamp her.

She wanted to stop thinking and start feeling, to leave her head and be immersed in the scent, taste and feel of him. She wanted hot and hard and fast, for him to brand her, to burn away her thoughts of fidelity and forever.

Garrett gripped the side of her face in his long, gentle

fingers and pushed her back to look into her eyes. "Slow down, baby, I want to savor this. I want to savor you."

No, soft and sweet would rip her apart, and she wasn't sure if she'd be able to cobble herself back together. Jules turned her head and bit his thumb. "I want hot and fast and out of control. Think you can manage that, Kaye?"

He was a guy and, like all alpha men, couldn't resist a challenge. His eyes narrowed, and the glint in those blue depths tempted her. "Are you sure you can handle that, Jules?"

Hell, she never backed down from a challenge, either. He lifted her chin, and she returned his challenging stare. "I can take anything you dish out, Garrett. I'm not a fragile flower."

"No, you're not," Garrett said, dropping his hands to grip her hips. He lifted her off him and deposited her on the edge of the bench, before dropping to his knees in front of her. He spread her legs, looked at her and sat down on the floor, crossing his legs. He placed his hands on his knees and sent her a wicked, wicked smile.

"You're already wet… That's so hot, Jules. Bet I can make you come without me touching you at all."

Yeah, she didn't think so. Jules shook her head. "Contrary to what you've heard, Garrett Kaye, you're good, but you're not that good."

Garrett just smiled. "Take off your sweatshirt, baby."

Jules wanted to demand that he come up and do it himself, but his dark eyes asked her to trust him, to play this game with him. To make this memory…

She slowly lifted her sweatshirt, exposing the skin at the top of her thighs, her stomach, her rib cage and her breasts. Then she deliberately dropped the shirt and started the process again, enjoying the way Garrett's eyes turned to molten teal.

"Tease," Garrett murmured.

"But you like it," Jules replied, finally tossing her shirt to the floor. He picked it up, buried his nose in its folds and inhaled.

"You smell so damn good. You always do," Garrett told her, placing his hands on the floor behind him and stretching out his long legs. He looked at her feet and slowly made his way up her body, stopping to stare at her feminine folds. Jules, feeling exposed, fought the urge to close her legs, but the appreciation in his eyes kept her knees apart, and she felt a low throb pulse at the edge of her womb.

He was right. This was hot.

"Touch your breast, Jules. Roll your nipples through your fingers," Garrett commanded her.

Jules did as he ordered and then stopped, frowning. "Hey, you said you can make *me* come without any touching! This is cheating."

"No, I said I can make you come without *me* touching *you*." He grinned. "Always read the fine print, darling. Touch yourself, Jules. Feel your marvelous skin, the texture of your nipples, the curve of your breasts."

Jules closed her eyes, lost in his deep voice, the sensations he pulled to the surface. She was so hot, so turned on, and when he told her to run her hand across her stomach, she was eager to follow his order. Her hand dipped down, and he shook his head.

"I didn't say you could do that."

Jules pulled her hand back and allowed her gaze to drift over him. His eyes blazed with barely harnessed desire, and a muscle ticked in his jaw. He held himself rigid, as if he were forcing himself not to reach for her, all leashed power and masculine grace. Her eyes drifted over his T-shirt-clad chest, over his flat stomach. His erection pushed the thin fabric of his sweatpants up, showing her exactly how much he wanted her.

And that was a lot.

Jules felt her pleasure build, knew that if she touched herself, she'd come. "I need—"

"I know exactly what you need," Garrett growled. "Push your hands between your legs, down your thighs, but don't touch yourself."

So near but so far. Jules rested the back of her head against the windowpane and stared up at the ceiling, not caring that she was utterly, incredibly exposed to Garrett. He could see every part of her, and she didn't care.

She just wanted all the pleasure he could give her.

"You're so sexy, Juliana. I'm so hard for you."

"Are you touching yourself?" Jules asked, her eyes still closed.

"No. Are you close, Ju?"

"So close," Jules whispered. "I want—"

"What do you want, baby?"

"To fly," she whispered.

"Then do it. Come now, sweetheart, come for me."

Jules didn't hesitate, her fingers finding her sweet spot, and with one swipe, two, she shuddered and tipped over into that abyss of pleasure. She screamed and shuddered, clamping her thighs together against her hand, drawing the pleasure out.

When her shudders calmed down to the occasional tremor, she opened her eyes to see Garrett watching her. She couldn't help her fierce blush, embarrassed at her screams and that she'd forgotten he was there.

"Sexiest thing I've ever seen," Garrett told her. He stood up slowly and held out his hand. Jules slid her palm into his and allowed him to pull her to her feet.

"Come back to bed with me, baby."

Jules nodded, knowing that when he looked at her like that—like she had hung the moon and stars—she'd follow him wherever he wanted to go.

Literally a minute after he exploded inside her, Jules heard Kate's melodious voice floating up the stairs.

"We're back! Get your lazy asses out of bed."

Garrett groaned, rolled off her onto his back and slapped his forearm over his eyes. The door was open, they hadn't been quiet, and ten minutes ago Jules had been plastered against the bay window, naked and exposed.

"Am I going to be met with the business end of a shotgun when I walk down the stairs?"

Jules knew that Kate and Peta were probably doing a happy dance downstairs at the thought of Jules having a man in her bed—*Sex is natural and a great way to relieve stress, darling*—but couldn't help teasing Garrett, just a little.

"Maybe," she told him.

"Awesome," Garrett dryly muttered. "Maybe exiting the house via the third-story window is a reasonable option."

She grinned at him as she shoved back the covers and stood up. She picked up a throw lying on the end of the bed, wrapped it around herself and walked over to the open door. She slammed it closed and moved back to the window and sighed at the cold, clear day. The mountains were in-your-face close, and the sky was a sharp blue. Gorgeous, she thought.

Judging by Kate and Peta's return, the roads were navigable, and she had to think about leaving Kilconnell Ranch. She was flying to Cancun soon, and from there she was heading to Montego Bay.

She'd only return to the States in three weeks.

The thought did not excite her.

But it was her job and a well-paying one. Garrett hadn't found anything in Kate's books that would suggest a way out of her financial woes, so she'd be supporting Kate and Peta for the foreseeable future. To do that she needed to earn more, and that meant increasing her workload. She'd have to look at doing more TV and cooking shows, endorsements, demonstrations.

She wouldn't have time for a lover or even a fling. And dropping in and out of Garrett's life would be like repeatedly stabbing herself between the eyes with a rusty fork. Seeing him again would be a high, sex would take her higher, and leaving him would drop her like a sack of concrete.

And if she fell in love with him—and that was a distinct possibility—those highs and lows would increase exponentially. She needed to be emotionally upbeat to do her job, and she couldn't see how she'd feel anything but miserable when she was away from him.

No, it was better to call it quits, while she still could. She turned to look at him and opened her mouth to speak, and her words caught in her throat. With his hand tucked behind his head, he looked relaxed and lazy, satisfied. And years younger than the tense man who'd stepped off the plane yesterday.

She'd give him—them—a few more hours. She'd tell him in Portland.

"Is there anything at all you can do about Kate and saving her ranch?" she asked.

Garrett sighed, flung back the covers and walked over to his clothes, yanking on his sweatpants. They rode low on his hips and showed off his sexy hip muscles and Jules felt that now-familiar surge of heat and need. She'd just had a series of orgasms, and she wanted him again!

She needed to change the subject and get confirmation of her suspicions. "So what's your final diagnosis on Crazy Kate's state of health?"

"I didn't find anything that would help the situation, Jules," Garrett bluntly told her.

Jules sat down on the edge of the bed, feeling like he'd gut punched her. "Nothing at all?"

"She needs thirty million to cover her debts, to pull herself out of the hole she's in. This place is only worth five to seven million, on a good day. So unless she finds thirty mil in the next two weeks, she's going to lose her shirt no matter what."

Jules gripped the bridge of her nose, blinking away hot tears. "So there's nothing she can do?"

Garrett lifted his powerful shoulder. "Unless she has a secret stash of shares or an investment she's forgotten about, and it would have to be a hell of a honeypot, then it's over, Jules."

Jules frowned, his words pulling up a vague memory. She scratched her forehead, trying to grab hold of it.

"What is it, Jules?"

Jules looked at him, frowning. "Her husband was a speculator, he played the stock market. He bought a lot of speculative shares."

"When he died, those shares would've passed to Kate, and they would've been included in his estate. I'm sure the accountants would've found them. I understand that you are clutching at straws but—"

"I need to know that I've done everything I can. I can't have any regrets, Garrett. I want to be able to say that I did everything I could. How do I check?"

Garrett rubbed the back of his neck. "I can get one of my people to search, but it would help if we knew what we were looking for. Does Kate still have the computer he used?"

"Yeah, in the study. It's in the cupboard." Jules winced. "It's pretty old. I don't know if it still works."

"I'll ask Kate if I can take the hard drive, and I'll get my PA working on it. He knows his way around computers."

"Thank you," she quietly stated, allowing her turbulent emotions to coat her words. "Thank you for coming with me, for trying to help Kate, for introducing me to amazing sex. For this weekend."

Her eyes slammed into his, and she held her breath as his fingers skimmed her cheek, her lips. His eyes were a soft teal, tender as hell, and she sucked in her breath. If there was anyone in the world she could trust completely, it was Garrett.

However much she was tempted, she refused to allow that to happen.

"Breakfast is ready. Get down here!" Kate yelled, breaking the tension between them.

"I'll use my en suite bathroom to shower," Garrett told her, standing up. He scooped up his T-shirt and pulled it over his head in an economical movement. "I'll see you downstairs."

Jules nodded.

"I'd like to leave in a couple of hours. Does that suit you?"

Jules forced herself to nod. Their lovely, out-of-step weekend was over, and it was time to go back to reality.

She wanted to stay here, with him. Going back to reality didn't hold any appeal, at all.

When they arrived at the airport, his Bentley Bentayga, as per his instructions, was waiting for him in the pickup zone. He threw their bags into the trunk, helped Jules into the passenger seat and slid behind the wheel, settling into the super luxurious leather seats. Pulling into the traffic he glanced at Jules, saw that she was looking out the window and sighed at her remote expression. They'd eaten a late breakfast with Kate and Peta, and she'd made an effort to be sociable, but on the drive to the airport and the flight back home, she'd barely spoken. His gregarious girl was gone, and a sophisticated stranger had taken her place.

It was odd. He normally liked stylish, quiet women, but he didn't like the look on Jules. She was energetic and vivacious, wide smiles and warmth. Playing it cool didn't suit her.

"I need directions on where to take you," Garrett told her, as he pulled into traffic. The next words escaped before he could pull them back. "Or you can just come back to my place."

Jules plugged her address into the onboard GPS—the car's computer could power a spaceship—and shook her head. "I thought we agreed that we weren't looking for anything permanent, Kaye."

"It was an offer for you to come back to my place, not an invitation to move in," Garrett replied, keeping his voice mild. The fact that she didn't want to extend their time together hurt him, far more than it should.

What the hell?

Jules half turned in her seat, and he saw the frustration on her face. "Okay, say I come home with you and spend the night? The day after tomorrow I'm flying to Cancun, from there I'm off to Jamaica. I'm not going to be home for three weeks."

"So, I'll see you in three weeks, then."

Jules looked irritated. "And then what? We carry on sleeping together?"

Sleeping, laughing, talking… He was up for any and all of it.

Garrett checked his mirrors and moved over a lane. "Would that be a problem?"

"Maybe not for you, but it would for me. I'm not cut out—I don't think—for a no-strings affair. Neither can I commit to anyone, so I'm stuck in this weird place, a no-man's-land." Jules pushed a curl behind her ear.

He hadn't wanted anything more than to sleep with her, but sometime over the last thirty-six hours, that had changed. He didn't want to let her go, couldn't allow her to walk out of his life, not just yet. He didn't know where this was going, how it would pan out, but the thought of never seeing her again, hearing her laugh, tasting her smile, talking to her, was not something he was prepared to accept.

"What if I said that we should see where this went, how it could grow?" Shit, what was he saying? Was he really prepared to consider a relationship with this woman, someone who buzzed around the world like a bee on steroids? He'd never see her, would have minimal time with her, and he'd be constantly saying goodbye.

But anything would be better than nothing. Of that, he was convinced.

"I'm not what you want, Garrett."

The finality in her words, her complete conviction, annoyed him. "I'm thirty-five years old. Do not tell me how I feel."

Jules threw her hands up in the air. "I can't, Garrett. I have to walk away from you, now, *today*."

He banged his hand against the leather steering wheel "Why?"

"Because if I don't, I'll fall for you, and I can't do that I can't be with anyone like that. I can't give that much o myself, and I will never be a man's possession."

"I've never treated a woman like my possession, *ever* I don't believe in that shit."

"That's what my mom believed about my dad, and look how well that turned out!" Jules shouted.

Garrett slapped his hand against the leather steering wheel again. "I am not your goddamn father! I would never, ever hurt you." Jesus, they shouldn't be having this conversation while driving; he needed to concentrate.

Jules's curls bounced. "My heart knows that, but my brain won't get with the program. My brain thinks it's better, safer, to be free, to be unattached. Attachment equals hurt. Staying in one place, with one person, means I'll be trapped. I can't be trapped, Garrett."

"I'm not going to lock you in a goddamn cage, Jules! I just want to be able to see you, talk to you, make sure you're okay, enjoy your fabulous body. For you to enjoy me."

"But in no time at all, I'd find myself emotionally trapped."

She was scared, Garrett realized, terrified of repeating her mom's mistakes. He understood that, could even empathize, but she was throwing away something incredible, an amazing connection, because she was scared. That was unacceptable.

"Stop being a wuss and trust yourself, Carlson!" he snapped. "You're being a coward."

He glanced at her, saw the anger flare in her eyes and jerked his eyes back to the road. He was expecting an eruption and was surprised when she spoke in a calm, measured tone.

"Aren't we all scared, Garrett? Even you?"

He frowned. "What do I have to be scared about?"

Sure, he was a little concerned that he might drop to his knees, throw his arms around her legs and beg her not to leave, but apart from that...nothing much affected him.

"You're terrified of acknowledging that you are James's

son because you'll have to deal with the drama of having a new family, of disappointing your mother. You'll have to deal with all those pesky people and their emotions. It's far, far easier to walk away than embrace a new reality."

Her words hit him like poison-tipped arrows, piercing his skin and setting his cells on fire. He didn't want to acknowledge the truth of her statement, that every time he thought about the Ryder-Whites, he imagined Sunday lunches, catching a game with James, teasing his sisters, playing pickup and trash-talking with their guys, enjoying family holidays at one of his many, never-used vacation homes.

He wanted that. Wanted it so much it hurt to breathe.

But that was a dream, a mirage, a bubble that would immediately burst as soon as he reached for it. No, it was far more realistic to assume that any relationship with James would be a minefield, that Tinsley and Kinga would resent him, that Penelope would hate him.

Besides, where would he find the time for a family? Kaye Capital already took up all hours of the day. His lack of time was a valid excuse. "I have enough on my plate without taking on the running of a massive, international company, Jules!"

"You wouldn't have to run it on a day-to-day basis, and you know that. They have excellent people, and with James there, you'd only have to make the big-picture decisions. Running Ryder International isn't the issue, as you well know! What terrifies you is having a father, sisters, people to care for you."

"You're assuming that Kinga and Tinsley would even like a brother!" Garrett retorted. He liked them. Admired their strength and work ethic and obvious intelligence and would be proud to call them his sisters. But the reverse might not be true. He had a reputation in the business world for being a bastard, and they'd resent him for horning in on their inheritance, on their lives. They were Ryder-Whites. He wasn't. He just carried James's genes.

And Callum's. God help him.

"The Ryder-Whites are nice people, Garrett. You should give them a chance."

"Stop, Jules! Look, this is my problem, and I'll deal with them," Garrett shouted, frustrated. They'd been talking about their relationship—or nonrelationship, whatever the hell they had or didn't have—not about his family.

"If you hurt them, Kinga and Tinsley specifically, I'll never forgive you."

Her words sucker punched him, and the impact was followed by searing pain, a mental kick in the head. She was so ready to defend them, to fight for them but not for him. She wasn't worried about how he'd come through this situation, how he'd feel. Her friends were a priority; he wasn't. He was just the guy who introduced her to sex.

It had always been like this. He was expected to deal with his shit in his own way. On his own. Nobody, not even his mother, had ever been prepared to stand in his corner and fight for him, protect him.

He was alone. And Jules was telling him that was the way it would always be.

To hell with her. To hell with them all! He didn't need Jules. He knew a dozen women he could hook up with at a moment's notice, and he had his own business to run, the business he'd built without any help from anyone.

That wasn't true. He'd had the money from the trust James had set up for him, and he'd used that cash as the building blocks of his business. He owed him for that.

That could be easily rectified. He'd repay James his money and tell him that he wasn't interested in having anything to do with him or Ryder International. He'd drop off Jules and put her, and this weekend, out of his mind. He was giving too much importance to a two-day fling. He'd forget that he had sisters and that he was part of, genetically at least, the Ryder-White clan.

As he knew, connecting and then being rejected hurt like hell, and he was better on his own. Tough, hard-assed, self-reliant.

Put a fork in him. He was done.

Ten

Garrett heard Sven's knock on his office door and hastily minimized Jules's Instagram account. But the photograph of her, dressed in a flame-orange bikini top and a matching patterned sarong knotted low on her hips, standing next to a beach bar, was burned into his brain.

He'd licked that belly button, traced the curve of those fabulous breasts with his tongue, kissed that wide, smiling mouth.

How dare she look so happy when he was as surly as sin?

"What?" Garrett looked up when Sven cleared his throat.

Sven sent him a steady look and lifted one pierced eyebrow. "Do you know how long this mood of yours is going to last?" he politely inquired.

Garrett glared at him. "I am not in a mood!"

Garrett glanced at the window and waited for the bolt

of lightning to hit him for verbalizing that whopper. When it didn't, he felt vaguely disappointed. "What's it to you, anyway?" Garrett demanded.

Sven shrugged. "Well, if you are going to mope around for another week or two, I might be able to get through it without stabbing you. Any longer than that and I might end up in jail," Sven mused.

Garrett winced, silently acknowledging the point. Since returning from Colorado, he'd been in a foul mood. He couldn't concentrate, was barely eating and hadn't exercised since Jules left a week ago.

He'd spent a day and a bit with her, and he was acting like a lovesick fool. God, he was pathetic.

Garrett spun his chair around and stared at the boats bobbing in Portland's harbor. He shouldn't be missing her this much. There was no rhyme or reason for it. He'd spent one night with her...

And they hadn't done much sleeping.

But she knew him better than anyone else in the world, and he knew her secrets—secrets she'd never shared with her best friends. With Jules, he felt better, calmer, more relaxed, easier to be with, simply nicer.

But Jules was ten, twelve, hours away on a goddamn beach, and he hadn't had any contact with her in ten days. That was nine days and twenty-three hours too long.

Was she okay? Working too hard? Sleeping with someone else?

Garrett gritted his teeth, and he imagined flecks of enamel hitting the inside of his cheeks. He couldn't stand it, being away from her, but what choice did he have? She didn't want him in her life.

"I came to tell you that I found something on that hard drive you wanted me to investigate," Sven said.

What hard drive? What was he talking about? Garrett spun around and asked for an explanation.

"The hard drive you brought back from Colorado with a 'See if you find anything interesting on this hard drive'?"

Right. The hard drive he'd taken from Kate's husband's computer. Garrett placed his forearms on his desk and nodded. "Okay, I'm following you… What did you find? And no, porn isn't interesting."

Sven smiled at his weak joke. "I found a lot of financial documents on the drive. Whoever owned the laptop was a hell of a businessman."

Yeah, he knew that. "He left Kate a ton of money, and that's how she financed the reopening and expansion of Crazy Kate's."

"I found share certificates and a list of bank accounts. But upon further investigation, they all became part of his estate when he died."

Not a surprise, Garrett thought. "So, what else did you find?"

"Bitcoin."

Of everything that he'd expected Sven to say, that wasn't the sentence he expected to hear. "Bullshit," Garrett said.

Sven grinned. "I know, it sounds improbable, right? I mean, there are so many urban legends out there about people who find old computers with Bitcoin stashed on them, but they are all BS. It never happens."

"But there's cryptocurrency on that computer?" he asked, excitement coursing through his system.

"There's a wallet, but without looking inside it, I can't tell if he owned any crypto."

"So look inside it," Garrett told him. "Do you need a code?"

Sven looked insulted. "I was hacking computer wallets when I was a kid, so no, I don't need a code."

"Excellent." Garrett pushed his chair back and walked to the door. "Let's go look and see what's in the wallet. I'm not getting my hopes up. It's probably nothing. Up until relatively recently crypto was an obscure concept and few people knew about it. Here's hoping Kate's husband knew about the digital currency early on."

"Only one way to find out," Sven said.

In his office, Sven sat behind his messy desk and, with fingers flying across the keyboard, brought up an old-fashioned screen filled with icons. Sven pointed to the wallet, and Garrett's heart thumped in his chest. He couldn't make Jules happy, love her for the rest of her life or give her security and stability and babies, but maybe he could save Kate's beloved ranch for her.

You're getting your hopes up, Kaye. This is a million-to-zero long shot.

The screen went black, Sven's fingers danced on the keyboard, and code rolled across the screen. He issued a satisfied grunt and stared at the code for a minute before switching back and opening the wallet.

A log-in screen appeared, and Sven punched in the twelve-digit alphanumeric code from memory. The screen changed, and Garrett stared at the figures on the screen.

"Does that say that there is crypto worth more than forty million?" Garrett asked, his voice coming from a place far, far away.

"Forty-two million to be precise," Sven said, leaning back in his chair, a satisfied grin on his face.

"Holy shit," Garrett said, looking at the screen again, just to confirm. That was more than enough to pay off the bulk of Kate's debts and, most importantly, save Kilconnell Ranch.

Garrett gripped Sven's shoulder with a shaking hand. "I need to get to Colorado, so get my pilot to file a flight plan. I'll leave for the airport immediately."

Sven nodded and reached for his phone.

"And disconnect the hard drive. I'm taking it with me," he added.

He could call Kate, but he preferred to tell them this momentous news in person. And being with the people Jules loved most made him feel closer to her.

What a sap.

"I would, and I could, but James Ryder-White will be here in five minutes," Sven stated.

Garrett stared at him. God, he couldn't cope with his biological father at the moment, didn't want to. He'd tell James that he was uninterested in running Ryder International when he returned from Colorado.

"Call him and cancel," Garrett told Sven.

"I'm already here."

Garrett spun around to see James standing in the doorway to Sven's office, the Kaye Capital receptionist at his elbow. Crap. Oh, well, he could give the guy a few minutes.

How long would it take to get James to understand that he wasn't interested? Two minutes? Three?

Garrett gestured to James to follow him. He'd get this done and then head to the Rockies. Saving Kate's company and the ranch was far more important than anything James had to say.

"He's with someone at the moment," a tired-looking nurse told Garrett when he asked to see Callum Ryder-White.

Garrett suspected he knew who Callum's visitor was. "Slim woman, platinum-blond hair?"

The nurse nodded. "My mother," Garrett explained. "She works as his assistant."

Short on sleep and just in from Colorado—with Kate's and Peta's screams of joy and relief still ringing in his ears—he didn't have any patience for bureaucracy so he stared the nurse down. She eventually nodded, gave him directions to Callum's room and admonished him to not stay long. Garrett jammed his hands in the pockets of his chinos and walked down the long corridor, the smell of antiseptic tickling his nose. A doctor brushed past him— young, pretty and female—but all her concentration was on her clipboard, and he could've been a fly on the wall for all she noticed.

It didn't bother him in the least. There was only one woman whose attention he needed, and she was in Montego Bay, making cocktails on a freakin' beach.

He'd lost her, but having had Jules in his life, even so brief a time, made him realize that he didn't want to live a solitary life. It was time to accept that he needed people in his life, as messy as they made it. He needed his rough edges, and his spikes, rubbed off, his views tempered and challenged. He became a better person around people, was at his best with Jules.

But if he was going to be less antisocial, then he might as well start with the people who were related to him. James, Kinga and Tinsley...

But not with his grandfather; he didn't see them having a relationship. James had already told him that if you weren't for Callum, then you were against him. And he'd already chosen to join Team James.

Do not lose your temper with Callum, Garrett reminded himself. *Or your mother.*

Garrett rapped on the door and heard his mom's voice telling him to come in. He stepped inside the room and looked around. It looked nothing like a normal, sterile hospital room. Callum's bed was covered in expensive linen, a huge bouquet of lilies sat in a vase, and two laptops sat on a small table in the corner. There were crystal glasses on the bedside table, and a cashmere blanket lay across the end of Callum's bed.

Emma frowned at him. "Garrett, this is a surprise."

She had no idea. And he had a lot more of those up his sleeve.

He looked from his mom's puzzled face to Callum's cool one and walked over to where the man sat, his hand outstretched. Callum's grip was frail, and the old man looked terrible, Garrett decided. Gaunt and washed-out, a shell of who he'd been at the Valentine's Day Ball.

"I'm afraid we don't have another chair for you," Callum said, as his mom sat down at the table opposite Callum.

"That's fine. I'm not going to take up too much of your time."

Callum's sharp eyes rested on his face. "Why are you here? Your mother might work for me, but our paths have never crossed."

He wasn't surprised that Callum didn't remember their previous meeting. Garrett walked over to the wall and pushed his right shoulder into it, deliberately keeping his posture relaxed.

"You tasked James with finding Ryder International a CEO," Garrett stated. He heard his mom's sharp inhale and, out of the corner of his eye, saw her face pale.

"I did, and he's been, as he always does, dragging his feet," Callum snapped. He gestured to the pile of paper next to his elbows. "Emma and I are working through the résumés."

"James offered me the position," Garrett informed

them. Callum's eyes narrowed, and his mom released another low, shocked gasp.

"Why?" Emma asked, in a shaky voice. Garrett met her
eyes, thinking she looked old and more than a little scared.

"You know why, Mom."

"He told you?"

"Yeah, he did. And it was something you should've
done a long, long time ago. You had no right to keep his
identity from me, keep him from me."

"I did what I thought was best," Emma protested.

"No, you did what was best for your career," Garrett
countered. "You were worried that if Callum found out
who made you pregnant, you might lose your job. Or that
they'd take me away from you. But I think you were more
concerned about your career than your child."

"That's not fair," Emma whispered.

"He wanted to be my dad. He wanted to acknowledge
me, be in my life. But you made that impossible," Garrett
stated, his voice hard.

Emma's hands bunched into tight fists. "Did he tell you
what I did to make him back off?"

"No, but judging from your petrified expression, it
must've been a pretty shitty card you played."

Callum's hand slapping the table brought Garrett's attention back to him. "What are you talking about? What
are you saying?"

Here goes, Garrett thought.

"James and Emma had an affair before he was married. I am a result of that affair. I am James's son and
your grandson." Garrett pushed a hand through his hair.
"God help me."

Callum stared at him for a long time before lifting a
bony finger and pointing it at his face. "You will have a
DNA test to prove that you are related to me," Callum said,

his hand shaking. "When that test comes back positive, I will continue this conversation with you."

Garrett rolled his eyes. "Emma isn't disputing that James is my father, you and I both sneeze when we walk into the sunlight, and Jesus, I look exactly like you did when you were young. But sure, let's put your mind at ease with a DNA test."

Callum stared at him, and Garrett knew his mind was going a mile a minute, no doubt trying to work out how to turn this to his advantage. When Callum started to speak, he held up his hand. "No, Callum, you're not calling the shots. Not today, and never with me."

"But—"

"Today you are going to listen," Garrett told him. He stood up straight and folded his arms across his torso, thinking that he was so tired. But more than sleep, what he wanted to do was lay eyes on Jules. Enfold her in his arms, bury his nose in her sweet-smelling curls.

But for that to happen, Jules had to trust him, and he didn't think she would. Not him or any other man.

Garrett pulled his attention back to his mother and grandfather. "James has an emergency power of attorney, one the lawyers kept on file in case you were ever incapacitated. Using that power of attorney, James hired me as a CEO-slash-consultant to Ryder International. He will be making the day-to-day decisions and calling on me, and Tinsley and Kinga, for help with the bigger decisions."

"I am not happy with that," Callum blustered.

"Well, the board is, including the representative of the person or entity holding the huge block of shares not owned by Ryder-White."

"Do you know who owns those shares? I want to buy them!"

James had told him that Callum was obsessed with

getting those shares back under his control, that they'd once belonged to his brother Ben but had passed out of the family's hands.

"Who owns those shares is not important right now, Callum," Emma told him, patting his hand. Garrett saw the affection in her eyes... No, it was more than affection: it was love. She loved and adored Callum. Had James just been a substitute for the man she could never have?

Possibly. It was something to think about.

"James told me that if you ever found another close male relative, you'd write him out of your will. That's a pretty crappy thing to do."

"He sided with my brother over me," Callum immediately responded. "I promised him he'd pay for it someday."

Really? Hadn't that happened nearly forty years ago? What a waste of energy. And if Garrett continued to argue with Callum, he'd be wasting his. No, it was better to focus on the issue at hand.

"Once I have concrete proof, DNA proof, I will leave everything to you, but only if you change your name to Ryder-White," Callum stated.

God, the old man was stubborn. "I have no plans to change my name. James doesn't care one way or the other, and it's his opinion I value. As for your will..."

Callum cocked his head when Garrett hesitated.

He waited a few more beats before handing his grandfather a cold smile. "You can take your will and shove it, Callum. I don't need your money, your influence or your possessions. I don't need a damn thing from you." He only needed Jules, standing by his side, walking through life with him. But if she couldn't trust him, what was the point?

Callum's jaw dropped open, shock flashing across his face. "What?"

"And if you decide to leave everything to me, the first thing I will do is instruct my lawyers to divide it three ways, with your son and your granddaughters getting an equal share. Personally, I think you should leave it to James—he's earned every cent of it—but if you can't wrap your stubborn brain around that concept and you do leave it to me, I promise you that's what will happen."

"You can't do that!" Callum shouted. "I can put a clause in that will stop you from doing that."

"Okay, do that. But then I will run the company into the ground, strip it out and sell it off. The proceeds will be split between my father and my half sisters. Those are your options, Callum, and I suggest you choose carefully."

He'd backed him into a corner, and Callum knew it. He glared at Garrett, spit forming in the corners of his mouth. "I don't think I like you, Kaye."

Garrett's lips lifted in a small smile. "That's okay, I know I don't like you." He looked at his mom, who hadn't yet managed to pull her eyes off him.

"You really should've told me, Mom."

She nodded, devastation in her eyes. "I know. Can we talk again?"

Along with needing people, he also needed a dad. He'd missed out on thirty-plus years of having a father and that was long enough. His mom's actions were inconceivable. "You kept my dad from me, a person I needed, who wanted to be part of my life. That's pretty harsh and unforgivable." He lifted his shoulders, and when they fell, he felt a hundred years old. "I don't know about talking, I really don't. I'll let you know when I figure it out."

Feeling like the walls were closing in on him, Garrett walked across the room and yanked the door open, pulling it closed behind him. Turning around, he rested his pounding forehead on the cool wall, tears burning his eyes.

Family drama wasn't his thing. It would all be so much easier with Jules by his side.

But she wasn't, so he'd just have to deal.

One weekend... One and a half days.

She'd spent thirty-six hours with the guy—give or take—and she was moping around like Eeyore on a very bad day.

Jules, standing on the balcony of her Montego Bay hotel, looked down at the poolside bar and noticed the staff replenishing the stock. She was due to give a cocktail demonstration in a little while, and she looked like road-kill. A flattened, dried-out husk of an opossum.

She needed to do her hair, slap on makeup, find her happy face and smile, dammit. But doing that on the beach yesterday almost killed her. She didn't know if she had the energy to give the hotel's guests what they wanted this afternoon. Or tonight.

Jules walked back into her hotel suite and placed her hands on the back of a sofa and lowered her head. She was in another exquisitely decorated suite in another foreign country, and next week, next month, she'd be somewhere else, doing the same thing.

This was what she wanted, she told herself, what she'd always wanted. To be free, untethered, able to dart across the world at a moment's notice. She didn't want a house, a family, a man tying her down, someone she had to consult before she made a decision.

She was *not* her mother... She would not dance to the beat of a man's drum.

But she missed Garrett. And she couldn't understand why as she'd spent so little time with him. But he got her, like no one else ever had, and she'd told him things that she'd kept buried for so long.

She trusted him, and she knew she could love him. And that's why she'd run. Because he made her feel too much, made her question her life, her beliefs, her lifelong plan.

If she spent a week with him, she'd be completely under his spell; a month with him and she'd not be able to make a decision without him.

No, it was better to be on her own. She'd get over this hump, this blip, and would be back to herself in a few days.

She hoped.

Hearing a knock on her door, Jules straightened, shaking out her fingers. She'd ordered a power smoothie from room service earlier—peanut butter, banana, milk and protein powder—in the hope that it would give her the lift she so desperately needed.

It couldn't hurt.

Jules walked into the hallway and yanked open the door, blinking when she saw two very unexpected faces. Then she blinked again.

Tinsley, dressed in a blueberry-colored sundress, dropped a kiss on her cheek and gave her a quick hug before Kinga nudged her aside to repeat her sister's action.

Okay, so this was *waaay* better than a power smoothie for a pick-me-up.

"What are you doing here?" she demanded, putting her hands to her cheeks.

Kinga pushed her hand into her ultrashort blond hair as they walked onto the balcony and into the warm air.

"Tinsley saw the video you posted yesterday and asked me what I thought about it. We both agreed it was terrible," Kinga said, dropping into a chair and putting her bare legs up onto the balcony railing. Like Tinsley, she wore a short sundress, but hers was a bright yellow. She looked like a worried sunbeam.

Jules rubbed her hand up and down her jaw. She knew

she'd been a bit off yesterday, but she didn't think she'd been *that* bad.

Tinsley rubbed her shoulder before sitting down on the sofa. She patted the space next to her. "Relax, Ju. Kinga is being melodramatic."

Jules sat down, her gaze bouncing between her two friends.

"But it wasn't your best work," Tinsley continued. "You smiled and laughed and said everything you needed to…"

"But?"

"But your smile wasn't genuine, and your eyes were dull and sad," Kinga stated. "And because that's unusual for you, we commandeered a plane and headed south."

"Whose plane?" Jules asked. "Cody's or Griff's?"

Tinsley smiled. "Callum's."

"We figured if we were going to lose access to it soon, we might as well get some use out of it," Kinga cheerfully added.

Jules frowned. "What are you talking about?"

"Ah, that's a long story, but right now, we want to find out what's going on with you," Tinsley said. "But we can't do this without a drink. I need a margarita."

Jules glanced at her watch. "I've got to work in an hour or so."

"We don't," Kinga said, climbing to her feet. She pointed her index finger at them. "I'll call room service and order. Don't start interrogating her until I get back, Tins."

When Kinga disappeared back into the suite, Jules looked at Tinsley. "How's Cody?"

Tinsley's smile bloomed, and happiness hit her startling blue eyes. "Lovely, thank you."

Tinsley's former brother-in-law was going to be her

new husband, and Jules knew that she was finally with the right Gallant brother. "And your folks? And Callum?"

Tinsley rolled her eyes. "There's drama, lots of it. Callum has been moved to a private room and is being his normal, irascible self."

"Whatever happened about those DNA tests you took, the ones Callum gave you for Christmas?"

Tinsley shrugged. "God only knows. They were for a genealogical website so that we could trace the history of our DNA. Also, if anyone else has some of the same DNA, indicating a family tie of some sort, it flags it. But our tests haven't come back, and none of us are on the website. And that's weird because a friend of Cody's did his in the middle of February, and he got his results back within two weeks and was up on their website a day later."

"Weird."

"What's weird?" Kinga asked, dropping down into her seat.

"I was telling Ju about the delay in the DNA tests," Tinsley explained.

Kinga waved her words away. "On the scale of stuff to worry about, that is way down the list. We want to know what's upset you, Ju."

Jules turned her head to look at the beach and the azure waters of the Caribbean Sea. It was beautiful, but she'd far prefer to be at Kate's ranch, watching the snow fall on the Rockies. But with Garrett. Only with Garrett.

"Jules, talk to us," Tinsley implored.

She should. She needed to talk to someone. But where to start? With her childhood, with Kate losing her ranch, asking Garrett for help? The Valentine's Day Ball? Going to his office?

Did it matter? They were all tied up with each other.

Jules sighed and started to recount what had happened

between her and Garrett. She spoke, interrupted only by
the delivery of the margaritas. And then spoke some more
while her friends simply listened.

When she finally wound down, Tinsley put her hand
on her knee and passed her a bowl-like glass. "Drink,"
she ordered her.

"I've got to work soon!" Jules protested.

"A sip, or even a half glass, won't hurt you," Tinsley insisted. Jules, seeing the determination in Tinsley's
eyes, caved and sighed when the tart liquid hit her tongue.
Lovely.

Kinga sat up, placed her heels on the edge of the chair
and wrapped her arms around her shins. "Right, let me
make sure I have the highlights. You bounced around the
country, fleeing your abusive dad. You met Kate, who let
you spend summers with her. Your dad found your mom
in Denver and put her in the hospital, and he ended up
dying in a car accident? Right so far?"

Jules nodded, appreciating Kinga's matter-of-fact voice.

"As a result, you vowed that you would never tie yourself to anyone or anything, ever? Not to a place or a man
or a home?

"Kate is about to lose her ranch, so you asked Garrett Kaye—the man with a reputation for stripping companies, not rehabilitating them—to see if he could save
Crazy Kate's? And you spent the weekend with him, and
you slept with him?"

Tinsley picked up where Kinga left off. "And he asked
to see you again, but you told him no, that you can't because you might fall in love with him and that's unacceptable?"

Jules nodded. Yeah, basically. She'd omitted the part
about being, technically, a virgin, and how Garrett cured
her of her aversions to bedrooms. She glanced inside and

wrinkled her nose. Well, that wasn't true. She'd only managed to sleep in a bedroom, in a bed, with him. She'd slept on couches, in her apartment, Cancun and here in Montego Bay, since leaving Colorado.

"You're in love with Garrett," Kinga stated, on a delighted hoot.

"I am *not* in love with him! I spent two days with him, not even that! People don't fall in love that quickly!"

"You did!" Kinga crowed.

"I did not!" Jules shot back, knowing she was lying. Of course she was in love with him, that arrogant, big, powerful, confident man. Dammit.

"Jules?" Tinsley softly asked.

She met Tinsley's sympathetic eyes and bit her lip, annoyed at the tears in her eyes. "I don't *want* to be in love with him. I don't want a man in my life, telling me what to do, how to act."

Tinsley and Kinga stared at her, their eyes wide with astonishment. They exchanged a long glance, and Tinsley put an arm around Jules's shoulder. "Baby girl, that's not fair."

Jules pulled away from Tinsley and moved into the corner of the couch, her body rigid with tension.

"No, don't get huffy, Jules," Tinsley said, in a clear but tough voice. "Look, we understand that you have some trust issues when it comes to guys. Who wouldn't when the first man who was supposed to love and protect you was a total bastard? But you know, you *know*, Garrett isn't like that!"

"I don't know that. How would I know that?" Jules demanded, her voice rising.

"Because you would never, ever have slept with him if you didn't trust him," Tinsley told her. "Your subconscious knows that he's a safe bet. That's why you were

able to make love with him and fall asleep with him. You
did fall asleep with him, right?"

Yeah, she had. With her head on his shoulder, her hand
on his heart. She'd slept deeply, waking up feeling wonderful.

"Your head, your intellect, is just trying to protect you,
but your heart knows that he would never physically hurt
you," Kinga told her, sounding so very serious. "He's the
guy for you, the first guy you've had sex with, the first
guy you've fallen asleep with, the first guy you've trusted
enough to let him share a bedroom with you. You've been
waiting for him."

Jules stared at her, in total shock. "How did you know
about me being a virgin, about not being able to sleep in
a bedroom?"

Kinga sent her a smile full of love. "Remember that
girls' weekend we spent in Vail, and you got so drunk on
Dom Pedros and Irish coffees? You told us you were a virgin but not why. We've always wondered. As for not being
able to sleep in a bedroom, on every trip we've taken, despite there being a bed for you, you've slept on couches,
in hammocks, on decks. When you've stayed over at our
places, despite us both having beautifully decorated guest
suites, you've always slept on the couch. It's not rocket
science, sweetie."

Well, shit. So much for thinking she had some secrets
left.

Kinga dropped her legs and leaned forward, the fingers of her right hand playing with the enormous diamond on her left hand. "I never thought I'd find Griff,
didn't think I needed love. But he makes my life better,
in every way." She grinned and pulled a face. "Look, he
annoys and frustrates me, and he calls me out, and I call

him out. We're both strong-willed people, but it's an equal partnership, Jules."

"As is mine with Cody," Tinsley told her. "We think you could have the same type of relationship with Garrett, Ju."

"How do you know that?" Jules cried. "How do you know that, when I commit to him, he won't turn into a freak who'll try to control me?"

"Because if you look for them, there are signs that he respects women, Jules," Tinsley told her. "He's the son of a working single mom, and Emma would've slapped down any misogynistic ideas he had as a teenager. He doesn't have a gender pay gap at his company, and he has more women as managers in his organization than he does men. His exes only have good things to say about him, and his staff says he treats everyone the same—he's demanding but fair."

"And respectful of their time and appreciative of their efforts," Kinga explained.

"The point is, he might be tough and hard-assed, but he's a good guy," Tinsley added.

"Jules, what if you are wrong? What if you are making a choice based on fear? What if you miss out on the *one* guy who makes life a little brighter, more colorful, who rocks your world? In ten days or ten months or ten years, are you going to regret walking away from him?"

"But what if—" She couldn't complete the thought.

"What if it doesn't work out?" Kinga asked. "Then it doesn't work out. What if he's dominating? You call him on it, and if his behavior doesn't change, you walk. If he threatens you physically, you walk. If he hurts you, even if you just break a goddamn nail, we kill him," Kinga said, her tone matter-of-fact again. And Jules suspected she wasn't joking.

Tinsley gripped her hand in hers. "He won't hurt you, Jules, ever. Of that we are sure."

Jules saw the conviction in her friend's inky-blue eyes and moved her gaze to Kinga's. Kinga nodded her agreement, and Jules relaxed, just a fraction. She trusted her friends, trusted their intuition, far more than she trusted her own. If they believed she was safe, she would be. They would never encourage her to enter a situation that would cause her pain.

"We're not asking you to make a decision now, Ju," Tinsley told her, after draining her margarita glass. "We're just asking you to think about what we've said."

Kinga glanced at her watch. "You have a gig in twenty minutes, sweetie. While you're thinking, might I suggest a shower and a change of clothes? You look like hell."

Jules nodded. "I know. I do not want to go and throw bottles around and talk crap."

Honestly, she didn't know if doing pop-up bars, openings and celeb events was what she wanted to do at all anymore. She didn't know what she wanted to do, but darting around the world had lost its appeal. If she didn't have to support Kate and Peta, she'd pack it in tomorrow or, at the very least, take a long break. Actually, she did know what would make her heart sing... She wanted to see Garrett every day, go to bed with him, wake up with him, spend as much time as possible with him.

She stood up and wiped her sweaty hands on the seat of her denim shorts. "What if he tells me he's not interested?"

They smiled at her, bright, blinding smiles. "He won't," Kinga told her, oozing confidence. "But if you want to see him, check where he is first. He's been spending a lot of time in Colorado lately."

Colorado? Why on earth would he be there? The only link between him and Colorado was Crazy Kate's, so what was he up to? Was he buying out her assets, stripping her company?

There was only one way to find out, so Jules lunged for her phone and made an international call.

And later, when she made it to the beach and her temporary bar, her steps were lighter, and her eyes brighter.

She couldn't wait to return to Portland, to take a shot at the life she so desperately wanted.

Garrett straightened his silver tie and did up the button on his dark gray suit jacket. He stood by the bar and anxiously cast glances at the door to the restaurant, waiting for the arrival of the Ryder-Whites.

Earlier in the day, when James had called him to check his schedule for the next board meeting, his dad—God, he had a *dad*—told him Tinsley and Kinga were aware they had a brother and, before he could recover from that statement, invited him to join the family for a meal in the private dining room of Siena, one of Portland's best restaurants.

The entire family expected him to be present.

Garrett, supposedly the toughest, baddest ass in business, had butterflies in his stomach, and his mouth was as dry as ten-day-old bread.

He wanted to have a drink, take a Valium, hightail it out of the restaurant. What the hell did he know about being part of a family? God, he barely had a relationship with his mother.

"You look like a guy who needs a drink. Or a hug."

He slowly turned, and there she was, wearing a black-and-red plaid dress and thigh-high boots, the dress's asymmetrical hem showing off her thighs. Her hair hung down her back, and her smile, normally so bright, was turned down a notch.

"Uh…" He glanced at the door, expecting to look back and see that she'd disappeared.

But nope, Jules was still there and standing in front of him, a long black coat over her arm. "What are you doing here?" he asked, his voice scratchy.

"Depending on how the next few minutes go, hopefully I'll be joining you for dinner," Jules told him. She looked around at the crowded bar and jam-packed restaurant. "Can we talk somewhere quiet? Maybe outside?"

She'd be an icicle in two seconds flat. Garrett shook his head and lifted his hand. Within ten seconds, a concierge materialized at his side. "If the Ryder-White family arrives, can you seat them at the bar? I will come and get them in due course."

"Certainly, sir."

Garrett locked his hand around Jules's wrist and led her down a small hallway, pushing open a frosted-glass door.

She walked inside, saw the flowers and the candles and the exquisitely set table and sighed. "It's perfect for a family dinner."

Family. He still wasn't used to the word. Garrett closed the door behind Jules and leaned against it, crossing his arms and trying to look casual. "You asked if we could talk. What's on your mind?"

Jules placed her coat over the back of the nearest chair, bent down to sniff a rose and showed him a good portion of her thigh. All that golden skin… His lungs held his breath, and his heart spluttered. How was he supposed to have a rational conversation when he was unable to think of anything but taking her to bed, making her his? Permanently.

"I hear you've acquired a family," Jules said, her gaze inquisitive. Seeing his frown, she quickly continued. "Tinsley told me, on the understanding that I promised not to tell anyone. And I haven't."

"Yeah, it's a concept I am still wrapping my head around," Garrett replied.

"Well, they are thrilled. They've always wanted a big brother to torment."

She laughed at his expression, something he imagined to be somewhere between horror and...well, horror. "Relax, they'll go easy on you, for the first few days."

"Wonderful," Garrett dryly replied.

"If they ignore you, then you have a problem. If they tease and torment you, you're part of the family," Jules explained.

Right, that didn't make him feel any better.

"I'm thrilled for you, Garrett, and I'm thrilled for them. You need a family, and they need you."

He needed her, but he was damned if he was going to beg. Love wasn't love if it had to be coerced.

Jules played with the heavy silver bracelet on her arm, and when she finally looked up at him, he saw the sheen of tears in her eyes. "But that's not why I am here." She hauled in a deep breath and waved her hands in front of her eyes, as if trying to dry her tears before they fell. "I came to say thank you, for what you did for Kate. You saved their business and the ranch."

No, that was going too far. His guy just found an investment nobody thought to look for. "I didn't do anything, Ju. It was there, my guy noticed it and he did the heavy lifting."

"Your guy is amazing," Jules said, her eyes a deep gold. "You're amazing, and I can't thank you enough. What can I do, what can I say to show you how grateful I am?"

"Your goddamn gratitude is not what I want from you!"

His half shout surprised him, but Jules barely reacted. She just held his stormy eyes and slowly tipped her head to the side. "What do you want from me, Garrett?"

Why not just tell her? He was already miserable. If she walked out on him again, nothing would change. "I want you."

Her curious expression didn't change. "How do you want me? Exactly?"

It would be too easy to say *Up against the wall* or *Over the back of the couch*, but the time for hedging, fudging and playing word games was over. He wanted that. Of course he did—he'd never stop wanting her—but he wanted more. He wanted everything.

"I want you in my life, permanently. I want to wake up with you, play piano for you, ply you with decent coffee—"

She sighed. "I could do with one of your coffees right now."

He glared at her. "Really? That's what you went with?"

She waved her hand and pulled a face. "Sorry. I didn't mean to interrupt. What else do you want from me?" she politely asked.

Oh, what the hell. He'd come this far, he might as well throw it all out there. "I want to be with you, have you be with me. But right now, the thing I want the most is your trust, the assurance that you know, deep down know, that I would never hurt you. Because if you can't give me that, nothing else matters," he added.

Jules saw the frustration in his eyes, the insecurity, the fear that she was, once again, going to turn him down. How brave he was! He was embracing a new family, getting to know his dad, wanting a relationship with his two willful sisters. And he'd just put himself out there, for her.

She felt humbled by his strength and his honesty.

"Before we get to that, I do just need to thank you once again, from the bottom of my heart, for saving

Kate's ranch. I will forever be grateful to you, and from now on, you will be treated like a god when we visit Kate and Peta."

Garrett waved her thanks away.

"You asked me if I trusted you, and I thought I didn't but... I do." Jules walked over to him and slid her hand under his suit jacket to find the spot above his heart. She picked up his hand and placed it on her chest, above her heart. "It was pointed out to me, by your sisters, that I would never have made love with you if I didn't. They also made me realize that you are the only person who has ever gotten me to sleep in a bedroom. I couldn't, not even at the ranch or when I was with them, do that. I haven't slept in a bedroom since I was a kid, but I did with *you*."

"Oh, baby."

Jules ignored the slow slide of tears running down her cheeks. "Only you, Garrett. That's how much I trust you. I also love you, by the way," she added, lifting her shoulder. "So much."

Garrett's big hands clasped her face, and he used his thumbs to wipe away her tears. He placed his forehead against hers and dropped a hard kiss on her mouth before abruptly pulling back. "If I kiss you, I won't stop. I've missed you so much, Juliana."

"I missed you, too," Jules said on a tiny hiccup. "I dropped two bottles of tequila and a bottle of Cointreau because I couldn't concentrate. My mind was too full of you."

Garrett placed his thumb in the center of her bottom lip. "How much time do we have together before you have to fly off again?"

"How much time can you spare me? I asked my agent to cancel my bookings for the foreseeable future. She squawked and squealed, but I'm currently unemployed."

"Why did you do that?" Garrett asked.

Jules held his wrists, her eyes tracing his beloved face. "I wanted to give this, our relationship, a little time to settle, for us to get to know each other better." She saw the satisfaction in his eyes and smiled.

"Now that I know that I don't have to support Kate and Peta, I can rethink my career. I'm tired, a little burned-out, so sick of sleeping on hotel-room couches. I want to be with you, but I also want to see what else I can do, be. Maybe write a cocktail book, a travel memoir. I'll get back on the road at some point, sometime, but I don't ever want to go back to the frenetic pace I was working before."

"Tell me where you need to be, how you want to do it, and I'll rearrange my schedule to be with you."

"You'd do that for me?" she asked, shocked at his generous offer.

"I'd do anything for you, Ju. This is a partnership. We have to be able to compromise. I can work remotely. I do it all the time. My career doesn't take preference over yours, ever. We sink or swim together."

Jules stood on her tiptoes to brush her mouth against his. "Does that mean you love me?" she asked, her heart bouncing off her ribs.

"Oh, Jules, how can you doubt that? I love you with everything I have, everything I am. My world doesn't make sense without you. Be with me. Be mine."

Jules clasped the back of his neck. "Always."

And when he kissed her, Jules could taste the love on his lips, feel it in the big hands that held her, in the body that he'd placed between her and the world. He'd love and protect her, cherish her. Of that she had no doubt.

She was home, and he now owned her heart.

Jules sighed when he deepened their kiss, and desire flashed, hot and fast, through her. She groaned into his mouth and smiled as he bent his knees to wrap his arm behind her thighs to lift her. She fumbled for the button to open his suit jacket, found it and slid her legs around his waist, desperate to get close to him.

Their kiss burned hotter, more desperate, and Garrett placed his hands under her dress, kneading her butt cheeks. She needed him. Now.

From a place far, far away, Jules heard the door open and the trill of feminine laughter. Pulling her mouth off Garrett's, she peeked over his shoulder to see his sisters, doubled over with mirth.

She tried to shoo them away, but they just shook their heads. Kinga, the brat, in a singsong voice, was the first to speak. "*Da-ad*, Garrett has his hand up Ju's dress."

Garrett groaned, and Jules grinned as she slid down his big body. "And so it starts," she told him. "Strap in for a hell of a ride, Kaye."

He grinned at her. "As long as I have you at my side, I'm good." He kissed her before turning around to nail his sisters with a mock-hard look. "I told the concierge to ask you to wait. Do you ever listen?"

Kinga and Tinsley strolled over to them, and both of them kissed Garrett's cheek. "No, we never do. We do what we want, when we want."

Griff O'Hare looked at Cody, and they both nodded. "We can vouch for that. We blame James."

James grinned at them, his arm around Penelope's waist. "There were days when we were convinced they'd be the leaders of a prison gang."

"Funny," Tinsley muttered, scowling at her father.

"You're just excited to have another male in the family to dilute the estrogen," Kinga informed James.

"What are we, fairy dust?" Griff protested, his hands on his hips, scowling at Kinga.

"Play nicely, children," Penelope said, walking up to Garrett. "Welcome to the madness, Garrett. I hope you have a spine of steel."

Jules grinned at Garrett. "Having second thoughts about your ready-made family, darling?"

He looked at his sisters, then at his father, and smiled. "A thousand and one, but I'll deal. Once I commit, I stick." He bent his head and kissed her, and Jules knew that it was a promise he'd never break.

To his family and to her.

* * * * *

COMING SOON!

We really hope you enjoyed reading this book.
If you're looking for more romance, be sure to
head to the shops when new books are
available on

Thursday 12th May

MILLS & BOON

THE HEART OF ROMANCE

A ROMANCE FOR EVERY READER

MODERN

Prepare to be swept off your feet by sophisticated, sexy and seductive heroes, in some of the world's most glamourous and romantic locations, where power and passion collide.

HISTORICAL

Escape with historical heroes from time gone by. Whether your passion is for wicked Regency Rakes, muscled Vikings or rugged Highlanders, a the romance of the past.

MEDICAL

Set your pulse racing with dedicated, delectable doctors in the high-pressure world of medicine, where emotions run high and passion, comfor love are the best medicine.

True Love

Celebrate true love with tender stories of heartfelt romance, from the rush of falling in love to the joy a new baby can bring, and a focus o emotional heart of a relationship.

Desire

Indulge in secrets and scandal, intense drama and plenty of sizzling action with powerful and passionate heroes who have it all: wealth, s good looks…everything but the right woman.

HEROES

Experience all the excitement of a gripping thriller, with an intense mance at its heart. Resourceful, true-to-life women and strong, fear face danger and desire - a killer combination!

To see which titles are coming soon, please visit

millsandboon.co.uk/nextmonth

LET'S TALK
Romance

For exclusive extracts, competitions
and special offers, find us online:

 facebook.com/millsandboon

@MillsandBoon

@MillsandBoonUK

Get in touch on 01413 063232

For all the latest titles coming soon, visit
millsandboon.co.uk/nextmonth

JOIN US ON SOCIAL MEDIA!

Stay up to date with our latest releases, author news and gossip, special offers and discounts, and all the behind-the-scenes action from Mills & Boon...

 millsandboon

 millsandboonuk

millsandboon

might just be true love...

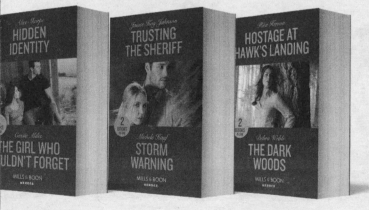

MILLS & BOON

MODERN

Power and Passion

Prepare to be swept off your feet by sophisticated, sexy and seductive heroes, in some of the world's most glamourous and romantic locations, where power and passion collide.

Julia James
Heiress's
PREGNANCY SCANDAL
MILLS & BOON
MODERN

Jennie Lucas
Chosen as the
SHEIKH'S ROYAL BRIDE
MILLS & BOON

Kim Lawrence
A WEDDING
of the
ITALIAN'S DEMAND
MILLS & BOON

Sharon Kendrick
The
SHEIKH'S SECRET BABY
MILLS & BOON
MODERN

Eight Modern stories published every month, find them all

millsandboon.co.uk/Modern

MILLS & BOON
True Love
Romance from the Heart

Celebrate true love with tender stories of heartfelt romance, from the rush of falling in love to the joy a new baby can bring, and a focus on the emotional heart of a relationship.